Deborah Challinor is a freelance writer and historian living in the Waikato. *White Feathers* is her second novel, following the highly successful *Tamar*, and she has written several nonfiction titles.

WHITE FEATHERS

The second volume in a three-volume family saga.

In 1914, Tamar Murdoch's life is one of ease and contentment at Kenmore, a prosperous estate in Hawkes Bay, as storm clouds over Europe begin casting long shadows. Tamar's love for her children is sorely tested as one by one they are called, or driven, into the living hell of World War One. During the Boer War, Joseph, her illegitimate eldest son, fought as a European, but this time he is determined to enlist in the Maori Battalion. As loyalties within the Murdoch clan are divided, and the war takes Tamar and Andrew's only daughter far from her sheltered upbringing, the people and experiences their children encounter will shape the destiny of the Murdoch clan for generations to come.

Books by Deborah Challinor
Published by The House of Ulverscroft:

TAMAR

DEBORAH CHALLINOR

WHITE FEATHERS

Complete and Unabridged

CHARNWOOD
Leicester

First published in 2003 by
HarperCollins*Publishers* (New Zealand) Limited
Auckland

First Charnwood Edition
published 2005
by arrangement with
HarperCollins*Publishers* Pty Limited
Australia

The moral right of the author has been asserted

This novel is a work of fiction. Any references to
historical events; to real people, living or dead; or to
real locales are intended only to give the fiction a
sense of reality and authenticity. Other names, places,
characters and incidents are either the product of the
author's imagination or are used fictitiously, and their
resemblance, if any, to real-life counterparts is
entirely coincidental.

British Library CIP Data

Challinor, Deborah
   White feathers.—Large print ed.—
Charnwood library series
   1. Immigrants—New Zealand—Fiction 2. New Zealand
—Social life and customs—20th century —Fiction
   3. Domestic fiction 4. Large type books
   I. Title
   823.9'14 [F]

   ISBN 1–84395–826–0

Thanks to my husband Aaron, who once again forked out for everything while I was writing this. Thanks also to the team at HarperCollins, to Anna Rogers for her great editing job, and to Ian Watt, who took a chance on the first book in the *Tamar* series.

This one is for my nieces,
Rachael and Rebccca

Part One

Joseph

1914–1916

1

Joseph Deane's strong brown hands gripped the ship's rail as the trans-Tasman steamer *Dolphin* eased into dock at the port of Wellington. The salt-spiced wind, blustering aggressively through Cook Strait, blasted his heavy dark hair back from his forehead. He inhaled deeply and closed his eyes, savouring the smell of his homeland. He had been away for well over two years this time and was very much looking forward to seeing his family again, although a growing sense of unease and nervous excitement lurked beneath his anticipation.

Below him on the quay a small crowd milled and jostled, necks craning to catch a glimpse of the *Dolphin*'s passengers. Joseph looked for his mother, who would no doubt be wearing the latest fashion and looking as young and as lovely as ever. As the gangway was lowered ponderously on creaking chains, he hefted his bag over his shoulder and moved to join the queue waiting to disembark.

'*Joseph!* Joseph, darling, over *here!*'

He looked up to see his mother, Tamar Murdoch, waving wildly with one hand while the other clutched the edge of a very wide-brimmed hat that threatened to take flight in the strong wind. No, he thought, smiling to himself, she hasn't changed at all. He was, however, surprised

3

to see the tall, elegantly dressed figure of his father beside her, a proprietorial hand at her elbow and a look of amused fondness on his dark face. Attractive and fashionably attired, they appeared the perfect couple, except that Kepa Te Roroa, his father, was obviously of the Maori race while his mother was European, and they had never been married, and never would.

Joseph dropped his bag at his feet and stepped forward to hug his mother enthusiastically, dodging the long peacock feather adorning her hat.

'Joseph, you look more handsome than ever!' she exclaimed, her eyes moist with tears. 'Damn, I'm going to cry,' she muttered as she blotted her eyelashes with the tips of her gloved fingers. 'I said I wouldn't, but it's been such a long time. I'm sorry, darling, but I'm so pleased to see you home at last.'

Joseph glanced at his father, who smiled indulgently. They shook hands and *hongi*-ed, forehead to forehead, nose to nose.

'I didn't expect to see you here today, Papa,' Joseph said.

'No, but Parehuia wanted to shop for something or other in Wellington, so we decided we might as well come down to meet you. I deposited her at Kirkcaldie and Stains earlier. I expect she has bought half the shop by now,' he added, looking faintly disconcerted. 'It is good to see you, boy.'

Joseph nodded. 'It's good to be back,' he said, and turned to Tamar. 'Is Andrew here as well?'

Andrew Murdoch was Tamar's husband of

twenty-seven years. A wealthy Hawke's Bay station owner, he adored his wife and, even though together they had produced four wonderful children of their own, he had never begrudged his wife's love for Joseph, her illegitimate and half-Maori first-born.

'Yes, but he's at a meeting this morning. Something to do with increasing wool exports to Britain because of this new war, I gather. He's promised to meet us later at the hotel and we're all to have dinner together. But there's someone else here to meet you, Joseph.'

He raised his brows inquiringly.

'But you have to close your eyes,' Tamar added mysteriously. 'It's a surprise.'

Joseph did as he was told, and immediately felt a pair of small, cold hands slide into his own. 'Can I look now?' he asked, smiling broadly.

'Yes!' crowed a jubilant voice.

Joseph opened his eyes and laughed in delight. He snatched up his half-sister, swinging her around and hugging her tightly before depositing her gently on her feet again. 'Keely!' he cried. 'I thought you were busy learning to be an angel of mercy!'

'I am, but I've got a day off! Oh Joseph, it's so *lovely* to see you!'

Joseph stepped back and took a long and appraising look at his sister. She had been away at school the last time he was briefly home and the young woman in front of him bore little resemblance to the thin, rather flighty girl he remembered. They had corresponded fairly regularly but he'd had no inkling she'd grown into such a beautiful young woman. She looked remarkably like her mother with her heavy auburn hair and wide laughing mouth, except she had her father's blue eyes. Of all of Tamar's children only Joseph had inherited the brilliant near-emerald of her eyes.

'God, you've grown up,' he said, surreptitiously eying her curvaceous figure and the slim ankles revealed by her modern, daringly short skirt. 'You're quite the young lady now, aren't you?'

'Well, no, not according to Da,' replied Keely, smiling mischievously. 'Apparently young ladies don't clean bedpans and hold bowls for people to be sick into!'

Tamar frowned. 'There was a slight fracas when Keely told Andrew she wanted to train as a nurse,' she explained, biting her lip at the memory of the bitter and protracted fight between her husband and daughter, 'but Keely had her way in the end and she's nearly finished her training now. Andrew had hopes of her marrying and starting a family after she finished school but, well, you know your sister.'

Joseph did indeed. Keely had always been very good at getting her own way, and he could imagine Andrew's dilemma at trying to reconcile his dream of a happily married daughter with the idea of her racing about the countryside, professionally trained, unfettered and thoroughly independent.

'Are you enjoying it?' he asked. He had also had to battle for the right to do what he wanted with his life and knew that such victories were not easily won. *His* father and his late great-uncle Te Kanene had plotted to orchestrate his own future from an early age, grooming him for an illustrious life in Maori politics, but he had rebelled and gone to work as a drover instead, then volunteered to serve in South Africa during the Boer War. After returning home he had been restless and unable to settle down, and he'd left New Zealand again almost immediately. He'd visited England for a time and been back to South Africa, but had found no antidote to his wanderlust there, and had finally settled, if settled could be considered the right word, in Australia where he'd been droving for the past six years on huge outback sheep stations. But now he was home again. At heart he was a New Zealander, and by all accounts New Zealand would have her work cut out in the very near future.

Keely answered enthusiastically, 'Yes, I love it. It's so rewarding. Erin loves it too.'

'Good, I'm pleased,' said Joseph as he kissed her quickly on the cheek. 'And how are our brothers?'

'James is still in the army of course. He's a full lieutenant now, and absolutely loving the life, but then he's always been good at bossing people around. He's here at Trentham but he couldn't get away today. Thomas is in his last year at Otago. Did you know he isn't doing medicine any more? He decided he didn't want to wallow in blood and guts for the rest of his life after all and swapped to the new law school. And Ian . . . '

Tamar interrupted. 'Ian is at home, trying to decide what he wants to do with himself. He's only eighteen, of course, and has plenty of time to make up his mind, but Andrew's hoping he'll take over Kenmore eventually. He loves the station and seems quite happy to potter about mending fences and chasing sheep day after day, so I expect he will. Uncle Lachie's no spring chicken either now, you know, and someone will have to pick up the reins when he and Andrew retire, which I constantly hope will be sooner rather than later.'

At the age of sixty-three Andrew Murdoch was eleven years older than Tamar, and she had been on at him for some time now to slow down and put his feet up. But sheep farming was his passion and he refused to budge. Tamar suspected he might concede to semi-retirement when Ian had learnt the ropes, but she feared that until then he would continue driving himself as if he were twenty years younger.

'And what about Huriana and Haimona?' Joseph asked Kepa, referring to his half-sister and brother from his father's marriage to Parehuia.

Kepa pulled his well-cut coat tightly about him against the sharp wind. 'Haimona is still at sea, and Huriana is teaching at Gisborne. She married eighteen months ago, as you know, but there is no sign of children yet. God only knows whether Haimona will ever settle down.'

Joseph could hear the grumpy note in his father's voice; none of his children had obliged him yet by providing the *mokopuna* he wanted,

8

and he seldom let it be forgotten. At fifty-four he considered it his right to be blessed with grandchildren, but was on the verge of giving up hope. Huriana was too immersed in her teaching, Haimona seemed wedded to the sea and Joseph was still wifeless at thirty-three.

'Still, it is good to have you back, boy,' Kepa said again. 'Perhaps you will stay this time?'

Joseph didn't answer immediately, and bent to pick up his bag. As he straightened up he said, 'I need to talk to you both about that, but not here. Do we have accommodation in Wellington tonight?'

Tamar and Kepa looked at each other uneasily, wondering what their errant son was about to spring upon them this time.

'Yes,' said Keely, rubbing her hands together briskly to restore the circulation. 'But I'm back at the hospital tomorrow and Mam and Da are *motoring* home, in their new *automobile*, the day after that.'

Joseph looked to his mother who smiled and said, 'You know Andrew and his machines. He had to have one.'

'We are returning home tomorrow,' added Kepa, 'providing your stepmother has finished her shopping, but we will be travelling by train. Shall we get off this quay before we freeze solid?'

★ ★ ★

That evening, in the vast dining room of Lambton Quay's luxurious Club Hotel, Joseph watched with interest as the two very different sides of his family chatted and laughed together. Andrew was looking as distinguished as ever, although the grey in his light brown hair had spread noticeably and the lines on his tanned face were deeper. His father's wife, Parehuia, had also joined the group, wearing a smart new outfit and looking very well-preserved for her age, if considerably plumper than she had been two years ago. Joseph thought his father was ageing very handsomely too. There was a definite slash of silver at each temple now, and lines about his dark eyes, but he had retained his youthful physique and the years had only enhanced his charismatic good looks.

But, as usual, it was his mother who astonished him most. At fifty-two she looked close to ten years younger, the auburn of her hair as vibrant as it had been in her youth and her figure still slender and firm. There were distinct laughter lines on her face now, and the faint scar on her brow had never quite disappeared, but Tamar wore both as if they were badges of honour. The first testified to the contentment of her years with Andrew; the second was a physical legacy of what had come before that, her marriage to the unfortunate Peter Montgomery and her adulterous liaison with Kepa. Joseph knew the story of his birth intimately, but still he marvelled at his mother's remarkable strength of character.

But perhaps even more remarkable was the fact that they were all so comfortable in one another's company. It was not common for Maori and Pakeha to mix socially, and

10

particularly not in public, as Joseph was reminded by the covert sidelong stares from other hotel diners, but no one at his table had been concerned about social propriety or public opinion for years, and were blithely ignoring the interest they were attracting. But it was more than just a matter of race. Andrew accepted Kepa's infrequent but continuing presence in Tamar's life with consistently good grace. Parehuia, too, knew of the history her husband shared with Tamar, but had philosophically relegated the episode to the distant past, although from time to time Joseph had sensed some unvoiced competition between the two women.

And then there was Keely, who had been raised in a monied and privileged Pakeha home but who was so proud and fond of her part-Maori brother. He remembered with amusement and anger the day some years ago when they had been shopping in Napier together and a middle-aged woman had approached them and announced to Keely that she should have more pride than to walk out in the company of a Maori man, even if he was dressed in fancy European clothes. Joseph had thought for a horrible moment that his sister would strike the opinionated creature, but she had controlled her temper, quite a rare feat, and simply suggested that the woman mind her own business. Keely was headstrong, very self-confident and, if everyone were honest, spoilt, but she was unerringly loyal to her family.

Joseph knew, therefore, that she would support

11

him in what he planned to do next. It was time to tell the family of his news. He took a small sip of wine and cleared his throat.

'I have an announcement to make,' he declared, looking around the table at the faces of those who loved him most. 'I've come home to enlist. I'm going to war again.'

There was a prolonged silence. War. There had been talk of little else since the news of Archduke Franz Ferdinand's assassination in Sarajevo in June. New Zealand had followed Britain in declaring formal hostilities against Germany on 5 August, and ever since the press had been full of the preliminary arrangements for the raising of a New Zealand Expeditionary Force.

Kepa banged his fork sharply onto his dinner plate, splattering his front with gravy. 'For God's sake, boy!' he exploded. 'You have already been to one bloody war!'

People at neighbouring tables turned to look.

'Yes,' replied Joseph calmly, aware that his father's belligerence spoke of love and fear, rather than anger, 'and now I'm going to this one. I was thinking of enlisting in Australia but I'd rather go as a New Zealander.'

There was another silence. 'At least this war has a little more merit than the one in South Africa,' said Andrew. 'By all accounts that bloody Kaiser Wilhelm has stepped well beyond his boundaries.'

Tamar pushed a slice of carrot around her plate briefly, then said without looking up, 'I suppose there's no point in asking you this, Joseph, but do you really feel you must go?'

12

Joseph looked at his mother with tenderness. 'I'm sorry, Mam, but yes, I do.'

'Why?'

Joseph had pondered the answer to this question for some weeks now, and he still hadn't been able to adequately explain, even to himself, his need to go to war again. 'I'm not sure. I can't put it into words. After the last one I came home feeling as if there was something I hadn't finished, or something I hadn't done. So perhaps this time I'll actually do whatever it is I'm supposed to do.'

'And what might that be?' demanded Kepa sarcastically, wiping gravy off his waistcoat with his linen napkin. 'Die?'

Joseph shrugged. 'I don't know, Papa. This is coming from my heart, not my head. You and Mam have always told me to listen to my heart, and that's what I'm doing.'

Kepa looked across the table at Tamar as if such advice had never passed his lips and therefore she should take full blame for their son's latest folly, but she pointedly ignored him.

'Well, you're a grown man this time, Joseph,' she said. 'We can't prevent you from following your heart, and neither should we, but think carefully about your decision, won't you?'

'I have, Mam, and I've made up my mind.'

'Well, that's that then, isn't it?' declared Keely cheerfully, knowing that her brother would never change his mind to suit someone else, not even his mother and especially not his father. 'You'll be a hero all over again.'

'I wasn't a hero last time,' Joseph said sourly.

13

Oh dear, so that's the problem, Tamar thought astutely. 'Well, I'm sure you will be this time, my love,' she said, patting Joseph's hand placatingly. 'Just as long as you come home safely,' she added.

Andrew shook his head. For such a shrewd and sophisticated woman, his lovely wife could be very naïve sometimes, especially when it came to her children.

'I'm afraid this war looks as if it could be on a much larger scale than South Africa, dear,' he said. 'All of Europe could be involved, they say.' He felt Joseph's boot nudging him under the table and countered, 'No, Joseph, we have to be realistic about this. You, us, Bill Massey, King bloody George, everyone. It could go on for years.'

'Erin hopes so. She's thinking of volunteering,' said Keely blithely.

'Erin volunteering? What for?' Andrew asked in astonishment.

'The war. They'll be calling for our nurses to serve overseas if it goes on for longer than a few months, and Erin's considering putting her name forward.'

Andrew and Tamar glanced at each other across the table in dismay. Erin was Keely's cousin, the only child of Andrew's sister Jeannie and her husband Lachie McRae, who also lived at Kenmore. With only eighteen months between them, Erin and Keely had grown up together and were both at Wellington Hospital completing their training as nurses.

'Surely not!' said Andrew, outraged. 'Do

Jeannie and Lachie know about this?'

'Well, of course not, Da. They'd just try to talk her out of it, wouldn't they? And please don't say anything to them just yet. But why shouldn't she go? Plenty of women have been to war, you only have to read the history books.'

'We have some very famous *wahine toa*,' said Parehuia unhelpfully.

Andrew said, 'Aye, but Erin's hardly soldier material, is she?'

'No, but she wouldn't be a soldier, would she? She'd be a nurse,' replied Keely. 'I don't think they're planning to send women to fight just yet.'

Joseph said, 'This doesn't sound like the Erin I know. I realise I haven't seen her for four years but I've always thought of her as the kind of girl who would rather sew and arrange flowers and read books than get her hands mucky. I can't believe she's changed that much.'

Keely gave her brother a withering look. 'Well, she has and she's an excellent nurse. Matron's always saying so and the patients love her.'

'And she didn't say anything at all to me the last time I saw her,' Joseph continued. 'In fact, she was so shy it was embarrassing.'

Yes, well, there's a reason for that, reflected Keely, although she had no intention of divulging it. Not here, anyway.

'I take it you're not thinking of volunteering yourself, Keely?' said Andrew rather pompously. 'It would be out of the question, of course. And I very much doubt whether Jeannie and Lachie will let Erin go, either.'

'She's twenty-four. I can't see how they could

stop her. And anyway it's just something she's thinking about.'

Andrew made a humphing noise, picked up his dessert spoon and concentrated on his poached pear. Only Joseph and Tamar noticed that Keely hadn't answered her father's question.

★ ★ ★

The trip by train from Wellington to Napier took over nine gloomy, rain-sodden hours, most of which Kepa used to try and persuade Joseph not to enlist. By the time they reached their destination, however, Kepa had resigned himself to sending his son off to war for a second time, and during the wagon ride to Maungakakari, the Ngati Kahungunu village north of Napier, he finally, reluctantly, gave his blessing. He wanted everything to be well between himself and his son, just in case something untoward did happen. They had been close when Joseph was young, although the boy had been raised by Kepa's sister Mereana, and their relationship was a good one, but they were both stubborn and there had been several prolonged differences of opinion resulting in temporary estrangements. Those episodes had blown over, but when Joseph had been away for so long after the Boer War, Kepa had come to realise how much he loved and valued his eldest son. He also dearly loved the two children he had fathered with Parehuia, but Joseph was Tamar's son, and despite Kepa's deep affection and immense respect for his wife, Tamar remained uppermost in his mind and in his heart, even after more than thirty years.

The inhabitants of Maungakakari had gathered to greet Joseph after his long absence and a small feast had been prepared in his honour. He greeted his *whanau* with undisguised fondness, hugging Mereana fiercely and engaging in a heartfelt *hongi* with Te Roroa, his ageing grandfather and the village chief. Te Roroa's health was failing rapidly, and Joseph reflected sadly that he could well be overseas again when the old man died and the chief's cloak passed to Kepa. He had not been present at his great-uncle Te Kanene's *tangihanga* fourteen months ago, and was loath to miss that of his grandfather as well, but sometimes such things could not be helped.

Joseph was also very pleased to see Wi and Ihaka, his two closest boyhood friends. Both had taken wives and Wi now had two young children, but Joseph could still see the spirit and sense of adventure that had bound the three of them together in their youth.

Ihaka, always the most vociferous and bellicose of the trio, clapped Joseph heartily on the back and asked in Maori, 'So what has brought you home this time, *e hoa*?'

Joseph contemplated the bulging muscles of his friend's thighs and the straining width of his chest and arms. 'The war has, Ihaka. I have come home to enlist.'

'Ah!' Ihaka exclaimed excitedly, his heavy eyebrows shooting up over his rather protuberant eyes. 'Then we will do that together! Wi and I are volunteering as well. We are fit and we are ready!'

'Is married life not suiting you?' asked Joseph, grinning slyly.

Wi, physically slighter than both Joseph and Ihaka, and much more given to jokes and a steadfast refusal to take anything too seriously, laughed. 'He married Miripeka Huriwai, remember,' he said, as if that explained everything.

It did. Joseph recalled Miripeka, a good-looking and intelligent woman but with a mind so much her own it was doubted she would ever find a mate. Only Ihaka had dared court her, and he was evidently now paying the price.

'Yes, married life suits me,' replied Ihaka huffily, 'but this is an opportunity for *war*! You have already proved yourself as a warrior, Joseph, but we have not. Now it is our turn.'

Joseph nodded. During the Boer War he had enlisted as a Pakeha: officially no Maori had been permitted to serve during that conflict, but his pale skin and European name had encouraged the recruitment officer to turn a blind eye and he had been accepted into the First Contingent.

'Papa told me that the government may not allow Maori to fight,' said Joseph carefully, not wanting to disappoint his friends.

Ihaka flapped his hand dismissively. 'Then your father should not believe everything he reads in the newspapers, or wherever that came from. The Maori Members of Parliament sent telegrams to the government offering the services of our warriors overseas as soon as the war was declared, and it is true that the offer was

18

declined, but the government will change its mind,' he said confidently, crossing his arms over his chest aggressively. 'Will you be coming with us, Joseph, or will you be serving with the Pakeha contingents again?'

'With my own people, Ihaka,' replied Joseph without any hesitation at all. 'With my own people, this time.'

Ihaka's face was suddenly illuminated by a wide and rather fierce grin. 'Then we will have two celebrations tonight! One to welcome you home and one to celebrate the birth of our war party!'

★ ★ ★

As he trotted up the long, tree-lined lane that led to Kenmore homestead, Joseph struggled to put together in his mind what he needed to say to Tamar. The British government had agreed that a Maori contingent could be raised to go to Egypt and to German Samoa for occupation duties, and Joseph, Wi and Ihaka had enlisted immediately. Now he was on his way to say goodbye to his mother, to Andrew and to his half-brother Ian before he left for the training camp near Auckland. There would be no opportunity to see James, Thomas or Keely as, with luck, he would be leaving for camp very soon, although he hoped that if the contingent departed from Wellington he would perhaps catch up with Keely and James there.

Slowing his horse to a walk, then finally coming to a complete halt at Kenmore's imposing iron gates, he paused to survey the Murdoch family home. The elegant two-storeyed masonry house with its chimneys and porticos, grand balconies and verandahs, and expanse of beautifully manicured garden always awed him — not because of its grandness, which meant little to him, but because his mother, the daughter of an impoverished Cornish miner, had managed to find her way here. She deserved it, of course, and she deserved even more the love and support of a man as kind and as generous as Andrew Murdoch, but to Joseph it still seemed like something out of a fairy tale.

Urging his horse on, he followed the carriageway around the side of the house to the stables, then dismounted and tethered his horse next to a water trough to rest and drink. Inside a large shed sat Andrew's new motor vehicle, a 1911 Ford Model T tourer painted a gleaming midnight blue.

'She's a beauty, isn't she?'

Joseph glanced over his shoulder to see Ian standing behind him. 'Absolutely. Been out in her lately?'

Ian replied enthusiastically, 'Yes, Da let me take her into town the other day. Did the trip in just over two and a half hours. It's incredible, really, when you think how long it takes by wagon or horseback.'

Joseph watched with amusement as Ian, gesticulating vigorously, described his motor trip into Napier. At eighteen he was a fit, long-limbed young man with wavy hair the colour of almost-ripe wheat, freckles scattered across his tanned nose and a wide and infectious grin. As the youngest in the family he was still occasionally treated as the baby, especially by Tamar, and consequently went to considerable lengths to prove that he wasn't one by throwing himself into, and usually succeeding at, every new experience that came his way. He wasn't the brightest of Tamar and Andrew's admittedly talented children but his disposition was perpetually sunny, he was universally popular and already sought after by some of the local station owners' daughters. He loved Kenmore, he loved his family and he idolised Joseph.

'So you're definitely off, are you?' he asked, a look of open envy on his face.

Joseph nodded. 'Yep, to Avondale. We're going up by train, but I'm not sure when we're actually going overseas. I don't think anyone is.'

'I wish I were going,' said Ian. 'I suggested it to Mam the other day and she tore strips off me, saying it was bad enough with you and James. *And* she said it'll all be over soon anyway, so there'd be no point. Is that true?'

Joseph shrugged and replied truthfully, 'Who knows? When's James off, have you heard?'

'On the twenty-fifth, apparently,' Ian replied. 'Actually, are you staying tonight? James has got leave and he'll be here this afternoon some time. He telephoned last night and said he and a friend are motoring up to say goodbye. Poor Mam, all these goodbyes.'

'Really? That's good news, I thought I'd miss him. Where's Mam?'

'Up the hill behind the house picking daffodils, I think.'

Joseph found Tamar on the hillside above Kenmore's small family cemetery, standing with her back to him and staring intently at the ground. She was wearing a voluminous pair of Liberty print harem trousers tucked into rubber boots, a short jacket belted at the waist and a large straw hat with a ragged hole in the brim. She jumped as he came up behind her.

'Hello darling!' she said brightly. 'We weren't expecting you!'

He kissed her smooth cheek, appreciating the faint scent of lavender he had associated with her since early childhood.

'Well, I've got some news,' he responded, then added quickly, 'Ian says James will be home this afternoon.'

'Yes, he's bringing someone with him, and I think I know who, too. Well, not *who* perhaps, but *what*.' She gave a small smile, her eyes shining with anticipation. 'He's been a trifle secretive lately, has our James. I hope he doesn't arrive early — Andrew says these trousers are dreadful and I shouldn't be seen in them in public, so I ought to change. I quite like them, actually, they're very comfortable. But I'm glad you're here, dear. I seem to have lost my daffodil basket. You're definitely going away, aren't you?'

She turned her face away, but not before Joseph had seen the tears welling in her eyes. He put his arms around her and hugged her to him. Her hat fell off and, with her head against his chest, she watched absently as the breeze snatched it and rolled it down the hill.

'It will be all right, Mam. I'll come home again, I promise you.'

Tamar said nothing, and hung on to him even more tightly.

2

James arrived late in the afternoon accompanied by a man in uniform and a very pretty young woman.

When Tamar hurried to meet them at the front door, James introduced the man as his very good friend Captain Ron Tarrant, then announced proudly, 'Mam, I'd like you to meet Miss Lucy Mason, my fiancée.'

Tamar smiled brightly and feigned surprise. James was a private person by nature, but he had hinted in recent months that there was someone special in his life, and she had been wondering when he might bring her home.

'Your fiancée, James? How lovely, we had no idea!'

James smiled wryly; not much got past his mother.

Tamar stepped forward and touched cheeks with the girl. 'I'm delighted to meet you, Lucy. Please come in, and you too, Captain. Your father will be in at five, James. He's been out in the paddocks all day.'

As she ushered James and his guests into the formal parlour, Joseph and Ian could be heard kicking their boots noisily off at the back door and skating down the polished wooden hall in their socks, Ian laughing uproariously. They came to an abrupt halt outside the parlour door when they saw there were visitors.

'Hello,' said Ian immediately.

James rose to shake his brothers' hands, then grinned broadly as he broke the news about the impending end to his bachelorhood.

'Really?' said Ian, genuinely surprised and delighted. 'I say, that's good news, isn't it?'

'Yes, we think so, don't we, sweetheart?' said James, sitting down again next to Lucy and taking her hand. 'We're planning to marry as soon as we can make the arrangements. Here, actually, if that's all right with everyone. We're in a bit of a hurry, what with the Expeditionary Force leaving so soon, Mam, but we were sure you'd understand.'

Tamar allowed herself a very quick, very discreet glance at Lucy's waistline before exclaiming, 'Well, of course it will be all right, dear!' The girl was not displaying any overt signs of an imminent arrival but pregnancy was not always easy to discern under the fashionably loose and high-waisted clothes women were wearing today.

Lucy Mason was very smartly dressed in a straight skirt of terracotta tweed with a matching short jacket over a cream silk blouse, worn with amber beads, beige gloves and a hat sporting a long rust-coloured feather. She looked poised and elegant but rather nervous. Her hair was an attractive shade of dark blonde and she had wide blue eyes, a small upturned nose and full lips enhanced by a subtle application of pink gloss. Her voice was educated, her manner gracious, if somewhat subdued. Tamar guessed that she came from a well-bred family, so why was she

25

running about the countryside with two young army officers, evidently about to be married and with no sign of her parents anywhere?

Never one to beat about the bush, she asked, 'And will your mother and father be attending the wedding, Lucy? We'd love to meet them.'

The young couple exchanged quick glances, then James said, 'No, unfortunately they won't, Mam. Lucy's father is very busy with war work at the moment but we visited them in Wellington a few days ago and they gave their permission. They understand that we want to be married before I leave.'

Tamar looked steadily at James for a moment, waiting to see whether he would add anything to his explanation. He didn't, but he had never been a good liar and was unable to look her in the eye.

Joseph had decided fairly quickly that he didn't like Ron Tarrant. The man looked to be about James' age, twenty-five, or perhaps a year or two older, and was good-looking in a dark, slightly fleshy way. His hair was sleek and black and had a dent in it where his uniform cap, now balanced on one crossed knee, had sat. A large and luxuriant moustache covered his upper lip and his eyebrows almost met above a strong nose. There was a heavy gold and onyx ring on his right hand and he swung his leg as if he were just a little bored by the family tableau before him. Next to him, James, with his nut-brown hair, blue eyes and rather classical profile, his long legs stretched out before him, looked far more at ease.

Although somewhat surprised to learn that he was about to gain a daughter-in-law, Andrew took the news with good cheer and expressed hearty congratulations, but he voiced his doubts as he and Tamar dressed for dinner.

'Is she pregnant, do you think?' he asked, fastening his tie and frowning at himself in the full-length mirror.

'Oh, Andrew, what a dreadful thing to assume!' replied Tamar in an admonitory tone as she bent over to look for something under the bed.

Andrew laughed but didn't turn around, content to view his wife's still very shapely bottom reflected in the mirror. 'Now don't tell me you haven't already had a good squiz at the poor girl's middle, Tamar. I know how your devious little mind works!'

Tamar stood up, her face flushed and her hair escaping from its pins. 'I'm not devious, Andrew. You're fully aware that these things happen and if it is the case, I'd prefer to know about the arrival of our first grandchild sooner rather than later, that's all. Have you seen my harem pants anywhere?'

'You're not wearing them to dinner, dear,' said Andrew mildly. 'They're hideous. Wear one of your lovely dresses.'

Spotting a minute scrap of patterned material sticking out from under the heavy cherrywood blanket box at the end of the bed, Tamar discovered her cherished trousers crushed underneath. She shook them out and said bemusedly, 'Now, how did they get under there, I wonder?'

Andrew said nothing.

'Damn, I'll *have* to wear a dress now,' she said, and burst into tears.

Andrew whipped around, appalled by her sudden distress and ashamed of himself for having hidden the ugly pants in the first place. He took Tamar in his arms and stroked her hair. 'It's the boys going, isn't it?' he murmured gently.

'Yes,' she said into his shirt front. 'I desperately want to plead with them not to, but they're men now, Andrew. I can't stop them and I've no right to.'

'Aye, I know,' he said. 'I feel the same way but young men have always gone off to war, Tamar. This time won't be any different.' He shut his mouth before he could add that, as far as he could see, this one could well be worse than anything they had seen in their lifetime. He adored his children, and had grown very fond of Joseph over the years, but he knew he was powerless to prevent them going. At a pinch he could probably blackmail Ian by offering him the carrot of Kenmore. He believed that Keely had no interest in serving as a nurse overseas, and was convinced that going to war would be the last thing Thomas, with his gentle and sensitive ways, would want to do, but Joseph was already an experienced war veteran and James was a professional soldier.

'We have to let them go, dear, and support them while they're away and when they come back,' he said, 'but beyond that, this is something they have to do for themselves. They're not children any more. Now come on, dry your tears and make yourself beautiful and we'll go down to dinner. If we are to have a new daughter-in-law we don't want her to think we're a pair of old miseries, do we?'

Tamar drew back, looked up at his kind face and gave him a watery smile.

★   ★   ★

In the end Tamar dressed in one of her best evening outfits, in honour of James's impending marriage and as a gesture to her departing sons. Under a silk kimono in a mauve and black oriental print, she wore a grey silk Charmeuse sheath dress styled on one of Parisian couturier Paul Poiret's latest designs, which she had copied from an illustration in a magazine. On her feet were mauve satin heels with an ornate silver buckle trim. To complete the look she pinned her hair up in a series of coils that covered the tops of her ears but revealed a pair of large pearl drop earrings matched by a lustrous double rope about her throat.

Joseph and Ian both whistled as she entered the dining room.

'You look marvellous, Mam,' said Ian appreciatively.

'Thank you, darling,' said Tamar as she regarded the long, beautifully set dining table. Everyone was seated, including Jeannie and Lachie. Glancing at Lucy she noted that the girl

29

was also fashionably attired for dinner in a lilac silk tunic over a ruched but straight skirt so was clearly not travelling light. Both James and Ron Tarrant had changed into smart three-piece lounge suits, and next to them Ian, in his shirtsleeves, looked even more of a boy than he was. Joseph, who, unlike his father, had never bothered too much about fashion, was also in shirtsleeves.

'Mrs Heath's serving the first course in five minutes,' announced Jeannie.

'Is she? Good,' said Andrew. 'Would anyone like another drink?'

Avis Heath, Kenmore's housekeeper and cook, had replaced the dauntless Mrs Muldoon upon her retirement four years ago. A small woman in her mid-fifties with apparently limitless energy, Mrs Heath cooked expertly, ran the house with extreme efficiency, thoroughly approved of good manners and proper etiquette and was therefore occasionally a little perturbed, but privately of course, by some of the goings-on at Kenmore. This afternoon she had been asked by Tamar to 'do something special' for dinner and had done her mistress proud, even if she did say so herself.

'Yes,' said Tarrant in answer to Andrew's question. 'I'll have a little more of that brandy, thanks.'

For the last half-hour he had been regaling the men with amusing stories from the training camp at Trentham, although Joseph had not been overly impressed when Tarrant had begun describing the less educated enlisted men in his company as 'oicks'. Now, he was soaking up

30

Andrew's best brandy as if he were a sponge, although he had said nothing else offensive and had indeed been very entertaining and quite charming. Still, Joseph felt uncomfortable for some reason he couldn't pinpoint, and wondered what it was that drew James to Tarrant.

Lucy Mason, on the other hand, was a dear little thing. Slender and fair, and altogether too 'fluffy' for Joseph, who preferred his women to possess considerably more physical substance and spiritual fire, she was nevertheless rather appealing and it wasn't difficult to see why James was infatuated with her.

As Mrs Heath bustled about serving the first course, Lachie asked Ron Tarrant conversationally, 'And where are you lads off to first, or is that a secret?'

'No, no,' replied Tarrant as he buttered a roll. 'I should imagine everybody knows where we're going — it's been hinted at in the papers for long enough. England and then on to France, I'd say.'

Andrew said, 'Pass the bread, will you, Ian. So, Captain, do you think the Expeditionary Force is in good shape? For active service, I mean?'

'Oh, definitely,' replied Tarrant. 'The Territorials have been training for years, and most of the NZEF is made up of Territorial volunteers. There's no doubt Major-General Godley's got an effective fighting force together. At the moment we've an infantry brigade of four battalions, a mounted rifles brigade of four regiments, and support units of artillery, engineers and field ambulances.' He turned to Joseph and said, 'And there'll be you Maori

31

chaps, too, of course, doing garrison duty and what have you. I don't expect you'll be allowed to do any of the actual fighting, but we'll all be glad of your efforts, I'm sure.'

James looked very embarrassed. There was an awful silence, which Andrew broke by saying rather coldly, 'Actually, Joseph is a Boer War veteran, Captain. He's a very experienced soldier and has already served the Empire with some distinction.'

'Yes, quite, James told me about that,' said Tarrant. 'But surely an all-native contingent won't be expected to fight alongside, well, everyone else?'

Joseph finished chewing a mouthful of food, swallowed and took a small sip of wine. 'And why would that be the case, Captain?' he asked evenly.

'Well, I suppose there mightn't be a problem if the contingent were to be under non-Maori command, but, well, you have to admit that most Maoris haven't had much experience fighting in a real war and it'll be pretty serious over there.'

Oh my God, thought Tamar, closing her eyes.

Jeannie, equally appalled, pushed back her chair and said quickly, 'I'll just ring for Mrs Heath, shall I, and tell her we're ready for the second course?'

At the same time Lachie loudly asked Ian if he had finished moving the sheep out of the top paddocks, even though he knew he had, and Tamar asked Lucy what she was planning to wear on her wedding day.

Lucy replied, 'I brought two dresses with me,

Mrs Murdoch, but I'm not sure which one to wear. I was hoping to ask for your advice on that, if you don't mind. James said you're very knowledgeable about fashion.'

'Of course, Lucy. I'd love to and I'm very flattered, but it's your wedding day and you must wear what you feel best in.'

Tarrant suddenly cleared his throat, turned to Joseph and said abruptly, 'Look here, old man, I apologise if what I said sounded patronising. I certainly didn't mean it that way.'

Joseph returned his gaze for several seconds, then replied, 'No offence taken, Captain. You're right, in fact. It may not be easy to combine the two fighting styles, but I'm sure we'll all manage when it really matters.'

There was another short silence, then Lachie said, 'Our boys seem to be doing well in Samoa.'

'Well, they should be,' replied Andrew. 'We sent nearly fourteen hundred troops just to capture a wireless station on an island occupied by eighty Germans and a handful of reservists. We'd be looking rather silly if we weren't doing well, wouldn't we?'

'Is it true that when the New Zealand government asked the British War Office about the German defences in Samoa, they said to look it up in *Whitaker's Almanac?*' asked Lucy. 'I read that in the papers,' she added hesitantly.

James smiled at her fondly, ignoring Tarrant's look which suggested that pretty young ladies should not confuse themselves by trying to keep up with current affairs. 'Well, that's the story going around, but I wouldn't think it's true.'

'No, I doubt it,' laughed Tarrant. 'I'm positive the intelligence we had on Samoa would have been a little more specific than that. Britain hasn't taken the decision to enter this war lightly, as you must know, and certainly wouldn't send one of her best colonial forces into a potentially dangerous situation unprepared. No, the Empire and her soldiers are much more wily than that,' he added bombastically, 'and I'm predicting that the Kaiser is in for a very rude shock. You don't antagonise Britain and her colonies without paying a very hefty price.'

Tamar wished she felt as confident as the captain sounded.

'In fact,' Tarrant continued, 'I'd like to raise a toast to both James and Lucy's marriage, and to all of us who are going off to war. I'm sure that the former will be a very successful union, and the latter, well, victory can be the only conceivable outcome.' He stood and raised his glass. 'To James and Lucy, and to the Dominion's soldiers, heroes to a man!'

★   ★   ★

Making herself comfortable on the guest room's upholstered couch, Tamar watched as Lucy carefully withdrew two dresses from a suitcase that looked far too full for a short visit and laid them across the bed. One, in cream chiffon, had a nipped-in waist under a neat box jacket with full lace sleeves. The other, less formal in design, was a pale blue silk with a high-waisted straight

34

skirt that fell softly from a fitted bodice to just above the ankle.

Lucy sat on the bed and asked shyly, 'What do you think, Mrs Murdoch?'

Eying the two dresses critically, Tamar said, 'Well, which do you prefer?', then moved over to the bed to inspect the gowns more closely. She didn't like the cream chiffon, which was rather old-fashioned for her tastes, but it was Lucy's wedding and she might prefer something traditional.

Lucy hesitated, then said, 'I like the cream.'

Tamar, intent on examining the fine embroidery around the neck of the blue dress, nodded, then looked up in alarm as she heard a stifled sob.

Lucy's hand was over her face but behind it Tamar could glimpse the tears beginning to trickle down the girl's cheeks, pink with the effort of trying not to cry.

'Oh dear,' said Tamar sympathetically. 'Something's not right, is it?'

'I like the cream,' Lucy repeated, from behind both hands now, 'but it doesn't *fit*! I'm getting too big for it!'

Ah, thought Tamar. She sat down next to the girl and put her arm around her. 'Do you mind if I ask *where* you're getting too big?' she enquired gently.

'*Here*,' Lucy replied in anguish, a hand moving to her belly. 'I'm expecting, Mrs Murdoch! I'm so sorry. We didn't mean to.'

Oh James, you careless boy, thought Tamar reprovingly. But then she was a fine one to talk.

'How far along are you, dear?'

'Just over three months, I think. Maybe closer to four. I'm not entirely sure. It's James' child,' she said. 'I haven't, you know, been with anyone else.'

'Of course you haven't.' Tamar sighed inwardly but patted Lucy's shoulder placatingly. 'Look, these things happen. It's not the end of the world. I understand that you want to be married as soon as possible.'

Lucy sniffed noisily, extracted a lace handkerchief from her sleeve and wiped her nose. She cleared her throat, took several deep breaths and said in a rush, 'My parents threw me out. When James talked to them about us getting married they wanted to know what the hurry was and James said it was the war but Father didn't believe him and I finally told them I was expecting a baby and that was that. Father has a very important job and the scandal could ruin him, and Mother always does what Father tells her to do, and now I've nowhere to go and James is going away soon and I'm quite frightened.'

'Do you love James?'

'Yes, I do, very much. He's all I've ever wanted. And I believe he loves me.'

Tamar had no doubt about that; she'd seen it in her son's eyes the minute she had opened the door.

'How old are you?' she asked.

'I'm twenty next month.'

'And there's no chance at all that your parents will take you back while James is away?'

Lucy shook her head and blotted the new

tears collecting on her long eyelashes. 'No, they were absolutely livid. I was hoping that perhaps after the baby comes and they see it, they might change their minds, but I really don't know.'

'Has James made arrangements for somewhere for you to live?'

'He's going to send me all of his army pay so I can find a little place until he comes home.'

Tamar snorted inelegantly and said, 'Well, that's silly when we've got endless spare rooms here. You're more than welcome to stay with us, Lucy.'

This announcement made Lucy cry even more, and Tamar waited patiently until she had herself under control again.

'We'll all sit down and talk about it in the morning, shall we, after you've had a good night's sleep. And, under the circumstances, I think you should perhaps choose the blue for your wedding. The fall of the skirt will easily hide your little bump, if that's worrying you, and the colour suits you better.'

'Isn't it worrying you?' Lucy asked. 'I was sure you wouldn't want a daughter-in-law who gets herself into this sort of predicament.'

Tamar laughed out loud. 'Then you've a lot to learn about me, my dear!'

Lucy nervously folded her handkerchief into a series of small damp squares. 'James said you would be very understanding. May I ask then, well, I had noticed that Joseph, your son, he isn't, um, he's not the same as . . . '

'Joseph is half-Maori, Lucy. He's my firstborn, and the man I was married to at the time wasn't his father, so I'm in no position whatsoever to take the moral high ground just because my first grandchild will be born less than nine months after the marriage of its parents. And this child will be the product of a genuine loving union, won't it? Who could ever be censorious of that?'

'Thousands of people, I should imagine,' Lucy replied, pulling a wry face and displaying the first hint of a sense of humour Tamar had seen in her so far.

★　★　★

Downstairs, James, Joseph and Andrew sat in front of the fire in Andrew's study, smoking cigarettes and drinking a late-evening cognac.

Joseph said, 'I'm sorry James, but I don't think much of your friend Ron. He's a bit, well, arrogant in my view.'

'Aye, he did rather come across that way, didn't he?' agreed Andrew, swirling his glass and watching the way the flames added richness to the colour of the brandy.

James shifted in his seat uncomfortably. 'Yes, I'm sorry about that, Joseph. He can be a little overbearing at times and he does tend to go on about the glory of fighting for one's country and all that, but he's a decent sort of bloke, really. He's an exemplary officer, enthusiastic, dedicated and very highly trained, and he's been very helpful to me and truly cares about his men, even if he is a wee bit of a snob. Did a stint at Staff College in England not so long ago and it's expected this kerfuffle in Europe will be the start of a very illustrious military career.'

'Is he married?' asked Joseph.

'Only to the army.'

'He doesn't seem to have a very high opinion of your young lady.'

'Oh, no, he approves. In fact, he was the one who introduced us. But he does believe that women should look pretty, keep quiet and produce babies, in that order. He's not too keen on them using their brains any more than absolutely necessary.'

'Yes, well,' muttered Andrew, 'he wouldn't last too long in this family. It's full of women who insist on using their brains. He'd never get on with Keely and Erin, and I don't think your mother fancied him much either.'

James grinned. 'Aunt Jeannie gave him a filthy look behind his back as well, I noticed. Poor old Ron. He gets so carried away with the idea of being a hero and the nobility of war and all that that he doesn't realise he's offending people.'

'Or boring them,' added Joseph dryly. 'I hope he's not disappointed when he gets overseas. There's a lot of 'hurry up and wait' even on active service, and then when things do happen they hardly ever go according to plan.'

'Perhaps not,' agreed James as he reached for the decanter, 'but we've been training hard out lately. We've practised a whole range of strategies and manoeuvres, the officers know their stuff and the men know exactly what they should be doing and when. I think we'll be all right.'

Joseph raised his eyebrows but didn't say anything: if his service in South Africa was anything to go by, James could be in for a very rude shock.

'So, this Lucy of yours,' said Andrew, 'are you sure you're doing the right thing, marrying her?'

'Oh, definitely. She's a wonderful girl.' James paused for a moment, idly twiddling a button on his suit coat, then looked his father directly in the eye. 'Her parents gave us permission to marry, Da, but they don't exactly approve.'

'Why on earth not?' said Andrew indignantly. 'Who could ask for more in a son-in-law!'

'Ah, well, it's not *me* they've a problem with, exactly,' replied James, going red. 'It's more to do with what we've, ah, done.'

Andrew looked at his son over the rim of his glass for a moment, then exclaimed in exasperation, 'Oh James, for God's *sake*! I expected you to have had more sense. When is it due?'

'Some time in February, we think. Her parents went berserk. I'm delighted myself, and I would have asked her to marry me anyway. The only thing that bothers me is that I might still be away when she has it, but if I am I expect I could apply to come home on leave.'

'Well, congratulations,' said Joseph, leaning forward in his chair to shake James's hand warmly. 'A child is worth celebrating no matter what the circumstances. Consider yourself lucky, James — you'll have a loving wife and a child to come home to.'

'Yes,' said James, smiling softly as if this had not really occurred to him until now. 'I will, won't I?'

3

James and Lucy were married quietly on the
19th of September in the drawing room at
Kenmore, the officiating Methodist minister,
Bernard McKenzie, already accustomed to
marrying couples at a moment's notice. The
family regretted the absence of Thomas, Keely
and Erin, but there had just not been enough
time for them to travel to Napier.

James and Ron Tarrant left for Trentham the
following morning, and Joseph returned to
Maungakakari to wait impatiently with Wi and
Ihaka for the call to go into camp.

After the Main Body of some 8500 troops had
finally sailed on the 16th of October, word at last
came through that the Ngati Kahungunu
contingent from Hawke's Bay would be entrain-
ing for Avondale on the 21st. Joseph, already a
combat veteran, was more subdued than his
companions and took a book to read on the way,
much to the disgust of Ihaka, who accused him
of acting as if he were going on an ordinary old
trip to town for supplies, not to war.

It took a week for the First Maori
Contingent's volunteers to assemble at the
tented campsite on the Avondale Racecourse. In
the days that followed the men milled about
aimlessly, their confusion fuelled by wildly
spreading rumours and long-held intertribal
rivalries that surfaced with a vengeance. Joseph

41

watched it all patiently, with the wisdom of one who knew the idiosyncrasies of both army life and Maori culture, and waited quietly until some order had been established.

Initially the Maori Contingent had been intended as a garrison force in both Samoa and Egypt, freeing up other New Zealand troops to fight elsewhere, but after only a few days at Avondale it became clear that the Maori volunteers, backed by their tribal leaders, had no intention at all of being separated and sent to serve in two different places. There was more trouble when the volunteers were divided into two companies that arbitrarily threw members of different tribes together.

Ihaka complained bitterly to Joseph, 'What a stupid thing to do. How can we uphold the name of the Maori race and take with us into battle the brave reputation of our ancestors if we are all mixed up? I will not fight alongside tribes who have been our enemies for generations. Will you?'

Privately, Joseph expected that intertribal rivalries would be forgotten the moment he and his cohorts came face to face with the enemy, but he knew how important Ihaka's warrior heritage was to him. He finished winding his puttees firmly about his calves and stood up, stretching until his spine cracked; he had grown a little soft sleeping on mattresses and pillows since his return from Australia. 'In the end, Ihaka, we will fight next to the men we're told to fight next to. This is a Pakeha army, remember, and we may not end up in battle at all. And don't speak *te reo*, eh? It upsets the Pakeha officers.'

Ihaka hissed through his teeth, but switched to English. '*Ea*, I am going to Egypt to *fight*, not to dig latrines for some fat Pakeha officer's arse to sit on! I'll run away to join the fighting soldiers if I have to, and I won't be the only one, eh!'

Probably not, reflected Joseph. Ihaka, like many of the volunteers, had been angry to discover that while officers up to the rank of captain would include Maori, commanding officers above that would be Pakeha only. But Joseph believed the men would accept the arrangements once they discovered that much of the practical direction in battle comes from non-commissioned officers. In South Africa he had never bothered too much with orders given by the more senior officers but had relied almost solely on the advice and instruction of Sergeant Thornton, who had led the section.

'We'll see. Things will sort themselves out soon enough,' he said philosophically.

As it turned out, two things happened that greatly improved the morale of the camp in general. First, after much protest, the two companies were reconfigured so that men from the West Coast, South Island and North Auckland tribes made up A Company, while B Company comprised the East Coast tribes. This minimised, although it did not entirely eradicate, intertribal rivalry. Then, early in November, the men were told that the whole Maori Contingent would be sent to Egypt.

After that, they settled down to train with an enthusiasm that impressed many observers. The job of instructing the new recruits, however, was not made any easier by the seemingly continual arrival of family members at the camp. By the time parents had located and removed errant sons, and wives had done the same with husbands who had been seduced by the prospect of war and adventure overseas, holes were beginning to appear in the ranks. Also vanishing were the men judged unfit by the medical officer, Major Te Rangi Hiroa, an old schoolmate of Joseph's, as well as those who had changed their minds about joining the army and had quietly deserted. However, a constant stream of reinforcements, in the form of new arrivals, meant that the contingent was never under-manned.

Because of his age and his previous combat experience, Joseph was promoted almost imme-diately to the rank of sergeant, a development he found moderately embarrassing but also pleas-ing. He was grateful to find that the composition of his section, which included Wi and Ihaka, did not change, and within the first week of serious training he was proud to report that his men were progressing well and working admirably within the platoon. This was not strictly true, for Ihaka was displaying a rather reckless indepen-dence, but Joseph was quietly convinced that, when the time came, his friend could be relied upon to perform in the best interests of his fellow soldiers.

Finally, on the 10th of January 1915, the two companies of the Maori Contingent paraded proudly down Auckland's Queen Street to the wharf where the SS *Warrimoo* was waiting to transport them to Wellington.

Joseph, marching along with his head up and his rifle against his left shoulder, felt oddly ambivalent. Here they were, five hundred of the Maori race's best warriors on the eve of departing to fight an imperial war in a foreign land, and there was barely a murmur from the predominantly Pakeha crowd lining the street. As the slap of a thousand booted feet echoed off the tall buildings, he wondered what the bystanders were thinking. Were they asking themselves why these five hundred had volunteered to fight in a war that was essentially nothing to do with Maori? If they were, Joseph didn't blame them; from time to time he had caught himself wondering exactly the same thing.

Then he glanced at Ihaka, marching energetically beside him with his chin thrust out and a ferocious look on his dark face, and smiled to himself. Yes, he was doing the right thing.

★ ★ ★

The reception in Wellington was much more enthusiastic. The citizens cheered as the Maori Contingent, together with reinforcements for the New Zealand Expeditionary Force, marched through the city streets to Newtown Park. And Joseph was surprised and delighted to spy Keely waving furiously at him from the forefront of the crowd at the park.

Shouldering his kit he hurried over. 'What are you doing here?'

'Don't look so amazed, Joseph, we've come to

45

farewell you! Mam rang us and said you'd be here today.'

'We?'

'Yes, Thomas and Erin are here too, somewhere. On the other side of the park, I think, trying to find you. I must say, your contingent is looking good. Come on, let's go and find the others,' she said, taking his hand and yanking him along behind her.

Thomas and Erin were standing under a tree, gazing about in bewilderment, and turned in unison as Keely shouted, 'I've found him!'

Thomas hadn't changed much at all since the last time Joseph had seen him. A little taller, perhaps, but still lean and rangy and looking very much like his father with his light brown hair and mild blue eyes. At twenty-four he was the most retiring and reserved of Tamar's sons, but blessed with a very quick mind and a sense of commitment he applied diligently to everything he did. His sense of humour remained hidden from most but he was a kind and earnest young man with plenty of friends and the respect and admiration of his tutors at Otago law school.

Joseph grasped his hand and shook it warmly. 'Good to see you, Thomas! I thought you were still down south?'

Thomas grinned in pleasure. 'Well, I was, but I'm back up for a little while to sort out a few bits and pieces. I'm on my way home to see Mam and Da but I thought I'd stop in and visit Keely.'

'Well, I'm glad you did. God only knows when I'll be back.'

46

'Yes,' replied Thomas, a worried expression replacing his smile. 'Are you sure you're doing the right thing, going off again?'

Joseph nodded. 'I think so, yes. And anyway it's a bit late now to change my mind.'

Thomas pulled a face and shrugged, then turned to the young woman beside him and said, 'You haven't said hello to Erin yet.'

Joseph, who'd had one surreptitious but pleasantly surprised eye on Erin the whole time, was intrigued to see her blush. Unlike Thomas, she had changed significantly. She had always been moderately tall, but now, at twenty-four, she had blossomed into a very shapely young woman with wide shoulders, a full bust above a neat waist and generously rounded hips. Her hair, heavy and dark like her mother's, was parted demurely in the middle and pulled back into a smooth bun at the nape of her neck, framing a face that made Joseph think of illustrations he had seen of women from ancient Rome. Erin's nose was certainly patrician and her mouth full but her eyes, slightly slanted and a deep, velvet brown fringed with long black lashes, almost completely dominated her currently rather pink face.

He took her hand and gave her a peck on the cheek, suddenly feeling unaccountably uncomfortable himself. 'Erin, it's lovely to see you. It's been a while, hasn't it?'

'Yes, years,' she agreed, extricating her hand from Joseph's grasp. 'It seems that whenever you were home, I wasn't. We kept missing each other.'

47

'Yes,' said Joseph unnecessarily. She really did have the most extraordinary eyes. 'How's the nursing going?' he asked lamely, feeling uncharacteristically tongue-tied.

'Fine,' she replied.

'Good,' he said.

At the periphery of his vision Joseph noticed Keely winking exaggeratedly at Thomas, and demanded, 'What?'

'Something in my eye, I think,' replied Keely, giggling and dabbing theatrically with her handkerchief.

Joseph was mystified, and Erin seemed even more embarrassed.

At that moment a piercing whistle sounded and Joseph said, 'Damn, I'll have to go now. Thanks for coming, and I'll see you all when I get home!' And with another quick kiss for each of the girls and a pat on the back for Thomas, he hurried off to rejoin his unit.

'What was that all about?' asked Thomas, perplexed.

Keely smirked. 'Erin has fancied Joseph for years and years, and I thought it would be nice for her to see him before he left. She hasn't seen him for ages, you know.'

Thomas shook his head reproachfully. 'You'll get into a terrible muddle one of these days, Keely, interfering in other people's lives.' He had never quite forgotten one disastrous assignation Keely had engineered a year ago involving himself and a nurse friend of hers. Although he had the normal instincts of a young man, his rather undeveloped social skills had let him

48

down badly and his face still burned at the memory of it. 'How do you know Joseph is interested?' he added, then turned to his cousin. 'I'm sorry Erin, but he might not be, and that's embarrassing for everyone.'

Erin, still looking rather mortified, said, 'I know, Thomas. It was Keely's idea and now I wish I hadn't let her talk me into it.'

'But he does fancy you, Erin!' protested Keely. 'Didn't you see the look on his face? You're exactly the type of girl who would appeal to him.'

'How do you know that?' demanded Thomas. 'And anyway, they're cousins.'

Keely tapped her nose conspiratorially. 'A woman can sense these things, Thomas. And they're only kissing cousins, no blood ties, remember?'

'Oh Keely, leave it alone, will you?' said Erin crossly. Now that Joseph had gone her excitement at seeing him had degenerated into a vague feeling of depression.

'Anyway, we might bump into him over there,' added Keely airily.

Thomas frowned. 'Over where?'

'France, perhaps, or maybe Egypt. Erin and I have both volunteered for service overseas with the New Zealand Army Nursing Service.'

★ ★ ★

Inside his tiny tent, Joseph shivered in his military issue shorts and light tunic as the temperature and the sun both went down.

Sitting cross-legged on his thin blanket spread over sandy but deceptively hard ground, he glanced up as the tent flap was flipped briskly back to see the grinning face of a fellow sergeant, Jack Herewini, peering in at him.

'*Kia ora*, mate. We're sharing, eh. Shove over.'

Joseph grinned himself and moved his kit out of the way, reflecting that although the tent was barely big enough for a single person he should have known he would be required to occupy it with at least one other. He didn't mind at all, however; Jack Herewini was an amiable and interesting character, strict with his men but always ready to see the humour in everything around him, and they had shared some memorable experiences during their training at Avondale. He was also a distant cousin of Joseph's, hailing from a village some thirty miles further up the East Coast from Maungakakari, and they had quite a few relatives and acquaintances in common.

The trip to Egypt on the *Warrimoo* had been long, tedious and unremarkable. Even Joseph, accustomed to the sea, was bored and impatient by the time they reached Suez at the end of March. Although the days were partially occupied with drill and training, the cramped conditions on board and the dull food made life monotonous. The exotic minarets, mosques and bazaars of Cairo made a welcome change but the contingent had little time to explore before being marched off to the New Zealand military camp at Zeitoun, a sprawling tent city squatting under the ancient obelisk of Matarieh.

'You got any food?' Jack asked, crawling into the tent and dumping his kit in a corner.

'No, but I could do with some,' Joseph replied.

As if in agreement Jack's stomach rumbled loudly. 'Me too. Go for a walk, eh, see what we can scrounge.'

Joseph quickly nodded; he wanted to check on his men anyway.

Outside, twilight stained the countryside a deep purple and made hazards of the guy ropes radiating out from the long lines of tents. Jack had fallen over three and sworn long and loud by the time they located a large tent filled with trestle tables, from behind which a handful of the Expeditionary Force catering corps were handing out cups of cocoa and bread spread with jam.

'Yous are lucky,' said one of them, a Pakeha soldier with a lance corporal's stripe on his sleeve. 'We were just going to close up but someone said yous were coming in late. Good on ya, too. My old man always said you lot were good fighters.'

'Thanks mate,' said Jack through a mouthful of bread. 'Glad to be here. Took long enough.' He swallowed and emptied his mug in one long draft. 'Seen any fighting yet?'

'Me? Nah, I come over with the Main Body and I been stirring bloody pots ever since. No doubt we'll be right in the middle of it, though, soon as we get face to face with Johnny Turk.'

'On the Gallipoli Peninsula, you mean?' asked Joseph.

'Yep. Can't wait. Are you lot coming with us?'

'Don't know yet,' Jack replied, helping himself to another slab of bread. 'Might be going on to Malta.'

'What for? There's bugger all happening there.'

'We haven't had our orders yet, but that's what we've heard,' confirmed Joseph gloomily. 'Anyway, thanks for the feed.'

'Welcome,' said the lance corporal congenially as he turned away to serve the next man.

As Joseph and Jack wandered back towards the Maori Contingent's lines, they stopped suddenly.

'Can you hear that?' asked Joseph.

'It's a war *haka*, eh?' replied Jack. 'Someone's doing a bloody *peruperu*!'

They wove hurriedly back through the lines until they came to an open space in front of the contingent's tents, which was quickly filling up with Maori soldiers. At the front and directly in the middle of the group stood Ihaka, a wild grin on his dark face. The whites of his eyes and his big, sweating chest gleamed in the dim light as he stamped his booted feet, swung his rifle and bellowed the *peruperu*. It seemed that almost all of the contingent had congregated, and the volume of the chant was rising by the second. Swarms of other soldiers, attracted by the noise, were appearing between the tents and jostling each other for a better look.

Joseph glanced at Jack. 'Well, shall we join them?'

'Might as well,' Jack replied, grinning widely himself and already stripping off his shirt. Then he paused and said, 'Shit, our rifles. I'll go and get them.' The *peruperu* would be incomplete without the brandishing of weapons.

When he returned a minute later they moved together into the front row next to Ihaka and picked up the rhythm. By now a great crowd had gathered to watch the spectacle, spellbound by the ferociously bulging eyes and protruding tongues of the Maori soldiers, all armed and jumping into the air with feet tucked beneath them, and the frenzied chant that alternated between a guttural hissing and blood-curdling yelling. In Maori, they chorused:

> *Gird yourself in the dogskin cloak,*
> *And leap into the fray!*
> *The battle, what of it?*
> *Warrior meets warrior man to man,*
> *Ha! The battle is joined!*

Then the lines parted to let through a dozen lunging, dancing men wielding *taiaha*, or fighting sticks, and Joseph laughed out loud to see the observers in the front row step back in alarm. Not the Pakeha New Zealanders, who were performing their own spontaneous version of a *haka* on the sidelines, but a handful of British and Australian visitors, whose expressions registered an uneasy mix of astonishment, fear and wonder.

As the *peruperu* neared its climax and Joseph began to sweat freely, his blood racing and his throat aching, he felt suddenly and wildly elated, as if all of his recent ambivalence about being part of this new war had flown away and left in his heart nothing but a burning desire to fight. He was aware of the spirits of his Ngati Kahungunu ancestors flooding into him, and he knew by their exultant expressions that the men beside him were also in direct communion with their *tupuna*.

The *haka* ended with a final, deafening shout and a massive leap into the air, followed by tumultuous applause and cheering from the onlookers. Panting from exertion and wiping trickles of sweat from his face, Joseph approached Ihaka, intending a half-hearted admonishment, but the triumphant look on his friend's face stole the words from his mouth.

'See!' demanded Ihaka, 'they know what we made of now! They have to send us warriors to the fighting, 'cos we the best!'

Joseph turned to Wi, who was never far from Ihaka, and shook his head benignly. There was nothing he could say.

* ★ ★

The contingent's blood lust remained high for several days and, in retrospect, Joseph would always wonder whether the *haka* that had so galvanised them had also contributed to the appalling shambles of Good Friday.

It all started when his company was on leave in Cairo with others of the New Zealand Expeditionary Force and a large party of Australian troops. Like many other soldiers caught up in the event, Joseph was unaware at the time of what had initially sparked the riot.

54

Some reckoned that the debacle had in no way come as a shock, others were surprised that it hadn't happened earlier. After all, relations between the Allied forces and their Egyptian hosts had been strained for some time, both at Zeitoun Camp and in Cairo itself.

Every soldier had been approached at least twice by the persistent and apparently deaf native men and boys peddling cigarettes, oranges and rude photographs whenever and wherever they saw an opportunity. The oranges were thirst-quenching but the harsh cigarettes immediately cancelled out any relief provided by the fruit, and the photographs were offensive to some, titillating to others, but eventually boring to all, especially when the real thing could be obtained for very little financial outlay, if a man wasn't too choosy about where he laid his hat.

The situation was even worse when the troops ventured into the city. A soldier could hardly take five steps down a street without being accosted by crowds of natives offering all manner of goods for sale, from muslins and silks to Sudanese beads, peanuts, sex, souvenirs, 'authentic' artifacts and other strange bits and pieces. When one of the more naïve young privates in Joseph's section purchased an exorbitantly priced scrap of textile said to have been wrapped around the actual mummified body of Rameses III, Joseph, sick of his men being rooked, lost his temper and told the soldier to return the disgusting piece of rag and get his money back. It stank too much to be that ancient and no doubt harboured all sorts of dreaded diseases. The private did as he was told but, unable to find the hawker who had sold him the 'artifact', thumped the nearest Egyptian with wares for sale and helped himself to the money he felt he was owed. The fracas that followed resulted in the lieutenant in charge of Joseph's platoon, a popular officer named Ropata McPherson, advising him to discourage his men from going into the city in future. Joseph however, believed they were entitled to learn to look after themselves, though after Good Friday he wished he'd taken heed.

But the New Zealanders and Australians themselves were more often than not guilty of arrogant and opportunistic behaviour. Running out of cafés before paying was a favourite, abusing the natives was another, but the biggest cause of resentment, on both sides, was the troops' attitude towards the Egyptian women. Prostitution thrived in Cairo, and although whores were usually easy to spot, many of the men still apparently had trouble distinguishing between the females who were for sale and those who were not, resulting in many outraged complaints to the authorities about respectable Egyptian women being, at best, insulted, and at worst assaulted. On the other side of the coin, many of the prostitutes were riddled with venereal disease, and had very little compunction about passing it on to their customers. The afflicted troops then blamed the women for their painful predicament and subsequent spells in hospital. All these pressures, together with the pent-up frustration of waiting to go into battle, fuelled the events of the 2nd of April.

Early on the evening of Good Friday, having just finished a moderately satisfying but atrociously overpriced café meal, Joseph, Jack, Ihaka and Wi were walking off their dinner and inspecting the stalls in the colourful Wazzir, a district known for its brothels. Suddenly they were forced to dodge a hail of items being hurled from a third-storey window. First came a flutter of women's clothing accompanied by loud screeching, which caused some laughter on the street below, but when this was followed by a very solid chest of drawers and then a piano, Joseph and his mates wisely took cover under the protection of a balcony. A crowd soon gathered and Australian and New Zealand soldiers began to appear as if from nowhere and contribute enthusiastically to the destruction; predictably, Joseph was unable to restrain Ihaka and he quickly disappeared into the mêlée. Brothel after brothel was entered and ransacked, the debris piled up outside and then set alight, and troops crowded into the bars and helped themselves to bottles, which they drank dry then threw indiscriminately into the throng. When fires broke out in several houses and the fire brigade arrived, the hose was slashed and the nozzle snatched up and used to smash windows.

Shortly after that the Red Caps, the universally unpopular military police, arrived and Joseph decided it was time to leave, but not before he witnessed a phalanx of out-of-control troops turn on the MPs and launch into them with fists and make-do weapons. The grossly outnumbered police opened fire. Joseph heard later that one of the four soldiers wounded was a New Zealander.

Zeitoun Camp was in an uproar when Joseph arrived back, alone because he had lost contact with Wi and Jack. He rounded up the men in his section to find that three were missing: Ihaka and Privates Joe Witana and Hone Reti, whose father Joseph had sailed with on the schooner *Whiri*, and whom he had spied hurling furniture around the Wazzir with the best of them.

At midnight the lost trio drifted in, all bearing bruises and ripped uniforms and reeking of alcohol. Joseph lined them up in front of their tent and railed at them while the rest of the section slunk away, grateful they'd had the good sense to keep out of the fracas. After being yelled at for a good thirty minutes, the miscreants were dismissed with the threat that if they ever became involved in a similar situation again they would be shipped home immediately in abject disgrace.

All leave into Cairo was cancelled, the troops were confined to Zeitoun Camp for the remainder of their stay and relations between the New Zealanders and the Australians, camped fifteen miles away, cooled markedly as each blamed the other for starting the riot.

The shameful affair of the Wazzir seemed to mark a downturn in the Maori Contingent's spirits. As it seemed more and more likely they would be sent to Malta for garrison duty, their grumbles grew to a loud protestation that eventually manifested itself in an impassioned public plea from Major Te Rangi Hiroa for his people to be permitted to go to the Dardanelles with the main force. He also warned that any Maori *taua*, or war party, would be ashamed to go home without having even confronted the enemy and that such a prospect would have a dire effect on morale. But the decision had been made: the Maori Contingent was to go to Malta.

Once on the island they marched across a scrubby and dreary plain to a camp with the unpronounceable name of Ghain Tuffiah. There, they dug endless holes, took part in mock exercises and underwent interminable foot inspections, and Joseph thought of Erin McRae and her huge, luminous eyes far more frequently than he could ever have imagined. The men listened with mounting frustration to the news of the Gallipoli landing on the 25th of April and were awed into silence at the numbers of wounded evacuated from the Dardanelles and arriving at the hospitals on Malta. But then word was received that the Maori Contingent would be needed at Gallipoli after all.

4

As he hung over the ship's rail Joseph commented idly to Jack that the steep hills ahead of them reminded him a little of those in the Hawke's Bay. It was the 1st of July and their troopship had anchored in Mudros Harbour, the main port of the spectacular Greek island of Lemnos. There was no response and he glanced up to see Jack waving cheerfully to a group of sailors on a British warship cruising slowly past, its gentle passage forming small waves that whispered and sighed across the sapphire water.

'Who are you?' one of the sailors called.

'We're the Maoris!' Jack bellowed back.

The sailors looked at each other and shrugged, then another responded, 'Oh, the *Maoris*! Three cheers for the Maoris!' He and his mates cheered loudly and enthusiastically, and grinned hugely as the New Zealanders came back with, 'Three cheers for the Jacky tars!'

The men were kept on board ship until they transferred to a steamer the following day, where they waited until they finally set sail for the Gallipoli Peninsula at five o'clock in the afternoon.

Few of the men slept easily that night, if at all. Joseph calmed himself by rereading a long and gossipy letter from his mother, written at the end of March, which had arrived before the contingent left Malta.

My Dearest Joseph,

I hope this finds you well. At the time of writing we were unsure of your destination but Andrew said to write something and post it off anyway in the hope that it will catch up with you wherever you are.

I have a fair amount of news so I hope you're well settled with a cup of tea! Lucy has had her baby, a very healthy boy she has named Duncan Robert. Both are well, although I believe Lucy is feeling a little depressed about James not being here with her for the birth. Jeannie is fussing like mad over the baby, which is good because it's giving Lucy plenty of time to get back on her feet, so I expect she'll be feeling right as rain again in no time. Duncan doesn't look like anyone yet, although Lucy insists he's the spitting image of his father.

I suppose you haven't bumped into James at all? Andrew says I shouldn't be so silly — the two of you are bound to be in different places — but we've been reading in the papers lately that the New Zealanders are being sent to the Dardanelles because of the Turks, so I thought your paths might cross. We've had several postcards from James, from Egypt, so I'm assuming that's where you are too.

The most shocking news I have for you is that Keely and Erin have both volunteered for nursing service overseas. I must say I was rather upset when they turned up a month or so ago and told us, and so were Jeannie and Lachie, but there really isn't much we can do.

Andrew has been affected the most, I think, because he had such high hopes of Keely settling down. He only let her go nursing in the hope that she would get sick of it, give up halfway through and find herself a suitable husband instead! As of course you know I had a little trouble settling myself, when I was her age, so I can understand a little of what they feel but Andrew is incapable of seeing it from their point of view. Poor Andrew — it's been bad enough James going off, and you, but Keely as well! He went into a decline for several days but I think he's resigned himself to it now, although he certainly isn't happy about it.

I suppose we're lucky they didn't just hare off to England to offer themselves for service over there, which so many of our nurses have been doing lately. They're due to sail out some time early next month, and we think they'll be going to England. At the moment they're in Wellington sorting out their uniforms, which sound positively dire — grey wool with scarlet trim and brass army buttons, ugly boots and a rather silly hat — and doing extra training and what have you. They telephone once a week with the latest news, but we'll be going down to see them off, of course. But Keely says she's written to you about it, and so has Erin, so you might already know all of this.

The other bit of news concerns Thomas, who was here last month and said he saw you in Wellington just before you left. He had a long talk with Andrew and me about the war. He says he doesn't believe in war, that it's barbaric and futile and a shocking waste of human life. I must say I agree with him, and so does Andrew, but I'm afraid, given the government's view and the enthusiasm most people seem to have for the war, he's chosen a very hard row to hoe, especially if conscription is introduced, as some doom-mongers are predicting. He plans to finish his law degree at Otago, which will be towards the end of this year, but isn't sure what he'll do after that. He has a vague idea about setting up a law practice for returned servicemen, because he thinks some will need a hand when they come home, but I doubt that will be enough to keep him out of the services if the war does drag on. It's not that he's frightened of going into battle, I don't think, but you know how he's always been with his ideals and his beliefs. Once he gets an idea into his head it's very hard to dissuade him from following it up, and there is apparently quite a strong movement within the universities against the war. Well, we'll just have to wait and see how it goes for him, I suppose. If, as they are saying, it will all be over by Christmas, it probably won't matter anyway.

That announcement didn't really surprise us much, but Thomas' other news did. He has a young lady now, a girl called Catherine Ferris, the sister of one of his university friends. You could have knocked us over with a feather when he told us, he's always been so shy and reserved! But he's a lovely, kind person and he deserves someone nice. He said he hadn't mentioned it to the family because he wanted to be sure of Catherine's feelings towards him (and, I suspect, because he didn't want Keely rushing down there poking her nose in), but it's my guess that there could well be another Murdoch family wedding this year. Fingers crossed!

Ian is fine, although Andrew is worried he might get carried away with the idea of volunteering for the army. To 'head him off at the pass', so to speak, he's been involving Ian in all sorts of things to do with the station. When he isn't sweating over the books (and I have to be honest here, darling, he doesn't seem to have inherited my head for figures, or his father's) or chasing lambs up hill and down dale, he's gallivanting about the countryside with some girl or other to the various farewell dances and functions everybody seems to be having for the men who are off overseas. But I'm not taking any of it too seriously — he's far too young to settle down and he knows it. I just hope he doesn't do anything unwise which means he might have to settle down, like James has. But Lucy is a lovely girl, and she loves and misses James desperately. And he obviously loves her, if the number of letters she's received from him are anything to go by.

Your father is well — I saw him a couple of weeks ago in town. Have you heard from him yet? He said he's sent you two letters. In case you haven't received them, your brother

Haimona has joined the Merchant Navy, but Kepa doesn't know where his ship is at the moment. Huriana is still teaching and, to your father's absolute delight, finally expecting a child, so I expect she won't be working for much longer. I'm glad that something has cheered him up — he has seemed rather depressed since you left. Parehuia is fine, although if I were her, and you'll have to forgive me for being catty but it's true, I'd cut down on the amount of cakes and potatoes I was consuming — the last time I saw her she was looking really quite porky! But still magnificent, of course.

The heat here has finally broken, and we're all looking forward to a cooler autumn, although I expect we could be very busy if a lot of the young men are still away at shearing time later in the year. We're all fundraising again. Almost all of the women I know are knitting like mad, and when we're not doing that we're packing parcels to send overseas.

Which reminds me, I had a letter from Riria Adams the other day telling me how involved she's become with the Maori Soldiers' Fund in Auckland, which quite surprised me, I must admit, after the dreadful struggle she had getting over poor John's death in South Africa. But she says she's getting a lot of satisfaction from her work. Both her boys, Simon and David — you remember them, don't you? — have enlisted. David went first, as a lieutenant with the Main Body, but Simon is training at Narrow Neck with the Second

Maori Contingent.

I must finish up now — we're off to see a patriotic carnival in town, the fourth in as many months! I asked Andrew to come with me, but as I spied him sneaking off up the hill on his horse an hour ago I suspect it will be just Lucy and me. And Lachie, who will be driving us in the motor. Andrew has been teaching me to drive lately, but has decreed that I am not to take the motor out onto the road until I can get through the front gates without banging into one or other of them, which is a little cheeky coming from a man who killed a poor defenceless sheep the other day!

I'll write regularly and hope that my letters find you. Take care, my dear. I know you think I'm a silly, fussy old mother sometimes, but my children are worth more to me than anything else in the world.

All my love, Mam

Joseph smiled as he folded the letter and slipped it back into his kit. The bit about his stepmother Parehuia made him laugh but the news about Thomas disturbed him. He admired his brother for taking a stand on something in which he truly believed, but he suspected Thomas might be aligning himself with a dangerously small minority.

And he had received a letter from Keely, full of news about her impending embarkation, and a parcel from Erin containing a letter and a pair of rather misshapen and holey socks. She might be an excellent nurse with gorgeous eyes, but she couldn't knit to save herself. He'd been a little surprised at how disappointed he was by the rather impersonal nature of her letter: it was full of chatterings about getting ready to go overseas but little else. He'd been sure he had detected something more than just friendship in her face when they'd met at Newtown Park.

Stretching out in his cramped bunk, he put aside thoughts of home and concentrated instead on what awaited the contingent on the Gallipoli Peninsula tomorrow. The troops had all heard numerous stories of the disaster that had befallen the New Zealand and Australian Division after they had landed at Anzac Cove, on April the 25th. It was now common, though unofficial, knowledge that the troops had been dropped at the wrong landing site, that they should have been landed at a beach several miles further south. And the defending Turks, assumed to be present in the area in very small numbers and displaying only a dubious fighting ability, had proved a formidable enemy. The resulting casualties had been horrendous.

Joseph, with his Boer War experience, was subdued and very wary of what they might find when they landed. Ihaka, on the other hand, had no such worries and remained convinced that the Maori Contingent would succeed in wrestling the ridges of the Sari Bair Range from the Turks when everyone else had failed. Joseph had long since given up hoping to temper his friend's enthusiasm but had continued to drum into his men the need for a cool head, common sense and restraint, especially in the heat of battle.

* * *

Standing on deck, fully kitted and armed and sweating despite the coolness of the early dawn air, Joseph quietly watched his men as they prepared to disembark. There was Ihaka, at the head of the line and waiting eagerly for the first of the small landing craft to bump up against the side of the transport, followed by Wi, who turned to Joseph and winked. Joe Witana and Hone Reti, standing motionless and listening keenly to the crack of rifles up on the heights, both acknowledged him with a calm nod. Behind them stood Nugget Dawson, Billy Parawai and Belter Paki, three mates from Wairoa, and Pare and Matiu Black, brothers from the Tuhoe tribe, nudging each other nervously.

Wi, Ihaka and Joseph were the oldest in the section; the others were aged between twenty-one and twenty-six, and Joseph considered them a capable bunch, notwithstanding the fact that Belter, the one who had been cheated by the Egyptian hawker, was a little slow off the mark at times. They were all very fit men, hardworking and willing to do their share without complaint, and certainly up to the job. Joseph liked and cared about them all, and hoped like hell he could keep them alive.

There was a grunt and a curse as Ihaka launched himself into the landing craft and hit the deck sooner than he expected, misjudging the distance in the dim light. This set the rest of the section off giggling as they clambered in after him, followed by Joseph who hissed at them to keep quiet. They were rowed in to shore and let off at a makeshift jetty at the northern end of the short crescent of beach where, crouching on the damp sand, they eyed the dark shapes of mountains of boxes, supplies and ammunition and the maze of shelters and dugouts: the beach was obviously a frequent target for shellfire. The smell of the sea was strong in Joseph's nostrils, but underneath it lurked the oily hint of a far more offensive odour, that of death and putrefaction.

When the last of the contingent had come ashore, the platoon lieutenants scurried about mustering their men and calling out their NCOs. Lieutenant Ropata McPherson, his shoulders hunched as if he expected to be shot in the back at any moment, approached Joseph and said nervously, 'Tell your men to put their smokes out, Joe. We're not on a picnic. And get them organised, will you? We're going up there in a minute, to a spot called Number One Outpost,' he added, turning away from the beach and pointing towards a roughly dug sap that led straight up into the sharply angled foothills, increasingly visible now in the growing dawn light.

Joseph rounded up his section, fell in with the rest of B Company and began the long slog up the steep trench. The men muttered and cursed as they stumbled and slid on the loose clay surface and Joseph marvelled afresh at how people whose first tongue was Maori could swear so fluently in English. As the gradient of the track increased, the stench of rot became stronger and Joseph could see why when the sun's rays spilled over the ridges towering above. All around them, lying in shallow depressions in the soil, jammed into tight crevices and snagged on the branches of low, thorny bushes, were corpses, black, rotting and buzzing with flies energised by the sun. The bodies, Joseph was appalled to see, wore the remains of New Zealand and Australian uniforms. Why hadn't the corpses been retrieved and buried? By the time their path had transected more gullies and ridges, he had his answer: there were so many bodies that it would have been an impossible task. As they neared their destination, artillery fire started up and, looking back down to the beach, he could see the small black figures of men scuttling for cover like ants whose nest had been rudely disturbed.

Number One Outpost was a position chipped into the side of a hill at the base of a spur. The contingent was directed to Number Four Section, part of the post's defence line, to join the New Zealand Mounted Rifles Brigade, unmounted because of the terrain and bitterly missing their horses. The men immediately set to digging themselves in, fashioning terraces from the hillside and making themselves as comfortable as they could, given the rapidly rising temperature, the flies and the constant whine of sniper fire overhead.

Joseph, sitting with his back against a wall of cool, freshly excavated clay and his canteen tilted to his lips, started when he heard a voice say, 'Don't drink it all, mate. There's fuck all of it around.'

In front of him stood a scruffy-looking soldier with sunken, bloodshot eyes and a deeply sunburned face. 'Tom Jones, Sergeant, Mounted Rifles,' he said by way of introduction. 'You blokes just get here?'

Joseph nodded, wiped his lips and got to his feet. 'Joseph Deane, Sergeant, First Maori Contingent.'

'Keep your head down, mate, or you'll get it shot off, and don't guts all your water — there's a shortage, in case you didn't know. It all tastes like bloody kerosene anyway,' the sergeant added gloomily. 'Are you going to be doing the digging?'

'Not sure yet,' replied Joseph.

'Well, if you are, you'll be fighting as well, I guarantee it. We're in the shit here.'

'I gathered that,' Joseph replied, looking around. 'Been a tough few months, has it?'

'Fucking oath it has, mate. We've lost fucking thousands! It's like a bloody rabbit shoot here some days.' The sergeant shook his head in disgust. 'I'm supposed to be giving you the guided tour. This here where you're sitting is your new home, down there's the beach where you'll collect your water, supplies and rations for the delicious meals we enjoy here, and along there is the shit pit. You'll be spending a fair bit of time there, I'd say.

71

'The most important thing you have to remember is keep your heads down. Johnny Turk's sitting just up there on that ridge and there's a bloody nasty little sniper's nest just to the left of it. See?'

'Where?' asked Pare Black excitedly.

He stepped up onto a mound of dirt for a better look, and before anyone could utter a single word there was the sharp crack of a rifle and he collapsed instantly. No one moved for a second, then Matiu, his brother, rushed forward to crouch over the still body, followed closely by Joseph. He looked down at the neat hole in Pare's forehead, just above his wide-open eyes, and knew immediately the boy had been killed outright.

Matiu gazed up at him with a stricken expression and cried, 'He's dead! My brother! They've killed him already!'

Sergeant Jones shook his head woefully and said, 'Ah Jeez, I'm sorry, mate, but this sort of cock-up happens all the time.'

He didn't even see the punch coming. Ihaka stepped up to him, swung back his fist and hit him full in the face. 'Don't you call this a *cock-up*!' he raged as the sergeant fell over backwards. 'The death of a *toa* is never a *cock-up*!'

'Fucking hell,' yelped Jones, his hand over his copiously bleeding nose as he scrambled out of Ihaka's way. 'Get him off me! Fucking bastard's mad!'

'*Corporal Kerehi*!' bellowed Joseph. 'Stand down *now*!'

Ihaka stepped smartly back, coming dangerously within range of the sniper himself. He was
panting heavily, not from the effort of punching
the sergeant, which he already regretted, but
from the shock of seeing Pare healthy and alive
one minute then dead on his back the next.
Always a man to whom honour came before
anything else, he said stiffly, 'I apologise,
Sergeant Jones. You can put me on a charge if
you want.'

'Oh, Christ,' said Jones, sitting up and dabbing
gingerly at his nose with the tail of his already
filthy shirt. 'I bloody should, you know, but I
won't, long as my big-ears lieutenant doesn't get
to hear about it.' He looked up at Ihaka, paused
for a moment, then continued. 'When you've
been here for a while you'll understand what it's
like whenever someone cops it. You don't stop to
think about it, you *can't* stop, 'cos if you do
you'll start bawling and never be able to put a
cork in it and then next thing you know they'll
be carting you off to the nearest mental hospital,
mad as a two-bob watch.' He sniffed deeply and
hawked a gob of bloody snot onto the ground.
'You just got to get used to it, mate. That's all
there is to it.'

Joseph held out his hand to pull the sergeant
to his feet. 'Joe and Hone, go and find the MO
and the chaplain. Where can we put him,
Sergeant?'

Jones, still holding his nose, replied, 'There's a
spot down the hill a bit where we been burying
people. He'll go there.' He didn't want to add
that the private's remains would probably be

73

blown sky high the next time a shell landed in the immediate vicinity of the makeshift graveyard: it happened all the time and, like all the other horrors that had assaulted them over the past months, the men had grown appallingly used to it.

* * *

Pare Black was buried the next day. His brother wept openly and unashamedly at the shallow graveside, and as many men from the contingent attended as could be released from duties. The chaplain, Reverend Wainohu, officiated at the funeral and the Tuhoe members combined in a soulful *manawa wera* to honour their dead brother. Joseph closed his eyes against tears as they sang:

> *From where comes the darkening of the*
>   *heavens?*
> *It comes from the mountain tops*
> *Rest in peace on the sacred marae of the*
>   *Big Fish, the Long Fish,*
> *The Fish of Maui-tikitiki-o-Taranga*
> *Lying here*
> *Farewell, sir, the pride of our ancestors*
> *The nobility of Tuhoe*
> *The canoe is overturned*
> *Indeed overturned.*

Although he could understand that it was often too risky to bury the many corpses that were decomposing all around them, the prospect

74

of the bodies of his own men lying scattered over the foothills of the Sari Bair Range bothered Joseph. Traditionally, and until very recently, his people had followed the custom of burying their dead in very shallow graves, and after a year or so when the flesh had fallen from the bones and been absorbed back into the earth, the bones were dug up, cleaned and settled in their final resting place. He imagined that, like him, his men would probably not mind if their earthly remains lay around for a while, as long as they stayed more or less in one piece, because the flesh was not considered sacred. But who would collect the bones of the warriors after the weather had stripped the meat from them and bleached them white? Who would come back to this harsh, isolated corner of the world to carry them back home to New Zealand where they could be buried with honour and in peace next to their ancestors?

5

The day after the burial, Lieutenant McPherson came to Joseph and suggested he keep an extra watchful eye on Matiu Black, the dead boy's brother: it would be shocking for his parents to lose both of their sons. Privately, though, both men were equally aware that if fate intended Matiu to die on the peninsula, there would be nothing either of them could do to prevent it.

His mates absorbed the impact of Pare's death in different ways. His brother was grief-stricken for a matter of days then seemed to pull himself together, remaining quiet but apparently determined to ensure that the name of Black would not disgrace itself by demonstrating any form of weakness, emotional or otherwise. The others were upset but philosophical, and had learnt a lesson in self-preservation that knocked the edges off their collective bravado. Ihaka, on the other hand, was angry and remained so, which made him impulsive and at times blatantly careless of his own safety.

The contingent was put to work enlarging the sap up which they had traipsed on their first day, so that eventually it was eight feet deep and wide enough for two stretcher teams to pass each other with room to spare. Digging, carving terraces out of the heavy clay, clearing freshly excavated dirt from the ever-expanding trenches and dragging supplies and huge water tanks up from the beach was exhausting work, made even more gruelling by searing heat, permanent water restrictions and poor food. But the Maori soldiers adapted quickly enough and soon took to working shirtless in the high temperatures — only they and the Indian Transport Corps could do so without risking severe sunburn after a matter of minutes. At times it rained with torrential force, turning every gully and ravine into a raging watercourse, then the sun would reappear, its heat sheathing the ground in warm, steaming mist, and workings that had taken days to excavate would have to be redug.

Joseph lived in a recess gouged into the back of one of the terraces at Number One Outpost, an area that soon came to be known as the Maori Pa. His cave went back about six feet, providing just enough shelter from shellfire when he was lying down, and was extended at the front by a canvas cover held up by sticks and fortified against blast by sandbags. He shared his possie with Jack Herewini and two other sergeants, although there was little segregation of ranks on the cliffs. The same could not be said of the heavily reinforced bivvies just above the beach which accommodated most of the commanders and those lucky enough to secure a 'soft' job away from the trenches. Beach-dwellers had first pick when new supplies were landed and the opportunity to buy or trade for black-market items offered by sailors working the barges, not to mention comparatively easy access to the sea for bathing and cooling off between shell bursts.

Although there was plenty of it, the food that

reached the upper slopes of Anzac Cove was extremely basic. After only a week Joseph had grown heartily sick of bully beef, bacon and cheese, and longed for a piece of succulent chicken or fresh fish. The meat was salty and stringy, and did nothing to assuage a man's thirst, and the cheese ponged and melted everywhere in the heat. The almost indestructible biscuits, four inches square and rock-hard, were occasionally employed to write home on when paper ran out, and generally accepted as being more useful left in their boxes and piled up around bivvies as protection against shell blast. Some men threw their biscuits at the Turks, and it was rumoured that more often than not they were hurled back. Now and then there was bread, although usually stale and never enough to go around, and jam to go on it, and, on memorable occasions, eggs, but otherwise rations remained soul-destroyingly predictable. Fresh fruit and vegetables were non-existent, and Joseph and his men agreed that they would have traded almost anything for a bushel of *puha* or even a single *kumara*.

They soon succumbed to signs of the malnutrition that afflicted most at Anzac Cove: even minute cuts and scratches developed into great infected sores. Nugget Dawson developed huge boils on both buttocks and was unable to sit down for days, and in a matter of weeks Hone Reti had three of his back teeth pulled by a sweating and harried young man from the New Zealand Dental Corps, while Billy Parawai lost four in the front, giving him a very nefarious

78

look whenever he smiled.

Then there was diarrhoea, followed more often than not by dysentery or even enteric fever. On the way back from the vile and reeking latrine pit one day, Joseph calculated that of the time he had spent at Anzac Cove to date, at least a fifth had been wasted crouching over a stinking hole in the ground while his bowels emptied noisily and extremely painfully. So far he had not become ill enough to be considered a casualty, and for this he was truly grateful. Every day men, groaning in agony in pools of their own green slime, were carted by stretcher down to the beach to be evacuated. Even worse, were the blanket-wrapped bodies awaiting burial. But he had lost a lot of weight and had resorted to a length of twine threaded through his belt loops to hold his shorts up. Like many others he had forsaken underwear some time ago — it was almost impossible to keep clean and only made a man hotter when he was working — but he was uncomfortably aware that he stank, although he doubted his body odour was any worse than anyone else's.

More detested than even the Turks were the lice that infested the belongings and possies of every man at Anzac Cove. They filled trenches and dugouts, burrowed into clothes and skin and laid their eggs everywhere. The itching drove the men insane — more than one had to be invalided off the peninsula, pushed to mental collapse by a psychotic obsession with the tiny vermin. It was widely rumoured that one soldier, who had recently committed suicide by deliberately walking into the range of a Turkish sniper, had done so to rid himself of the incessant need to scratch. Joseph himself spent many of his off-duty hours sitting with his shorts, now cut off at the groin, around his ankles, patiently but determinedly running a lit cigarette up and down the seams in an attempt to kill the lice lodged there; this common and acceptable pastime was also useful because it gave the weeping and painful sores that many men had developed around their genitals an opportunity to dry out.

Occasionally they would be allowed down to the beach for a swim and a temporary delouse, usually when the Turk's big gun, affectionately dubbed 'Farting Annie', was taking a rest. On such jaunts Joseph was as enthusiastic as everyone else, almost running by the time he reached the beach and naked well before he splashed into the water, not caring by then whether he was hit by a shell or not and leaving his filthy clothes to float about in the shallows until he was ready to get out. It was a comical sight, the array of generally undernourished bodies standing about in the sea, arms, legs and faces burnt brown but buttocks almost shining in stark, white relief. Except for the backsides of the Maori Contingent, of course. Joseph would float out beyond the gentle waves and swim parallel to the shore, relishing the feel of the salt water on his dirty, parched skin, stinging his sores and sluicing the dust and grease from his hair. He would then swim back in to a point where the water was only waist deep, scoop up handfuls of sand and rub it all over his body in an attempt to remove some of the ingrained filth. After that he would climb back into his reeking shorts, shirt, socks and boots and trudge back up to Number One Outpost, on the way getting thoroughly covered in sweat and dust again.

Running a close second behind lice as a universal source of hatred were the flies, always plentiful in the area but attracted in even greater numbers by the filth of the men's living arrangements and the presence of unburied corpses. They settled inches deep on and around the rotting remains, hovered and crawled over the latrine pits day and night, and tormented the troops incessantly. They seemed indifferent to swatting and dragged themselves with somnolent arrogance over everything and everyone; it was impossible to sleep with your mouth open without running the risk of swallowing at least one, and preparing food was a nightmare as they would immediately descend in great, buzzing droves, falling into stews and floating about in cups of tea. Joseph's men joked that at least they were getting some fibre in their food but they, like almost everyone else on the peninsula — the Turks included — longed for the cooler weather to arrive in the hope that the flies would depart.

At the beginning of August Joseph was plodding along a trench below Quinn's Post one morning when he stumbled and stood heavily on an oustretched ankle. When the owner of the ankle swore loudly Joseph mumbled an apology, then took a closer look at the bundle of rags he had inadvertently stepped on.

'James!' he exclaimed in delight. 'How the hell are you?'

James squinted up from the bottom of the trench, then sat up properly. 'Joseph! Bugger me, I've been wondering whether we might bump into each other!'

'Yes, me too. I've had my eye out, but we're usually stuck up the other end.' Joseph sat down next to his brother, waving in the general direction of the northern reaches of Anzac Cove.

James appeared to be utterly exhausted; his clothes were in an even worse state than Joseph's, his eyes were hollow and shadowed and he had a filthy bandage tied loosely about one ear.

'Have you been here the whole time?'

James nodded wearily. 'We were in on the landing, but I've been down and back to Helles a few times since then. A sergeant now, eh? Not before time.'

Joseph shrugged off the compliment. 'So what do you think of it all?'

James's reply was delayed while they shuffled out of the way of an Australian stretcher party coming back from Quinn's Post. When the bearers had squeezed past he said simply, 'It's a cock-up, Joseph. A complete fucking cock-up.'

Joseph was surprised at the barely suppressed anger in his brother's voice. James, the career soldier, had always held the military in the highest regard.

'We're sitting here like a pack of idiots,' James continued vehemently, 'not going forwards, can't go backwards, half of us are shitting ourselves to death and the other half don't give a stuff any more, and what're Godley and bloody Hamilton doing? Playing silly bloody games with attack timetables that are doomed to failure before the whistle even blows! The only one with any brains is Malone, and they won't give him the time of day!' He rubbed a grimy hand across his eyes and sighed. 'Oh, look, I'm sorry mate. I'm just knackered. Take no notice.'

'She's right,' said Joseph easily. 'My lot have just about had enough as well. Have you heard from Mam lately?'

'Yep. Got a letter a few weeks ago, plus some photographs of Duncan, my son. He was born in February and he looks a real little trooper,' he said proudly. 'Oh, but you probably know all that already. They all seem to be all right at home. What about you?'

'I've had a couple. Mam said your boy's a real little champion. Congratulations. And Keely and Erin are in Egypt now?'

'So Mam says. They've got guts, those two.'

Joseph nodded. 'Is your mate Ron Tarrant here? This would be right up his alley, wouldn't it? Glorious charges over the top and all that?'

'No, he's not, actually. He got an offer just before we left Egypt to do some sort of extra training with the Australians, so I expect he'll turn up soon. I think he was a bit miffed about not coming with the division but it was an order, apparently.'

Joseph asked, 'Is what they're saying about a push for Chunuk Bair true, do you know?'

'Well, you know, I'm only a lowly lieutenant,' James replied sarcastically, 'but yes, something's in the wind. We've heard Hamilton's got this idea about taking Chunuk Bair, Hill Q and Hill 971 in one massive push at the beginning of next month — that's why we've got these reinforcements coming in — and I suspect it'll start from up your end, too, although I hear there's to be diversionary attacks at the same time from Helles and Lone Pine.'

'How do you know all this?' Joseph asked curiously. 'We don't hear anything.'

James pointed to his bandaged ear. 'It pays to keep these things open. Mind you, a piece of shrapnel nearly chopped the bloody thing off the day before yesterday,' he added with such indignation that Joseph had to laugh.

'Could have been worse,' he said. 'Could have been your entire head.'

James grinned.

'Well,' said Joseph, getting to his feet, 'now that I know more or less where you are I'll try to keep in touch. You know where the Maori Pa is?' James nodded. 'We're bivvied along there,' continued Joseph, 'when we're not digging holes somewhere else, that is. Drop by if you get the chance.'

'I'll do that. Good to see you, Joseph. Keep your head down, won't you?'

'You too, eh?'

★ ★ ★

84

Under cover of darkness the Maori Contingent was kept busy digging communication trenches, new roads and dugouts for the reinforcements who continued to land, as unobtrusively as possible, at Anzac Cove. On August the 5th orders were issued for the major offensive scheduled to begin at nine o'clock the following evening: A Company was divided among the four New Zealand Mounted Rifles regiments to fill the gaps left by those who had succumbed to illness and wounds, and B Company was told it would wait in reserve. This piece of news was not received at all well by B Company, who had been looking forward to the opportunity to prove themselves as warriors. The battle orders also said that bayonets only, not bullets, would be used in the opening minutes of the surprise attack, and that no man was to stop for wounded.

As the evening of the 6th drew in, both companies gathered for a religious service conducted by Reverend Wainohu. Quietly and gravely he exhorted them to remember that they held the *mana*, the honour and the good name of the Maori people in their keeping, to go forward fearlessly and do their duty to the last, and to never turn their backs on their enemy. The troops responded with a hymn in Maori, the poignancy of which was slightly spoiled by the applause of a large group of British soldiers who had gathered to listen.

The offensive began with a naval bombardment followed thirty minutes later by the order to advance, and it wasn't long before Joseph and

85

the rest of B Company, waiting anxiously in trenches well back from the fighting, could hear the wildly jubilant *peruperu* of A Company as they bayoneted their way through the Turkish lines.

No one said anything, but no one needed to.

Then, stealthily, like stoats slinking away from a raided henhouse, a handful of shadows slipped out of the trench and began to make their way up the gullies towards the battle on the higher slopes. By dawn only two platoons remained.

Joseph led his men quickly up to the heights where they slid into enemy positions now occupied by Anzac and British troops. Panting heavily from the dash up the scree-covered slopes, they crouched at the bottom of a trench and waited for orders from Lieutenant McPherson. Joseph's throat was painfully dry and the blood in his head pounded, but he felt elated and more alive than he could remember. To his left squatted Ihaka and on his right hunched the rest of his section, eyes round with fear and excitement but all of them grinning madly. At the sight of their faces, black in the darkness but with the whites of their eyes and their teeth shining, he fought a brief urge to giggle as adrenalin roared through him.

When McPherson gave the order to go over the top Joseph sensed Ihaka gathering himself to vault out of the trench and prepared to follow him; in theory he should be going first but he doubted that Ihaka would be wasting too much time on matters of military protocol. He dug the toe of his right boot into the crumbling clay of the trench wall, noting with detachment that whoever excavated this one hadn't done a very good job of shoring it up, rested his rifle briefly on the ground in front of him, and heaved himself up and over. Rifle and shellfire cracked, whistled and boomed overhead, but through it he could still hear the mighty sound of a hundred Maori war chants echoing along the ridges. Ahead of him he saw the dark shape of a low mound, and signalled to his men to spread out and follow him toward the minimal shelter it afforded.

As he moved forward he suddenly realised, with a dreadful sinking sensation in his gut, that there was an occupied enemy entrenchment between his section and the mound. McPherson clearly had not seen it before he gave the order to advance. But they were too close now to do anything but keep running forward. Out of the corner of his eye he caught a flicker of downward movement as Joe Witana stumbled and fell to the ground, his rifle tumbling away from him, but did not check his own stride. Instead, he glanced around to ensure his men were with him, increased his speed and launched himself into the trench ahead, landing with a bone-jarring thump directly on top of a terrified face peering up at him from the shadowy depths.

He used his momentum to drive his bayonet through the throat of the wretched Turk, grunting with the effort of yanking the blade out again and grimacing as he felt it grate against bone. To his left Ihaka was despatching another Turk rather more messily, and Joseph could feel rather than hear his friend's yells of victory.

In less than a minute the handful of enemy had been disposed of, and Joseph squatted on his haunches, gasping and trying to slow his galloping heart. Most of his men had made it to the trench with him, although they had had to leave Joe Witana where he had fallen. He noticed Billy Parawai nursing what appeared to be a badly wounded shoulder, and wondered fleetingly how they would get him back down to the beach. The other thing he noticed was Ihaka, bending over his dead Turk and preparing to decapitate the corpse with his bayonet.

'Kao!' Joseph bellowed, kicking out with his boot and knocking Ihaka's rifle out of his hand. 'Whakamutu!'

Joseph saw with a jolt of dismay that Ihaka's eyes were bulging with naked fury and his teeth bared. He raised his clenched fist at Joseph for a brief moment, then, shouting words that didn't make any sense at all, he leapt out of the trench, turned his back on the line of Turks dug into the ridge above them, bent over and deliberately bared his buttocks in the traditional and ultimate Maori gesture of disrespect. Without thought, Joseph lunged out of the trench and made a grab for his friend's ankle, hoping to pull him off balance and out of the direct line of fire, but he was too late. He had a moment to register the look of affronted astonishment on Ihaka's face as the single bullet tore through his back and into his heart, then opened his arms in a clumsy attempt to catch the big man's body as it tumbled back into the trench.

Wi crawled over, his mouth hanging open in shock, and gazed uncomprehendingly at the body of his boyhood friend. 'What did he do that for?' he yelled over the rifle fire.

'You know as well as I do, Wi,' Joseph yelled angrily back in Maori. 'Because he was who he was, and because nothing else would have been as good as this, as far as he was concerned. This is what he wanted, and now he has it.'

Wi said nothing but reached out and gently touched Ihaka's face, relaxed now in death and looking somehow triumphant. 'Ae, you are right,' he agreed eventually. Then, to himself, he said flatly, 'The ancestors will be pleased.'

★　★　★

At ten o'clock the following morning the Maori Contingent received orders to reassemble and move on to Table Top, a position slightly to the north of Rhododendron Ridge and below Chunuk Bair. They did, under a constant hail of rifle fire, then were told, confusingly, to get off the hill again and wait at the bottom. They gathered there in comparative shelter, comparing notes on the previous night's work while Major Te Rangi Hiroa worked steadily to sort out who had been wounded and to what extent, and whose bones would have to be left behind on the peninsula.

The remainder of that day was spent resting, crouching among the low bushes and snatching sleep whenever possible. Joseph, as weary as everyone else, was not at all surprised to find himself nodding off from time to time, and not particularly perturbed when others succumbed to sleep even as he spoke to them. Billy Parawai's shoulder wound was declared serious enough to warrant his evacuation from Gallipoli, and a gory but not life-threatening gouge across Belter Paki's broad back required stitching, a painful process he endured stoically. The section, now reduced to six, had been blooded and were proud of their achievements, but utterly exhausted. Much later in the night they roused themselves, ate, smoked, emptied nervous bladders and bowels in the bushes and prepared for the morning's pre-dawn attack on Chunuk Bair.

Concealed in shadows not yet banished by the faint light of the impending dawn, the Maori soldiers crept in a column led by Brigadier-General Johnston up the ridges of Chunuk Bair and moved quickly onto the summit. But as the sun ascended the Turks were afforded better visibility and began to pick off the reinforcements moving up to join Johnston on the heights, and after that the situation began to deteriorate. The New Zealanders hung on until they were relieved under cover of darkness the following night, but on the 10th the British forces who had taken their place on Chunuk Bair were swept off by a massive Turkish counter-attack. The newly gained Hill Q was also lost.

The offensive had failed. Lieutenant-Colonel Malone, one of the few New Zealand officers who had inspired respect and admiration in his men, was mortally wounded and although his death was keenly felt particularly among the Pakeha units, the loss of one man paled into insignificance compared with the overall allied casualties: the Maori Contingent alone had lost seventeen men, eighty-nine were wounded and two were missing in action.

6

Joseph was only ever able to remember brief slices of what happened to him after the shell landed near his bivvy on the morning of the 10th of September.

He could recall the moments immediately before the blast — stirring his stringy stew half-heartedly and thinking how sick and tired he was of bloody bully beef — then lying flat on his back with flies crawling all over his face and not being able to make his arms move to swat them away and Wi's face hovering over him saying, 'Hang on, *e hoa*, I get them off for you.' After that there had been a few mumbled words from a serious-looking face that might have belonged to Major Hiroa, then a feeling of great tiredness and an odd sensation of weightlessness.

His next memory was of the sharp smell of disinfectant in a room with thick pipes criss-crossing the ceiling and of being lifted off a stretcher by a pair of medical orderlies who chattered to him nonstop. After that he was unpleasantly lucid for a considerable period of time. He was carefully transferred to a narrow table, then told that the doctor would be with him in a few minutes. Both of his legs ached monstrously and he wanted desperately to sit up and have a look at the damage, but a searing pain in his back wouldn't let him. When one of the chatty orderlies asked him if he wanted more morphine, he nodded and closed his eyes gratefully as the drug flowed through his system. He must have only dozed off for seconds, though, because when he came to again the same orderly was still there, helping a rather plain-faced and tired-looking nurse cut his stinking shorts off him with a large pair of shears.

'Am I on the hospital ship?' Joseph asked, his voice rasping dryly.

'That you are, Sergeant Deane,' replied the nurse cheerfully, snipping through the waistband of his pants, apparently immune to the sight of male genitals. 'You're on the *Maheno*. You'll be fine now, just wait and see. Doctor Forster will be along in a moment.'

'What's wrong with me?' he asked, struggling weakly but failing to sit up.

'No, you don't,' said the nurse kindly but firmly, pushing his shoulders back against the table. 'You need to lie completely still until Doctor's had a chance to examine you.'

Joseph licked his dry lips and asked, 'How long have I been here?'

'Just arrived,' said the orderly. 'You copped it this morning, according to the blokes that brought you on board, and it's five in the afternoon now. You've been lucky, mate, you didn't have to wait long. Want a smoke?'

Joseph nodded and the orderly lit a cigarette and held it to his lips while he drew in shallow lungfuls of soothing nicotine, then immediately felt dizzy and turned his head away. 'Maybe later,' he mumbled.

'Right you are,' replied the orderly, nipping the end off the smoke and slipping it back into its packet. 'Doctor's here now anyway.'

A surprisingly young man in wrinkled battledress with a major's pips on the shoulders loomed over the table. His eyes were baggy and he had at least a day's growth on his chin, but his voice was hearty enough.

'Righto lad,' he said, as if Joseph were years younger than himself, 'what have you done to yourself? Let's take a look, shall we?'

'*I* haven't done anything to myself,' Joseph muttered. 'My legs and back hurt.'

Both the nurse and the orderly smiled but Forster was too busy prodding Joseph's chest and belly, then snipping layers and layers of soiled field dressings off his legs. He dropped the bloodied bandages and pads on the floor, poked around for a few minutes, then bent down and sniffed. Apparently satisfied, he straightened up and said, 'You're lucky. Sergeant Deane, isn't it? No sign of infection yet — that's a definite plus, I can assure you.'

The doctor moved closer to the head of the table, sighed and said in a voice leaden with regret, 'Well, old chap, I'm sorry to say you've lost your right leg below the knee but I'm pretty sure we can keep the left one for you, providing you don't develop septicaemia. It looks a bit of a dog's breakfast now but it should come right.'

As Joseph stared blankly up at him, Forster scrabbled around for some better news. 'You got a fair knock on the head, I'd say, which is why you've been in and out of consciousness, and

94

you lost a lot of blood up on that hill by the looks of it, but I wouldn't worry about that side of things. And your back might just be wrenched, I can't feel anything particularly out of place, and if that's the case we've got a couple of excellent masseuses on board who can sort that out for you. But we'll do some x-rays, and I'll have to tidy up this stump and some bits and pieces on the left leg, which should do the trick. You're well out of it now, though.'

Joseph's eyes moved away from Forster's face and fixed unseeingly on the cat's cradle of pipes traversing the ceiling above him. Eventually, he said without any emotion at all, 'I can still feel both of my legs.'

'Sorry, but it's phantom pain. We see a lot of that.'

But Joseph didn't hear him; he was thinking back to when he was a boy and he and Ihaka and Wi used to swing out over the river on a long rope and let go over the deepest point, screaming and laughing, and the times they would run along the beach as fast as they could, racing each other then splashing into the surf, breathless and giggling. He thought about the horse he had bought himself after his return from Australia, put out in the paddock behind his father's house now, waiting for him to come home, and what he would do if he couldn't ride and be a drover any more. He thought about Erin McRae, who wouldn't want a man with only one leg, about his mother's face when she found out, and of his unspoken and faintly embarrassing desire to return home from the war a hero.

'Fuck,' he said quietly.

'Indeed,' said the doctor, more than a little relieved to see that his patient appeared to be taking the news calmly. He cleared his throat. 'They're making some pretty good artificial limbs these days. I hear a man can get around almost as good as new. You'll get one before you go home, I expect.'

Joseph nodded absently. 'Where will I go from here?'

'Well, the ship's leaving tomorrow morning for Mudros and you'll be transferred from there to Egypt, either to the New Zealand hospital at Port Said or the one at Cairo, I don't know which. After that you'll probably go on to the one that's just been set up for New Zealanders at Walton-on-Thames in England. Then home, I'd say.'

Home.

* * *

An hour later Forster operated on Joseph's legs in one of the *Maheno*'s two theatres, cutting away the shredded flesh below his right knee, trimming the bone and stitching skin and muscle over the wound to make a decent stump. Although it was intact, the left leg was a trickier prospect: neither the tibia nor fibula was broken but there was gross tissue damage requiring painstaking debriding and repair. By the time he had finished, however, Forster was reasonably satisfied with his work and expected that Sergeant Deane would regain more or less full use of his leg, provided infection was kept at bay and he received good medical care after he arrived in Egypt. But if septicaemia did set in, then it was possible that he would lose the left leg as well, and not just the portion below his knee. Forster was in fact surprised that Deane had survived his injuries at all; the extent of his wounds suggested he'd been very lucky not to have been blown to pieces. And if the *Maheno* had not been in Anzac Cove at the time, he would undoubtedly have died waiting on the fly-infested beach.

But Joseph did develop a major infection, and the hours before the surgery were the last he could remember with any clarity for some time. By the time the *Maheno* weighed anchor to sail back to Mudros Harbour the following morning, he lay in his cot sweating and shivering as bacteria swept through his body, one of four hundred soldiers packed like sardines in the belly of the ship. Forster was disappointed, but not inexperienced enough to blame himself; the *Maheno* was one of the better hospital ships but if casualties came on board having already developed septicaemia or, worse, gangrene, then there was little anyone could do, bar chopping the infected bits off, which Forster thought would be premature in Sergeant Deane's case.

Joseph was unconscious during the trip from Lemnos to Port Said, a town perched on the Egyptian coast near the Mediterranean end of the Suez Canal. He did not regain consciousness until some days after his arrival, and even then he was only partially awake for minutes at a time.

He dreamt of something huge and dank and dark that chased him and wanted to hurt him, and when it caught him it did, crushing his legs and making him scream out loud. He dreamt of Ihaka sitting at the end of his bed telling him to hurry up and make up his mind — was he coming or was he staying, because the pair of them had a lot of things to do together if he wasn't going to hang around here in this hospital with its lovely view of the sea. Ihaka's hair was long again, and tied up in a top-knot from which two black and white feathers protruded, and he was naked except for a woven *tatua* about his waist and his grandfather's treasured dogskin *korowai* over his shoulders. He had a full-face *moko* now, too, one befitting a man who had fought with honour on the battlefield.

Joseph also dreamt of Tamar, and of his father and his brothers and sisters, of one-legged Cassius Heke who had captained the *Whiri* all those years ago, and of the girl Emerald with whom he had almost lost his virginity at the age of twelve in a dirty little room above a bawdy tavern in Wellington. He dreamt of the terrifying old woman Te Whaea who had once prophesised that his blood would be spilt on foreign shores, and realised, even through the heavy fog of his delirium, that she had been right. Often, he imagined he was a boy again but when he tried to jump out of bed to run outside and play he felt himself being held back, and cool hands on his brow and gentle voices telling him things would soon be all right, but he knew they wouldn't because the *taniwha* that lived in the river outside the village had finally got him and was chewing his legs off and he'd never ride a horse again. Sometimes the hands belonged to Erin McRae and sometimes they belonged to angels who wore long white veils and smiled sadly at him. And it was so hot, and when it wasn't he thought he might freeze to death.

He came very close to dying. The surgeon in charge of his case, Doctor Birch, took him into the operating theatre twice to debride the wounds in his left leg, saying in worried tones to the theatre sister after the second operation, 'If we have to bring him in again, I'm afraid it'll be to take the leg off.'

But somehow Joseph defeated the rampant poisons in his blood and twelve days after his arrival at Port Said he opened his eyes and croaked, 'I'm thirsty.'

There was no response so he said it again, louder this time, or as loud as his parched throat would allow.

'Jesus Christ, mate. We thought you'd had it.'

Joseph swivelled his eyes to the right, feeling his eyeballs grind painfully in their sockets, until he could see the owner of the voice, a freckle-faced man sitting up in the bed next to him wearing a blue pyjama jacket and matching trousers rolled up well past his knees to reveal a pair of short, heavily bandaged stumps.

'You've been yelling your head off for nigh on two weeks now,' the man said conversationally, as if he and Joseph had known each other for years.

'They've been expecting you to pass any day but I says no, you're bloody wrong as usual, just you wait and see.' He leant over and extended his hand. 'Bert Croft. Private, the Wellingtons.' When Joseph didn't move he said, 'Oh, sorry mate, I expect you're still feeling a bit wobbly. I'll get someone, shall I?' He opened his mouth and bellowed '*Nurse!*' at the top of his voice, making Joseph wince and close his eyes.

'All right, all right, Private Croft, we're in the next ward, not the next country,' remonstrated a nurse, the soles of her boots squeaking as she hurried down the centre of the room. 'What can I do for you?'

'It's him,' said Croft, pointing at Joseph.

The nurse stopped and a slow smile spread across her face. 'Well, Sergeant Deane, I see you're back in the land of the living!' She moved to the side of his bed, picked up his hand and placed two fingers over the pulse in his wrist. 'Well, that's better, isn't it? We were quite worried about you for a while! How are you feeling?'

'Thirsty,' replied Joseph. 'My leg hurts.'

'Yes, I expect it does. I'm Sister Griffin. We'll get Doctor to give you something for it, shall we? He'll be very pleased you're back with us. He's done a lot of work on you, you know.'

Joseph, pain fraying his temper already, wondered if he should apologise for being such an inconvenience, but couldn't summon the energy. 'Could I have some water, please?' he almost begged.

'I'll bring a jug for you after I've fetched

100

Doctor Birch,' Sister Griffin replied.

As she marched away Croft rolled his eyes and complained, 'I don't like that one much. Got a face like a horse's arse and no sense of humour. The others are pretty good, though. Except for Matron, she's a real bitch, won't even let us smoke in bed. Nurse McRae'll be dead chuffed you're back.'

Joseph froze. 'Who?'

'Nurse McRae. Erin, I think her first name is, except we're not allowed to call them by their first names. Spent no end of time sitting by your bed holding your hand. You belted her once, right across the tits, but she didn't seem to mind. Does she know you or something?'

Joseph swallowed but didn't turn to look at Croft. 'Yes, we're cousins. Sort of.'

'Well, that explains it then. She cried a lot and Sister bloody Horse-Face had to tell her to pull herself together a couple of times.'

They were interrupted by the arrival of Doctor Birch, a tall man in his forties wearing a white coat flapping open over a New Zealand Army uniform, with a stethoscope draped around his neck and a packet of cigarettes sticking out of his tunic pocket.

'Him and Sister don't get on,' whispered Croft, loud enough for the entire ward to hear.

'That will do, Private Croft,' commented the doctor as he rested his rump against the end of Joseph's bed and crossed his arms. 'Welcome back, Sergeant. You're at Number One Stationary Hospital, Port Said, Egypt. How are you feeling?'

101

'He's thirsty and sore,' interjected Sister Griffin as she padded up with a glass jug of water. 'Do you think we could sit him up?' she asked, then, without waiting for a reply, proceeded to raise Joseph's head and fluff his pillow. She poured a tumbler of water, added a measure of white powder, swirled it and held the glass so he could drink. 'Morphine to help with the pain. Now, not too much water to start with. You've had nothing of substance in that stomach of yours for nearly a fortnight and you don't want to overdo it.'

Joseph slurped greedily, his eyes darting about, taking in the other beds in the ward and the men in them. Several, who were watching with interest, waved. The cool water trickled down his gullet and he grimaced as his stomach responded immediately, contracting violently and noisily ejecting the fluid. Sister Griffin wiped the mess off Joseph's chin and front and said, 'Have another go now, but slowly this time. You've nothing to hurry for, you'll be fine.'

When Joseph had had enough, Birch said calmly, 'Get him another jacket, thanks, Sister.'

'Yes, that's a good idea,' piped up Croft who had observed the entire procedure with interest. 'That one'll stink to high heaven now.'

Sister Griffin glared at him and whipped his curtain across on her way out.

Birch tapped his front teeth thoughtfully with the end of his stethoscope, then said, 'You know you've lost your right leg, don't you, Sergeant? Well, the bottom half of it anyway.'

Joseph nodded. 'Yes. How's the other one? It's

still there — I was worried it might not be.'

'Oh, it's fine, don't worry about that. Or it soon will be, despite the fact that we seriously considered taking it off. You'll have some scarring which won't be pretty but providing you're able to build the muscles up again you'll walk on it all right. It's a bit of a miracle really — a lot of men with the level of infection you had die, even after they arrive here. You must be made of stern stuff.'

'I'm Ngati Kahungunu,' Joseph replied matter-of-factly. 'We don't give up easily.' His eyes felt leaden and he was having trouble keeping them open.

'Well, you're not on your own then. When you're feeling a bit better you can introduce yourself to the rest of the lads in the ward. We've got legs in this one, or rather, patients without legs, and a couple of them are from the Maori Contingent. But take your time, you've been extremely ill and you mustn't overdo it if you're planning to be up and about as soon as you can.' Birch stood up, patted his tunic pocket and said, 'Well, time for a cup of tea and a smoke, I think. Sister Griffin will look after you, although I'll be around twice a day to see how you're getting on. She's pretty good, Sister, and so are her girls. I suggest you try and get some sleep.' He lowered his voice to a conspiratorial whisper. 'Sister and I do actually get on, but we pretend we don't so Croft here has something to entertain him. He's in a bad way and it's turned him into a bit of a wet blanket, although I suppose he could have been one of those before he even joined the

Army. But he's being transferred to the UK soon for convalescence and hasn't got long to go here. I know you've a lot to come to terms with yourself, but see if you can't jolly him along and set him a bit of an example, will you?'

Joseph wondered whether this was a genuine request, or a ruse designed to take his mind off his own semi-legless state. He thought of Erin and was overcome by an intense sense of shame that she should see him like this. He allowed his eyes to close and was asleep even before Birch had left the ward.

★ ★ ★

She was sitting next to his bed when he next woke, staring sightlessly across the room at a spot on the opposite wall. He watched her in silence for several minutes, noting her great dark, expressive eyes, the strands of hair struggling to escape from beneath her veil and the rather uncomplimentary cut of her stiff, white apron. It made her breasts look enormous. Her fingernails were bitten to the quick and her hands red and dry-looking. He wondered how long she had been there.

'Hello, Erin,' he said quietly.

She jumped and went pink. 'You're awake,' she said.

Neither said anything more for a moment, then to Joseph's absolute mortification he began to cry. Not great loud sobs, but a slow and helpless trickle of tears that ran across his temples and into his ears.

'Let them come,' she whispered, fighting to conceal her own embarrassment and despair at this shocking and desperately intimate manifestation of his pain. She took his left hand and squeezed it gently, averting her eyes so he could weep with a modicum of privacy. He had always been such a vital and essential man, and always somehow larger than life. Seeing him now, lying in this cot broken in both body and spirit, was something she wasn't sure she could bear.

He held her hand tightly, feeling the dryness of her skin against the clamminess of his own, and was grateful for her presence.

Presently, when his tears had slowed, she said, 'I wired your Mam, and asked her to pass the news on to your father, and sent a message to Keely as well. She's stationed at Number Two Hospital in Cairo. I told them you'd been seriously wounded but that you'd be coming home soon.'

Joseph nodded and wiped his nose on his pyjama sleeve as unobtrusively as he could.

'Do you want a handkerchief?' Erin asked, feeling silly and redundant. She was a thoroughly trained and highly skilled nurse, and this was all she could offer him. She wanted to reach out and lay her hand on his brow again, to gently smooth away the furrows of hurt and sickness as she had for so many hours when he had been unconscious, but she was too embarrassed now that he was awake.

He examined her face closely for signs of pity, but there were none. 'No,' he replied, 'but could you give me a hand to sit up?'

She slid an arm under his back and levered him up with surprising strength, rearranging his pillow so he was more comfortable.

He eyed the unnatural-looking hump at the foot of his bed, then leant forward and quickly flipped the sheet off it. Underneath was a metal frame enclosing his legs, or what was left of them. His left lower leg, swathed in bandages, appeared almost twice its normal size. He gazed at the space below his right knee in numb silence, feeling dizzy and breathless at this horrible and blunt proof of his loss.

Erin bit her lip to stop herself saying that he would get used to it in time: right now it would sound trite and empty.

'So, that's it, then,' he said, because he couldn't think of anything else to say. More than anything, he felt a fool. For putting his hand up for a war he needn't have become involved in, for so blithely assuming he would come through it unscathed — because, underneath his caution and his occasional misgivings, he *had* assumed that — and for being stuck now with this gross and irreversible insult to his body.

They sat in silence for a minute longer, then Erin said, 'I know this probably won't make you feel any better now, but for a traumatic amputation it was quite a tidy and convenient one.'

Joseph stared at her in amazement, then surprised himself by laughing out loud. 'A *convenient* one?'

'Well, yes,' she replied cautiously, wondering whether she'd said the wrong thing after all. She ploughed on regardless. 'You've still got a bit of your lower leg left, which means that when you get your prosthesis you might not have much of a limp at all if it's a good fit. Losing your leg above the knee can pose much more serious problems.'

'Oh, well, I should feel grateful then, shouldn't I?'

Erin's face reddened slightly before she responded, and when she did she forgot her inherent shyness and hissed rather more forcefully than she had intended, 'Yes, you should, Joseph, so don't start going down that road. Look around you. Look *next* to you!'

Joseph remembered Croft and immediately felt ashamed of himself. He rubbed his hand across his eyes and said, 'Oh God, Erin, I'm sorry, I really am.'

She patted his hand forgivingly. 'Yes, I know.' Then she stood up and smoothed her apron. 'I've been on my break but I have to go back now. I'll come and see you whenever I have a moment, shall I? I'm not on this ward today but I probably will be later in the week. In the meantime you could get to know your roommates. They're not a bad bunch, if you don't mind bad language and having your bottom pinched, but then I don't expect that yours will be,' she added wryly.

When she had gone Joseph looked around the room, saw that everyone was staring back at him with undisguised curiosity, except for Croft who was on his back snoring, and introduced himself. There were five others sharing the ward, two of them Maori whom he recognised but didn't know by name, a man from the Otagos who introduced himself as Lofty Curtis, and another from the Mounteds, named Henry Ormsby.

'Sonny Tahere, Ngati Maniapoto,' announced the man opposite Joseph. 'I seen you on that hill at Anzac. She was rough, eh?'

His neighbour, who introduced himself as Eru Te Moni from Ngati Tuwharetoa, said, 'You in B Company, eh? We was in A. Yous were up near us at that push on the Sari. That's where I got it,' he added, pointing ostentatiously at his truncated left lower limb.

'Eru, shut up about your bloody leg,' said Sonny benignly. 'You always going on about it.'

'Well, it was a good one. It suited me,' Eru replied with an affronted dignity that made Joseph smile. 'What do I do with only one bloody leg?'

'Same as you done before. Nothing,' replied Sonny.

Joseph listened as the two traded amiable insults, suspecting, from the amused looks on the faces of Lofty Curtis and Henry Ormsby, that this was a routine the pair of them had been polishing for some time and thoroughly enjoyed. Henry looked over and gave him a broad wink and it occurred to Joseph for the first time since he had been wounded that, notwithstanding Erin's unexpected presence, he might not have to face his recovery alone.

* * *

He came to know the men in his ward very quickly — it would have been very difficult not to. They lay within feet of each other, shared the minute details of each other's progress, heard and smelt each other farting and emptying their bowels, and became very familiar with each other's personal habits and idiosyncrasies. Their intimacy reminded Joseph of his relationship with the men in his section, and it comforted him.

With the exception of Croft, they all seemed, at least outwardly, to accept their injuries and subscribed strictly to the soldier's creed of never exhibiting signs of weakness, never talking about dead mates and never admitting out loud that it hadn't been worth it. But occasionally at night one of them could be heard weeping quietly; Joseph thought it was probably Lofty Curtis, whose right leg had been amputated almost at the hip and the other, shattered and deformed, was suspended by a complicated series of pulleys and weights above his bed, but he never asked and certainly nobody else ever mentioned it.

Croft, though, regularly slipped into deep troughs of depression that made him totally uncommunicative on some days, and on others sullen, sarcastic and aggressive. Because he could not get out of bed by himself, and the rest of his roommates had learnt to ignore his unpleasant behaviour, he often directed his unhappiness at the nurses. He would find fault with everything they did, complain that they didn't treat him as well as they did the others, and make extra work for them. When he was especially miserable he would shit in his bed and sit in it until the smell wafted over to someone else's nostrils and a nurse would have to be summoned to clean up the mess.

After the third time he had done this, Joseph, who vacillated between feeling intensely sympathetic for the man and despising him, threatened to drag himself out of his bed and belt Croft one. This elicited a round of cheers from the rest of the ward, and prompted Croft to retreat into a sulk that lasted three days because he'd thought he'd found an ally and it was clear he hadn't. But Joseph was left with an unpleasant taste in his mouth: Croft could be quite pleasant when he wasn't feeling down and it seemed obvious the man was suffering from some kind of serious emotional disruption. In the end Joseph more or less gave up — he had enough adjustments of his own to make without worrying about Croft.

After a week Joseph was allowed up and into a wheelchair, which gave him an immense sense of freedom and alleviated the crushing boredom of being confined to bed. Eru, Sonny and Henry were already mobile, either on crutches or in wheelchairs, and had regularly congregated around either his or Lofty's bed to play cards or dominoes. Doctor Birch would not let him use crutches yet, as his left leg still hadn't healed sufficiently to take his weight, but it now required only a light bandage at night, under which it itched fiercely and constantly. His stump was healing well, too, and in some ways was in better condition than his intact leg, but he was still having trouble with pain in places where there was no longer any flesh and bone. Birch assured him it would go away eventually and Joseph, sick of waking up in the middle of the night and catching himself in the act of reaching to massage non-existent toes, wished heartily that it would, and sooner rather than later.

His days were occupied, like everyone else's, with resting, talking, writing letters assuring everyone at home he was fine and recovering well, going for short trundles around the hospital in his chair and outside for a smoke, speculating on what would be served for breakfast, lunch and dinner and then complaining when it arrived. Croft left, and was not missed. His bed was taken by a man called Noah Jackson who had lost both feet and was such a persistent joker that Joseph suspected he did it to stop himself from slitting his own wrists.

Joseph's mood had improved markedly since his arrival, and he thought he knew why. Somewhere between his first week at the hospital and the third, it occurred to him that he might just have fallen in love with Erin McRae. She had been as good as her word and had come to sit with him at every opportunity. When she was assigned to his ward Joseph happily spent hours watching her tend to the other men, bathing poor old Lofty who was still attached to his traction device, changing dressings on the others, tidying their beds and generally jollying them along. He noted that when she worked her shyness fell away like the outer petals of a rose opening into full bloom, and she shone. She chatted away, joked, laughed and cheerfully

111

tolerated endless well-natured teasing — daily proposals of marriage from Henry, or Eru announcing that he had a shocking itch in his groin and could Nurse McRae please scratch it for him. Every nurse on the ward received the same treatment, except for Sister Griffin whose glare could freeze even Sonny's backchat.

This was a side to Erin that Joseph had never seen before, and it enchanted him. She had always seemed so shy and self-conscious, but time and perhaps her nursing training had obviously allowed some very charming and appealing facets of her character to blossom. Or was it that perhaps he had just never looked hard enough? She was patient and kind and sympathetic without conveying a sense of pity for her charges.

He wondered how she felt about him, and spent much of his time devising ways of asking her. If Keely had been here it would have been easy — she would have confronted Erin and asked outright, then relayed the answer back to Joseph immediately. He couldn't summon the nerve to ask Erin himself, fearing that her extra attention and frequent blushes and the intensity of her gaze when she thought he wasn't looking might just be symptoms of her compassion for a man crippled by a random shell blast.

7

October, 1915

In the end, he didn't need to ask, for Erin made her feelings perfectly clear herself. Until now, she had avoided taking him for his bath and shave in the bathroom down the corridor — whether deliberately or not, he didn't know — but on this day she came to his bedside with a fresh towel folded under one arm and a very determined look on her face. She positioned his wheelchair at his bedside, toed the brake on, lowered the armrest and motioned for him to transfer himself into it, a manoeuvre he was now quite good at.

'Where are we going?' he asked, still on the bed and somewhat perturbed by the look of fierce resolution on her flushed face.

'It's time for your bath,' she said, not looking at him.

'Oh,' he said uncomfortably. 'One of the other nurses usually helps me with that.'

'Yes, but I'm doing it today,' she replied stiffly.

'Oh,' he said again, then lapsed into silence.

There was a short interlude during which neither moved, then Erin said, 'Joseph, can you get into the chair, please?'

'What? Oh, yes, sorry.'

He shuffled his backside over to the edge of his bed, put one hand on the outer arm of the wheelchair and heaved himself into the seat. She checked that his legs were in place, his left foot resting securely on the footplate, snapped the armrest back up and pushed the chair briskly towards the door.

Passing Sonny's bed Joseph caught a smirking, head-nodding wink, and as they went through the doorway he heard behind him the voices of several of his room-mates joined in a gleeful and speculatory, 'Ooooh, eh?'

He resisted the temptation to turn and look up at Erin to see if she'd also heard, but evidently she hadn't, or if she had she was doing a good job of ignoring it; in silence she wheeled him at a vigorous rate down the corridor, not even giving him the opportunity to propel the chair himself. Parking him outside the bathroom, she propped open the heavy door, wheeled him through, then locked the door behind them.

The bathroom was cool and smelt of disinfectant that masked a suggestion of mould, its thick walls tiled in white and the polished porcelain of the two urinals gleaming in the diffused light spilling through a single high window. There was also a heavy cast-iron bath on clawed feet, and two toilet stalls he hadn't been able to avail himself of yet because they would not accommodate his wheelchair. He yearned for the day Doctor Birch promoted him to crutches; they would not only mean more mobility, but also the luxury of sitting on the toilet to move his bowels instead of the humiliation of perching on a pan in his bed and trying to clean himself up afterwards.

Erin reached over and turned on the taps, and they waited in silence as the plumbing clanked and rattled and slowly filled the bath with tepid water.

Joseph could not think how to diffuse the suddenly amplified tension between them. Instead he sat dumbly in his chair, watching the water swirl around the tub. Eventually Erin judged the bath full enough and briskly turned off the taps. She secured the wooden board Joseph would use to ease himself down into the tub, then stood back.

She looked him in the eye at last, took a deep breath and said, 'I'll need to help you in, and I'm not leaving you alone in case you have an accident.' Then, when he didn't move, and with another flush staining her cheeks, she added, 'Er, you'll need to take your pyjamas off.'

Joseph nodded and fiddled with the buttons on his jacket, then stopped, struggling with an urgent and overwhelming urge not to reveal to her his body and his ruined legs.

She read his mind and said gently, 'Oh, Joseph, I've seen so much worse than what's happened to you. You're still the same person to me. Please.'

In that instant he was aware she was encouraging him to lay himself open to her, to let her see him as he was now and allow her to accept him.

'Here, let me help,' she murmured, leaning over and undoing his jacket. This close to her, he could smell the chemical acidity of the dressings and lotions she handled in the course of her work, the warm scent of her skin and a faint hint of fresh, feminine sweat. She slid the jacket off his shoulders and down his arms, tugged it out from between him and the back of the wheelchair, and let it fall to the floor. Then she knelt in front of him, untied the cord securing his pyjama pants at his waist and ordered, 'Lift.'

He placed his hands on the arms of the chair and raised his buttocks an inch off the seat, allowing her to slip the cotton trousers down over his slim hips and across his lap, where his penis, flaccid with his shame and discomfort, lay in its nest of wiry black pubic hair. Finally she slid the trousers down his brown thighs and to his knees. Filled with sudden panic, he grabbed her wrists and said, 'Stop.'

'No,' she replied.

'Yes.'

'*No*, Joseph!' She sat back on her heels and gazed up at him. 'Can't you see? It doesn't make any difference to me. How you were before and how you are now, it hasn't changed anything. It hasn't changed how I feel at *all*!'

He heard urgent desperation in her voice, as if she were the one broken and scarred and craving reassurance, not him. But he also heard her words, and they gave him hope.

To Erin the moment was critical: she had of course already seen the state of his legs, many times in fact, but this was different and they both knew it. This was about what they might be *together*.

Joseph, for his part, knew that if he shut her out now, there would be no possibility of a shared future; she would dart back behind her emotional armour and he would be left alone to flounder in a morass of misery and paralysing self-pity. He let go of her wrists then and, almost imperceptibly, he nodded.

With a touch as light as thistledown she drew the pyjama pants down to his ankles, lifted his foot and pulled them clear. Then, so gently he could barely feel her fingers, she traced the path of the deep purple scars scoring the inside of his left leg from knee to ankle, then did the same to the puckered seam running across the stump of his right leg. He lay his hand on her veiled head and closed his eyes.

They sat that way for several minutes, both motionless and silent and aware that together they had sent the invisible blocks of some great, emotional barricade tumbling to the ground.

He ran his hand down her cheek then and, in a voice hoarse with feeling, asked, 'Are you sure, Erin? Will you be with me? After this, I mean? For always?'

'Yes,' she replied simply, as if in her mind at least there could never have been any other answer. She had wanted him for so long, and in such aching silence, and she marvelled that he might now feel the same way about her.

'Good,' he said softly. 'Good. I need you.' And he enveloped her in his arms and brushed his lips against her forehead.

She smiled and said, 'You need a bath, too.'

He raised his left arm and sniffed at his armpit. 'Oh. Sorry, I do too,' he laughed, suddenly feeling absurdly light-hearted and as if, after this, nothing else could really matter.

He kissed her again, on the lips this time, then

gently disentangled her from his arms. 'Help me?' he asked.

She nodded and positioned his chair parallel to the bath, dropped the armrests and watched while he hoisted himself onto the wooden board, admiring the well-defined muscles of his arms and chest and noting with pleasure the amount of condition he had regained since arriving at Port Said. From his perch on the board he was able to lower himself into the water until he was immersed up to his armpits. He closed his eyes again, enjoying the luxurious feel of the warm water on his skin, then submerged himself completely. Suddenly worried that he might have slipped, Erin grabbed for him but he popped up by himself, shaking his head and flinging drops of water everywhere.

He wiped the water out of his eyes. 'God, I miss the sea.'

'You'll be able to swim as much as you like when you get home,' she countered, pushing the wheelchair out of the way and settling herself on the floor beside the tub. She began to soap his back with a facecloth, fascinated by the brown smoothness of his skin and the long, graceful muscles that moved sleekly under it. 'Your hair's getting long again,' she added softly.

'Yes, a bloke came around yesterday doing haircuts, but I decided against it.'

'I know. Corporal Bell. He's an orderly, you know, not a barber.'

Joseph had a vision of the dreadful haircuts his roommates had suffered at the hands of the singularly unqualified corporal, and laughed out loud. 'Yes, I could see that.'

'Will you cut it again?' she asked, hoping he'd say no.

'I don't think so. Well, I won't have to now I'm not a soldier any more.'

'No, but you'll still be in the military until you get home and get your discharge, and that might be months away yet.'

'Then I'll just have to be a soldier with scruffy hair, won't I? I've done my bit, Erin. I'm not giving up anything more.'

She rubbed soap onto her hands and ran them through his wet hair, working up a lather and massaging his skull slowly as he relaxed against the end of the tub. He closed his eyes and sighed at the heavy sensuality of it, aware now that he had an erection.

Erin noticed it too, and was grateful he couldn't see her face. She'd experienced this before, of course — patients becoming aroused during the course of her professional ministrations — and had learnt to ignore the embarrassment it caused her and all but the cheekiest of men, but this was not like that. This erection belonged to the man she loved, and although not naïve she was sexually inexperienced and wasn't at all sure what to do about it.

'Do you want to rinse the soap out?' she asked.

He ducked under the water, rinsed his hair, then reappeared, noting her pink cheeks.

'I can do the rest,' he said, not wanting her to do anything she didn't want to do.

She nodded. He completed his wash, wrung

out the facecloth and draped it over the edge of the bath.

'I'll need a hand to get out. I can put some weight on my left leg now but if you could help pull me up, I'll dry myself sitting on the board and then get into the chair.'

They clasped wrists and she pulled him out of the water, then guided him onto the board and handed him his towel. He dried himself quickly while she repositioned the wheelchair next to the bath, then held it still as he moved into it. Seated, he bunched the towel in his lap, self-conscious now about the erection which refused to go away.

'No,' said Erin, 'leave it.'

'What?'

'The towel. Put it down.'

He did as she asked, and gasped involuntarily as she reached out and hesitantly stroked the soft, silky skin of his rearing penis.

Then she withdrew her hand and plucked out the pins that held her veil in place, and untied her dark hair so it fell straight and shining down her back. She took off her apron, unbuttoned the bodice of her uniform, then drew aside the folds of her chemise, revealing full, white breasts tipped with firmly erect nipples in the centre of large, dark areolae.

As she began to raise her skirt Joseph said, somewhat reluctantly, 'You don't have to do this, Erin.'

'I want to,' she replied, defiant now. 'And I'm going to.'

With her skirt tucked temporarily under her

arms, she hooked her thumbs into the elastic waistband of a pair of very utilitarian knickers and drew them down past the tops of her stockings, secured midway up her firm, white thighs by plain garters, and let them fall to the floor.

She stepped out of them, pulled a face and said, 'Lovely, aren't they?' Then she smiled apologetically and added, 'I don't feel comfortable taking everything off here. I'd rather, well, do it this way.'

Joseph nodded and held out his hand. She came to him then, raised her skirt again and straddled his thighs. He looked down at the dark, glossy mass of curls between her legs and almost lost control of himself.

'Am I hurting anything?' she asked.

'Could you move up just a little?'

She did and they both clutched at each other in fright as the chair lurched backwards.

'Bloody hell!' Joseph exclaimed. 'Is the brake on?'

Erin, giggling madly, couldn't answer.

'Perhaps you'd better check,' he said, beginning to laugh himself now.

She climbed off him and checked the brake. 'No, it wasn't. We could have ended up in a toilet cubicle,' she said, still giggling.

'Come back here,' Joseph said softly.

She manoeuvred back onto him but as she moved to settle her buttocks on his thighs, he guided her so that she was positioned over his penis instead.

'Sure?' he murmured, examining her huge,

expressive eyes for even the smallest sign to the contrary.

She answered by adjusting the angle of his penis and sitting down on him, using her thigh muscles to balance her weight so that the initial depth of his penetration would not be too extreme. He immediately realised what she was doing and moved his hands under her buttocks to help her. She grunted involuntarily as he entered her, but she was ready and there was only a slight sensation of resistance for both of them as he slowly slid in. He stopped then, wrapped his arms around her, pulled her to him and held her tightly.

He whispered in her ear, 'I'm sorry, I can't hold on.'

'Then don't,' she whispered back.

So he didn't and his release came with such intensity that he wondered for a moment whether he might pass out. As his shuddering subsided he let his head fall backwards, feeling her cool hands gently smoothing his dark hair back from his temples. When he opened his eyes her face was only inches from his, and she looked concerned.

'Are you all right?' she asked.

'Oh, I'm more than all right,' he replied, smiling. 'Are you?'

She sat back and smiled back at him, a slow wide grin that told him everything he could have hoped to know.

'There's more to it than this,' he said, still smiling but somewhat ruefully now.

'Oh, I know that, but we've plenty of time.'

He enfolded her again and pressed his cheek against hers, hugging her to him.

'Ow,' she said as she felt his bristles. 'We forgot to shave you.'

They laughed again, and then he started to cry and she held him tightly for a long time.

★ ★ ★

Noah Jackson turned to Joseph and said, 'That was a bloody long bath. Nice and clean now, are we?'

'Squeaky,' replied Joseph shortly, settling himself against his pillow. Although quietly elated and almost giddy with the knowledge that the woman he loved loved him back, he was bone weary and the stump of his right leg throbbed monstrously from his recent exertions. He thought, or at least hoped, that he might have shed his final tears for his lost leg against the solid comfort of Erin's breasts, but whether he had or not, he knew now that he wouldn't have to adjust to a life of disability alone, and that seemed to him a miracle.

'Well?' Sonny demanded.

'Well what?' said Joseph.

'Me and Eru was having a bet with everyone. We got five bob on you and that Erin girl. Are we rich then?'

'A bet on what?'

'You know. What us fellas would all pay fifty quid for right now, eh?'

Eru sat up in protest, flipped his bedcover off and reached for his crutches. 'No, no, you *fool*,

123

that wasn't it! Jeez!' He got up and hobbled across to Joseph's bed and parked his bum on the end of it. 'We was betting sooner or later that one of yous'd get round to telling the other one that yous fancied each other.' He took in Lofty, Henry and Noah with a sweep of his arm. 'Them others said nah, but me and Sonny, eh, we seen it.'

'Is it that obvious?' asked Joseph, startled.

'Like a dog's balls,' Henry called laconically from his bed by the window. ''Cept we didn't think you'd do anything about it. That was the bet, that you would or you wouldn't.'

'And did yous?' persisted Sonny.

Joseph considered for a moment, then decided he had no right to spoil their speculation. 'We came to an agreement, yes.'

'*Aaaah*!' crowed Eru gleefully. 'Come on yous jokers, cough up!'

There was much muttering and groaning as the losers reluctantly handed over their money to a jubilant Sonny, who had also got out of bed and was hopping around the room with an empty teacup collecting the winnings.

At that moment Doctor Birch walked in and raised his eyebrows enquiringly. 'Fundraising, are we? Good, I could do with a new shaving kit,' he remarked as he sauntered over to Joseph's bed. 'Morning, Sergeant Deane. Good news. *I*,' he said with a flourish, 'in my capacity as quite possibly one of the finest orthopaedic surgeons to serve in this miserable war, have decided that today is the day for you to have a go on crutches. Only up and down the corridor, mind, and certainly not outside, but you can get up whenever you want. I'll get someone to bring you a set, shall I?'

'Nah, hang on,' interjected Eru, offering Joseph his pair. 'I aren't rushing off anywhere. Have a go on mine, mate!'

Oh God, thought Joseph, whose strength hadn't yet quite returned after his performance in the bathroom. He swung his legs over the side of the bed and grasped Eru's crutches, settled them under his armpits and gingerly put his left leg on the ground. Then, as Birch moved over to steady him if necessary, he stood slowly, experiencing a momentary but disconcerting rush of dizziness, and leant his weight on the sticks, testing the strength of his leg before he took a few tiny, hesitant steps forwards. He looked up and grinned, astounded at the altered perspective his newly regained height gave to the room. Shuffling carefully, he moved to the end of the bed then, after a brief reconnoitre of the obstacles he would have to negotiate, headed towards the doorway for the second time that morning.

'Don't you go out without your slippers!' admonished Lofty.

As he reached the door, Birch hovering behind him like a father with an anxious eye on a child just learning to walk, his roommates burst into applause. Joseph raised a crutch to acknowledge their support, and came close to losing his balance.

'Steady now,' said Birch solicitously, grasping Joseph's arm. 'Now, up and down the corridor a couple of times, all right? Then have a rest. We don't want to put too much pressure on that leg just yet.'

Joseph hobbled from one end of the corridor to the other twice, hoping that Erin would appear and see how well he was doing, but when she didn't he went back and almost collapsed on his bed, shocked at how weak he felt. He spent the rest of the morning dozing, but woke up feeling a lot better and went for another walk, this time with Eru and Sonny. He did find Erin this time, and she smiled delightedly at his new mobility, tucking her arm under his in the pretence that he might need some support. Eru and Sonny winked knowingly at each other, but said nothing.

They wandered back to the ward together and found that mail had been delivered. For Joseph there was a letter from Tamar, as well as one from his father. He had received several cheerful and morale-boosting notes from Keely in Cairo since he had been at Port Said, but these would be the first letters from his parents since he was carted off Gallipoli. As he was deciding which one to open first Sister Griffin appeared, striding purposefully down the ward, her ample and powerful buttocks flicking the back of her skirt out as she walked.

'Nurse McRae? A word if you please?' she said. She wasn't smiling.

Erin followed her out into the corridor apprehensively, half guessing what this might be about.

'Nurse McRae,' began the Sister brusquely.

126

Then she stopped, looked over her shoulder at the open doorway, took Erin's arm and steered her further down the corridor. She lowered her voice. 'Look, there's no discreet way for me to broach this matter. It has come to my notice that you assisted Sergeant Deane with his ablutions this morning.'

Erin blinked. 'Yes, Sister, I did.'

'But you're not on this ward today. What did you think you were doing?'

Erin said nothing.

'It's rumoured that you and Sergeant Deane have developed some sort of an understanding. Is that true?'

'We're cousins, yes.'

'That's not what I mean. People talk, Erin, and you know it's absolutely forbidden for nurses to fraternise with the patients. Were you?'

'What?'

'*Fraternising!*'

Erin gazed at the sister's stern face and decided she had better tell the truth, or at least most of the truth. 'We did have something we needed to sort out, yes.'

'And what was that?'

Erin suddenly didn't want to confess that she and Joseph had discovered, gloriously and ecstatically, that they loved each other; it sounded so childish and unprofessional, standing here now in front of Sister Griffin in a corridor that smelled of disinfectant and boiled greens from the midday meal. But she blurted it out anyway. 'I love him.'

Sister Griffin sighed wearily and blew her

cheeks out, her breath smelling faintly of tea and cigarettes. 'For God's sake, girl, do you realise what will happen if Matron hears about this?' Erin nodded but she went on regardless. 'You'll be bundled onto the next ship home before you even know what's happening, that's what, in complete disgrace and with your career in tatters. Did you not listen to anything during your selection interviews? The need for the strictest of moral codes, the highest standards of professionalism and all the rest of it?'

'Yes, I did listen. But it's not like that.'

'Oh, no, it never is, is it?'

Sister Griffin rubbed her hand over her face; she didn't want to lose this young woman — Erin McRae was a highly competent and compassionate nurse and God knew they were short of those at the moment.

'Look,' she went on, 'believe it or not, I do understand, Erin. Just between you and me, the same thing happened to me during my service in South Africa. You develop feelings for the young men, especially when they're lying there hurt and confused. They're lonely and frightened and some of them cry out for their mothers, and I don't know about you but that *always* touches me,' she said, tapping her ample breast. 'But there's only so much you can do for them. You can tend their wounds, feed them, comfort them by talking to them, but you *can't* fix them, my girl. That's someone else's job, not yours. And yes, I'm sure they'd all perk up if you gave yourself to each of them, and I'll speak plainly here — every man wants the comfort of a woman's arms when he's feeling afraid and miserable — but let's face it, you'd never get any work done, would you? Leave that side of things to the women who do that for a living. You are a nurse, a dispenser of medical care, and a very good one, I might add, but that's all.'

'But it isn't *like* that, Sister! This was something that started well before the war. I didn't know he was going to turn up here!'

'Well, that's as may be, and I can't say I blame you if that is the case — he's a very attractive man, Sergeant Deane — but it doesn't change anything. He'll be sent on to England shortly for convalescence, and then home, and you'll be left behind here because you've got a job to do. A very important one. Yes, you could plead nervous exhaustion or something and go running back after him, but somehow I doubt you'd do that, would you?'

'No, I certainly wouldn't.'

'Right, so where does that leave you? God knows how long this war will go on — you could be apart for years. What future is there for either of you? Be practical about this, Erin. Think about it.'

'I am thinking about it, Sister. I've done nothing else since he arrived.'

'Good, and there's something else you need to think about too, now. We've been warned to be ready to move at short notice.'

'The hospital?'

'Yes. I don't know where we're going but wherever it is, it will be soon. Lemnos perhaps, no one's sure yet.'

'And we'll all be going?'

'As far as I'm aware, yes. Orderlies, doctors, nurses, everyone. So you wouldn't have had your young man for much longer anyway, which is just as well as far as your career's concerned, if nothing else. But until we do go, Erin, for God's sake please watch your step. I don't want to have to be talking to Matron about you, all right?'

Erin nodded; she would indeed watch her step. 'Yes, Sister. Thank you.'

'Don't thank me, dear. All I ask is that you heed me. You've a lot at stake here.' Sister Griffin looked at the watch pinned to her apron. 'Good God, is that the time? One more question. What sort of cousins are you?' she asked curiously.

'Not incestuous ones, if that's what you mean. Joseph is the illegitimate son of the woman who married my mother's brother.'

'Oh, well, that's all right then,' replied the Sister, looking relieved, if slightly confused.

As she turned and hurried off, Erin called out after her, 'Sister, may I ask what happened to your young man?'

There was a brief silence as Sister Griffin turned back, and when she finally spoke, her voice cracked with long-suppressed feeling. 'He was declared fit for duty again, and he died on the veldt a month later.'

★ ★ ★

Joseph read the letter from Kepa first. His father had received an official telegram advising him that his son had been wounded but there had been no details, which had been very worrying. Then a message had come from Tamar saying Erin McRae had wired that Joseph had lost his leg but was expected to survive and would be coming home soon. It was terrible news but how was he feeling now and when did he think he'd be sent home? Joseph gathered from this that his father, and therefore Tamar, had not yet received his letters. His father then offered a long list of occupations, mostly involving politics and the law, that he believed a highly educated and intelligent young man with one leg could successfully master in civilian life. Joseph shook his head in disbelief — would his father never give up trying to manage his life?

There was also news about the imminent arrival of Kepa's first grandchild, expected within the month, and his campaign to get Huriana and her husband to move back to Napier so he could have more to do with the baby, as was his traditional right. So far he was not having much success, but he had not given up yet. Haimona was still at sea, and safe as far his father was aware. Parehuia had not been well of late and he had taken her to some Pakeha specialist doctor who diagnosed that her heart was under some strain and had advised her to lose a significant amount of weight. Parehuia had not been at all pleased to hear this and had refused to discuss the matter since. Joseph's grandfather, Te Roroa, was failing fast and not expected to see the year out. The shipping business was doing moderately well, although in Kepa's opinion its days were numbered as a result of the extension of the railway, and if that were the case he would have to find some other way of financing Parehuia's shopping trips. After that came snippets of news about Joseph's various cousins and aunties and uncles, and a mention that he had bumped into Joseph's mother in Napier the other day and that she was looking extremely well, as usual. Joseph smiled at this: in his opinion his father had never quite been able to let go of his feelings for Tamar.

His mother's letter was in a similar vein. She too had been desperately worried about his condition after receiving Erin's communication, and hoped that he would be home soon. And, like Kepa, she offered advice on the type of thing Joseph might want to do once he had fully recovered, except that her proposition was infinitely more appealing. She suggested he might like to take up a position at Kenmore if he decided not to look for work beyond Hawke's Bay; he was an experienced drover and God knew they needed more young men on the station these days. She hadn't heard from James for quite some time and they'd read in the papers that the Gallipoli campaign wasn't going well. She and Andrew were both worried about him, as was Lucy. It was for Thomas, however, that they were most concerned.

He has only a month or so to go at Otago before he finishes his degree, then we expect he might come back up here, for a short while at least. He has asked Catherine to marry him and she's accepted, and we're delighted about that and hope they'll have the wedding here, although there is her family to consider too, of course.

All that's excellent news, but what's been worrying us is the fact that he's apparently received several white feathers in the mail. He rang the other night and told us, rather casually in passing, I might add, as if he wasn't too bothered by it. Well, he might not be, but I am! This whole white feather business nauseates me, it really does. It makes me feel ashamed to be a New Zealander.

Joseph's eyebrows went up: this was the first time he had ever heard Tamar refer to herself as a New Zealander. Usually she staunchly insisted on calling herself a Cornishwoman, despite the fact she'd been settled in New Zealand for over thirty years. She must really be annoyed.

This insistent need to persecute is a nasty, poisonous little disease worming its way through our communities, and women are almost entirely responsible for it. The feathers, as far as I can gather, come from the women whose menfolk have already gone away. I can understand that they might be upset about being left without husbands, sons and brothers, but the death and maiming of even more men surely won't remedy that! I have two sons and a daughter overseas and I certainly don't feel the need to persecute anyone! This war really is bringing out the worst in people and 'shirker-hunting' seems to have become a national pastime. I'm not saying that there aren't men going to some lengths to avoid service, but really, must every man be shamed into volunteering?

Thomas says quite a few of his fellow students have received white feathers and nasty, anonymous notes as well, so he doesn't think he's been singled out, but obviously his personal beliefs will have generated at least some of this animosity. Thank God he has Catherine now to give him support.

Joseph finished the letter and put it away. He couldn't be bothered thinking about shirkers and their persecutors. Both parties were puerile as far as he could see — the first didn't have the guts to stand up and say publicly that they opposed the war and would not fight in it; and the second hid behind feathers and unsigned letters instead of honestly expressing their feelings. He thought it was a peculiarly Pakeha thing, and didn't even pretend to understand it. He was concerned for Thomas, but credited his brother with enough brains and fortitude to manage his affairs with honour.

Tamar's proposition about him working at Kenmore, though — that was worthy of very serious consideration. Providing he could still get on a horse, it would be the ideal solution when Erin came home and they were married.

8

The news that No. 1 New Zealand Stationary Hospital was on the move became public knowledge within days. The exact date of departure was unknown but the already busy pace increased as equipment was sorted and packed and patients prepared for transfer to other hospitals.

Lofty Curtis, his shattered leg now out of traction, and Noah Jackson were both informed that they were to be sent to No. 2 Hospital in Cairo, while Joseph, Sonny, Eru and Henry, whose wounds had healed sufficiently for them to travel some distance, would be transferred to the New Zealand War Contingent Hospital at Walton-on-Thames on the outskirts of London.

Erin felt ambivalent about the impending move. Although she had resigned herself to being separated from Joseph, she was very loath to see him go. She didn't mind where she was stationed, as long as she could continue to nurse New Zealanders, but she would have liked a little more time with Joseph. He, too, viewed their separation with a wistful but resigned acceptance. In the days before the hospital's departure they found time only for some snatched, private moments together.

When word came that the hospital would be embarking from Alexandria in a week's time for a destination still unspecified, the ambulances began to arrive to collect the recuperating men. When Joseph's turn came to be loaded into one of the motorised transports, solid trucks with a red cross and NZEF stencilled onto their canvas sides, Erin almost missed him. She had been on duty in another ward that afternoon, busy changing the dressings on a man whose right arm and torso had been badly burnt in an explosion, when Sister Griffin appeared at her side.

'I'll finish this, Nurse McRae,' she said. Then, under her breath, she'd added, 'Your young man's getting ready to go. He's out the front. You'd better hurry.'

Erin hesitated long enough to give the sister a quick, grateful smile, then ran swiftly though the echoing corridor, down the stairs and outside to where the ambulances were parked in a line outside the front door. She scanned the small crowd standing on the steps, then, unable to see any sign of Joseph, grabbed an orderly she knew and asked breathlessly, 'Bob, Sergeant Deane. Which truck is he in?'

'End one, I think, love. Better hurry, though — they're moving out any minute now.'

Erin hurried over to the last ambulance in the line and stuck her head through the opening in the back. 'Joseph?' she said, and then she saw Sonny, his dark face even darker in the dim interior, and knew she was in the right place.

Joseph, propped on his elbows on a precariously narrow bunk, looked profoundly relieved. 'Erin, thank Christ, I thought I might miss you!'

She hitched up her skirt, climbed into the

back of the truck and made her way along to him. It was sweltering inside the ambulance already, the atmosphere made even more oppressive by that fact that everyone seemed to be smoking, and she didn't envy them their long and uncomfortable trip. 'Sister Griffin told me. I thought you weren't going until tomorrow morning.'

'So did we,' said Joseph, turning on his side to face her. He leant forward so their faces were only inches apart. 'I love you, Erin McRae,' he said quietly.

But obviously not quietly enough because there was a muted scuffling as the occupants of the other bunks did their best to turn away and give them a few private moments together. Erin felt absurdly grateful. She would miss these men — their solid stoicism, their cheek and their fiercely disguised love for one another.

'I know.' She rested her forehead against his for a moment.

'I'll go home and wait for you,' he said.

She raised her hand and brushed his hair back from his temples. 'I don't want anything more than that,' she replied, tears stinging her eyes.

In the gloomy light he saw them. 'Please take care,' he said, then roughly cleared his own throat. 'Everything will be all right if I know I have you.'

'You do have me, Joseph. You always did.'

There was a rasping clank as someone began to lower the canvas flap at the rear of the ambulance. 'Oh, oops, sorry,' said an orderly as he spotted Erin. 'Time to go now,' he added apologetically.

Erin took Joseph's face in her hands and kissed him on the lips. His hand came up to briefly clasp her wrist, then moved to touch the dampness on her cheek, and they broke apart.

'Safe journey,' she said, smiling softly at him.

'You too.'

As she left she touched each of the others in turn as a gesture of farewell.

'You look after yourself, eh, missy?' ordered Sonny.

'Oh, I will,' said Erin as she climbed down over the tailgate.

She and a handful of the staff stood on the steps and watched as the ambulances pulled out and set off towards the sun, low in the sky now, their tyres raising plumes of dust as they slowly picked up speed.

★　★　★

It took another two days to completely pack up the hospital, and then a train journey through the night took everything and everyone to Alexandria. They arrived at 3 a.m. on the 20th of October and embarked immediately on the SS *Marquette*, a good-sized steamship with a huge central funnel and only just enough room for her seven-hundred-odd human passengers, the men of the British 29th Divisional Ammunition Column and the New Zealanders, plus five hundred mules. The animals did not appreciate being squashed into stalls in the bowels of the ship, and brayed dismally and without respite.

Erin, tired and scratchy from being unable to sleep on the train, located the cabin she was to share with three other nurses, drank a cup of pale, tepid tea, then lay down on her cramped bunk and fell asleep only minutes later, lulled by the gentle roll of the transport as it moved slowly out of the harbour and into deeper water.

When she awoke some hours later, feeling stiff and grubby, the sun was up and Egypt well behind them. She had a rudimentary wash and went in search of food. During breakfast she learnt that their destination was Salonika, a small town on the Greek coast where the hospital would care for wounded soldiers from the British and French expeditionary forces. Like most of her colleagues she was deeply disappointed that they would not be looking after New Zealanders.

Because of the persistent rumours of German submarines in the area, they practised lifeboat drill exhaustively over the next two days. In a way it was fun, but the exercise lost some of its lightheartedness after the French destroyer *Tirailleur* joined the convoy on the 22nd, although many on board the *Marquette* insisted on viewing the French vessel as a precautionary measure only, especially when it left the convoy the same evening.

The following morning the *Marquette*'s passengers were informed that they would be in port by midday, and a good number went up on deck to make the most of the sea breezes before they reached land. After breakfast Erin and two friends, Nancy Metcalfe and Louise Ryan, went up themselves and strolled the upper deck for several pleasant minutes before they stopped to lean on the starboard rail.

'What's that?' said Louise suddenly.

'What?' Erin squinted in the direction Louise was pointing.

'That thin green line coming towards us.'

'I don't really . . . ' Erin began, but she was interrupted by a muffled thud and a protracted shudder beneath their feet.

'Oh my God, I think it was a torpedo!' exclaimed Nancy, her hand over her mouth. 'We've been torpedoed!'

They looked at each other in horror, then staggered as the *Marquette* suddenly listed violently to port.

'Oh my God,' Nancy said again.

'Come on, we have to get to the lifeboats,' urged Louise.

She turned and hurried up the now-sloping deck toward the stern of the ship, heading for the port-side stations they had been allocated during their drills.

By the time they had circumnavigated the upper deck it was crowded with people hurrying towards the lifeboats in a grim but controlled procession. There was no noise — not even a single scream or raised voice. A large crowd milled about the boats, struggling to tie on the life jackets being rapidly passed out. The first boat winched down contained mainly nurses, huddled in the centre of the craft as it swung out beyond the ship's lower rails on rapidly unreeling chains and hit the water with a bone-shaking

140

jolt. But all did not go well with the next boat. The soldiers could not free it from its davits. As the ship rose the heavily laden boat swung forward and fell. Erin cried out in horror as it smashed down onto the boat below, throwing most of its occupants into the water and killing several outright.

Erin turned to Nancy and Louise and shouted, 'The other side! The lifeboats on the other side!'

As they fought their way starboard again, Erin's knee connected so forcefully with some solid object that she thought she might be sick with the stabbing agony of it. 'Take your coats off,' she said to the others as she staggered to her feet again, amazed at how calm her voice sounded. 'They'll drag us under!'

They clambered into the forward lifeboat and crouched together holding on to whatever they could as it descended quickly towards the water. Then all five nurses on board shrieked as it swung wildly and crashed against the side of the ship. Suddenly one of the suspension chains tore away and the boat's bow plummeted and emptied them all into the sea. Erin had a second's glimpse of flailing bodies tumbling to her left and right before she hit the water and went under immediately.

She was suspended briefly in the muffled and almost serene greyness of the shockingly cold sea water, and she wondered if she had drowned already. Then her lungs began to ache and it occurred to her that if she was still holding her breath she couldn't be dead yet. She righted herself, kicked and broke the surface several seconds later, gasping and choking.

Around her bobbed people and a few bits and pieces from the dying ship, almost fully submerged now, only the stern above the water, so she struck out to put as much distance as she could between herself and the *Marquette* before it went under completely and dragged her down with it.

She'd only managed a few yards before a mighty enfolding sensation tugged her backwards and she felt rather than heard a low hissing as the stern slid beneath the water a short distance behind her. Filling her lungs with as much air as possible she let herself relax as she was sucked under, and drifted bonelessly as she waited for the downward pull to ease off. When it did she kicked madly toward the surface and bobbed up again like a champagne cork, noting with something close to almost hysterical amusement that her boots had been sucked right off her feet and her knickers were down around her knees.

Nancy floated several feet away, floundering slowly and apparently blindly. Erin swam over, cursing the long skirt and heavy undergarments tangling around her legs and constricting her movements, and rolled Nancy onto her back. There was a deep gash across the side of her skull and her uncoordinated movements suggested a serious head injury. Erin glanced around and, fixing her sight on the hull of an overturned lifeboat, set out for it, towing Nancy's limp body along behind her.

There were already over a dozen people hanging onto loops of rope attached to the boat's sides, including Louise who, to Erin's relief, appeared uninjured. Hands reached out to pull Nancy in closer as Erin gasped, 'Can we turn it back over again?'

A man with a flattened and bleeding nose said through chattering teeth, 'No, bloody great hole in it. We've had it.'

'We have *not*,' Erin snapped as she gripped the side of the boat. Shock had filled her with adrenaline and she felt outraged at what had happened to them. 'We'll be spotted soon. We'll be rescued. We just have to hang on.' She had no idea whether this was true, but she was damned if she was going to give up as meekly as this man seemed to have done.

Around her there were several intact boats, the right way up, crammed with people. Even more held onto the looped ropes encircling the keels, although most of the survivors seemed to be in the water, grimly clutching anything that might keep them afloat. She could also see bodies, floating face down, and wondered how many had died already. There were mules everywhere too, paddling about frantically with their noses and ears sticking up out of the water; other animals were dead. Erin felt desperately sorry for them — they wouldn't understand what was happening and wouldn't have the sense to keep still and conserve their energy. The only sounds were the slap of the sea against the wreckage, some people moaning and crying and a woman singing a hymn in a reedy, cracked voice.

Louise let go of her section of rope and paddled carefully around to Erin. Her lips were blue and she was very pale. 'Are there sharks?' she whispered in Erin's ear.

Oh God, thought Erin. 'I don't know,' she whispered back, 'but don't say anything, all right?'

Louise nodded, closed her salt-stung eyes for a moment, then opened them again.

Erin said, 'Have you seen Sister Griffin?'

'She was over there before.' Louise gestured vaguely to her left. 'I think she was dead. She wasn't moving.' She coughed violently and retched. 'Oh God, what are we going to do?'

'We're going to hang on here until someone comes for us. And we're going to help. We're nurses.'

'Help?' Louise let her head loll against the side of the boat. 'I'm already so cold I can barely move.'

'We're not going to give up. That's help.'

But Erin was feeling the cold now too, an aching chill that bit deeply into her bones and made even the most conservative of movements, even speech, an insurmountable effort. She wondered detachedly whether you knew you were drowning if it happened while you were asleep.

After some minutes, or it might have been hours, she realised she actually was dozing, but woke when her hands lost their grip and her head sank beneath the water. She was horribly thirsty as well, her throat parched and sore, but knew better than to deliberately drink the sea water. When she needed to pee she just let go, dimly appreciating the brief waft of warmth around her thighs.

What was Joseph doing now? Had he reached England yet? Was he thinking about her? Did he know she was drowning?

She dozed again, and was woken this time by severe cramps in her shoulders, arms and back. She was unaware of how much time had passed, but estimated by the position of the sun that it was well past midday. There were noticeably fewer people — had they died or had they just given up and let themselves float away? — and they were drifting further and further apart. She looked for Nancy but she'd gone and her spot had been taken by someone else. A woman was sobbing hopelessly and on the other side of the boat an unseen man babbled incoherently, his ramblings punctuated by an eerie, childish wailing.

Louise was dozing too, and Erin watched almost dispassionately as her hands slowly opened and she slid noiselessly under the water. When she didn't bob back up again Erin shot out her arm, croaking with the sudden spasm of pain snaking across her shoulders, grabbed her friend by the hair and yanked her head above the water.

Louise coughed and spluttered. Eventually she fixed her dull, reddened eyes on Erin and rasped, 'If I go under again I want you to leave me.'

'No,' replied Erin with weary resolution.

Louise's lips were cracked and bleeding, or perhaps she had bitten them. 'I'm tired, Erin. I want to go to sleep. I've had enough.'

'Someone will come soon.'

'No they won't,' Louise said bleakly.

Was she right? They had all watched in disbelief as several ships had steamed past, apparently too far away to see or hear the *Marquette*'s survivors. Those who still had the energy screamed themselves hoarse, but none of the vessels stopped or even slowed down. Eventually a man, a major judging by the crown on his shoulder tabs, said they were not stopping because they were neutrals and therefore not prepared to come to their rescue, and Erin felt like drowning him herself.

Her legs and lower body were totally numb now, except for the excruciating cramps that seared and convulsed her muscles with dreadful and unrelenting regularity, but she was far too exhausted to kick or paddle in an effort to ward them off. She felt sad at the thought of never seeing Joseph again, and wished fervently she'd said out loud in the back of the ambulance that she loved him too. The idea of just going to sleep and drifting away was very seductive. She wouldn't be the only one.

But she couldn't give up.

★ ★ ★

Erin knew nothing until she was dragged out of the water and laid in the bottom of a rowing boat by a sailor with a very thick French accent and an appalled look on his face. What happened next was a blur. Erin became properly aware of her surroundings only when she realised she was being winched up the side of a ship in some sort of harness. Strong hands caught her at the top and she was helped onto the deck, wrapped in a blanket and given a mug of hot coffee, which she gulped greedily but coughed up again as the generous tot of brandy it contained caught in her throat. She sat for some minutes, sipping more slowly now, her limbs leaden and unresponsive, then lowered her head to her knees and finally, in the darkness and confusion, allowed herself to cry. But the brandy did its job and began to warm her stomach and return the feeling to her arms and legs, actually a rather unpleasant and painful sensation. She clutched at a rail and tried to pull herself up, but her legs gave way and she slumped sideways again, defeated.

The French destroyer was not her final destination. Erin and other survivors were transferred first to a French hospital ship where they were given some dry clothes, supper, tea and hot wine. Soon afterwards, they were taken to a British hospital ship.

As Erin boarded, she collapsed again. A woman in a nurse's uniform bent down next to her and helped her to sit. 'Are you hurt?'

Erin shook her head. 'No, I'm just so tired.'

'That's to be expected, love. You've had a terrible shock,' the woman responded kindly in a distinctly Australian accent.

She stood and beckoned to a medical orderly, and Erin felt masculine arms lift her to her feet and support her as se walked unsteadily across the deck. They passed through a door and down a short corridor to what appeared to be a medical examination room, where she was helped out of her borrowed overcoat by another nurse, then interviewed by a doctor.

He explained that she and at least some of her colleagues were on board the hospital ship *Grantully Castle*, staffed by Brits and Australians, and that they were preparing to sail for Salonika shortly. Erin's lack of response concerned the doctor, who proceeded to give her a thorough examination, shining a light into her eyes, waving his fingers in front of her face and asking her to count them, feeling all over her skull and checking her limbs. He pronounced her physically sound, apart from scrapes and severe bruising, but exhausted, severely dehydrated and in shock, and recommended fluids, plenty of rest and a draught to steady her nerves. Erin was almost asleep on her feet by the time she was led out into the corridor again, where she saw Louise leaning heavily on the arm of another orderly.

The two women stared at each other dumbly for several moments. Then Louise's face crumpled and they hugged in silence, hanging onto each other in an agony of shared grief and disbelief. How many of them had been lost? *Who* had been lost? What would happen to them now?

The nurse gently disentangled them and led Erin away to a cabin, where she was helped into a bunk with another hot drink and advised to get some sleep, even though other survivors would be coming in on and off. Erin slept fitfully, despite her exhaustion, and stirred each time someone entered the cabin. But she did not dream, and thanked God for that.

When she woke some hours later it was light and she thought for a brief moment she was still on board the *Marquette*, but then, with a jolt that nauseated her, she remembered what had happened.

She sat up slowly and her hand strayed to her dully aching lower belly. Then came a sharp, twisting pain and, taking care not to wake anyone, she left the cabin in search of a toilet, finding one after several minutes of increasingly desperate searching. She went in and shut the door, lowered her borrowed underpants and perched on the seat, grimacing at the stiffness of her thigh muscles. Her abdomen spasmed again but instead of the expected bowel movement, a gush of something warm slid out of her vagina and dripped with frightening heaviness into the bowl. She wiped and inspected the tissue; it was covered with thick, bright blood. Another cramp caught her and she leant over with her elbows on her knees and her face in her hands while she waited for it to pass. It did, with another sliding gush.

Her period, finally? It was late by nearly a month. Or was it something else?

It had taken her a few weeks to allow herself to consider the possibility she might be pregnant, because by her calculations the timing hadn't been right, but a growing tenderness in her breasts and a queasiness around eleven each morning had begun to convince her. Her eyes squeezed shut in an attempt to hold back bitter tears as she realised that if she had been pregnant with Joseph's baby, she certainly wasn't now.

The cramps continued but their force began to abate. Someone came into the bathroom and knocked on the toilet door.

'Is someone in there?'

'Yes,' called Erin. 'Erin McRae. I'm having a bit of trouble. Who is it?'

'Elizabeth Barclay.' Another nurse. 'Is it serious? Can I do anything?'

'I need a sanitary towel.'

'Oh.' A brief silence, then, 'It's probably the shock. I'll ask one of the Australian girls for you. Won't be a minute. Hang on.'

The door to the bathroom clanged shut as she went out. She was back five minutes later. 'Erin? Here, I managed to get a couple.'

Erin opened the door and a hand passed her a brown paper bag. 'Thanks,' she called gratefully.

'Anything else I can do?'

'No thanks, Elizabeth. I think I'll be fine now.'

Erin blotted herself again, folded the cloth into the crotch of her knickers, stood and pulled them up. Then she took a deep breath and flushed the bowl, deliberately not looking as the contents swirled away. She opened the door and stepped out.

'You look very pale,' Elizabeth observed, concerned. 'Have you been crying?'

Erin nodded.

Elizabeth touched her hand, her own eyes filling with tears. 'I know, it's been a terrible shock, hasn't it? I keep crying on and off myself.'

Erin turned to the mirror above the hand basin and disinterestedly surveyed her bleached, dark-eyed face. The only spots of colour were on her nose and cheeks, chapped red by salt water. There was a bruise on her left temple and her lips were cracked and sore.

'How is Matron, have you heard?' she asked.

Elizabeth's voice wobbled. 'Very ill, apparently. She might not live.'

Erin turned away from the mirror to face the other woman. 'How many, do you know?'

Elizabeth held up both hands, splayed her fingers, said, 'Ten of us.' She struggled to contain her tears. After a moment she sniffed inelegantly and added, 'And eighteen from the Medical Corps, they say.'

The two women gazed at each other in horrified silence.

The hospital ship steamed into Salonika later that morning, where the survivors disembarked with hugely appreciated gifts of clothing, hairpins, toothbrushes and other necessities from the Australian nurses.

After two days in Salonika, which proved to be a dirty, malodorous town, the survivors returned to Alexandria. Some of the more severely distressed women were sent home to New Zealand to recuperate. The others, including Erin, stayed on and, after a short rest, went back to work in one of Alexandria's four British General hospitals. Erin wired home as soon as she could; she also wrote to Joseph at Walton, unable to bear the thought of how he might feel

151

when he heard what had happened. But only about the sinking; she would not burden him with her sadness regarding their more personal loss.

* * *

By the time Joseph arrived at Walton-on-Thames, everyone knew that the Maori Contingent, seriously battered and reduced in number by its service at Gallipoli and subsequently withdrawn to Lemnos for recuperation, was to head back to Egypt for rest, reinforcement and further training.

Joseph wondered how Wi and the rest of them were getting on, and who had taken over as the section's sergeant. There were also rumours that the Anzacs and the British could be evacuating from Gallipoli altogether, now that the campaign seemed doomed to such costly and inevitable failure.

It was the news about the *Marquette*, however, that chilled him. He had been at Walton only a matter of days when the rumours began to circulate: the ship had been torpedoed six or seven times, more than half of its passengers had been drowned, there were very few survivors from the New Zealand Medical Corps and even fewer from the NZANS party. He scoured every newspaper, growing more and more agitated as time passed. At the beginning of November he read that ten of the almost 170 who perished had been from the NZANS, but this did nothing to assuage his mounting concern as no names were provided.

When Erin's letter arrived a week after that, he locked himself in the toilet and wept with relief. She was alive. His spirit and demeanour changed dramatically and neither Sonny nor Eru needed to ask whether he had received good news. He wrote back immediately, his letter brimming with words of love and expressions of his profound sense of gratitude at her survival, then threw himself into the process of his recovery with renewed determination and vigour.

Walton-on-Thames was a tranquil-looking hospital beside the river, set in beautiful grounds with artfully laid-out walks, flower beds, mature trees and manicured lawns. Even the food was good. But more than that, it was staffed and run by New Zealanders, which helped to relieve the homesickness of many of the men, although such sentiments were never openly admitted. Joseph and the other patients also found the hospitality of the locals a welcome comfort — there were frequent invitations to private homes, boating parties and picnics and even the occasional motor trip to Windsor, which meant little to him although he enjoyed the scenery.

Best of all, though, was the river. Joseph swam until his shoulder muscles burned, ignoring the cold for as long as he could until it finally defeated him and he was forced to find another outlet for his steadily increasing energy and his obsessive desire to improve his physical condition.

His left leg was progressing well and his stump

had healed to the extent that the orthopaedic surgeon overseeing his treatment had suggested trying an artificial limb. When the time came he found himself inordinately nervous. Sonny told him not to worry — there was nothing to it; he'd been lurching around on his for a fortnight now and could even manage a fair distance without a stick.

But there was a little more to it than that. Joseph's stump was extremely tender and his prosthesis had to be remodelled several times to reduce irritation of the scar tissue. The surgeon had stressed how important it was that the surface of the stump not break down, because if it did the artificial limb could not be worn. Joseph complied wholeheartedly, taking extra care of the area.

What was left of his right leg was ugly now, withered, bereft and foreign-looking, and he felt a vicious pang of regret every time he looked at it, although his thigh muscles hadn't atrophied as much as those of many fellow amputees. But once the prosthesis had been refitted, and he was beginning to master its use without the need for a cane, his optimism returned. The artificial leg felt as if it weighed a ton, however, and the harness attaching it was just as unwieldy, fastening around his waist, then over both shoulders and buckling again across his back. Apart from giving him something to walk on, its only other advantage was that its weight was building up his thigh muscle again. Joseph complained it was worse than full field kit, but as Eru pointed out at least once a day — in an

154

effort, Joseph suspected, to reassure himself — there was no point moping or grizzling about something that could not be changed.

A snow-blanketed Christmas came and went, and a few weeks into the new year Joseph was informed that he could expect to be sent home to New Zealand within a month. A representative from the Repatriation Department visited the hospital at the end of January and all men earmarked for going home were ordered to attend his lecture in the hospital's dining room.

The envoy, a short, nervous-looking man in a three-piece worsted suit, talked earnestly about 'increasing the functional activity of the individual', and the benefits of training convalescent veterans to 'strengthen them for suitable tasks in civilian life' so that they could effectively 're-enter the workaday world'. The 'final stage of recovery and restoration' would take place in one of the numerous military hospitals or convalescent homes in New Zealand — and here he rattled off a list of who would go where, according to which part of the country they called home — before veterans would go on to a programme of suitable vocational training.

He talked about cabinet-making and basketry, leather-working and schoolteaching, upholstering and small business loans, and tailoring and motor mechanics. He discussed jobs that sounded so thoroughly alien to most of his audience that a profound and disbelieving silence descended over the room and he looked up from his notes to see if anyone was still there.

Joseph glanced at the faces of his neighbours,

most of whom appeared as incredulous as he imagined he did. Basketry? But they were labourers, many of them, wanderers. Farm hands, drovers, builders' mates, odd-jobbers, some of them fishermen, others hunters. Most of them knew they wouldn't be going back to that, not with missing or useless limbs, but how could they settle to something like bloody *basketry*?

And this was only a fraction of the information they all craved. Earning a living would be important, but would any woman love them now with their scarred bodies and faces, their nightmares and private, unspoken horrors; would their children know them, or even want to; would they be seen as heroes or as the ones who didn't make it and had to come home early? Had they been missed, had what they done *counted*, had they paid too big a price? And, most of all, what would everyone at home expect of them?

Joseph shook his head, grateful that at least something was being done for the veterans, especially the badly mutilated and the mentally unbalanced, but knowing that none of this would be for him.

He was a drover; nothing would turn him away from that. Or from Erin.

Part Two

The Murdoch Children at War
1916–1918

9

Kenmore, May 1916

Andrew's lips were pressed into a thin, grim line and his face was white except for an isolated smudge of angry colour high on each cheek.

'Over my dead body you will!' he exploded, spittle flying. 'This family's given *enough*! There's no need for you to go as well!' He lunged out of his chair, strode angrily to the French doors and gazed unseeingly at his immaculate gardens. He spun around to face Ian again. 'It's all a bloody great adventure to you, isn't it? Have you any idea what it will do to your mother, having you away as well?'

Ian sat still and waited patiently; he had anticipated this.

Andrew, hurt and frightened, was still winding himself up. 'First Joseph, home with a *leg* missing, in case you hadn't noticed, Ian. A *leg*! Then Erin, torpedoed and nearly drowned, Keely at some hospital putting up with God knows what filth and disease and horror day after day, James in bloody France, and Thomas not able to set foot outside his front door without someone accusing him of cowardice! And finally, *finally*, it's driven even him away!' He returned to his chair and collapsed into it, deflated. 'He could have done an enormous amount of good work here, for the war effort and for the veterans, if people had just left him alone.' He sat in silence for a moment, then looked wearily over at his youngest son. 'Is that what's behind all this? That bloody feather? Fear of what other people might think?'

'No,' Ian replied calmly. 'I don't give a toss what anyone else thinks.'

And that was true. Over the past two years Ian had matured into a broad-shouldered, impressive-looking young man, although his freckles and tousled blond hair seemed destined to lend him a perpetually boyish air. At the age of twenty he was self-assured and gregarious, and had lost little of his happy-go-lucky outlook and infectious enthusiasm. Unlike Keely he wasn't usually headstrong, and he didn't have either James' need for order and justice or Thomas' soul-deep sensitivity, but he had of late discovered within himself a driving need to establish who, and what, he was.

The anonymous white feather he'd received in the post last week hadn't bothered him at all, however, because he agreed with the sentiment behind it: only concern for his parents had stopped him enlisting until now.

But he was restless. He had mastered and befriended the stroppiest horses on the station, mustered across the high country for more gruelling hours in the saddle than anyone else, swum the deepest rivers in full flood, and bedded the most interesting and alluring girls in the district, both from within his own social class and beneath it (although he had never shared these particular victories with his parents), but none of this was enough. He needed to prove himself on a grander scale, and going to war seemed the only way of doing it.

'Well, if that isn't it, then *why?*' persisted his father, knowing full well that the reasons were more or less irrelevant, and wondering how many fathers had asked their sons the same pointless question.

Ian stared back at him with compassion, sensing Andrew's disappointment and fear.

'Because I can,' he replied simply. 'Because I'm old enough, because it's expected of me, but mostly because I want to.' He pulled determinedly at a loose thread on the cuff of his faded work shirt. 'I'll never know if I don't, Da.' Another pause. 'And I have to know.'

Grimly, Andrew responded, 'Aye, well, *I* don't expect it of you and I won't give you my permission. Or my blessing.'

'I'm sorry, Da, but I don't need either.'

'I'll say you're needed here to work on the station. I'll say you're indispensable.' Andrew felt childish and somehow shamed at saying this, but his despair at the prospect of losing the last and youngest of his children to the war had blinkered him against rational argument of any sort. And it was true: Ian was needed to help run Kenmore.

Ian, more perturbed by his father's uncharacteristic demonstration of guile than by the anger that had preceded it, said, 'Conscription's coming in soon. Surely it would be better for me to volunteer now and get the unit I want, rather than wait and be shunted any old where?'

He felt terribly guilty saying this: he had already secretly enlisted and was due at

161

Trentham for training in less than a week's time. He'd considered joining the Mounted Rifles, because of the horses, but there was talk that the brigade was bound for the Sinai Peninsula and he wanted to fight wherever the New Zealand Division — and therefore James and Thomas — was, and that was France. So he'd signed on as an infantryman, despite his equestrian experience, and would be leaving, with or without his parents' endorsement, in a day or so.

'It's infantry they'll be wanting, Ian. You've had no other specific training so you'll end up with them whether you want to or not.'

Ian nodded. 'Infantry would be all right.'

'So then why don't you wait until conscription comes in? There's a chance you might not even be called up.'

'Because, Da, I want to go now.'

Andrew could see there was no point trying to reason with his son while the boy was in such an obstinate mood, so he stamped outside to find Tamar.

She was in the courtyard at the back of the house, repotting plants. She was wearing gloves, an old shirt and a pair of his work pants, and had managed to smear a streak of dirt across her cheek; he took out his handkerchief and wiped her face clean.

'I've been talking to Ian,' he said glumly.

Alerted by his tone, Tamar put her trowel down on the potting table. 'What about?'

'This enlisting business.'

She waited for him to go on.

'He says he wants to go, and that he'd rather

162

volunteer than be conscripted.' Andrew inspected his now grubby handkerchief before stuffing it back into his pocket. 'I must admit I agree with him on that one — better to get the unit you want if you have to go at all. Not that I told him that, of course, but if he waits his name might not even come up.'

'Was it that feather?'

'No, I don't think so. I suspect this has been on his mind since Joseph came home. And Thomas joining up — Thomas, who's so opposed to the war — was probably the last straw. I know he isn't fighting, but he's still over there. I think Ian feels left out.' Andrew shook his head sadly and his face crumpled for a moment. 'I just can't make the boy see sense, Tamar. I'm afraid he'll just run off.'

Tamar sat down on an overturned flower pot and pulled her gloves off. 'Has he said that?'

'No, but he did point out he doesn't need our permission to enlist.'

'Yes, well, he hasn't needed that for a while, has he?'

'No, but he seems a lot more serious about it this time.'

'Ian is very seldom serious about anything, dear,' Tamar observed benignly.

'He is when it comes to proving himself. He might always do it with a joke and a smile on his face, but you can't deny there's something driving the boy.'

Tamar said nothing because privately she agreed. Especially of late, and particularly since Thomas had gone away. Poor Thomas, who had rung them out of the blue one day to tell them he'd enlisted in the New Zealand Medical Corps as a stretcher bearer. Because of his medical training he'd been accepted immediately, despite his openly declared status as a conscientious objector and his refusal to carry arms, and had been sent overseas only a month later, headed, everyone assumed, for France.

She absently pulled an errant weed from between the cobblestones at her feet. If Ian went, then all her precious children would have been sucked into the maelstrom. Although she had a deep and unshakeable conviction that each would return, she'd been profoundly distressed by what had happened to Joseph; he was her firstborn, a vital and dynamic young man so like his father, and he had come home shockingly maimed. He was adapting to his disability quite well, riding again already and determined to return to droving, but she fancied she could see through his optimistic words and demeanour to the pain and disillusionment locked inside.

The news that he intended to marry Erin had been received with utter delight in all quarters, and not least of all by Jeannie and Lachie who had grown very fond of Joseph over the years, and they were all looking forward to their daughter's return home, although now she was in France and God only knew how long for. Their marriage would symbolise a new start for the family, something positive to help them all put this upheaval and turmoil behind them, and there would no doubt be babies who would grow up with all Tamar's other grandchildren to become the generation that would live in peace, well beyond any shadow of war.

She looked up at Andrew and asked quietly, 'Do you think he *will* run off?'

But before he could answer Lucy came out of the house, squinting against the sun as she held a wriggling, grizzling Duncan in her arms. He was almost fifteen months old now, the image of his father with his rich brown hair and blue eyes, and just as prickly when crossed.

Lucy's pretty face was flushed and she looked distracted. She thrust the baby at her mother-in-law and beseeched, 'Could you please take him for a few minutes? I've been trying to feed him but he's been . . . ', and here she glanced at Andrew and her cheeks grew even redder, ' . . . well, he's been biting me and his teeth are so *sharp*! I've told him not to bite and now he's having a tantrum but he has to learn.'

Andrew thought it was high time his grandson was weaned, but he understood that Lucy's insistence on continuing to breast-feed the child gave her more than a little comfort and perhaps some sort of connection, no matter how tenuous, to James, whom she had not seen for over a year and a half.

He said, 'I'll take him, Lucy, if you like.'

In his view Tamar spoiled Duncan, and in a household populated mainly by women, he saw himself as the rightful dispenser of masculine discipline. He took the child from his mother and cradled him in his arms. Duncan's face was very red and angry-looking, and he was now bellowing his head off, but there was not a single tear in his blue eyes; it was plain to Andrew that the boy was having them all on. After years of raising Keely he was good at spotting this sort of manipulative and opportunistic behaviour in children, and prided himself on being immune to it. But he wasn't.

'Are you a thirsty wee man, are you?' he crooned. 'Aye, well, you mustn't bite your Mam. It isn't polite.' And he wandered off across the lawn where he put Duncan down to see how many unaided steps he might take today.

Tamar and Lucy looked at each other and rolled their eyes. 'Did he hurt you?' Tamar asked.

'Yes,' Lucy replied reproachfully, 'the little ferret. He can be very impatient sometimes. And I'm sure he understands when I tell him no, but it doesn't seem to have any effect on him.' She blinked as her eyes filled with tears. 'I wish James were here. Things would be so much easier.'

Tamar stood up and brushed off the seat of her pants. 'I know, dear. I wish they all were. But they're not, and we just have to accept that for now.'

The following morning, when Ian did not appear at the breakfast table at his usual time, Tamar's unease rose up in her like a particularly nasty surge of indigestion as she recalled his excessively fond goodnight to her the previous evening.

'You've not seen Ian this morning?' she asked Lachie as he sat down.

'No, I haven't. I've just come down,' he replied. 'Why?'

'He's normally up and about by now but I haven't seen him.' She glanced up as Andrew came in and asked, 'Have you seen Ian this morning, dear?'

Andrew stopped in his tracks and looked at her sharply, and in that instant they both knew. He went out again and Tamar could hear him pounding up the hall stairs. When he returned he had a note in his hand, which he flung angrily at the table; it fluttered to the floor.

'What is it?' asked Lachie sharply.

Andrew replied stonily, 'He's gone.'

'Oh,' said Lachie, knowing full well what his brother-in-law was talking about: Ian had been going on about enlisting to anyone who would listen for months now.

Tamar bent and retrieved the note from under the table. She read:

Dear Mam and Da,

I expect I'll be on the train to Wellington by the time you read this.

I'm sorry I wasn't able to break the news to you face to face, but I've enlisted. I did it last week but couldn't bring myself to tell you because I knew how upset you'd be.

It's for the best — I don't think I could live with myself if I didn't go and I would always be asking myself, why didn't I?

I'll write, and will try to get home for a quick visit before I go overseas.

I love you both and hope you can be proud of me.

Your loving son, Ian

France, August 1916

Ian pressed his face against the grimy glass of the troop train and watched as the French countryside rolled past. It was coming into autumn here and rain had fallen steadily since they'd arrived, but the land looked clean and crisp because of it.

He was one of a number of reinforcements who had been temporarily stationed over the past few weeks at Sling Camp, the main New Zealand base in the heart of the great Salisbury Plain, and was extremely pleased to be shot of the place. It was damp, dismal and desperately bleak, the only sign of welcome a huge, shallow kiwi carved into the chalk of the bare hills rising behind the camp. The food was mediocre at best, the rats tenacious and the huts cold and draughty. Long route marches and remorseless training were daily occurrences, with endlessly repeated drill, rifle and trench-digging practice, Lewis gun instruction, wiring, bomb-handling and gas-mask drill. Recreational facilities were sparse, and once a man had visited Bulford and Tidworth villages a couple of times, and perhaps the ancient town of Amesbury if he had an interest in history, there was very little else to do.

So Ian and his cohorts hadn't been at all sorry to farewell Sling, and had enjoyed the short trip across the Channel from Folkestone to Boulogne in a rather decrepit paddle-steamer, then on to the New Zealand infantry base at Etaples. Yesterday they had entrained for Armentières and hadn't stopped for any length of time since. The train's inadequate toilets had backed up long ago and men had taken to peeing out of the windows. They were bored now, and concealing their apprehension regarding their imminent arrival at the front beneath a veneer of irritatingly schoolboyish rowdiness, if the pained expressions on their officers' faces were anything to go by. But they would reach Armentières soon and join up with the New Zealand Division shortly thereafter.

The Division had been in France since April, and was currently holding a nine-mile stretch of the line south-east of Armentières on the River Lys. The rumours of conditions at the front that filtered back to Sling Camp had been pretty grim, but Ian was relishing the anticipation currently fluttering in his stomach. Back home they had trained hard, honing their shooting skills, drilling and traipsing over the Rimutakas from Featherston Camp back to Trentham in dreadful weather, then done it all again at Sling, and the time had almost come for them to put their new skills into practice.

When the train finally arrived at Armentières the light was fading but the reinforcements were ordered to march to New Zealand Divisional Headquarters at Estaires, some five miles further south. They got there too late for dinner, causing a swell of grumbling and a stern warning from officers against scrounging or stealing produce from the locals. By the time full darkness had descended the cookhouse had been reopened and was serving warmed-up bully and biscuits and cups of strong tea, but by then the men had been diverted by the fuzzy-edged glow on the horizon interspersed with brighter flashes coming from the battlefield. The rumble of guns was muffled by the atmospherics but the noise of heavy artillery was clearly audible, and Ian was surprised at how much of the sky was lit up. He went to sleep that night, stretched out under his greatcoat with his head resting on his kit, wondering how he would perform once he got into the middle of it all.

In the morning it was raining again, and Ian squelched through sticky, thoroughly churned mud to the latrines, holding his nose against the stink when he got there and piddling on his boot as a result. When he got back to his section everyone was present and accounted for and eagerly awaiting breakfast after last night's meagre fare. The quality of this morning's meal wasn't much of an improvement but at least there was a decent amount of it, and Ian washed down a heaped plateful of porridge with several cups of fortifying army tea; this morning they would be marching into battle and he didn't want to do it on an empty, nervous stomach.

As they sat waiting for the order to move out, having post-breakfast smokes and checking their gear yet again, he looked around at the men beside whom he would be fighting. Or at least he hoped that would be the case — they had trained together in New Zealand, but it was highly likely they would be split up and slotted into whichever units needed replacements.

'Fluffy' Johnson, so named because his mother had made him a lovely rabbit fur hat and posted it to Trentham with a note entreating him to wear it pulled down over his ears on cool days, was sitting on a crate letting off a series of loud, regularly spaced farts. 'Sorry, lads,' he apologised sincerely, 'it's me guts. Always plays up when I'm feeling nervous.'

'Yep, my old mum always reckons better out than in,' commented Trevor Neill, a soldier with whom Ian had become firm friends since his early training days at Trentham.

Trevor was twenty-two years old, good-looking in a way that seemed to appeal to most women he met, a farm hand in civilian life, self-willed and utterly fearless, a hard drinker and a perpetual optimist. He'd been repeatedly hauled in front of the company commander during training, once or twice for cheek but more seriously for arriving back from leave shatteringly drunk, or not arriving back at all and having to be fetched by the military police, but none of this had even dented his spirit. It was rumoured that while on the mat he had once told the commander to stick his army rules up his arse, but because Trevor was such a good fighting man the major had declined, and quite gracefully too, apparently. Ian thought Trevor was splendid, almost as good a role model as Joseph, and thoroughly enjoyed his rough and ready company.

'Although I think I prefer in,' Trevor added, waving a hand in front of his face. 'What you been eating, Fluffy?'

'Same as you.'

'Well, you stink.'

Fluffy looked affronted. 'I said sorry, didn't I? I can't help it.'

Trevor made a show of getting up and moving away. 'Safer over here,' he said as he sat down again at a distance of at least ten feet.

Ian laughed loudly with everyone else, then sobered abruptly as a junior officer hurried toward them.

'Mount up, men,' he said officiously, which Ian thought was silly as none of them had horses. 'We're on our way in ten minutes.'

There was general milling about as the reinforcements rose and formed a long column in anticipation of the march out, after which they stood about shuffling their feet for another forty minutes. Finally the order came and they headed off, adjusting their step until they found the rhythm and marching with their heads up and their arms swinging.

The road out of Estaires was flat and dreary and rain smothered the countryside in miserable grey mist. Trees were still visible, however, spectral and silent in the fog, some already bare and others harbouring crows that cawed harshly as the men passed. They soon began to encounter bedraggled-looking groups of soldiers, who didn't even look up as they trudged ghost-like out of the mist towards the rear. Blatting motorcycles also passed them, together with wagons drawn by listless-looking horses, and occasional trucks and ambulances. Here and there on either side of the road were discarded vehicles, tipped onto their sides or bogged down in the mud, and the carcasses of dead horses with teeth bared grotesquely behind shrinking, drying lips. As the column's smart march degenerated into an unsynchronised plod and the surrounding landscape became increasingly ravaged, the chatter died away, silenced by the scale of destruction.

'Christ,' Ian said to Trevor, 'they've had a good going over here.' He glanced at his friend. 'You nervous?'

'Nah,' Trevor replied cheerfully. 'Too late to be getting windy now. Why, are you?'

'Not really,' Ian replied honestly. 'It's worse than I expected though.'

Trevor nodded, because he could only agree.

They reached the reserve line just before lunchtime, a deep trench running parallel to the front line but further back and more or less beyond the range of all but the heaviest artillery. Then, after a short rest and a rudimentary meal, they continued on towards the front. On their way through the trenches of the support lines, situated equidistantly between the reserve and the front trenches, they passed a group of New Zealand troops, crouched hollow-eyed, unshaven and plastered with mud around a billy suspended over a small fire. Ian's hello was met with grunts but little else.

'Miserable bastards,' observed Trevor.

The column was signalled to a halt and they rested, squatting with their backs against the damp earth walls of the deep central communication trench and trying to keep their feet clear of the filthy water.

'What are we stopping for?' asked Fluffy.

No one answered. They lit up and waited. Presently Ian noticed a lieutenant sloshing down the trench toward them; he kicked a groove into the base of the opposite wall, settled his heels in it so he wouldn't slide into the water, and squatted down.

'We'll be splitting up when we get to the forward trenches,' he announced. There were groans of disappointment, which he waved away with an irritated flap of his hand. 'Come on, you all knew it might happen. We've tried to keep as many of you together as we could.' He then proceeded to designate who was to go where, explained that the column would be moving again in another fifteen minutes and told them for God's sake to keep their heads down.

When they reached the front line, with its breastworks and deep zigzagging trenches that bordered No-Man's-Land for miles and miles in both directions, the reason for the marked lack of enthusiasm they'd encountered earlier from the New Zealanders became clear. There was mud as far as the eye could see — on the ground, in the trenches, all over the troops who peered from dugouts like filthy, glittery-eyed rats, on sinking duckboards optimistically but fruitlessly laid in areas of heavy traffic, and oozing down the sides of the deep, foul-smelling, water-filled craters that pocked what had once been verdant farmland. The whole area was a sea of dense, viscid mud, and it stank of death and, strangely, Ian thought, cat shit, and it sucked at a man's boots with a life of its own.

They dropped into the main trench and were

herded along to their new sections, Ian, Trevor and Fluffy to a unit that had been under-manned for some time. The original section had burrowed back into the trench walls in an attempt to protect themselves from shellfire, although not altogether successfully as one dugout had received a direct hit five days ago and four of their number had been killed instantly.

They were greeted by a red-eyed sergeant who introduced himself as Blakely.

'Welcome, lads. You can bivvy in here,' he said tersely as he flipped back a heavy curtain of mud-plastered sacking.

Inside was a small, dim, low-ceilinged cave smelling of dirty humans and reinforced with pit props and sandbags piled near the entranceway. A biscuit box and an upturned bucket served as furniture, and two bodies lay huddled on the floor.

'The rest are next door,' said Blakely, 'and all asleep by now, most likely. We've just come in.' He yawned hugely himself.

One of the bodies sat up, peered blearily at the newcomers and queried, 'These the reinforce-ments, Sarge?'

Blakely nodded. 'Settle them in, eh, Owen? I'm off to talk to Ross,' he said, and was gone.

'Sit down,' invited the man. His narrow face showed several days' growth and even in the gloom his skin had a pale, unhealthy sheen. Ian, Trevor and Fluffy squatted down as he introduced himself. 'Morgan, Owen Morgan. Welcome to our lovely abode. That's Toby,' he said, pointing at the other body curled on its side in a foetal position, snoring gently.

They all looked.

'What's that thing he's cuddling?' Trevor asked curiously.

'A fox cub.'

'Eh? A real one?'

Owen nodded. 'Found it a couple of days ago wandering around outside and he's taken a bit of a shine to it.'

They bent over Toby's prostrate form and gazed interestedly at the creature nestled in the crook of his elbow. It had curled itself into a compact ball, its bushy tail folded over its nose, and was sleeping fitfully.

'And it's a baby one?' Ian asked, fascinated. He'd never seen a fox before.

Owen nodded again. 'Well, a few months old, probably. Broken leg, though. I can't see it lasting. It's too young to be without its mother, I suspect. A bit like Toby, really.'

'Why? How old's Toby?' asked Trevor.

'Just sixteen. Lied about his age.'

'Jesus, that *is* young.'

'Yes, and the poor little bugger's not coping too well, either. We think it's shell shock. And we should know,' Owen added wryly. 'That's where the sarge has gone now, to talk to Lieutenant Ross about it. We're trying to get him sent home but you know how bloody useless army bureaucracy is.'

Ian felt uncomfortable discussing someone as if he were out of earshot, which Toby clearly wasn't. 'Can't he hear us?'

'I doubt it. He sleeps like the dead. We used to wake him up just to make sure he was still breathing, but then it occurred to us that sleep's probably his way of blocking everything out, his buffer if you like, that and that little animal of his. I hope to God it survives.'

'Can't he be sent back to the rear or something?' asked Fluffy.

'The MO's a bastard and says there's nothing wrong with him. And his papers say he's eighteen, so therefore the esteemed doctor doesn't believe there's a problem. I'd like to strangle the prick, myself.'

Ian sat down again. 'How long have you been here?'

'Three months, but we've had a couple of trips back to Estaires for a decent sleep and a bath. Oh, and we had a little bit of leave.'

Trevor asked, 'What's it like? Really?'

'Leave?'

'No, *here*,' Trevor replied impatiently.

Owen rummaged in his shirt pocket, withdrew a bent, thinly rolled cigarette and lit it. 'Put it like this — I was a schoolteacher back home, and I sincerely wish I'd stayed there being one.' He spat out a shred of tobacco. 'It's not what I thought it would be, and I don't mind admitting that at all. Ask most of the lads — they'll all say the same if they're being honest.' He took in the dugout with a sudden, angry sweep of his arm. 'There's no honour or glory in any of this. All we do is sit in a bloody great mud hole getting shelled and shot to buggery. It's a fucking *joke*, really.'

The others gaped in shocked silence at his vehemence. Even Trevor seemed startled.

Owen shook his head. 'Christ, I'm sorry lads. I don't mean to be such a misery. It wears you down though, you know? It *really* wears you down.' He pinched out his smoke and put the dog-end back in his pocket for later. 'But anyway, I'm sure this isn't what the sarge meant by settling you in. You'll be dossing here when we're not out, and by out I mean in the listening post out the front there in No-Man's-Land. Or patrolling or digging. Or scrounging. We sleep and eat as often as we can — usually the grub's pretty basic but most days there's enough. You'll get used to Fritz lobbing shells at us night and day, and he's got some pretty sharp snipers so be careful where you stick your head. It rains a lot and there's always mud so you'd better hurry up and get used to that, too. Mail arrives irregularly, but it does come, and it's always something to look forward to. Providing you've got someone writing to you, of course. But it's deathly boring a lot of the time.' He raised his eyebrows hopefully. 'You don't happen to have any . . . '

His monologue was abruptly cut off by a piercing whistle followed by a bone-jarring crump that shook the earth and dislodged a shower of dirt from the ceiling. The newcomers dived for the ground with their hands over their heads.

A long minute passed before they heard Owen say almost apologetically, 'You can get up now. It probably hit further down.'

They sat up and looked at him sheepishly. He

178

hadn't moved at all and Toby was still asleep; even the fox hadn't stirred.

'As I said, you'll get used to it,' Owen reiterated. 'I was asking if any of you had any books with you? You'll find blokes here will kill for something to read.'

10

Ian settled in fairly quickly, if getting used to living in a muddy hole in the ground could be called settling in. He kept a sharp eye out for James and Thomas but had so far encountered neither, which disappointed him as he had visualised their brotherly reunion often. To his surprise the noise and the smells of the battlefield ceased to bother him after a few days, although he suspected he would never get used to the ragged and rotted remains of corpses scattered almost everywhere. They floated languidly in shell craters, rose slowly and stinkingly up from the mud after every rain, and their tattered skulls stared out at him as he slipped and slid his way between dripping trench walls. But he accepted their presence, as he accepted almost every other aspect of this foreign, unreal existence.

As Owen had warned, the routine of life in the trenches *was* extremely boring, despite the more or less constant shelling, sniping and bombing, and more work was done by the New Zealanders at night than during the day. In daylight hours teams of four or five would crawl out to shell holes in No-Man's-Land, covering gaps in the wire and listening for German activity, but at night almost everyone set to improving the defences. Sandbags were piled higher and extra barbed wire laid in front of the trenches, gun emplacements and loopholes were reinforced, and ammunition, water and stores were brought forward. It was only when the daylight routine started that men could rest; those not on listening or sentry duty would gobble down tepid stew and tea brought up from the company cookers in the support lines, then doss down, ignoring the constant stream of traffic passing them in the trenches, and try to sleep.

Physically Ian was fine, which was more than could be said for Fluffy, whose thigh had been shattered by a German bullet on the way back from a listening post two nights ago; he had been evacuated to the rear, 'Blighty-bound' already, but not before Trevor informed him he'd been the author of his own fate by not wearing his rabbit-fur hat. But, emotionally, Ian had taken a few knocks: things were simply not the way he had expected them to be.

For a start, he'd assumed there would be an immediate sense of comradeship, similar to but perhaps more intense than he'd experienced in training camp. He'd also thought that, as reinforcements, they would be welcomed by the New Zealanders already at the front with, if not open arms, then at least some appreciation. Since his arrival, however, he'd been constantly and uncomfortably aware of the covert circumspection demonstrated by his section mates: they were never unfriendly, but they kept themselves to themselves. So far, only Owen had openly offered the hand of friendship, and when he talked to reinforcements who had gone to other sections, Ian discovered that their experience had not been dissimilar.

After a week he felt compelled to ask Owen about it.

'Why are they so standoffish? The rest of the blokes?' he enquired with studied indifference one morning. It was raining as usual and from the entrance to their dugout he was idly watching assorted waste and rubbish as it bobbed and swirled along the bottom of the trench.

Owen, who was an extremely perceptive man, had been waiting for this question. 'Don't take it personally,' he replied. 'It's not you, it's just the way things work around here.'

Ian said he didn't understand.

'No, I expect you don't,' Owen replied, 'and it's not the sort of thing that gets discussed over the tea billy, either. It's about mates.' He said this last word as if the mere act of uttering it would make everything clear to Ian.

'What about mates?'

Owen got out his tobacco and rolled a smoke. After parking it unlit behind his ear he looked directly at Ian. 'It's superstition, it's fear, and it's self-protection. What if they'd all rushed up to you like bosom buddies when you'd first arrived and then the following day we went out — a jolly bunch of chaps all in it together — and you got everyone killed?'

Ian was too appalled to respond.

'They don't know how well you've been trained, and they don't know how well you'll stand up. Do you see? And you can wipe that affronted look off your face while you're at it, because I don't intend what I'm saying to be in any way an insult. It's simply the way it is. Everyone knows reinforcements are being rushed through the training camps at home then sent out here still wet behind the ears. It's not your fault, we know that, but what if you just aren't up to it? There are plenty who haven't been. Look at poor young Toby, and he's not the only one by a long shot. There he was, marching down the main street of Masterton playing soldiers in his lovely new uniform covered in shiny buttons and thinking he's the bee's knees and doing his bit for the Empire and all that, and look at him now. He can barely summon the courage to leave the dugout for a bloody pee!' Owen shook his head in angry bewilderment. 'I'd strangle his mother and father for letting him sign up if I could be bothered tracking them down when, or if, I get home. Of course,' he added, 'he might just have run off and if that's the case then they're probably worried sick about him.'

Ian averted his eyes guiltily.

Owen suddenly laughed. 'I'm going to be doing a lot of strangling before this war's over, aren't I? But that's the first thing, the lads not knowing whether you're up to it or not. You have to prove yourself, and I think you are, by the way. You've the makings of a good soldier. The second thing is that some of them might find they really quite like you, and it's hard to lose good mates. We might look like a pack of miserable, muddy bastards, but there's a unity here that you won't find anywhere else. It's never talked about but the blokes'll do just about anything to preserve both that and their own sanity.' He leant over and touched Ian briefly on the shoulder. 'Don't worry, you'll be all right, you and Trevor. Give it another week or so and it'll be like you've always been here. They're a decent bunch, really.'

Ian felt considerably more at ease after this conversation, although he felt a fool for having worried about it and not worked it out for himself. He soon found that Owen had spoken the truth: his feelings of being surreptitiously watched faded and were replaced by an awareness that he was indeed being accepted into the section. He'd never had a particular need to be universally liked, but he always had been, so his gradual assimilation had been a foreign and rather uncomfortable experience.

Although he was happy now to let personal relationships with the original members of the section develop in their own time, he went out of his way to befriend Toby. He felt immensely sorry for the boy, as did almost everyone else, and spent much of what little spare time he had trying to jolly him along, or at least occupy his mind until news came of his hoped-for discharge and return home.

Toby was a real liability now and it was tacitly understood that he was excused duties that involved him going any further from the section's dugouts than ten yards along the trench in either direction; when the others went out, he remained behind and cleaned the living spaces, tidied gear, cuddled and crooned to his fox, and slept. He seemed content with this arrangement, and it appeared to help his nerves, although everyone agreed that his condition was worsening. Lieutenant Ross had sent him back to the MO again in the deliberately threatening company of Sergeant Blakely, but both had returned, Toby with a note reconfirming his fitness crumpled in one hand, and Blakely with a black look on his already permanently grim face.

It was getting more and more difficult to converse with Toby, as Ian discovered.

'What's that on Foxy's leg?' he asked one evening, soon after coming in from a long stretch on sentry duty. He was tired and stiff from crouching immobile in a cramped hole for hours on end, and wanted nothing more than to shovel as much food into himself as possible then snatch an hour's sleep, but he thought it important to chat with Toby first.

'A splint,' said the boy proudly. 'I think it's helping.'

Ian didn't. The fox, which had surprised everybody by lasting so long, now appeared to be failing fast. It lay in Toby's lap panting shallowly, its pale eyes half closed and its russet fur rough and dull despite the boy's almost constant petting. He had bound a short stick to the animal's misshapen foreleg with strips of what looked suspiciously like his singlet, and Ian hoped for the fox's sake that Toby had aligned the bone correctly. It was crapping all over the place now, everything that Toby fed it evidently shooting straight through, but nobody had the heart to tell him to put it outside.

'Yes, he does look more comfortable, doesn't he?' Ian lied.

Toby nodded absently. 'I'm taking him home with me when I go.'

'Good idea.'

'I've got a dog at home, a terrier. He's called Patch because of the black bit over his eye. They could be friends.'

Ian couldn't think of a suitable response so they sat in silence for a few moments, then Toby said, 'I got the milk.'

'Milk?'

'Mmm. Mum asked me to, so I did it on the way back.'

'Oh,' Ian said cautiously. 'Right.' He looked around as Trevor came in and put a finger to his lips. Trevor sat down quietly.

'I told Mum we should get another house cow, but she reckons Daisy's enough. Not for me, I said. I love milk, it's nice and creamy.'

Ian and Trevor looked at each other in dismay, and Ian said gently, 'Where is it now?'

Toby stared at him uncomprehendingly. 'What?'

'The milk,' said Ian. 'Where's the milk now?'

Toby gazed around the dugout, a puzzled expression on his face. Then his bottom lip trembled and he started to weep, but soundlessly, and his hands crept up to cover his ears. A dollop of snot slid from his left nostril and plopped onto Foxy's fur.

'It was in the pail. I was going to ask if I could save some for Foxy,' he hiccupped, lowering his hands and running his fingertips protectively over the animal's fine skull. Then, as quickly as they had started, Toby's tears stopped and his face took on an eerie blankness as he began to rock slowly backwards and forwards.

Ian felt impotent and utterly wretched. Behind him he heard Trevor mutter, 'Bloody hell.'

'Perhaps we could give him some biscuit soaked in water instead?' Ian suggested, but it was clear that, in his head, Toby had gone somewhere else now.

'Poor little bastard,' Trevor spat. 'That bloody MO's got a lot to answer for.'

It was Owen who found him the following day, lying curled on his side at the back of the dugout, the underside of his thin forearms slit with a shard of tin — one deep, bloody, deliberate slice from elbow to wrist on each arm. His fur sticky with Toby's congealing blood, Foxy lay stiff and lifeless in the hollow between the boy's thighs and chest.

When Ian and Trevor came in Owen was sitting on the biscuit box with his head in his hands.

'What's up?' Trevor said, suddenly wary.

'Toby,' Owen replied, his voice muffled.

And then they saw. Ian crouched over the body and hesitantly touched the dead boy's cold cheek. 'How long?' he croaked. There was a terrible ache in his throat.

Owen lifted his head wearily. 'An hour? The fox longer.'

It was obvious to all of them what had happened: Foxy had died and Toby, left alone in the dugout, had either been unable or unwilling

187

to contend with his loss.

Trevor cleared his throat. 'I'll get the sarge.'

★ ★ ★

Self-inflicted wounds were not unheard of in the trenches. Such behaviour, if proved, could result in a court-martial and up to sixty days' field punishment. Men who harmed themselves deliberately were generally regarded with a minimum of compassion, but those who actually took their own lives were more often than not accorded a grudging posthumous respect for at least having the guts to do the job properly.

But everyone had known Toby was mentally unwell, and everyone agreed he should have been sent home long ago. His death symbolised for them not the shortcomings of the boy himself, but rather the army's merciless inflexibility, especially among its more senior officers, who refused to recognise a desperately ill, under-aged boy when they saw one.

At Toby's funeral, Blakely, in a display of sentiment that surprised everyone, ensured that Foxy's body was interred with him, and Lieutenant Ross made it known that his letter to the boy's parents would describe in detail the heroic deeds that had led to his untimely but noble death. After the brief and necessarily formulaic military burial, Toby's name wasn't mentioned again; it was as if his death had torn a hole in the flesh of the section itself, and only by keeping his name unuttered could the wound be healed.

A miasma of gloom settled over the unit and stayed there until word came that the New Zealand Division would be withdrawn from Armentières to a location outside Abbeville, a town near the French coast. There, they would receive further training in anticipation of their role in British Commander-in Chief Douglas Haig's grand attack against the Germans in the region of the Somme River.

To the original members of the division the break was welcome after more than three months in the line, but for Ian and Trevor, the prospect of redeployment was frustrating: they'd been in the thick of it for only a matter of days and were to be withdrawn already, even if only temporarily. The division's relief commenced on the 13th of August and five days later command of the sector passed to the Highlanders.

Ian and James were finally reunited at the train station at St Omer on the way to Abbeville. Ian thought his brother looked haggard and ill, and James told Ian he'd been a bloody little fool for enlisting.

'Mam wrote and said you'd signed up. I knew you'd been thinking about it, but why didn't you write and tell me yourself what you were going to do? I gather Mam and Da are pretty upset.'

Ian shrugged uneasily; he hadn't told his brother in case James tried to talk him out of it or, even worse, written to their parents and told them what he was planning to do. He hadn't written to Thomas or Keely either for the same reason.

'You're a beaut, aren't you?' James went on.

'You could have thought about the possible repercussions, with all of us being over here now.'

It irritated Ian whenever James spoke to him like this, something he'd forgotten during his older brother's long absence. He changed the subject.

'Duncan's the sweetest little thing. Well, actually, he's not that little any more. He looks just like you.'

James nodded. 'I know. Lucy sent me some photographs. How is she?'

'She's all right, but I think she misses you a lot more than she lets on. I used to hear her crying in her room sometimes. Your room, I mean. She's a nice girl, Lucy. Mam and Da give her a lot of support.' Ian thought he saw the glimmer of tears in his brother's eyes, and looked quickly away.

'And Joseph?' James asked after a minute. 'How's he getting on? Mam said he's riding again.'

Ian nodded. 'He's doing really well. He's got so good on his new leg you can hardly tell it's a false one. He was supposed to go to Napier Hospital for some sort of rehabilitation but he told them to get stuffed and he'd sort himself out.'

'Sounds like Joseph.'

'Da's offered him permanent work at Kenmore.'

'That's good.'

Neither of them said out loud that, after all, someone had to fill the gap left by Ian running off.

Ian asked, 'Have you seen Thomas at all? Is he

here with the division?'

'Yes, I've seen him and no, he isn't. He's gone on some training course with the Tommies, something to do with a new triage system, I think. He was unbelievably angry when he found out you'd enlisted. In fact, I've never seen him so pissed off.'

Ian let the thrust go. 'And what about Erin and Keely? We heard before I left that they're working together again.'

'Yes. They were here for a little while, although I didn't see them, but apparently they've been transferred to one of the New Zealand hospitals in England now. I haven't heard from Keely in a while.'

'It's good news about Erin and Joseph, isn't it?'

James smiled then, a rare, uninhibited smile from before the war. 'Yes, it's marvellous. Has there been any word about when Erin might go home?'

'No, and knowing her it probably won't be until the end.'

'I thought she might chuck it in after the *Marquette*.'

'No, she said in one of her letters that the survivors had been offered the choice, but she'd decided to stay on.'

'What did Joseph think about that?'

Ian shrugged. 'Nothing, I think. He seems to understand what her nursing means to her.'

'She's got guts, I'll say that for her.'

'Yes, she has. And speaking of guts, how's your friend Captain Tarrant? Been promoted to field marshal yet?'

A flicker of something dark crossed James's face. 'Not quite.'

Ian waited for his brother to elaborate, but the subject appeared to be closed.

After that they were able to meet again briefly at the camp at Abbeville on a number of occasions, despite being in different battalions, but the hectic training schedule of the three New Zealand infantry brigades meant the two brothers could never spend much time together. All talk was of the Somme push, and everything the New Zealanders did was in preparation for joining the campaign on the 11th of September.

The division was finally deemed ready, but before it went west again leave was granted. Ian's battalion furloughed at the New Zealand base at Etaples where they luxuriated in hot baths before heading into town for a feverishly anticipated night out. The bathhouse was in a large converted factory. A man went in, was issued with soap, a fresh towel and a full set of clean kit, then stripped off his filthy uniform and immersed himself in a vast tank of hot water before scrubbing himself to within an inch of his life. Discarded uniforms were whisked away by French laundry women and deloused, washed, mended, pressed and stored for issue to future soldiers.

Bathed, shaved and attired in fresh uniforms, Ian's section felt like new men; Ian himself had already almost forgotten what it was like to be clean, to feel his hair, unencumbered by mud and grease, lifted by the breeze and his hands, feet and backside free of sticky grime and filth.

He turned to Owen and remarked, 'You know, you don't look too bad, clean.'

'Oh, well, thanks very much.'

'No, I mean it. You look much younger and quite handsome.'

Owen screwed up his face in mock suspicion. 'You're not one of those pansies, are you?'

'Piss off,' Ian replied mildly. 'No, it's just that when we first met I got the impression you were quite a lot older than me. Now, all spruced up, you don't look it at all.'

'Well, I turned twenty-five in March, but since Gallipoli I seem to have developed a much older face. Can't think why.'

Trevor joined them, his own face scrubbed pink and his dark hair slicked racily back. 'Ready?' he asked them eagerly.

'God,' said Owen, wrinkling his nose, 'has Fritz shelled the local perfume factory?'

'No, it's skin tonic. One of the lads lent me some.'

'It's very subtle.'

'I like it,' replied Trevor, ignoring Owen's sarcasm. 'You'll be sorry when those pretty French girls come flocking around me and you're sitting all by yourself sobbing into your beer.'

Owen snorted. 'We'll see.'

By the time they got into town it was late afternoon. Owen expressed a desire to go down to the waterfront to look at the fishing boats, then visit a couple of the town's spectacular Flemish churches, but Trevor convinced him, admittedly without too much effort, that they should all go to an *estaminet* first for a meal and a few drinks.

Accompanied by Reg White and Jock Dow, two privates from their section, they found a likely-looking establishment almost immediately, although it was already full and the *proprietaire*, with the glimmer of profit in his eye, had to fetch extra seats. He arranged the stools around the table, waved his patrons into them and pointed to the blackboard menu propped on the bar.

'It's in bloody French,' complained Reg.

Owen said, 'Yes, well, we *are* in France.'

Ian asked, 'Can anyone read it?'

'I can, a little,' replied Owen. 'Enough to stop us poisoning ourselves, anyway. I hope.'

He turned to the *proprietaire* and asked for beer but was informed in very heavily accented English that, sadly, the beer had just run out. However, would the *monsieurs* like *vin rouge* instead? Owen said yes and the Frenchman, nodding and smiling ingratiatingly, took their orders and scurried away. Owen didn't blame him; his country was being blown to kingdom come and an appalling number of his country-men had recently been pulverised into the mud at Verdun, so who could blame him for grasping at the prospect of a small financial profit?

He returned with a large tin tray bearing five carafes of red wine and five stubby glasses, which he set on the table with a flourish. 'Are the *messieurs* ready to order yet?' he asked obsequiously.

By the time their meals arrived they'd disposed of more than half the wine and were

194

feeling quite relaxed, talking at the tops of their voices over the din of other diners and waving across the room at acquaintances.

'So what do you teach?' Ian asked Owen, his mouth full of delicious, meltingly fresh fish.

'History. Sort of fell into it, really. I read history at university for a year but then I got bored and chucked it in and travelled around doing a bit of farm labouring here and there for a while. I was in Dannevirke for a few months and I met the local schoolmaster in the pub one day and we got to talking and the upshot of that was I ended up teaching at the school there.'

'Will you go back to it after this?'

'I don't know, really. I enjoy working on the land. There's a certain satisfaction to it.'

Ian nodded enthusiastically. 'It's a good life,' he agreed.

''Course, we might be all dead soon,' commented Jock dourly.

Trevor wiped sauce off his plate with a chunk of bread. 'God, Dow, you're a miserable bastard.'

'No,' replied Jock stoically, accustomed to being had on about his pessimism, 'I'm just realistic.'

'Well, be realistic tomorrow. We're on leave tonight. Let's make the most of it, eh?'

And they did. By the time they'd finished their food, which even Jock had to admit had been 'fairly' good, they were well on the way to inebriation. They paid for their meal and wandered unsteadily out into the night.

'Right,' said Trevor, leering and rubbing his hands together. 'Where's the sheilas?'

They meandered down quaint, cobbled streets towards the waterfront where, Trevor insisted, there were bound to be whores.

He was right. Outside an *estaminet*, much less salubrious than the one in which they'd dined, and overflowing with rowdy Allied soldiers, they encountered three women leaning against the whitewashed wall chatting easily to each other.

'You sure they're tarts?' said Jock, squinting at them from across the street. 'What if they're just waiting for their husbands or something?'

'Well, there's only one way to find out,' declared Trevor. He adjusted his cap to a jauntier angle, slipped his hands into his pockets and stepped into the road. The women perked up and began to preen themselves provocatively.

'See?' Trevor said over his shoulder.

He wandered across, had a few words, then turned and beckoned to the others.

'You game?' Ian said to Owen.

'No, I value my health. I'm particular where I stick certain parts of my anatomy. What about you?'

Ian gazed wistfully over at the women, then sighed. 'Not sure I'm up to it. Had a bit much plonk, I think.'

Reg and Jock looked at each other, then slouched sheepishly across the street to join Trevor.

'They'll be sorry,' observed Owen dryly. 'Those girls have probably serviced half the New Zealand Division already tonight. Come on, we'll find ourselves a quiet little pub, shall we?'

They found a small bar not far away, settled

196

into a booth and ordered more wine. The establishment was full and moderately noisy, but comfortable. The patrons were mainly soldiers but here and there were tables occupied by civilians, hunched over their drinks and looking sourly around at every burst of laughter from the interlopers.

'Wonder if it pisses them off?' Owen speculated as he rolled a smoke.

'What?'

'Us being here, drinking their wine, eating their food, taking their women.'

'Why should it? We're helping them out, aren't we?' said Ian, pouring himself a glass and spilling a fair proportion of it on the white tablecloth.

'Well, think about it. We're only here because they're losing. Look what happened to them at Verdun, that must be making them feel bloody terrible for a start.' Owen touched a match to his cigarette, inhaled the smoke deeply then blew it out through his nostrils in a long, continuous stream. 'And now the Tommies have had to come and bail them out.'

'We're not Tommies,' Ian said pedantically. 'We're New Zealanders.'

'Well, it's the same thing to them. We're not *French*. It's a matter of national honour.'

'No it isn't,' Ian argued. 'England's their neighbour. The Germans have to be stopped by someone *somewhere*, don't they?'

'Yes, but how would you feel if New Zealand was invaded by some lunatic and you'd just been done like a dog's dinner defending Napier and now there's all these rowdy bloody foreign soldiers all over the place pinching your chickens and rooting your sister?'

'Or pinching my sister and rooting the chickens,' Ian giggled.

Owen smiled and refilled his glass. They sat in silence for a while, each thinking his own thoughts, which were getting progressively more disjointed as the level in their carafe went down.

'Did you say your family owns a station?'

Ian nodded. 'Kenmore, on the Tutaekuri River.'

'Big?'

'Quite. 'Specially when it's flooded.'

'No, the station.'

'Oh. Yeah, sort of. Thirty thousand sheep at the last count. Or is it forty? I forget. Da and my Uncle Lachie run it between them, but we've got a team of drovers that stay on the station. Well, we had a team, before the war. My brother Joseph's a drover, 'cept he's only got one leg now. He's my half-brother. You'd like him.'

Owen raised an eyebrow. Ian prattled on, the wine making him even more garrulous than usual. 'When Mam first came out, she's from Cornwall, you know, she married some bastard called Peter Montgomery but then she had an affair with this Maori bloke called Kepa and had a baby and that was Joseph.'

'Hang on a minute,' interrupted Owen. He waved his cigarette vaguely, then blinked painfully as smoke drifted into his eye. 'You sure you should be telling me all your family secrets?'

'Eh? No, it's not a secret. Anyway, she had Joseph and her husband, the first one, not Da, went berserk and she had to run away with her housegirl, Riria. Riria married a friend of Mam's, John Adams, who was a doctor. He died in the Boer War, but that was much later. Anyway they ran away to Riria's village but Kepa's Uncle Te Kanene, who was cunning as a shithouse rat but he's dead now as well, came and got Joseph and took him to the East Coast.' Ian paused for a slurp of his wine. 'Peter Montgomery died and Mam went to Auckland and ran a brothel for a couple of years.'

Owen choked on his drink. 'Pardon?'

'She ran a brothel. It belonged to this Scotswoman Mam met on the ship out and when she died she left it to my mother. I'm not sure why Mam decided to take it on, but she did. And then she met Da and they got married and he took her back to Napier.'

'And they lived happily ever after?'

'So far.'

'Good. I like a story with a happy ending.'

'Well, no, that's not the end because she found Joseph again. And his father.' Ian pulled an anguished face. 'God, where do you suppose the dunny is? I'm going to piss myself in a minute.'

While he was outside peeing against a wall behind the *estaminet*, Owen ordered more wine, knowing he would seriously regret doing so in the morning.

Ian returned and sat down heavily, narrowly missing toppling off his seat. 'Good-oh, more

199

plonk. It's bloody raining again. Now, what was I up to?'

Owen noted with amusement that Ian was enjoying telling the story. 'Your mother finding her son, I think.'

'Oh, right. That was Joseph. Did I say he was my half-brother? Except his name wasn't Joseph then, it was some great long Maori job he doesn't use any more that I can never remember. Anyway he stayed living with Kepa, or his aunty I think it was, actually — Joseph's aunty, not Kepa's — but Mam saw him quite a lot after that and he came to stay at Kenmore all the time so he really is like our real brother.'

'And your father doesn't mind this, what did you say his name was? Kepa, is it?'

'Mmm.'

'This Kepa being around?'

'Not as far as I know, but I wasn't even born when all this happened. And too bad if he does. Mam's always done exactly what she wants. But Kepa was married by then anyway, to this woman called Parehuia.'

Owen was beginning to lose track of who was who in this garbled, potted history of the Murdoch family, but Ian apparently hadn't finished.

'And then James came along, my eldest brother, not counting Joseph, that is. Then Thomas, then Keely, then me. And we had a younger sister too, but she died.'

'And all of you are over here now?'

'Yep, and my cousin Erin. She's Uncle Lachie and Aunt Jeannie's daughter. She and Joseph are getting married as soon as she goes home. She's a nurse, like Keely.'

'Can I ask how Joseph lost his leg?'

'He was with the Maori Contingent at Gallipoli and a shell blew up right next to him. He was lucky to survive apparently.'

Owen nodded. He'd had plenty of mates at Gallipoli who hadn't. 'And how does he feel about it now?'

'About losing his leg? Dunno, really. Haven't asked. I wasn't there when it happened of course, and I bet it pissed him off a fair bit, but he seems all right about it now. Joseph's never been the sort to let much get in his way. He got that from Mam, I think.'

'Sounds like an impressive woman, your mother.'

Ian burped, then swallowed quickly, aware he was fast approaching the outer limits of his capacity for alcohol. 'She is. I couldn't have asked for a better one. Or my Da.' He blinked as his mind conjured an unwelcome image of his parents' faces after they'd discovered he'd enlisted without telling anyone. 'I was a bit of a shit running off, really, now that I think about it,' he reflected.

Yes, you were, thought Owen, his suspicions confirmed, but he didn't say it. 'I'm sure they're proud of you anyway.'

'Proud of all of us, I think. James is career army so we knew he'd be off the minute the balloon went up. Suits him, the army. Always was a bit bossy and he loves things to be in order, our James, but not in a mean way because he really is

201

a decent bloke. Thomas is really decent too, but he's more quiet and very bright and incredibly . . . ' Ian searched for the appropriate word. '*Earnest*. Thomas really *believes*.'

'Believes what?

'Everything he gets involved in. He's dead against this war but he volunteered anyway. He's a conchie but he still wanted to do his bit so he's over here as a stretcher bearer. That takes guts,' said Ian proudly, 'but then Thomas has always had balls, despite what some people think.'

Owen sensed there was another story here, but he didn't pursue it.

'And Keely, well, Keely's a lot like Mam. She's beautiful and clever but she can be utterly bloody-minded sometimes. Mam says it's her fault because she and Da spoiled her rotten. She reckons Keely'll have to learn her lessons the hard way like *she* did when *she* was young.' Ian frowned and thought laboriously for a moment. 'Although I'm not exactly sure what she means by that.'

He reached for the carafe and was mildly surprised to see they'd finished this one as well. It was fortunate, because he was starting to feel rather sick. He looked blearily over at Owen, feeling uncharacteristically overwhelmed by these sudden and unexpected feelings of love for his family.

'I miss us all being together.'

Owen suspected that Ian's family missed him just as much — their vibrant, golden-haired, fun-loving boy.

The furlough ended the next day and the battalion, hungover almost to a man, headed for the Somme valley. It was raining as usual and the weather had turned bitterly cold. Then, as if especially for the division's march into battle, it suddenly improved as the 3rd Brigade, Ian's, moved through Le Quesnoy and then Vaux-en-Amienois. Still well to the rear, the three brigades met up and practised manoeuvres around the countryside for the next four days until they moved on again, this time passing through the modest villages of the Allonville area, crowded now with refugees, toward Dernancourt and Lavieville and the ever-increasing sound of battle. On the 8th of September the Germans hurled themselves at the length of the Allied line, and that night a corona of constant gun flashes stained the horizon the colour of blood.

The following day the 3rd Brigade set out along the main road to the Moulin du Vivier and then on to Fricourt where many thousands of British troops were already bivouaced on the slopes, the smoke from their cooking fires wreathing the hillsides with a fine, pungent haze. At nine o'clock on the morning of the 11th, the New Zealanders took over command of the sector between High Wood and Delville Wood, their objective to capture three of the enemy's major trench systems, the Switch, Gird and Flers Lines.

For Ian and his section, each man weighed

down with rifle, gas mask, hand grenades, digging tools, ammunition and rations, the days that followed merged into a chaos of tremendous artillery barrages, fountains of exploding dirt, drifting black smoke, fear, sleeplessness and adrenaline.

On the morning of the 17th, Ian's company was sent to the immediate rear for a brief eight hours' rest. They slipped and slid their way back, crouching in muck as artillery shells whistled overhead and exploded on all sides, throwing up great plumes of mud and debris that splattered down on them like hard, sharp rain. After one particularly close blast, Ian heard the piercing, high-pitched sound of an animal screaming and saw that two horses drawing a gun carriage had been blown into a vast shell crater. The carriage had come off but the limmer was dragging them under and in their panic they were flailing wildly in the liquid mud, eyes rolling madly and yellow teeth bared. The distraught driver was jumping up and down at the edge of the crater, stepping down into it then scrabbling back up as he began to slide.

'*Get them out!*' he screamed. '*They'll drown!*'

Ian ran over. 'You go that side, I'll go this! We'll unharness them, that'll help!'

'I can't swim!' wailed the soldier, crying now. '*Help them!*'

'Shit,' said Ian. He unloaded his kit and stepped down into the crater, ignoring Owen and Trevor bellowing at him not to be so fucking stupid.

He waded in, slipped immediately and sank up

to his thighs in the glutinous, grasping mud. Reaching for the bridle of the nearest animal he tugged on it to get the horse's head down then slid his hand along its neck to the heavy harness collar, murmuring in a low, gentle voice inaudible over the surrounding din. The horse heard, though, and its ears came forward and it seemed to calm a little.

Ian looked up at the lip of the crater and saw a small crowd had gathered, and raised his thumb as someone — Owen, he thought — threw down a coiled rope. The second horse had also ceased to struggle, but both were sinking rapidly and Ian knew they'd panic again at any moment. He himself was submerged up to his chest now, but judged that if he didn't let go, he'd be all right.

He leant his forehead against the horse's neck, breathing in the sharp, salty tang of its sweat, and took several deep breaths, all the while still stroking and soothing. He reached back and unclipped all points of the harness from the collar, and attached the rope. Then, still hanging on, he half waded, half paddled around to unharness the second animal. Now that it was no longer attached, the limmer fell away and disappeared into the mud. He turned and signalled to the men above him to start pulling.

For a few seconds it looked as if the manouevre might work and there was a spontaneous burst of applause. The horses were halfway up the side of the crater, still harnessed to each other and scrabbling frantically with their hooves to gain better purchase, when another shell crashed into the ground only yards away. The pair reared in fright, jerked the rope free, toppled over and careered back down into the pit. The hindquarters of one animal cannoned into Ian and he was knocked backwards into the mud, then the horse rolled on top of him and he went under.

Owen watched in horror as both horses floundered then sank rapidly out of sight. Beside him he could hear Trevor screaming, '*Give us a fucking rope!*' and had to grab him by the collar to stop him jumping in.

'No!' he shrieked only inches from Trevor's stricken face, the heat of his own rage and shock almost overwhelming him. 'He's gone!'

When Trevor bellowed, '*He has not!*' Owen delivered a punch that knocked him to the ground.

Then he helped Trevor to his feet again and they stood together, scrutinising the crater in rigid silence, but after nearly twenty minutes all that could be seen were several languid air bubbles which plopped obscenely on the scummy surface.

11

Kenmore, October 1916

Andrew risked a glance at Tamar, sitting next to him on the unyielding church pew, rigid and silent, cocooned in her anger and the darkness of her grief. And it was a risk, because to see her like this hurt him almost as much as the death of his beloved youngest son. Her lips were clamped shut, holding in her pain, and for the first time she was looking her age.

Behind them the small church was packed, with still more standing outside in respectful silence, and he felt a numb gratitude towards everyone who had come to mourn his son's death, even though he'd never even met some of them. Lachie, Jeannie and Lucy, holding an uncharacteristically still Duncan, sat on their left while Joseph, his face blank with his own suffering, sat on their right.

Reverend McKenzie had almost finished the memorial service, the hymns had been sung and soon they would shuffle out into the bright spring sunshine, having, in theory anyway, laid their memories of Ian to rest. But Andrew could, *would*, never do that, because to deliberately tidy up and pack away such a vibrant young life would be the greatest tragedy of all, a clear victory for the insidious, thieving *thing* that everyone so blithely referred to as 'the war'.

Outside, Kepa approached them, shook

Andrew's hand and hugged Tamar briefly. 'I am so sorry,' he said. 'Joseph was bad enough, but this is, this is . . . ' He tailed off.

Tamar nodded and Andrew said simply, 'Thank you, Kepa. We appreciate you coming.'

He meant it, but he had seen the deep, heartfelt compassion in the other man's eyes when he had embraced Tamar, and it pricked at him because he wanted to be the one to offer his wife the comfort she needed, not this annoyingly good-looking, fit, apparently ageless Maori man who had once been her lover. He knew he was being petty and foolish, but he couldn't help it; emotionally flayed, he lacked the strength to suppress all the mean little doubts and fears he'd so successfully kept at bay over the years.

'How is Parehuia?' he added, to ease the noticeable tension.

Kepa's wife had had a serious heart attack several months ago and was now more or less confined to her home, where she sat and continued to eat excessively in flagrant defiance of her doctor's warnings.

'She is not a well woman,' Kepa replied, and left it at that.

He thought Parehuia was eating herself to death, and they had argued bitterly about it, but she refused to change her habits, insisting that if she was destined to die soon, as certainly appeared to be the case, she intended to do it with a cake fork in her hand.

Andrew invited everyone at the church back to Kenmore for refreshments, although he knew Tamar would rather they all stayed away so she could shut herself in their room and mourn alone. But it was the socially expected thing to do, and Mrs Heath had gone to great lengths to prepare a fitting repast. Almost everyone accepted his invitation, and for an hour or so the house was crowded with friends and neighbours doing their best to console, but after they'd gone the rooms felt bereft and somehow cold, despite the sunshine streaming through the open doors and windows.

At breakfast the following morning Tamar looked up uninterestedly when Mrs Heath came into the dining room and stood twisting her hands in her apron, always a sign that something was upsetting her.

'Is anything wrong?' Andrew asked shortly.

The housekeeper nodded and frowned, then replied, 'There's something in the kitchen garden.'

'Yes?' Andrew prompted, irritated. Perhaps the house cow had got out again, and frankly he couldn't see why Mrs Heath couldn't shoo the bloody thing away herself.

'It's a baby,' Mrs Heath blurted, as if she couldn't quite believe the words coming out of her own mouth. 'Wrapped up in a box.'

Andrew and Tamar stared at her.

'What?' said Andrew.

'A baby. In a box.'

They hurried outside to find that there was indeed an infant, in a wooden crate nestled among the bean poles directly opposite the back door where it couldn't fail to be spotted by anyone coming down the steps. They gazed down at it in silence, turning only when Jeannie came out to see what the fuss was about.

The baby looked calmly back at them, apparently comfortable and contented, snug under a tightly tucked blanket. It was wearing a yellow knitted bonnet and matching mittens, one of which had almost fallen off.

Tamar bent down; there was a folded note tucked into the box. She opened it and silently read the few lines of neat writing.

Dear Mr and Mrs Murdoch
I was at Ian's memorial service yesterday. This is his child. His name is Liam and he was born on the 4th of July.
    I cannot look after him. I was hoping you would be able to. He deserves a real home.
Thank you.

The note was unsigned.

Tamar's mouth opened and then closed. She looked at the infant, then at the note again, and finally turned to Andrew. 'It says this is Ian's son!'

Andrew read it himself, then turned the paper over looking for clues regarding who might have written it. He said, almost to himself, 'Ian's son.'

Jeannie crouched, untucked the blanket and lifted the baby out; he gurgled complacently as she laid him against her shoulder and patted his back gently.

'Take his bonnet off,' she suggested.

Tamar untied the ribbons under the child's chubby chin and removed the hat. Then she

210

gasped and blinked back instant, hot tears, because the child really was the image of Ian as a baby. He had soft curls, almost white, that feathered up from his small head, bright blue eyes and dimpled cheeks. He was beautiful.

Andrew said, 'What are those things in the box?'

Under the blanket were folded a dozen clean nappies, two more knitted baby costumes and two cotton smocks. Tamar retrieved the bundle and touched the tiny garments wordlessly.

Lucy came out then, carrying Duncan. She stopped when she saw the infant in Jeannie's arms. 'Whose is that?' she asked in amazement.

Andrew handed her the note.

She read it and said, 'Is it really? Ian's, I mean?'

Tamar said 'Yes' at the same time that Andrew said, 'We don't know.'

'Oh Andrew,' Tamar responded crossly. 'Of course he's Ian's. *Look* at him!'

Then a very determined look crossed her face and she rushed inside, appearing again a minute later with a photograph taken of Ian a few months after his birth. The sepia tones had been hand-painted to enhance the image, but the resemblance between the child in the picture and the baby Jeannie held was extreme.

'See?' Tamar exclaimed triumphantly. 'They're exactly the same. Who else's baby could it be?'

Andrew closed his eyes briefly as Tamar took the child from Jeannie and settled him in the crook of her arm. He said gently, not wanting to hurt her, 'There isn't any proof, dear. This baby could be anyone's.'

But even he could see a remarkable similarity in the features that reminded him so painfully of those of his youngest son.

'Sometimes, Andrew, for such a clever man you can be very obtuse,' Tamar responded, not taking her eyes off the baby. 'He belongs here,' she added with a ominous note of finality.

'But darling, we can't keep him. He's not a puppy, for God's sake!'

But Tamar had already turned and marched up the steps by then, and her deliberate slamming of the back door cut him off.

France, 1916

James was also thinking about Ian, although he usually tried not to do because it distressed him so much. But then so many things did, lately. He told himself he'd come to terms with the death of his youngest brother, but he still felt sick and angry whenever he thought about the utter stupidity and waste of it. As he stared unseeingly at his boots, a thin, nasal voice interrupted his thoughts.

'If you don't mind, Captain Murdoch, your attention would be appreciated. We wouldn't want your men to die just because you'd nodded off during a briefing, would we?'

Sarcastic little prick, James thought, raising his eyes to meet those of the speaker.

Major Lydon was a short, round, odious man with a colossal ego who fancied himself a close confidante of the New Zealand Division's commander, Major-General Russell, although they'd probably only ever met once or twice, if that. Lydon commanded James' company and was universally despised for his pomposity, his arrogance and his general military ineptitude. At the moment he was whacking a large map with a stick to underline his instructions regarding tomorrow's battle orders. James let his eyes glaze over, although he was in fact listening; later he and the others would talk through the orders and, if possible, reinterpret them in a manner that would still perhaps achieve the desired outcome but minimise the number of men they would lose.

They were still on the Somme. Although only a matter of weeks had passed since the division had marched into the valley, it felt as if they'd been there forever and they were beginning to wonder if they'd ever leave the wretched place. It was still only early October, and already more than 1000 New Zealanders had been killed. The British and French had fared even worse; it was rumoured that their casualty lists numbered in the hundreds of thousands. The Germans kept coming, the Allies kept counter-attacking, a yard would be gained here, two lost there, and all the while men were being maimed, or killed, or just disappearing, buried forever under tons of putrid French mud.

James idly surveyed Major Lydon's spacious, heavily sandbagged dugout. In one corner there was a bed, a *real* bed, piled with pillows and a comforter, in another was an antique desk and in front of the currently assembled officers was a solid mahogany table on which Lydon dined and from behind which he held court during briefings. There were rugs on the floor, which Lydon's long-suffering batman was ordered to take outside and scrape and shake every morning, and on the wall a framed, badly executed portrait of a harried-looking woman everyone assumed was Lydon's poor wife. Over the past weeks James had been tempted many times by an extremely infantile urge to sneak in one night and draw a pair of spectacles and a moustache on it, but it would be the end of his army career should he be caught, although the chaps would all think it hysterically funny. These days they all laughed madly at situations and sights that would not have been considered even remotely amusing at home.

In his silly pseudo-British accent, the major was droning to a halt.

'Now, gentlemen, I know you're all feeling somewhat jaded, but things really are on the up and up and it's just a matter of keeping one's chin up, and of course honour and glory in one's sights. Dismissed.'

They filed out. 'Jaded?' James muttered to his friend and fellow captain, Ben Harper. 'Fucking *jaded*?'

'Ignore it, James,' said Ben, a tall young man with a shock of brown hair that flopped constantly over his forehead. 'He says it at the end of every briefing, you know it doesn't mean anything.'

James snorted in disgust. 'It's not as if he gets

out there and does anything himself, the windy little stoat.'

It was common knowledge that Major Lydon rarely got his own highly polished boots dirty, preferring instead to spend most of his time in his dugout issuing orders and criticising the performances of his junior officers. Everyone, however, assumed he was getting away with it as he hadn't been 'moved on' yet, which is what happened to at least some of the more inadequate officers who suddenly found themselves counting tins of bully beef back at the New Zealand base in Etaples.

Ben patted James placatingly on the shoulder, noting his friend's impatience with a slight frown.

'Don't worry about it,' he soothed. 'We'll get together later, shall we, and have a drink?'

Many of the officers drank in the privacy of their dugouts, and for all but the teetotallers it was the tacitly accepted method of relaxing. The enlisted men would have done the same if they could have got their hands on alcohol. Usually, their drinking was confined to the generous tot of rum issued before each scheduled attack.

James set off along the zigzagging, multi-branched trench system to check on his men and give them a quick rundown on what would be happening tomorrow. He found a group of them resting in a wide traverse; a handful were smoking and singing while others, oblivious to the noise, were asleep on the ground with their greatcoats over their heads. He allowed himself a smile as he listened to the latest song doing the rounds, and reflected that there'd be hell to pay if Lydon heard the men singing it:

> We're bombed on the left and we're
> bombed on the right,
> We're shelled all the day and we're shelled
> all the night,
> And if something don't happen and that
> mighty soon,
> There'll be nobody left in the fucking pla-
> toon!

In some ways James wished he hadn't been promoted to captain, since it alienated him to some extent from his men; he cared for them deeply, and perhaps somewhat to his own detriment, he suspected. He frequently wrote letters home on behalf of the illiterate ones, and his advice was often sought concerning wayward wives or the prospect of children who would not know fathers returning from the war. How would he know? He would be one himself.

More than anything else, however, his men wanted to know how to deal with fear, and he often lay awake thinking about the lives of which he was supposed to be in charge, because on some days it was all he could do to manage his own dread. But captains, and to an even greater extent lieutenants, were thin on the ground now and any junior officer who could still walk and talk often found himself propelled up the hierarchical ladder, whether he liked it or not.

As the men seemed to be enjoying themselves he decided not to interrupt them with news of tomorrow's inauspicious-sounding assault. He turned and headed back to his own dugout instead, the one he shared with Ron Tarrant.

He found Ron sitting on his cot, having a drink; at least he was still pouring his whisky into a tumbler before tossing it down his throat. Their bivvy stank like a brewery, with a faint but pervasive undertone of unwashed bodies.

Ron looked up. 'Want one?' he asked, proffering the bottle.

James nodded and subsided onto his own cot.

Ron's hands were shaking, an affliction that had appeared after his arrival at Gallipoli last year. Involuntary trembling was not an unusual phenomenon, and no one thought any less of a man if his hands shook from time to time, but Ron had soon begun to behave in less acceptable ways. He had been very unlucky with his health and had succumbed to every possible malady. He claimed a delicate stomach, a problem he'd apparently suffered since childhood, and as a result had been forced to spend a lot of time in his dugout, or even in the rear, recuperating. And he certainly had looked ill on those occasions — pale, sweating, dry-mouthed and often writhing in pain — but James and many others had managed to soldier on through similar ailments and the question was soon being asked, although not openly, why Ron Tarrant couldn't do the same.

To his extreme embarrassment, James had developed severe haemorrhoids after repeated bouts of dysentery, and often found himself sitting in the soggy squelch of his own blood, but the problem had never stopped him from performing his duties, although the pain almost drove him to distraction at times. He refused, however, to even contemplate being carted off the battlefield just because he had a backside full of piles.

The irrefutable fact of the matter was that Ron Tarrant was a coward. Everyone knew it — including the enlisted men who called him 'Captain Windy' behind his back — but more wretched than that was the fact that Ron himself knew it, and the knowledge of his own inadequacy only made his behaviour worse. He wasn't essentially a bad man, and genuinely loved the army, but the humiliating realisation that he was not cut out for active service had shattered and embittered him. Some of the other officers had discreetly complained to Major Lydon about Ron's inability to present himself for duty six mornings out of ten, but Lydon, perhaps subconsciously sensing the presence of a kindred spirit, had retaliated with, 'No, no, fine fellow. Dodgy guts, that's all', and had refused to entertain the matter further.

Initially James had felt sorry for Ron — no man could be blamed for experiencing fear in the face of the horrors they had all endured over the last eighteen months — but his sympathy had been tainted with a vague sense of anger at his own profound misjudgment of the other man's character. He had truly believed that Ron Tarrant was a hero in the making, and so, clearly, had Ron; now James had begun to doubt his own motives for initially fostering their friendship. Had he hoped that Ron's almost certain future as a military prodigy would somehow rub off on him? And if he now abandoned his friend, what did that say about him, about his ambition and his own moral integrity?

But then Ron's conduct had gone beyond that of a man who was simply frightened: he had become a deliberate shirker who was now a serious and dangerous liability to the men he commanded. When this happened, soon after the battalion arrived on the Somme and it became apparent that the ferocity of the fighting would surpass even that at Gallipoli, James had gone from doubting himself to covertly despising the other man, taking a perverse comfort from the fact that he was able to carry on.

In his heart James knew his attitude to be almost as discreditable as Ron's, but it was easier to damn than to take the time and emotional effort to consider what could turn a potentially excellent officer into a useless and even dangerous one. Above all, James feared that if he did think too much about it he might discover that he himself was just as susceptible to failure.

And there was the matter of the depression that had descended rather shockingly on him at Gallipoli, a paralysing and grindingly persistent dread that corroded both his waking and sleeping hours and left him with a dry mouth and a constantly racing heart. His state of mind had improved after the withdrawal from the peninsula, but when the division had rejoined the battle in France his deep despondency had returned almost immediately; in fact it had deteriorated and was now accompanied by occasional but violent episodes of weeping.

So far he had managed to keep this to himself, but he was terrified that one day he would publicly lose control. He had never avoided his duties, nor had he wanted to, and neither had he even remotely contemplated a self-inflicted injury — unlike Ron who was under suspicion for attempting to shoot himself in the foot, although he insisted he'd been firing at a rat — but the thought of his peers viewing him as a coward turned his stomach.

Now, in an attempt to avoid one of the embarrassing silences that occurred more and more frequently whenever they were alone together, he said, 'What did you think about Lydon's instructions for tomorrow?'

He had noted Ron sitting by himself at the back of the major's dugout during the briefing, his face blanching as detail after ill-conceived detail of the planned assault was presented.

Ron started, and turned to James a face from which the flesh seemed to be melting day by day.

'Sounds like an excellent tactical move to me,' he said, the patently false note of optimism in his voice belying his fear.

They both knew he was lying, but James let it go.

Then Ron said, 'I only hope the old stomach doesn't let me down. Been giving me a bit of trouble today.'

James deliberately didn't look up, unwilling to see the plea for understanding he knew would be in the other man's eyes, and even less willing to demonstrate his own distaste for it. He'd considered sharing a bivvy with another officer but, despite his repugnance at Ron's behaviour, he still couldn't bring himself to embarrass him so publicly. And he wasn't sure he cared any more, as long as Ron kept his fear to himself.

He said, still without raising his eyes, 'Get a good night's sleep then. That should help.'

* * *

The following morning James woke well before dawn. The assault was timed to begin just before sunrise and their instructions were to be in place and ready to go fifteen minutes before that. He splashed his face with water but didn't bother to comb his hair, and sat smoking, watching men plod backwards and forwards in the dark past the dugout, while last night's bully-beef stew reheated on a tiny kerosene stove. He didn't feel like eating but knew he should, and his piles were bleeding again.

Behind him he heard Ron stirring.

'How's the guts this morning?' James asked without turning around, too weary to keep the sarcasm out of his voice.

Ron sat up. His hair was wildly tousled and his eyes red and raw-looking after last night's whisky. He bent over and gave a great crackling retch, although nothing came up.

'Oh God,' he groaned.

James did turn then, and said, 'Not good, eh?'

Ron wiped his mouth then sat back gingerly.

221

'I'm all right,' he replied grimly.

'So you'll be coming with us then?' said James disbelievingly, although he still had the grace to feel a small stab of shame at his deliberate unkindness.

'Yes, why shouldn't I?' replied Ron in a tone that implied he had never once been left out of battle.

'Oh, well, I just thought with your stomach and that, you know.'

'No, it's fine,' Ron replied, and James recognised the expression on his pale, blotchy face — an uneasy mixture of petulance and bone-deep fear.

They were silent for a moment, then Ron blurted, 'Look James, I know what the others are saying about me, that I'm a coward . . . '

James waited for him to go on, but he appeared to have changed his mind and stayed silent.

The company gathered in the forward trench waiting for the artillery behind them to start the scheduled bombardment. It did, with an almighty roar, and continued for a full ten minutes, a carefully timed barrage designed to pulverise any Germans unfortunate enough to be in the trenches on the other side of No-Man's-Land. The strategy had been used countless times before during the Somme campaign, but seldom with the hoped-for degree of success.

James crouched at the bottom of the trench with his men, flinching involuntarily every time a shell passed directly overhead. He felt sick with anxiety, but was comforted by the knowledge that he wasn't alone in that; some men gazed unseeingly ahead, steeling their nerves as they

222

waited for the whistle, others mouthed inaudible prayers, and as usual there were the odd few whose nervousness spilled out via wisecracks and inane prattle. An unmistakable smell suggested that someone had lost control of his bowels.

The whistle blew and men began to scale the trench wall and slither over the parapets. With the toes of his boots digging briefly into purpose-dug slots in the clay, James shot over himself. To either side he could see waves of men following suit and, among them and to his left, Ron Tarrant, now lying motionless on his stomach a yard or so into No-Man's-Land. James crouched down and scuttled on an angle towards the precarious safety of the ridges and depressions of the cratered terrain that separated the two front lines.

As he passed Ron, still lying prostrate among the mass of bodies that continued to pour over the parapet, he glimpsed from the corner of his eye a hand reach out and grasp the ankle of a soldier named Jenkin, who was scrambling to his feet and preparing to run forward. The hand was Ron's, and it yanked Jenkin down so that the smaller man's body fell on top of him. Jenkin, already frightened half out of his wits by the noise and turmoil of the attack, was struggling as if the devil himself had hold of him.

James could see what was going to happen. Jenkin reared up in panic and was instantly struck in the head by a bullet. His body slumped forward, and Ron wrenched the now limp figure back over himself.

223

Incandescent with rage, James grabbed hold of Ron's webbing and dragged him back over the parapet, where they tumbled together into the trench, scattering the handful of men still waiting below. James was on his feet instantly. He knew he was screaming, although he couldn't hear himself. He snatched at Ron, who had curled up in the mud with his arms raised protectively over his face, and jerked him to his knees. The surrounding men had stepped away and were looking on with interest, instinctively aware that something extraordinary was about to happen.

James drew his service pistol and aimed it at Ron's head. 'Get up, you murdering *bastard*! Get back out there and bring his body back!'

Ron was crying now. 'I couldn't move! My ankle . . . '

'*Murderer*!'

'It was an accident! I didn't . . . '

'*Get up*!'

Ron babbled, 'I can't! I can't *move*! I tried. Oh, God help me, please! You don't understand!'

'Oh, yes I do,' James whispered, and fired the pistol.

He watched detachedly as a small red hole blossomed in the centre of the other man's forehead and his body collapsed slowly into the mud. Around him his men looked on impassively, then, as the second whistle blew, one by one they scaled the parapet, none of them looking back at the scene below them.

James opened his hand and let the pistol fall next to the body. Then he sat down to wait.

12

James sat on the neatly made cot. There were temporary bars on the window and a guard outside the door, but other than that his accommodation was not uncomfortable — he was, after all, still an officer. He was scheduled to be tried later that afternoon at a general court-martial convened by the divisional commander. There would be five officers acting as judge and jury, including Major Lydon, as James's commanding officer, and Lydon's senior, Lieutenant-Colonel George Chapley.

James was allowed a 'soldier's friend', an officer appointed to support him during the trial, and he and the court had accepted Ben Harper's offer to fulfil the role. Not that James had said much to anyone at all since the incident. The New Zealand Division was now in the process of being withdrawn from the Somme battleground, but James had been removed from the front line immediately and for the past two days had sat, silent and withdrawn, in this room in a house requisitioned from some French landowner.

But he hadn't been alone — Thomas had turned up only hours after James' arrest. Gossip spread like brushfire in the trenches and as soon as Thomas heard he'd requested and been granted permission to go to his brother. He hadn't, however, been allowed to represent him, despite his civilian qualifications as a lawyer.

Visiting his brother in a time of need, even if it did involve a charge of murder, was one thing, but representing him, especially if you were a well-known conscientious objector skilled in the arts of the courtroom, was quite another. Besides, Thomas was only a corporal.

He was almost at his wits' end over James's stubborn refusal to elaborate on the events surrounding Ron Tarrant's death. He would say only that he was guilty of killing the man but would provide no evidence of mitigating circumstances or provocation. But it was clear to Thomas that there was something very wrong with his brother: his speech was flat and monosyllabic, and he was unable to pay attention for more than a few seconds at a time. He was also physically unwell, to the extent that a medical officer had been summoned and had diagnosed chronic dysentery and acute haemorrhoids together with advanced neurasthenia, or shell shock.

Thomas and Ben both knew that shell shock was very unlikely to be considered a mitigating factor, especially after the recent edict from British High Command that left no doubt that a failure of mental equilibrium would not be accepted as an excuse for indiscipline. And a bleeding backside or the shits wouldn't help either, as many men, officers and enlisted alike, were suffering from the same unpleasant complaints. James knew this too, and perhaps that was why he seemed to have given up. But still, Thomas simply could not believe that his brother, normally such a stringently ethical and honourable man, could have shot someone in cold blood without any apparent justification.

'But why, James?' he asked again, almost desperate now. 'I just don't understand what happened. There must have been some reason, for God's sake!'

James, his head bowed, didn't reply.

'We've been over and over this,' said Ben reluctantly. 'He won't offer anything in his own defence.'

'And you were there but you didn't see anything?' Thomas had asked Ben the same question several times now.

'Yes, but I'd already gone over, and I didn't find out about it for quite a while. I thought James was out in front of me somewhere. And as for Tarrant, well, I hadn't even expected him to be there. I'd assumed he was holed up somewhere as usual, suffering from some dreadful, debilitating illness.'

'Will you say that? This afternoon, I mean?'

'That I thought Tarrant wasn't there?'

'No, that it wasn't uncommon for him to be left out of battle.'

'Oh, well, I shouldn't think I'd even need to mention that. I gather his windiness was fairly common knowledge.'

'Was it? To, what's his name? Major Lyndon, is it?'

'Lydon. Well, he's been told about it often enough, by the chaps, the other officers, if that's what you mean. Never did anything about it, though. Birds of a feather, I suspect.'

'And you think something happened with

Tarrant that might have pushed James over the edge?' Thomas turned to his brother. 'Is that what happened, James? Something that Tarrant did?'

Again there was no response, although Thomas waited for a full minute for one. Finally, he kicked out at the stone wall in anger.

'For Christ's *sake*, James, will you bloody well wake *up*! If you're found guilty you could be shot!'

Ben said, 'There are plenty of rumours flying about. Tarrant wasn't a popular officer. I've asked the chaps to keep their ears open, although apparently there weren't any officers there at the time. But, you know, the men talk.'

'What sort of rumours?' asked Thomas.

'Just what I've already told you. That Tarrant caused a lad's death, although nobody seems to be clear about exactly how.'

'And you'll bring that up as well?'

'Of course, but it's not really hard evidence, is it?'

James finally stirred himself. 'I'm tired,' he said, and lay back on his cot with his arm over his eyes.

Thomas and Ben looked at him, then at each other, and Thomas said gently, 'We'll leave you alone to rest for an hour then, all right?'

They banged on the door to be let out.

'There's something seriously wrong with him,' said Thomas as they stood in the garden behind the house. He began to roll a cigarette.

'Have one of these,' said Ben, offering a packet of Capstan.

'Oh, thanks.' Thomas lit the tailor-made and breathed the smoke in deeply. 'I really do think he's shell-shocked. And I should know — I see it every day.'

Ben agreed, 'Yes, the MO's report says that. Anyway it's obvious and it has been for ages, although he thinks no one else has noticed.'

'So why didn't he do something about it?'

'Well, Christ, I don't know. And think about it — would you, in his position?'

'What do you mean?'

'Well, here he is, a bright young infantry captain, good at his job, been trained for years to do it, loves the life, and now he's finally in the middle of it and he finds he can't cope. And of course it got worse after your brother was killed. It's not the sort of thing a chap puts his hand up about, is it?'

'Yes, but shell shock's a very serious illness. It's not just some bloody airy-fairy state of mind that only ever affects incompetents and cowards. We've plenty of quite outstanding soldiers sitting in hospitals in England right now because of it. Who do you think goes to those nice, quiet convalescent homes? And they're bloody well full too, I can assure you. In fact, it sounds like Tarrant himself should have been in one.' Thomas drew on his cigarette for a moment, then flicked the butt into an overgrown flowerbed. He asked, '*Is* he good at his job?'

'James? Yes, he's an excellent soldier. Sound, level-headed, certainly not lacking in guts, and genuinely popular with his men, which is no mean feat. He never avoided his duties no matter how rotten he was feeling, he always led from the front and he *always*, no matter what, thought of his men first. In fact, I suspect they'd do just about anything for him.'

'Really?'

'Yes, really.'

The two men looked at each other with thinly disguised hope.

'How serious is this?' Thomas asked eventually.

'Well, you know the law far better than I do. But they've been coming down hard lately, thanks to Major-General Russell's zeal for improved standards of discipline. No doubt you heard about Private Hughes' execution, and Sweeney just the other day. And James *has* been charged with murder.'

'So it's very serious?'

'Yes.'

'But would they execute an officer?'

Ben shrugged uneasily.

'Who brought the charge?' Thomas asked.

'Lydon. He had to, really, because he's James's commanding officer, but I'm sure he hasn't lost too much sleep over it. He never much liked James. Chapley, our battalion commander, he's a reasonable man as far as I can tell. We don't really have much to do with him. And I don't know the other officers on the panel, except for Lieutenant-Colonel Proffitt from the 1st Brigade. He's the president, I think.'

'And will there be witnesses?'

'I think so. There was talk of getting some of the enlisted men who were there to give eyewitness accounts, given that James won't provide any of the relevant details himself. Except to say he did it.'

'But he hasn't actually been appointed a lawyer, has he? He hasn't a hope in hell of defending himself in the state he's in.'

'Well, no, but this isn't a civilian court, remember. I'm supposed to be representing him but not in a legal sense, and anyway I don't know the first thing about law. I can give a character reference, though, for James. No doubt Lydon will be effusive about Tarrant's many virtues, although I think you'll find that otherwise the general feeling is that if James did kill Tarrant, he did us all a favour. It was only a matter of time before he made a horrible mistake.'

'Bit harsh.'

'Yes, but it's true. I don't know how it is in the Medical Corps, but with the infantry your life depends on the men on either side of you, and very little else. No one wanted to fight alongside someone they couldn't trust, myself included.'

★   ★   ★

The court martial, which began at three in the afternoon, was held in a large room of the house where James was being held. At the allotted hour he was led into what was clearly the parlour, although all the furniture had been removed except for a long, heavy table facing several wooden chairs, with extra seats arranged to the

231

left and a small desk each for the court clerk and the court scribe.

The five officers of the panel sat behind the table, with a carafe of water, a small sheaf of papers each and a copy of the *Manual of Military Law* arrayed in front of them; at the door stood two military policemen looking impassively ahead. Together with Ben, James was directed to sit in one of the chairs facing the table.

He felt nothing at all now, and was barely aware of his surroundings. Since Ron's death he had wanted only to sleep. He knew Thomas was here, but he had the strangest sensation that he wasn't the real Thomas, the one he had grown up with. And it was the same with Ben Harper, and everyone else he had seen since the incident — these were people he knew, but he could no longer quite connect with them. It was as if a huge black spider had come and spun a web around him, muffling him from the outside world, rendering him unreachable and, thank God, safe at last. In his cocoon he no longer felt dread, or pain, or despair, and he felt shielded from the smells and the noise and the faces of the dead.

Lieutenant-Colonel Proffitt shuffled his papers, cleared his throat and stood up. 'Captain James Andrew Murdoch, you are charged here today at this general court martial with the murder of Captain Ronald Stephen Tarrant. It has been recorded that you plead guilty. Is that correct?'

Proffitt sounded embarrassed, as if the murder

232

of an officer by a fellow officer was almost too unpleasant to contemplate and certainly not a matter to be discussed openly.

James didn't respond, and Proffitt repeated himself.

There was still no answer.

Proffitt turned to Chapley and whispered loudly, 'What's the matter with the man? Can't he speak for himself?'

Chapley thumbed through his papers and extracted several sheets. 'Er, no, apparently not. Says here he has acute neurasthenia, according to the MO.'

Proffitt snapped impatiently, 'Is he in a fit state to be tried then?' He turned to Lydon and waved the medical report at him. 'You're his commanding officer, aren't you? Is this true?'

'No,' said Lydon immediately. 'To my knowledge he's always performed perfectly well as an officer.' Then he promptly shut his mouth as it occurred to him that such ready confirmation of Murdoch's ability could well prejudice the charge against him.

'God,' muttered Proffitt. 'Well, someone's declared him fit for trial. Who was that?' He glared suspiciously at Lydon, who refused to look up, then said, 'Captain Harper, are you acting as Captain Murdoch's friend?'

'Yes, sir,' Ben replied.

'I plead guilty,' said James suddenly, his voice devoid of emotion. 'I killed Ron Tarrant.'

Ben closed his eyes in despair.

'Right then,' said Proffitt, 'the accused has accepted the charge.' He sat down. 'May I remind the court that we will be operating strictly within the rules of procedure as outlined in the manual. This is an extremely serious offence.'

The court clerk read the evidence as summarised by the accused's senior officer. On the morning of the assault Major Lydon, who had been unavoidably detained in his dugout, had been advised that there had been some sort of accident in the trenches just after the first whistle, and when he arrived at the site he had encountered Captain Murdoch sitting in the bottom of the trench near the body of Captain Tarrant. When Major Lydon asked what had taken place, Captain Murdoch confessed to having shot Captain Tarrant in the head with his service pistol. After it had been ascertained that Captain Tarrant was indeed dead, Captain Murdoch had been placed under arrest and escorted from the scene.

The clerk stopped and when it became clear he had nothing else to add, Chapley demanded, 'Is that it?'

'Yes, sir,' the clerk replied.

'No corroboration from anyone else as to what happened? No eyewitnesses?'

'Yes, sir. There were plenty of witnesses.'

'Well, then, why aren't there any other statements?' asked Chapley, clearly perplexed.

'Hang on,' interrupted Proffitt. 'Captain Murdoch, do you have anything to add to the clerk's description of the evidence. Major Lydon's statement, that is?'

James remained silent.

Proffitt shifted his gaze and addressed Ben. 'Captain Harper, do you have any knowledge that might in any way contradict what the evidence suggests, that Captain Murdoch shot Captain Tarrant? Anything he might have said to you in private perhaps, either before or after the incident?'

Ben wanted desperately to lie, but he couldn't. 'No, sir, I do not.' He added hurriedly, 'But I have known James Murdoch for over a year now and I can testify to his character and to the fact that there's more to this than . . . '

Proffitt held up a hand. 'That will do, Harper. I'm not asking for a character reference and you're not a lawyer.' He turned back to the clerk. 'Lieutenant-Colonel Chapley asked about witnesses. We'll hear from them now, thank you. One at a time, of course.'

The first witness, a short, stocky private with an exaggeratedly deferential air, was called into the room and ushered to a chair. 'Private Bob Smythe,' announced the clerk.

'Right, Private Smythe,' said Chapley. 'You understand the charge against Captain Murdoch?'

'Yes, sir.'

'And you were present at the time of the incident?'

'Yes, sir.'

'Good. Now, can you relate your version of the events, please.'

Private Smythe looked Chapley directly in the eye. 'I were waiting in the trench for the second whistle, sir, you know, to hop the bags, when I

235

looked up and seen Captain Tarrant come barrelling over the parapet. Then about two feet behind him come Captain Murdoch, that man over there . . . ' he added, pausing to point at James.

'Yes, yes, we know who Captain Murdoch is,' snapped Chapley. 'Get on with it.'

' . . . and they both fell in the trench,' continued Smythe as if he hadn't been interrupted. 'Then Captain Murdoch jumps up and yells at Captain Tarrant, something about him murdering one of the lads. Tarrant, I mean.'

'Yes, and what did Captain Tarrant do then?' asked Chapley in patiently measured tones.

'Nothing, sir.'

'Nothing?'

'Well no, sir, he were dead.'

'Dead? You mean after Captain Murdoch shot him?'

'No, sir, before that. He were dead when he come over the bags. Bullet right between the eyes. Hit the ground and just lay there. Captain Murdoch were screaming his head off at a corpse.'

There was a long silence.

Eventually Chapley made a few notes and said, 'Thank you, Private Smythe, dismissed,' and turned to the clerk. 'Get the next one in, will you?'

The next witness was Private Harry Villiers.

This time Proffitt initiated the interview. 'Private Villiers, do you understand the charge against Captain Murdoch?'

'Yes, sir.'

'Were you present at the time of the incident?'

'Yes, sir.'

'Tell us what happened please.'

Private Villiers looked thoughtful. 'I was standing at the bottom of the trench waiting to go over and I saw Captain Tarrant roll in over the parapet, followed closely by Captain Murdoch. Captain Murdoch got to his feet and accused Captain Tarrant of murdering someone, then he yelled at him to go and retrieve the body.'

'And did he? Tarrant?'

'No, sir.'

'Why not?'

'Captain Tarrant was dead, sir.'

'Dead,' said Proffitt woodenly.

'Yes, sir. It's my belief he was shot on his way back into the trench.'

'Shot by whom?'

'Well, the Germans, sir. It happened to lots of our men during that assault.'

Proffitt gave Villiers a withering look.

Chapley said, 'So you're saying Captain Tarrant was already dead by the time he fell back into the trench?'

'Yes, sir.'

'So why was Captain Murdoch yelling at him?'

'I don't know, sir.'

'You've no idea at all?'

'No, sir, except I suppose he might have been confused and thought Captain Tarrant was still alive.'

Chapley rubbed his temples where a headache was beginning to niggle. 'Well, then, did Captain Murdoch shoot at Captain Tarrant's corpse?'

'No, not to my knowledge, sir.'

And so it went on. There were three further witnesses to follow, three more men who had been present at the scene and who swore that Captain Tarrant was already dead when he fell back into the trench. After the third witness Chapley stopped making notes, and when they'd all given their evidence he cleared the court of everyone except the panel and the court scribe.

'Well, Lydon,' he said, 'you've gone rather quiet. Are you sure you weren't mistaken when Murdoch confessed to shooting Tarrant? Was anyone else with you when he did?'

Lydon's face held an expression of barely stifled rage. He admitted reluctantly through gritted teeth, 'I had my batman with me, but then he disappeared somewhere. Murdoch had already admitted to the murder by the time my batman reappeared.'

'Are you saying that in a busy trench, only a few minutes after the start of a major assault, there was absolutely no one else in the immediate vicinity?'

Lydon was compelled to tell the truth. 'Yes, that's right, sir.'

'How damnably odd,' said Proffitt, and there was a subdued mutter of agreement from the rest of the panel.

'Yes, wasn't it?' mused Chapley out loud. He gathered up his papers and tapped them into a neat and tidy pile with the outer edges of his palms. 'Right, well, what we have here is either a very unstable captain who thought he killed someone when he didn't, or five consummate liars.'

'I think they're lying, sir,' Lydon said quickly. 'Murdoch has always been difficult, always going off and doing what *he* thinks is appropriate, despite my orders. I've never seen eye to eye with him.'

'Yes, but you rarely see eye to eye with anyone, do you, Major?' replied Chapley sharply. 'Did he ever actually contravene or disobey your orders?'

Lydon opened his mouth and then shut it again. 'No,' he replied after a moment. 'Not in so many words.'

'Well, did he or didn't he?'

'No, he didn't.'

'Right. And Ron Tarrant, what sort of soldier was he, in your opinion?'

'Very conscientious and committed.'

'I gather he spent a significant amount of *his* time in his dugout or in a hospital bed. Is that right?'

'I wouldn't go that far, sir.'

'I would,' said Proffitt, sliding a sheet of paper down the table towards Lydon. 'This is a summary of his medical record. The chap was sick and out of action more often than not, and there's a discreet note here suggesting a possible unwillingness to fight. Is that true, Major? Based on your experience as his commanding officer, of course.'

Lydon sidestepped the question by blustering, 'Look here, are you suggesting Murdoch should be let off Captain Tarrant's murder just because Tarrant's service record was a little patchy?'

Chapley rounded on him. 'And are *you* suggesting that Lieutenant-Colonel Proffitt is condoning the murder of an officer by a fellow officer?'

Aware he had overstepped the mark, Lydon back-pedalled immediately. 'No, of course not, sir. It's just that the man confessed. That seems to be clear evidence to me.'

'Well, it doesn't to me. Captain Murdoch is clearly not in his right mind at the moment. In fact, his medical notes suggest he's been mentally unwell for some time now, even though he's still managed to perform reasonably successfully. And while he may have confessed to a murder, I don't think, especially in the light of the five eyewitnesses who have all given evidence to the contrary, that we can make any assumptions. As far as I can see, there is no clear evidence of murder.' He turned to Proffitt. 'What do you think?'

'I agree, although I suspect there is more to this episode than meets the eye. However, we can't condemn the man on the evidence presented today, and I vote we acquit him, but I also strongly recommend that he be removed from duties and sent somewhere well away from the front where he can get some rest. I'm not entirely convinced about this shell shock business myself, but if anyone is genuinely afflicted by it I'd have to say it's Murdoch. The fellow can barely sit upright in his chair, for God's sake!'

'Yes, it's rather awful, isn't it?' agreed Chapley. 'He's a mere shadow of the chap he was when we first arrived in France. And he showed so much promise. So, are we all agreed then? Acquittal with a recommendation of removal from the field for appropriate rest and medical treatment, with a possible view to retirement on medical grounds if things don't work out for him?'

Although the two other members of the panel gave their assent, Lydon's petulant silence was conspicuous.

Chapley repeated, 'Major Lydon? Are we agreed?'

Lydon looked as if he wanted to say no.

Proffitt said then, 'I'd also like to add a recommendation that the performance and welfare of commissioned officers at the forefront of active service be monitored more closely from now on. From the rank of major down, let's say. If Tarrant *was* a bit on the windy side and no one picked it up, he could have been a real danger at some point. I'd hate there to be other officers out there now in the same position, unable to carry out their duties to the standard required, I mean,' he added, looking pointedly at Lydon.

The major collected his papers and stood up. 'The aforementioned recommendations all have my official support,' he said stiffly. Then he saluted and walked out.

James, Ben and the remainder of the court were called back and the verdict and recommendations pronounced.

Ben shook James' hand in hearty congratulation, but the arm flopped up and down as if it belonged to a rag doll. Ben took his friend's elbow instead and whispered, 'Come on, old chap. You can get some real sleep now.'

When the room had emptied and they were alone, Proffitt turned to Chapley. They were old army friends and knew from long experience that whatever they said would remain between them.

He asked thoughtfully, 'Do you think he did it?'

'I'm not prepared to say, Victor. It wouldn't surprise me, judging by the state he's in, but the evidence just wasn't there.'

'But it's inconceivable they'd *all* lie for him. Isn't it?'

Chapley shrugged and pulled a face. 'Tarrant was rather unpopular, I gather. I didn't have much to do with him. Unlike Murdoch — the men think he's marvellous. There's incredible loyalty in the trenches, you know.' He tapped his pencil on the table, as if debating something with himself. 'I've never liked Lydon much. He has a style of command that doesn't inspire a lot of confidence. Time he was moved on, I think.'

'*Was* Tarrant windy?' Proffitt asked.

'One certainly heard rumours.'

'Well for God's sake, why wasn't something done about it then?'

Chapley sat back in his seat. 'I assume because he fell through the cracks, and as you well know, Victor, there are some bloody big cracks in this army. Plus he was the golden-haired boy. Tragic, really, for both of them. There's no bringing Tarrant back, of course, and the Murdoch boy's military career is in tatters.'

Proffitt sighed. 'Been a thoroughly unpleasant business all round, this, hasn't it?'

* * *

Thomas returned to his unit later that evening. James had been shuffled off to the field hospital and admitted for further assessment and to await his transfer to a facility in England, possibly Hornchurch near London, then perhaps on to the convalescent home for New Zealand officers at Brighton. Thomas would check on him in the morning in the hope that his acquittal might have bucked him up a little, but he had seen the flat emptiness in James' eyes, and knew its significance only too well. He wondered how he would break the news to his parents.

The field ambulance had been withdrawn from the Somme with the rest of the New Zealand Division, and was now preparing to move north to the Sailly sector not far from Armentières. The weather was packing up and winter proper seemed to have arrived, bringing with it icy rain and bitter wind.

Thomas had been in France for six months, which made him an experienced veteran, and he'd been in the line almost constantly during that period. At Trentham training camp back home, he'd been given a deliberately hard time because of his stance as a conscientious objector, but the taunts and attacks had subsided somewhat since he had begun work as a stretcher bearer. He wasn't the only conchie in the Medical Corps, and he soon found a cadre of men who held similar beliefs and with whom he had become firm friends. He ignored the jibes that did come his way with patient stoicism.

He found, somewhat to his surprise, that he was good at his work, and not just because of his medical training: he had adapted quickly to the appalling conditions and horrors of the battlefield. In many ways his duties put him at even more risk than the average infantryman — retrieving the wounded from the very heart of the fighting and delivering them to the nearest advanced dressing station regardless of the intensity of enemy fire.

He had been extraordinarily lucky. On many occasions he had run, or trotted — it was very difficult to run carrying a man on a stretcher — through a solid hail of German bullets and emerged without even a scratch. He had been blown into the air by artillery shells and walked away without so much as a concussion. He was aware he was regarded by his unit as someone who had somehow attracted divine protection, and as such he was never short of colleagues volunteering to be on the other end of his stretcher, convinced that his immunity would also extend to them.

He had become incredibly superstitious himself, which quietly amused him. He insisted on wearing his lucky socks day in and day out, pulling the reeking, barely recognisable tatters of the first pair he was ever issued on over his newer ones. He accepted that his behaviour was highly irrational but at the same time was convinced that if he didn't wear them something terrible would happen to him.

He had been promoted to lance-corporal after three months in France, then to corporal six weeks ago. This wasn't as auspicious as it sounded — stretcher bearers weren't renowned for their longevity. His senior officer, however, had gone to lengths to explain that his rapid promotion was a consequence of his performance, not because of holes in the ranks. Thomas had been grateful for and even proud of the compliment, and felt the good work he was doing justified his decision to enlist.

13

England, April, 1917

Keely stamped her foot. 'I don't care what you think, Erin. I'm going!'

Erin replied calmly, 'Don't you think it's time you grew up?'

Right now, her cousin, standing in her underwear with her hands planted firmly on her neat hips and a filthy expression on her face, looked exactly like Aunt Tamar on the rare but memorable occasions she lost her temper.

Keely said petulantly, 'You've changed, ever since Joseph, and I don't think I like it.'

'I know. You've said that lots of times already.'

'Well, it's true! You've gone insufferably holier than thou! Just because you'll be getting married the minute you get home doesn't mean *I* have to act like a nun, does it?'

'No, but it doesn't mean you have to act like an empty-headed schoolgirl, either. Or a tart.'

Keely's mouth fell open. 'What a rotten thing to say!'

They'd been arguing in this vein for weeks now, ever since, in fact, Doctor Ross McManus had arrived at Brockenhurst, the home of No. 1 New Zealand General Hospital.

They had been at Brockenhurst since June of the previous year when the New Zealanders had assumed responsibility for the hospital. In practice it was more like several hospitals: a main section known as Lady Hardinge Hospital, plus two large hotels nearby named Balmer Lawn and Forest Park, which had been converted for the duration, and several smaller auxiliary units, all of which could together accommodate 1500 patients at a time. Keely and Erin were based at Balmer Lawn and, after Egypt, their work had seemed almost leisurely until September when the flood of casualties from the big push on the Somme had begun to arrive. The pace had never really let up since and now, eight months later, they were still frantically busy. Time off was scarce, and to be made the most of.

Erin was content to spend her precious free hours writing to Joseph or daydreaming about him, or catching up on her sleep, but Keely was bored and, she insisted, socially deprived. She went into Southampton as often as she could with a group of other New Zealand nurses who found it easier to unwind away from the hospital. Lately, though, her companion of choice had been the dashing Doctor McManus, and Erin didn't approve.

'I'm sorry, Keely,' she said. 'I'm worried about you, that's all.'

'Well, don't be,' Keely replied stubbornly. She stepped into her skirt, fastened the hooks at the waistband and reached for her blouse. 'There's no need. I'm old enough to take care of myself, thanks very much, and I'm certainly old enough to enjoy a man's company.'

'And what's he enjoying in exchange?' asked Erin with uncharacteristic sharpness.

Keely shrugged into her jacket then fussed

about finding just the right angle for her hat. 'Not what *you're* thinking,' she replied, scrutinising the effect in the mirror. Well, not yet anyway, she thought as she snatched up her bag and marched out, not even saying goodbye, vowing that this would definitely be the last time she'd talk about her personal life with Erin.

Her outfit was new, purchased at great cost on leave in London a month ago, and this was the first time she'd worn it. The saleswoman in the shop had oohed and aahed over the contrast between her rich auburn hair and the deep burgundy of the suit, and Keely knew she looked good in it. The skirt fell straight and fitting to just above her ankles and the matching jacket with a black fur collar accentuated her small waist. Under it she wore a smart cream blouse with pearl buttons, and the outfit was topped off with an elegant black suede hat. She was freezing but didn't want to wear her overcoat as she felt it spoiled her silhouette. She had bought the suit to impress Ross and, as she waited at the hospital gates for him to appear, stamping her cold feet and rubbing her gloved hands together, she hoped he appreciated it.

He arrived ten minutes late but, as always, she forgave him his tardiness.

'Hello darling,' he said with his usual disarming smile. He glanced quickly around to make sure they weren't being observed, then leant forward and kissed her cheek. 'You look stunning. New outfit?'

'This?' asked Kelly disingenuously. 'I've had this for ages.'

248

'Well, the colour really suits you,' he replied, taking her hands in his. 'Now, are you sure about this? I've reserved a room at the Windsor, for Mr and Mrs McManus. I thought we might have a drink and a meal at the restaurant there first. It's quite good, I've eaten there before.'

Keely nodded happily. 'Yes, I am sure, and that sounds lovely.'

'And you managed to wangle a late evening pass all right?'

'Yes, Matron thinks I'm having dinner with a second cousin.'

Ross laughed heartily. 'You must have almost used up your stock of long-lost relatives by now.'

Keely laughed with him, but a little uneasily. She was in fact running out of excuses for permission to be out on her own, but he was so insistent she find a way to meet him unaccompanied, and so disappointed when she couldn't, that she dared not tell him so. In fact, she was a little annoyed at his cavalier attitude towards her availability — and his apparent assumption that she always would be available — but she almost always had been, so she supposed she couldn't really complain. And he was such a catch, she thought, as they set off down the street, and she couldn't help feeling more than a little smug at the thought that of all the nurses at Brockenhurst, she'd been the one to snare him.

'Where are we going? We're not walking into town, are we?' she asked in alarm as he steered her across the road. Her shoes, although elegant, were not made for long-distance walking.

'No,' he said as he stopped next to an automobile parked discreetly beyond the hospital gates. 'We're going in this!'

Keely's eyes widened as she took in the sleek lines of the gleaming yellow sports car. 'Is it yours?' she asked, impressed.

'Sadly, no,' Ross replied as he helped her into the quilted red leather of the passenger seat. 'Belongs to a friend of mine, bit of an auto enthusiast. It's a Stutz Bearcat, brought over from America. Nice, isn't it? I thought it would add an extra touch to our special evening.'

Keely was enchanted and flattered. 'It's wonderful.'

'No top, I'm afraid. Didn't you bring a coat?'

'I didn't think I'd need one,' Keely lied.

Ross opened the small trunk and passed her a woollen rug. 'Then put this over your knees, otherwise you'll freeze before we get there.'

She watched him closely as he started the motor. He was a ruggedly good-looking, charismatic man in his mid-thirties with dark brown hair, a moustache and piercing light grey eyes. He towered over her at six foot one, and was muscularly built — more like an athlete than the talented surgeon he was. He hailed from Auckland, had volunteered for service with the NZMC, and Keely had fallen in love with him the moment they'd met. That had been six weeks ago now, and as far as Keely was concerned every minute since had led directly and inexorably to this evening's encounter.

It had started with him catching her staring at him during ward rounds, then covert, private little winks and grins from him, and demure smiles from her. They started spending more time together discussing the progress of various patients, then she began saving him a seat in the staff lounge whenever she knew their breaks would coincide. His rank was major and hers only staff nurse, but expediency and limited space at the hospital encouraged ranks and genders to mix relatively freely, so that in itself was not considered too noteworthy, although the frequency with which they were seen together had raised eyebrows. A fortnight ago he had invited her into town for a drink; she had accepted and their mutual attraction had flared from there.

Last week he had followed her into the supply room, kissed her passionately, fondled her breasts through her uniform and thrust himself urgently against her and she'd never experienced anything so thrilling. She was hardly innocent in this area — she had kissed boys before — but Ross McManus was a *man*, big, powerful and blatantly virile, and it made her almost sick with excitement to think she aroused him to such an extent.

And tonight their relationship would reach new heights of intimacy. When he suggested booking a room at an hotel, she had barely hesitated. Losing her virginity to him was the logical next step, and she had no qualms about the wisdom of doing so. If lust was an indication of love, and Keely sincerely believed that it was, then Ross McManus was head over heels about her.

She hadn't said anything to Erin, whom she was convinced wouldn't understand, although she had wondered from time to time exactly how close she and Joseph had become when he had been in hospital in Egypt. Erin could be very private sometimes, and had steadfastly refused to divulge any of the more interesting details of their liaison, which suggested there was more to the story than Erin was prepared to confess. Erin had of course noticed something was up between Ross and Keely, and quite early on, too. Erin had been able to read her like a book ever since they were little girls growing up together at Kenmore. This had always been a comfort to Keely, but lately she had begun to find it more than a little irritating. She loved Erin dearly, but did not appreciate her cousin's rather blunt admonition that she was making a very big mistake. She'd also hinted that Keely's behaviour was causing increasing disapproval and rancour among her colleagues, who believed her infatuation with the dashing doctor was affecting her work, and that consequently it was unlikely to escape Matron's notice for much longer.

Keely, who *had* detected a certain coolness in the other nurses, believed they were jealous, and she couldn't blame them: Ross was an eligible and very attractive man. But she was convinced that none of her peers would be so small-minded as to inform the senior nursing staff of her clandestine romance. After all, if any of the other girls had been lucky enough to find the man of her dreams, Keely would be genuinely delighted. This apparent resentment of her good fortune

252

hurt her, but it did not stop her from seeing Ross.

She had, though, hoped for at least some support from Erin. She wasn't even sure why her cousin was still in England — Keely would have been off home at the first opportunity to marry her man. Privately she was jealous of Erin's situation, her joy and her quiet, steady confidence in her future with Joseph. But why was Erin being so censorious and reluctant to share in her happiness? Surely their experiences of love should have made them even closer.

Keely was tired of nursing. It had been wonderful to start with, that warm and gratifying feeling that came from being needed by sick and wounded young men, but there had been so many of them since then, and lately hopelessness and sometimes even indifference had crept into her attitude. She no longer saw her patients as people, but tagged them in her mind as 'the chest wound', or 'the double amputee', or the 'head injury'. If she did allow herself to contemplate them as individuals, they reminded her of poor dead Ian, who had never even had the chance to lie in a hospital bed, or of James, and those were images she refused to entertain. A perceptive psychiatrist might have recognised her malady as a product of chronic overwork, and her infatuation with Ross McManus as an unconscious but misguided attempt to escape it. But there were no psychiatrists at Balmer Lawn.

The damp evening air had turned Keely's feet into blocks of ice despite the heavy rug tucked around her legs, and she stumbled as Ross helped her down from the motor. Wishing she'd worn her coat after all, she scoffed silently at her own vanity.

'All right?' Ross asked solicitously as she righted herself awkwardly.

'Yes, I think so. Just pins and needles.'

'Best we get you inside then,' he replied, and turned and guided her up the hotel steps.

Inside it was significantly warmer, much to Keely's relief, and she surreptitiously blotted her dripping nose with a gloved hand as a waiter led them to a table near the roaring fireplace. Ross pulled her chair out for her and she sat down gratefully, hoping her face hadn't gone too pink from the cold.

The waiter returned with menus and a wine list and rattled off the evening's specials, then left them to make their selection.

'Shall I order for you?' Ross asked after he had scrutinised what was on offer.

Keely nodded. 'Yes, please.'

'Well, I don't fancy any of this. I wonder what else they've got?'

He clicked his fingers rather imperiously in the general direction of the waiter hovering a polite distance away. The man hurried over.

Ross asked, 'Anything available but, you know, not on the menu?'

The waiter made an ostentatious show of incomprehension. 'I beg your pardon, sir?'

Ross sighed at the obvious charade. 'Does the chef have anything special up his sleeve?' He slowly withdrew his wallet from his tunic pocket, placed it on the white damask tablecloth and tapped it deliberately.

'Oh!' exclaimed the waiter, as if it had only just occurred to him what was being implied. 'One moment please, sir.'

He scuttled off and returned a minute later. 'Pheasant, sir, in a brandy sauce,' he said out of the side of his mouth.

'Yes, that will be fine thanks. For both of us.' When the waiter had gone Ross leant over and whispered to Keely, 'I don't know what all the secrecy's about. The black market's rife and everyone knows it.'

She giggled. 'It's rather nice here,' she said, looking around at the décor.

'Well, it's not the Savoy, but it's comfortable. The rooms are nice.'

'Are they?' Keely said, raising her eyebrows in only semi-playful query.

'Yes, and before you come to the conclusion that I make a regular habit of entertaining women in hotel rooms, I had a look before I made our reservation. There's a sign at the reception desk that says 'We invite inspection', so I did.'

Keely laughed again. 'And what makes you think I *would* come to such a conclusion?'

He leant forward again, and Keely thought he was about to take her hand, but he didn't. Instead, he said in a low voice, 'Just so there aren't any misunderstandings, my dear. I wouldn't want that.'

Before she could ask him what he meant, their meals arrived. The pheasant was succulent and tasty, and went well with the claret Ross had chosen. Not that Keely was interested in the food — she was far too nervous. She was captivated by the sight of Ross deftly cutting his food, the strength of his long fingers with their neatly trimmed nails, and the way the silver cutlery accentuated the fading tan on the backs of his hands. He ate elegantly but with enthusiasm, and paused from time to time to dab with his napkin at non-existent traces of food on his lips. Keely approved — she couldn't stand a man with messy table manners — and wondered if he did everything with such confident and deliberate precision. Then she smiled to herself and almost shook her head as she recalled the frenzied touch of his questing hands on her body. Occasionally he would look up from his food and deliver one of his devastatingly slow smiles that made her stomach flip and her face burn. She pretended interest in her meal in the hope he hadn't noticed her reaction but knew by his amused gaze, which she felt rather than saw, that he had.

Keely had two glasses of the claret, and a brandy after dessert, and was feeling light-headed as they stepped into the lift that would take them up to their room. The lift was rather small, with a brass screen that had to be closed before the thing would move, and she didn't like the way everything jolted and rattled when it did. She was absurdly relieved to get out and follow Ross down the carpeted, subtly lit hallway. He unlocked the door of room number eleven and, before she realised what he intended to do, picked her up and carried her over the threshold.

'My God, Mrs McManus, you're heavier than you look,' he grunted as he carried her over to the wide bed and set her down with a bump. 'You don't mind being Mrs McManus for a few hours, do you?'

It was on the tip of Keely's claret-loosened tongue to say, 'What, only a few hours?', but really there was no hurry; after tonight there would be all the time in the world to plan their future. She sat up and looked around. The room was quite luxuriously furnished and very cosy with the open fire. Ross took off his uniform jacket and tie, lit a cigarette and sat down next to her.

'Would you like one?' he asked, offering her the packet.

'No, thank you,' replied Keely, a little put out that he'd apparently forgotten she didn't smoke.

'A drink then? I could have a bottle of something bought up.'

'Yes, another *small* brandy would be nice. But won't they think that's a bit odd, a married couple having a drink in their room when there's a lounge downstairs?'

Ross laughed. 'I doubt it. They probably see it all the time, especially since the war's been on. We're not the only couple to have done this, you know.'

Mortified, Keely stared at him. 'Do you think they *know*?'

'What, that we're not married? Why, does it matter?'

It did to Keely. She didn't want anyone to think she was just someone's mistress — she wanted the whole world to know there was much more to her relationship with this wonderful man.

Seeing the look of doubt on her face, Ross bent down to kiss her. 'Look, darling, it's very unlikely anyone's even noticed us. And if they have, why on earth would they care? Come on, surely you're not worried about it? I would have thought you much too sophisticated to be concerned about that sort of thing.'

He yanked on the bell-pull near the door to summon room service, then came back to Keely, smoothing her hair tenderly back from her face.

'Why don't we just forget about it and enjoy ourselves? We barely get time together as it is so let's not spoil what we do have.'

Keely nodded and turned her face to kiss his hand, then started as a discreet knock came at the door. She stood quickly and smoothed her skirt.

Ross opened the door and asked the housemaid for a bottle of good brandy. 'Remy Martin or Courvoisier, thanks, if you have either.'

The housemaid was busy eyeing Keely up and down. 'Well, I'll do what I can, sir,' she replied, and added rather impudently, 'but there's a war on, you know.'

'Do your best,' Ross replied, and shut the door in her face.

The brandy met with Ross's approval. He poured them both a glass then settled himself on the edge of the bed again.

'Take your jacket off, darling,' he said gently,

then patted the bedcover. 'Come and sit with me.'

Keely complied, draping the jacket of her new suit over the back of an armchair and moving over to the bed. She sat down nervously.

Ross entwined his hand in her hair and pulled her towards him, kissing her with real passion, running his tongue over her teeth and sliding it into her mouth. He tasted of brandy and cigarettes, and Keely could faintly smell his fresh sweat; the combination was heady and exciting. His hand came up and settled on her breast, lightly pinching the nipple, and she gasped. He pulled back and gazed deeply into her eyes. 'You, my dear, are the most enchanting creature I've encountered in a long time. Your lovely face and hair, and this gorgeous body of yours. You're enough to lead a man to make a complete fool of himself.'

Keely's pleasure was so intense that she involuntarily closed her eyes. Ross began to unbutton her blouse.

⋆ ⋆ ⋆

He'd been less than pleased to find she was a virgin. Keely thought he might have been flattered, but he'd acted as if taking her maidenhood was a rather annoying complication. But then his displeasure had been subsumed by the heat of his passion and he had ploughed on. And plough he did; by the end of the evening Keely felt as if she had been harrowed, sowed, hoed and thoroughly harvested.

She said to Erin the following morning, 'He said he thought I'd already, you know, done it. I thought he'd be really pleased I'd chosen him.' She had forgotten about her resolution never to talk to Erin again about her personal affairs.

If she hadn't felt such dismay, Erin might have laughed at the indignant look on her cousin's face. Although why *she* was upset, she didn't know: Keely was quite old enough to manage her own life. Erin just wished she wasn't risking so much in the process.

She asked, 'So you're serious about him, then?'

'Of *course* I'm serious. Would I spend the night with a man I wasn't serious about?'

Erin wondered; Keely had been a terrible flirt since at least the age of thirteen. 'Did you use any, ah, precautions?' she asked.

'What? Oh, I see what you mean. No, I didn't. But everyone knows you can't get pregnant during your first time.'

Erin made a conscious effort to stop her jaw from dropping. Where had Keely got that from? Certainly not her undeniably worldly mother.

'Well, you'd better sort something out, before something disastrous happens. I assume you'll be seeing him again?'

'Yes, do assume that. Tonight, as a matter of fact,' Keely replied, carefully ignoring her cousin's pointed comment about contraception. After all, becoming pregnant might not be such a bad thing — if she did Ross would be bound to propose.

'Are you going into town? You won't get a pass two nights in a row. And aren't you on night duty?'

'No, not to town, to his room after I come off duty at midnight.'

Erin shook her head. 'My God, Keely, if you're caught it will be the end of everything. Doesn't that bother you?'

Keely shrugged, then laughed. 'No, not really. Not any more. I mean, I'd have to give up work when I marry anyway, and Ross says the war will be over soon, so what would it matter?'

'Are you saying he's asked you to marry him?'

Keely couldn't prevent a smirk. 'Well, not yet, but I think I can say I'm confident. We're very much in love.'

Erin opened her mouth to protest, but suddenly realised that having said something very similar to Sister Griffin in Egypt about herself and Joseph, she was hardly in a position to cast aspersions.

'Well, for God's sake, be careful. I hope you know what you're doing,' she warned.

Keely pouted and sat down heavily on her bed, one of two jammed into the small room she and Erin shared. 'Oh, don't be like that, Erin. Please be happy for me. I'm thrilled about you and Joseph.'

Erin tidied her hair in the mirror and pinned on her veil. 'I'm sorry, I can't help it. I've a bad feeling about the whole thing.'

'He's a lovely man, and he treats me so well.

It's a wonderful feeling.'

'I've no doubt he is nice,' Erin replied, turning to face Keely, 'but this is wartime. He could be a completely different person when it's over. He could even be married to someone else.'

'Oh, he is *not!*'

'Have you asked him?'

'If he's already married? No, he'd think I didn't trust him.'

'Well, perhaps you should,' Erin replied, although she doubted very much that if Ross McManus was married, and inclined towards philandering, he'd readily admit his marital status while he had such intimate and ready access to a young woman as appealing as her cousin.

Keely rolled her eyes theatrically. 'Oh, all right then, I *will* ask him, if it makes you feel better. You'll see!'

★ ★ ★

But Keely didn't ask Ross, not for another ten weeks, and by then the question had been answered.

Those weeks were wonderful, filled with excitement and intimacy and passion. She went to him at every opportunity and, in the privacy and warmth of his bed, they lay together and explored each other's bodies intimately. He was a vigorous and evidently insatiable lover, and under his tutelage she learnt to satisfy his every desire.

So far their trysts had remained more or less

secret. Erin was aware, of course, but Keely knew she wouldn't say anything, and Ross had been close-mouthed as well. In fact, he'd made it very clear to Keely that he didn't want anyone else to know — it was to be their secret, he said, something just for them. But in a way Keely almost wanted to be discovered. Then, even if she were to be sent home in disgrace, they could announce their love to the world. She wouldn't mind going back to New Zealand if she knew Ross would be joining her when he had finished his service, and she would be more than happy to give up her nursing career in exchange for becoming Mrs Ross McManus. At least her father would be pleased, she reflected — he'd never been particularly thrilled by the idea of her having a professional career. And eventually there would be children, and perhaps, if they lived in the Hawke's Bay rather than Auckland, their children would grow up with Erin and Joseph's children, and they could go on being a big, noisy, happy family, despite having lost Ian.

She was thinking about this, and having a cup of tea and one of the hospital's rock-hard date scones in the staffroom, when she happened to look out of the window and see a yellow automobile park in the drive. A rather dashing man, dressed in a duster coat, goggles and driving gloves, jumped out and stood gazing about with his hands on his hips. He looked lost. Keely recognised the motor as the Stutz Bearcat in which Ross had taken her to town on their first night together, and she wondered if this were the owner, and what he was doing here.

She went outside and called to him from the steps.

'Hello! Are you looking for someone? Are you lost?'

The man removed his goggles and gloves, tossed them onto the passenger seat and strode towards her, his boots scrunching on the gravel of the drive.

'Hello,' he answered in a rather upper-class English accent. 'Well, possibly — I'm looking for Ross McManus, a friend of mine. He's a doctor here.'

'Yes, that's right. I can fetch him for you if you like,' Keely replied, smiling. 'May I say who wants him?'

'Oh, sorry. Gerald Halstead,' he said, extending his hand. 'He's been telling me I should drop in and see how the New Zealanders are set up, but I haven't had time until now. I'm a doctor myself, you see, with the military at the moment, of course.' He unbuttoned his coat to reveal a British Army uniform and went on chattily, 'Ross and I were at medical school together in London. Mind you, that was years ago now. Been great friends ever since though, despite him haring off back to New Zealand the minute he passed his finals.'

Keely smiled again, delighted to be meeting one of Ross' friends. She opened her mouth to say how enjoyable it had been to ride in such a glamorous motor car, and to thank him for allowing Ross the use of it, when Gerald patted his tunic pocket and added, 'I've a letter for him, from Evie. Apparently she's misplaced the address here so she forwarded it to me to pass on.'

'Evie?'

'Yes,' he replied casually, shrugging out of his coat. 'Evelyn McManus.'

'His sister?' Keely felt suddenly sick.

'No, my sister actually. Ross' wife.'

14

She slammed through the doors into the ward, almost knocking an orderly off his feet in her rage. She had never in all her *life* felt so hurt, angry and utterly betrayed. What an absolute fool she had been! What an *innocent*!

But still, beneath her fury there squirmed a little worm of hope hinting that this was all a dreadful misunderstanding, that even if there was a Mrs McManus already, her relationship with Ross would be barren and loveless, and that she, Keely, had revived in him the affection and passion of which he had been so tragically been deprived. But she was still outraged. How could he have lied to her like that?

Ross was bent over a patient and didn't look up as she approached.

'Doctor, a word!' she snapped.

He turned in surprise, his look of enquiry quickly fading to one of puzzled consternation.

Keely hissed in his face, 'You *bastard!*'

'I beg your pardon?'

'Your brother-in-law's here, with a letter for you from your *wife.*'

Ross had the decency to flush deeply, then the expression on his face changed from embarrassment to anger. He stood up. 'Not here, Keely, for God's sake.'

'Where then?' she almost screeched. 'The staffroom perhaps?'

'Keep your voice down!' He grabbed her arm and steered her out of the ward and into the corridor where he turned to face her. 'What the hell do you think you're doing?'

'*Me*? What am *I* doing? You cheating, lying bastard!' She drew back her hand and slapped him hard across his face.

He didn't retaliate but, suddenly aware of a nurse and an orderly who had stopped to stare in amazement, roughly took her arm again, propelled her into the supply room and kicked the door shut.

There was a knock immediately.

Ross yelled, 'Go away!'

He waited for the sound of receding footsteps, then rounded on Keely.

'Did you have to make a scene?'

'You *lied* to me!' Her voice was shrill and petulant now, and she hated herself for it.

'No,' he said slowly, 'I don't think I did.'

'You're *married*!'

'Yes.'

Keely was incredulous. 'Aren't you even going to try and deny it?'

Ross leant against a shelf and folded his arms. 'No, I'm not. And I haven't lied — *you* never asked.'

'Why the hell *should* I have asked? You were acting like the world's most eligible bachelor!'

'Yes, and you were acting like the world's most available good-time girl.'

Keely slapped him again. This time he took hold of her wrist and threatened, 'You do that again and I'll hit you back.'

She wrenched her arm out of his grasp and spat, 'Go on then, hit me! You've done everything else to me, why not that?'

Ross took a deep breath and rubbed his hands wearily over his face. 'Look Keely, I'm sorry. I hadn't realised you were quite so naïve. Really — you always seemed so sophisticated and self-assured. And you *didn't* ask, so I assumed it didn't matter to you. We are in the middle of a war, after all, and everyone takes what comfort they can these days.'

'Do they? Well, I don't. Not in the way you're suggesting anyway.'

'But you did though, and you certainly seemed to enjoy it.'

'Yes, I did. But I thought we . . . ' She faltered; she didn't want to make an even bigger fool of herself. 'I thought I was more to you than just a . . . *comfort*.'

He reached out for her but she stepped smartly out of range.

'Keely, I really am very fond of you and we've had a lot of fun together. I'm sorry if you thought there was more to it than that.'

'I suppose you're going to tell me you don't love your wife, that your marriage is one of convenience or some such rubbish?' she demanded, hoping he would say yes.

'Well, it is these days, more or less. We met when I was at medical school in London, and she became pregnant so we married and she came back to New Zealand with me. But, oh, I don't know, it just hasn't worked out, really.' He sighed as if he quite regretted this but it couldn't be helped, then dashed Keely's hopes completely by adding, 'I've no intention of leaving her though. We've three children and Evie thinks they need a father, even if it is me, and I've agreed to stay until they're grown.'

Something rather unpleasant occurred to Keely. 'Is this the first affair you've ever had?'

Again Ross went pink. 'Ah, no, not exactly.'

Keely closed her eyes and swayed as a wave of nausea swept over her. 'You don't deserve to be loved. I hope she leaves you one day and takes your children away from you.'

'I doubt that,' Ross replied confidently. 'For some reason she believes it's absolutely essential to keep up appearances.'

'And does your brother-in-law know about your, your *activities*?'

'No, and I'd rather it stayed that way if you don't mind.'

'God, you borrowed his motor car to take me out in!'

Ross shrugged. 'It was worth it, though, wasn't it?'

Wanting to hurt him as much as he had hurt her, Keely said vindictively, 'What if I told him? What if I wrote to your wife and told her what you've been up to?'

He looked mildly disconcerted for a moment, and his eyes narrowed. 'You wouldn't, would you?' Then he laughed, but it wasn't a pleasant sound. 'Actually, I rather suspect you just might. You're used to getting what you want, aren't you? Well, I've news for you, girl. Life doesn't work like that, and if you go spilling the beans to

Evie or even Gerry you'll only upset them, and probably a lot more people besides, and what will that achieve? Evie still won't leave me. But by all means tell them if you really think you need to. I'm sure it will help you to feel better. But the world doesn't turn around you, you know, Keely Murdoch, despite what you might think. Grow up before you cause someone some real harm.'

Keely was speechless — no one had ever said anything so nasty to her. She could easily have punched his handsome, aristocratic face, turned her back and walked away from him for ever, but then he spoke again.

'It's funny,' he added, 'I saw that in you the moment we met almost, but it never really bothered me. It was actually charming, in a way. I still think you're gorgeous and, really, you're the most fun in bed I've had in a long time.'

To her shock and consternation, and regardless of his cruel words less than a minute before, Keely realised she felt flattered. She was contemplating how to respond when someone banged loudly on the door and rattled the handle aggressively.

'Staff Nurse Murdoch, are you in there? It's Matron Carmichael. Open the door.'

'Oh Christ,' Ross muttered.

'Nurse Murdoch,' came the voice again, shrilly insistent now. 'Come out this instant!'

Keely opened the door.

'What's going on?' Matron demanded, her bulk almost filling the doorway.

She appeared extremely perturbed. Behind her

Keely could see a small crowd peering curiously in.

Keely stepped out but avoided everyone's eyes.

'Are you all right?' Matron asked. When Keely nodded she added crisply, 'Right then, I'll see you in my office. And you can get back to work, Doctor McManus.'

Ross did the sensible thing and disappeared as quickly as possible, although he still managed to saunter. Keely was left standing alone, her face flaming.

Matron glared at her. 'My office, Nurse Murdoch, now. And straighten your veil. You look a shambles.'

Keely strode off along the corridor, her head defiantly high now despite the stares that followed her. Outside the matron's office she sat down to wait, not nervous, just angry.

She waited for nearly an hour, and while she did, she thought very hard.

Was she that conceited and self-absorbed? She knew very well she was spoilt — her mother had told her as much many times — but it had always been a bit of a family joke, and she'd never really stopped to think about her own behaviour or what impact it might be having on other people. She had never wanted for suitors or friends, although apart from Erin she couldn't name any women with whom she was on truly intimate terms, and she tried to be kind and generous towards others. She hadn't meant what she'd said to Ross about telling his wife — she'd only wanted to hurt him — but he'd taken her seriously and come out with all those horrible things about her.

As the enormity of what had happened engulfed her, the shock of discovery and the harsh shattering of her dreams, she put her face in her hands and felt hot tears burning the backs of her eyes. Then she bit her lip hard and sat up again. She refused to cry. Crying was for silly, weak women, and she wasn't weak. She *wouldn't* be weak, despite Ross' appalling duplicity. Damn his smooth ways and his lies and his unforgettable lovemaking. She was a Murdoch, and she would retain her pride and her dignity no matter what. Even if her heart did feel as though it was being ripped in two.

She stood as Matron Carmichael swept in.

'Come in please,' she said stonily as she opened the door to her office.

Keely sat on the chair Matron indicated in front of her huge desk, feet together, hands clasped loosely in her lap and her head up. On the desk were tidy stacks of papers, charts and forms.

Matron sat down herself, her significant bulk forcing a protesting squeak from her chair, and cleared her throat. Without preamble she said firmly, 'I understand you've been having a liaison of a personal nature with Doctor McManus. Is this true?'

Keely replied without hesitation, 'Yes it is.' There was no pointing lying at this stage.

Matron frowned, as if she had not expected so frank an admission. 'Has this liaison reached a, well, let's say a physical level?'

'Yes.'

There was a short, very disapproving silence, then, 'You understand of course that such behaviour grossly contravenes both the regulations and the spirit in which you undertook to serve as a member of the NZANS?'

'I understand that *some* of my behaviour *could* be construed in such a manner, and if it has then I regret that. It's unfortunate.'

Stunned at Keely's arrogance, Matron glared. She had just spent the last hour quizzing various members of her staff, plus an orderly or two, about what the fracas in the corridor had been about. One sister, who seemed to have taken a shine to Staff Nurse Murdoch and was therefore reluctant to admit to any knowledge of the girl's alleged shenanigans, had finally talked, as had several of her colleagues, delighted to divulge more than Matron needed or wanted to know.

Apparently the affair was fairly common knowledge — indeed, Keely Murdoch had evidently been making a complete tramp of herself with that rather flashy Ross McManus — and Matron was annoyed with herself for not having been aware of the situation before now. She would certainly have put a stop to the business well before it reached such a public dénouement.

She said briskly, 'Yes, I'm sure you do regret it. And I expect there will be even more regrets after the Matron-in-Chief has been informed.'

Keely shrugged. She nibbled on a fingernail, then made what she thought was a mature and honourable offer. 'I will of course be requesting a transfer to another hospital.'

'A *transfer*! Staff Nurse Murdoch, it's highly likely you'll be sent home and discharged from the NZANS after this.'

Keely said nothing. Being sent home was not without its attractions. She had been very tired for a long time. Her family would understand, and they would forgive her because they always had. And Ross would probably be sent home too — he was, after all, equally to blame — and Napier wasn't that far from Auckland. Once he had thought things through, and spent a few months without her, he would realise how much he missed her and how inevitable it was that they should be together.

'Have you nothing to say?' asked Matron.

'Not really, except that I really am sorry,' replied Keely.

And she was, for the way Ross had lied to her, for this rather major hiccup in the blissful future she had envisioned and for the embarrassing manner in which their relationship had become public. But it would all be fine in the end because, in a way, Ross had been right — things almost always did work out for her.

Matron shook her head incredulously: this young woman seemed to have no idea of the impact this reckless and ill-considered affair would have on her future, both personally and professionally.

'I'm unlikely to have a decision from the Matron-in-Chief for a day or two. Until then, you're suspended from duties. I suggest you remain in your room. I don't want the staff distracted from their work. That will be all.'

⋆ ⋆ ⋆

Keely stepped down from the train and looked around for her luggage. Although the sun was bright and unobscured by clouds, the wind whipping off the Bristol Channel seemed to bite right into her flesh and she was grateful for her gloves and hat. This was her first trip to Avonmouth, and if the bleak grubbiness of the train station was anything to go by, she hoped it would be her last.

According to Matron Carmichael, the New Zealand hospital ship *Marama* was due in port this afternoon. Keely was to board later this evening and hand the matron a sealed letter. Keely could imagine more or less what it said. She was to work her passage home: the *Marama*, with a full complement of over six hundred patients, was on the eve of her voyage back to New Zealand, and another pair of trained hands would always be appreciated, even if they were attached to a woman of dubious morals.

Keely watched as a pair of porters began to unload boxes and cases from the guard's van, and sat down on a bench to wait for her luggage to appear. She would have to find somewhere to go until this evening, but she was sure there would be plenty of tea shops in the area. She would also buy herself a magazine or a newspaper, and perhaps a packet of cigarettes — given all that had happened it might be a

275

good time to start smoking.

Everyone, everywhere, seemed to be in a hurry these days. A trio of soldiers surveyed her appreciatively, but she returned their gazes with an icy stare. Why couldn't they keep their eyes to themselves? Did she have a sign around her neck or something? It had been like this during the trip from Southampton to Avonmouth, the other travellers in her compartment staring at her continually, as if her sins were advertised for all to see: censorious old ladies, accusing children, opportunistic men in uniform, and knowing, disapproving women who were obviously the wives of men away on service. Women like Evelyn McManus. She realised of course that no one had been looking at her — she was in England after all and the British simply did not stare — but her fatigue and her tattered nerves were making her imagine things.

It had been the same when she had been standing outside the gates of Balmer Lawn yesterday, waiting for the taxi to collect her and take her to the station. Erin, loyal as always, had come out to stand with her, but even so she had had the uncomfortable feeling that hundreds of pairs of judging eyes were peering down at her. She had turned quickly now and again, only to see the four imposing storeys of Balmer Lawn looking impassively back: there was no one there.

The taxi had arrived, she and Erin had hugged, then she had gone, leaving behind her friends, her nursing career and Ross McManus. Who had not lost his job — had not even received a reprimand for his part in their affair, as far as Keely was aware. Her mouth tightened again at the unfairness, and she looked down at the ground as a rush of blood flooded her face, then drained away again, leaving her normally glowing skin sallow and tired-looking.

It was so unfair that she should be the one to be publicly pilloried and made an example of. And for what? She had fallen in love — was that such a crime? He, not she, had lied and cheated and deceived. If he had been any sort of gentleman he would have volunteered his culpability, perhaps even insisted that Keely stay while he went home.

She must have dozed off, for suddenly there was a hand on her shoulder and a voice saying, 'Hey, lady. Excuse me, lady. Wake up.'

'What?' Keely murmured. How could she have fallen asleep on such a noisy, busy railway platform?

'Is this your luggage?'

It was one of the porters, a short elderly man, so pale and frail-looking Keely wondered how on earth he managed to heft baggage around.

'Sorry?'

'Is this your luggage?' the man repeated. He eyed her kindly and his voice softened. 'Been working hard have you, love? Never mind. It's a rum do all right, this war. Someone meeting you, are they? No? Get yourself a cup of tea then, you should. Perk you up no end, it will.' He stood there nodding to himself, as if tea was a panacea for everything.

He held out his hand and, with a surprisingly strong grip, helped Keely to her feet. 'There's a good tea shop just down the street. Don't drink the tea here, it's a disgrace and the scones aren't much better.'

He delivered her suitcase then tipped his cap and walked off, limping slightly. Keely suspected that if there hadn't been a war on, the little man would have retired years ago.

'Thank you!' she called after him, and he waved without turning.

She picked up her case and began to lug it towards the station gates. Only fifty yards or so down the street, as promised, was a tea shop. Sliding the case under a table near the window, she sat down, relishing the feeling of being out of the wind. She filled the next six hours by having five cups of tea, smoking, making three trips to the toilet and eating a rather sad sandwich and two pikelets. She also read two newspapers and a magazine, and nodded off again several times, to the thinly disguised disapproval of the waitress. At seven in the evening she rose and went outside to hail a taxi to take her down to the docks.

She walked along the wharves until she found the dock at which the *Marama* was berthed, ignoring the wolf whistles of the sailors as pointedly as she could. She climbed the gangway, then wandered along the deck until she encountered an orderly, who directed her down a series of corridors and a flight of stairs to the matron's office. She knocked on the closed door and waited expectantly until it was opened by a tall thin woman.

278

'Hello?' she asked, looking Keely discreetly up and down. 'Can I be of assistance? I'm Matron O'Connor.'

'Um, yes, I think so. I'm Keely Murdoch. I was nursing at Brockenhurst until recently but I'm on my way home now. I understand my passage on the *Marama* has been arranged?'

Matron looked at Keely blankly, then her eyebrows lifted almost imperceptibly. 'Ah. You're the one going home unexpectedly, is that right?'

'Yes. I have a letter for you from Matron Carmichael.'

Matron held out her hand for it, then said, 'Oh, I'm sorry. Please, come in and have a seat.'

She waved Keely into her office and pointed at one of the chairs in front of a rather imposing desk. Keely wondered as she sat down whether having a big desk was a prerequisite for being a matron, or a result of being one.

Matron scanned the letter quickly, then refolded the single sheet, slipped it back into its envelope and placed it on the desk in front of her. She put her hands together, the index fingers touching the tip of her nose, and looked at Keely over them.

'And how is Bea these days?' she asked.

'Bea?'

'Beatrice Carmichael. Matron.'

This wasn't the question Keely had been expecting at all. 'Oh. Well, ah, fine, I think. Although she wasn't very happy the last time I was speaking to her.'

'No,' agreed Matron, sitting back in her chair, 'I imagine she wasn't. She says you've managed to get yourself into a spot of trouble.'

'Yes. I, ah . . . Yes, I have.' Keely lifted her chin and said with as much dignity as she could muster, 'I made a regrettable error of judgement.'

'Indeed,' said Matron. 'Well, we won't go into that now. It's not as uncommon as you might think, and from my experience Bea Carmichael would be more likely to send you home for your own good, rather than just for propriety's sake. She wouldn't have made the decision lightly.'

Keely raised her own eyebrows.

'I see you're surprised, Nurse Murdoch?'

Keely nodded.

Matron continued. 'Bea Carmichael is a personal friend of mine — we trained together, years ago now, of course — and you might be even more surprised to hear she's quite a liberal-minded woman, and a real hoot after a couple of sherries. Yes, I know, her demeanour can be a little daunting but she's a good woman, and she has always put the welfare of her staff above anything else. If she'd had her way I expect the man at the centre of all this would have been sent home, not you, but she has no jurisdiction over NZMC staff, only her nurses. In any event, not all has been lost,' she added kindly. 'You can still nurse when you get home.'

'No I can't,' Keely responded. 'I've been dismissed from the NZANS.'

'No, I don't think you have, my dear. It says in the letter you've been stood down from active service due to fatigue, not dismissed.'

Keely stared. 'Are you sure?'

'Of course I'm sure. And you wouldn't be expected to work on the way home if you'd been dishonourably discharged. And you are, working I mean, there's no doubt about that, so I suggest we get a berth organised for you so you can get your head down and have an early night. You'll be busy learning the ropes tomorrow, and we're leaving on the late afternoon tide.'

Keely sat in stunned silence for a moment, then said, 'I thought I'd been dismissed. Matron implied, well, she never told me I hadn't.'

Matron tapped the letter in its envelope. 'No, she probably wanted you to reflect on the seriousness of your, ah, indiscretion.'

'What? You mean she wanted to teach me a lesson?'

Keely was incredulous now. What an interfering old cow! In the heat of her anger, she forgot how much worse it could have all been, how much worse she had thought it was.

'Now that I can't answer, and it isn't my place to. You're under my authority now, on my ship, so we'll put the past behind us and start afresh, shall we?'

★   ★   ★

By the time the *Marama* had passed through the Panama Canal, Keely had made up her mind: she would retire from nursing, even if did mean having to listen to her father telling her he'd known all along she wasn't really cut out for a profession, and stay on at Kenmore. She would have to find herself something to do, however.

She couldn't sit in the parlour all day arranging flowers and waiting for her friends and family to introduce her to a succession of young men deemed suitable as prospective husbands.

To her surprise she was enjoying life on the hospital ship. Some had considered nursing at sea 'cushy' — three to four months of changing bandages and giving sick and wounded soldiers cups of tea. In fact it was extremely hard work. The surgeons in the two fully equipped theatres worked almost constantly, removing infected flesh, beginning the long process of reconstructive surgery, performing exploratory operations to find out why a soldier might not be recovering when he should be. There were also the 'sick' wards, as opposed to those accommodating the wounded. God knew what diseases some of these men had: many had to be kept in isolation to prevent possible epidemics that might devastate the entire ship.

Keely worked shifts, as she always had, and found herself flopping, exhausted, into her bunk at the end of each eight-hour stint, her mind almost numb with fatigue. This was the way she wanted it, though — anything to keep her mind off Ross McManus, what he was doing and who he might be doing it with now. She still didn't quite know what she was going to tell Tamar and Andrew. No doubt her mother would understand — she always did — but her father never would.

She was looking forward to getting home now. She would see Joseph for the first time in ages, James should be home soon too, if he wasn't already, and Thomas and Erin, well, they would be back when they could be. Ian, of course, would never come home, and the thought of that still made her heart freeze.

Part Three

Keely

1917–1919

15

Kenmore, September 1917

James, followed at a wary distance by Lucy, went straight upstairs, while Tamar and Andrew collapsed on the sofa in the parlour and poured themselves generous brandies. Joseph found them still there when he came in half an hour later.

'Is he upstairs?' he asked, sitting down in his socks and shirtsleeves.

'Yes, he seems rather tired,' replied Tamar as she eyed the brandy decanter thoughtfully. 'No, perhaps not,' she murmured.

'Sorry?' said Joseph.

'I was going to have another drink, but it could be a long night, so perhaps I won't,' Tamar explained. 'He seems in rather a strange mood.'

James had arrived at Napier station that afternoon, to be met by his parents and Lucy.

Andrew looked pale and worried. Slouched dispiritedly on the sofa, he sat up abruptly and frowned. 'He just doesn't seem at all to be the same lad who went away. He's, I don't know . . . he's grown *old*, I think, Joseph.'

Joseph nodded. He'd seen this many times, of course.

'He barely said a word all the way home. He doesn't even want to see young Duncan yet, which has upset Lucy terribly. Mind you, I think he's probably still asleep. Duncan, I mean.' He looked at Tamar for confirmation. She nodded. 'They've gone upstairs, the pair of them,' he added, and sighed. 'I think poor wee Lucy will have a lot on her plate over the next few months.'

Months? It could be a damn sight longer than that before James gets back on his feet, Joseph reflected bleakly.

James and Lucy came down an hour later, then Lucy disappeared again to fetch Duncan from the nursery. She came back with him in her arms, a sleepy, grumpy, bronze-haired bundle of chubby two-and-a-half-year-old.

'Duncan?' she crooned as the little boy looked around through rapidly blinking eyes. 'Look who's here. Daddy's home.'

When his mother held him out towards the strange man in uniform Duncan began to wriggle and shriek, wrapping his plump arms around her neck and using his bare feet to climb up her chest. James, who had risen to take his son, sat down again, his lips pressed whitely together, and turned to stare silently out through the French doors.

Tamar thought her heart might break. 'Oh, James, you'll have to give him time. He's confused, he hasn't a clue who you are.'

James grunted, then sat back and rubbed his hands over his face. 'I'm sorry, Mam,' he said. 'I'm very tired, and it's extremely odd being home again after, well, everything. I'm bloody well confused, too.'

Tamar glanced at Lucy, who was rhythmically patting Duncan's back in an effort to placate him. The younger woman looked back, then quickly away again. Oh dear, thought Tamar, they've already had some sort of quarrel.

Fortunately, at that moment Mrs Heath appeared at the parlour door to take Duncan and announce dinner.

They filed into the dining room and sat down — Andrew and Tamar, Jeannie and Lachie, James and Lucy, and Joseph and Keely.

'Was Liam awake when you went up?' asked Tamar.

Lucy nodded as she unfolded her napkin and spread it over her lap.

'You should see him, James,' said Tamar, 'he's the absolute image of his father. Mrs Heath will bring him down after dinner. He and Duncan will be in the bath by now.'

This was the first time anyone had mentioned Ian in James' presence. Tamar desperately wanted to ask what his brother had said the last time they had been together. Had he been happy? Had he looked well? Had he made friends? Did he die alone? But her questions could wait a little longer. After all, Ian was never coming back, but James, thank God, had.

James put his soup spoon down with exaggerated care. 'Are you sure he's Ian's?'

'Oh yes, we're absolutely certain, aren't we, dear?' Tamar replied, looking across the table at Andrew.

He nodded. 'We had our doubts at first. Well, I had my doubts, but I think it's safe to say that Liam is Ian's. They look exactly alike, two peas in a pod. Even have the same mannerisms.'

'How can you tell?' asked James. 'The child's only . . . how old?'

'Just over a year,' Tamar replied. 'You'll have to wait until you see him, James. You'll know at once. He even has the same facial expressions Ian had when he was tiny. You might not remember, though — you weren't that old yourself at the time.'

'I remember, Mam. I remember every single thing about Ian.'

There was a heavy silence. Tamar blinked back tears and Andrew cleared his throat with an odd, high-pitched sort of whinny.

Lachie, always uncomfortable in emotional situations, lifted his glass and said, 'I propose a toast to you, James. Welcome back, laddie, you're a real sight for sore eyes.'

Everyone raised their glasses, clinked them together over the table, then drank briefly.

James lifted his drink a second time. 'And I propose a toast to the end of this fucking war.'

Tamar blinked again, this time in surprise. James had rarely sworn before he had gone overseas, and there was a tacit understanding that strong language was not to be used at the dinner table at Kenmore. In the paddocks, yes, but not while they were all gathered together to share a meal. She ignored it, however, assuming that James was either nervous, tired, or taking time to slough off his army habits. And anyway he was twenty-eight now, and she could hardly tell him off for swearing after all he had been through.

'Yes, to the end of the war,' echoed Andrew,

'and to Thomas and Erin coming home safe and sound.'

Joseph looked over at James' sunken eyes and sharp cheekbones — his brother must have lost stones in weight. And he might be safe now, but he certainly didn't seem sound.

He asked, 'Have you decided yet what you'll do? About the army, I mean?'

'It's been decided for me. I'm to receive an honourable discharge. I was informed on the troopship on the way home.'

'Oh,' said Andrew. 'That's all right, then. Isn't it?' he added hesitantly.

'It's the best I could have hoped for,' James replied flatly, 'considering I murdered one of my fellow officers. It's not really the done thing, you know.'

There was another uncomfortable silence. Then Tamar said, 'Yes, but you were acquitted, darling, declared not guilty. Surely that will have cleared your name?'

She knew, though, that James had been responsible for Ron Tarrant's death — even though she couldn't bring herself to accept that her son had shot someone in cold blood — because Thomas had written to describe what had happened. No matter what the details of the whole nasty business had been, she knew, in her heart, that her boy was not a murderer.

James shrugged. 'That sort of thing does rather stick, Mam.'

Joseph, watching James, asked carefully, 'How do you feel about leaving the army?'

James, looking down at the largely untouched

291

food on his plate, replied, 'Does it matter? I'm out now, or as near as, and that's it.'

Lucy began, 'Yes, but you could still . . . '

'No, Lucy,' James barked suddenly, banging his hand on the table so hard that his wine spilled and everyone jumped. 'I can't! I can't *still* do anything! Don't you understand? I wanted to lead men in battle, that's all I've ever wanted to do, and I fucked up and Tarrant's dead and so's Jenkin and all the rest of them and it's finished, all of it!'

Lucy's hands flew to her mouth in shock at the violence in her husband's voice, and her eyes filled with tears.

'James!' Tamar, too, was appalled.

'Well, I'm sick to bloody *death* of it! All they went on about in the hospital was how it wasn't my fault, that accidents happen and he was probably already dead when he fell back in the trench. But I *know*, all right! I know *exactly* what I did. I shot him in the head and I killed him! And do you know why?' James shoved his chair back and glared wildly around the table. 'Because he was *me*, that's why! He was a frightened, gutless little bastard and he was *me*!' He lurched to his feet and marched out of the room.

Tamar rose to go after James, but Joseph said, 'No Mam, leave him for a while. I think he'd probably rather be by himself for now.' He looked over at Lucy, feeling desperately sorry for her. 'He'll come round, don't worry. Shell shock can take a long time to recover from. This is pretty normal, I think. He just needs time.' He looked over at Keely for confirmation.

She nodded in agreement. 'He'll come right. Some of the men I nursed, some of the really badly affected ones, were still showing symptoms a year after being withdrawn from combat.' Then she realised what she'd just said — James had already been in hospital and then a convalescent home for almost a year. 'But it can come right just like that,' she added, clicking her fingers. 'All he needs is rest and quiet.' But even to her own ears she didn't sound very convincing.

After dinner Joseph went in search of James and found him in the garden, sitting on a bench in the dark, drinking brandy from the bottle and smoking. Joseph sat down next to him, but said nothing. The night air was warm, for September, and carried a hint of the delicious scents that spring would bring.

After a while James said tonelessly, 'I can't help it. It sounds pathetic, I know, but I can't seem to manage my temper any more.' He took a final drag on his cigarette, dropped it and ground the butt into the short grass under the heel of his boot. 'It just sort of roars up from somewhere in my guts and I can't control it and I always end up saying or doing something I regret. And I feel so wobbly and weak afterwards.' He turned to look at Joseph, and his brother saw in the light of the half moon that he had been crying. 'But I mean it, what I say. I mean it.'

Joseph nodded. There was no point to arguing — if James felt the need to persecute himself for his actions, then he would, until he found the strength to begin to live again. And that, Joseph knew, might be never. But he didn't — *couldn't* — judge his brother: Joseph himself, and any number of the men he had fought beside, would probably have done the same thing.

James took a swig from his bottle, and wiped his mouth on his sleeve. 'They all know what really happened, you know. Well, the ones that matter, anyway — Bob Smythe and Villiers and the others. And the boss knew, Chapley. He came and talked to me briefly after the trial before I was transferred to the hospital and he asked me outright. I wasn't talking much then, I don't think, but I do remember saying to him I definitely did it.'

'What was his reaction?'

'Can't remember, really. He shrugged, I think, and I *think* he might have said if that really were the case, I should keep my mouth shut about it. But I'm not sure. I might have imagined that bit. I was imagining a lot back then. God knows how much of it all was real. Chapley might not have been there at all.' James laughed, but it was without humour.

'And the people at the hospital? Hornchurch, wasn't it? How were they?'

'Oh, the doctors all wanted to believe I hadn't done it, because if I really had, what would that say about the Empire's glorious and noble officer class, eh? That we were a bunch of savages happy to casually murder anyone who didn't measure up? That if someone pissed us off we just shot them to get them out of the way? I don't think they wanted to treat confessed killers, so they chose to believe I was imagining things instead.'

'We were all confessed killers,' said Joseph eventually, after a silence.

'Yes, but we're not supposed to talk about that side of it, are we?'

Joseph reached for the brandy and took a long drink himself.

'Not many do. Not to outsiders anyway, people who weren't there. And do you really think the doctors were that naïve? That it might not have occurred to them that what you were saying was true?'

James was silent for a moment. 'No, I don't really. There were some really decent chaps there who didn't give a shit about the morality of it any more and just wanted us to get better and functioning normally again. They were absolutely knackered too, you know, the doctors. And some of them held quite openly pacifist views. They would have got on really well with Thomas.' He waved his hand dismissively. 'Oh, there was the odd arsehole who insisted it was just a matter of pulling yourself together and getting back to the war, but you never saw any of them volunteering for service in the field.'

Joseph grunted, then asked, 'So, do you think you *are* better?'

'No,' James said bluntly. 'I'm not 'neurotic' any more, as they say, but sometimes it still feels as if I'm right back there. I can hear it and see it and, worst of all, I can *smell* it. All that shit and blood and rot. And I'm still having the nightmares.' He turned to Joseph. 'Do you have those?'

'The odd one, yes. And sometimes I dream I've still got my leg and I'm running all over the place and then I wake up and realise it was just a dream. That's hard, sometimes.'

They lapsed into silence again for several minutes, then James said, 'Poor Lucy. She'll be wishing she hadn't waited for me. Now she's stuck with a mad husband invalided out of the army for conduct unbecoming.'

'Oh, bollocks,' Joseph replied immediately, a hint of anger in his voice now. 'You're being given an honourable discharge on medical grounds, like thousands of other blokes. And don't tell me you're the only officer to take drastic action to keep his men safe, because you aren't. I know that for a fact.' James opened his mouth to say something, but Joseph barged on; 'And don't be feeling sorry for yourself either, because that really is gutless, and for God's sake give your wife some credit because she deserves it. She *has* waited for you, and she's known since we got Thomas' letter what happened, and she hasn't wavered once. She's gone on raising your son and telling everyone what a hero you were at Gallipoli and in France and it's obvious she loves you and wants to stand by you, so don't go buggering that up, all right? She's a strong girl, and a decent one, and you're lucky to have her.'

James said nothing but took a deep swig of the brandy and lit another cigarette. He wanted to say that Joseph didn't understand what it had been like, but he knew that was untrue and that made him feel ashamed because he did sometimes feel sorry for himself. At other times he felt irrationally aggressive, but when he wasn't angry the fear came back in such monstrous waves that it paralysed him.

'Are you supposed to be having any more treatment?' Joseph asked, his voice even again.

James took a deep breath. 'If things go well, no. If they don't, yes.'

'What's 'well'?'

'Well, Christ, I don't know. I suppose if the nightmares and the anger and all that go away. Otherwise I'm supposed to go into town to the hospital for a 'rest' in the returned servicemen's ward they've set up there, but I'm buggered if I'm doing that.'

'But are you supposed to see anyone else in the meantime?'

'There's a trick cyclist at the hospital and apparently I'm booked in to see him every month or so.' James flicked his cigarette butt into the shrubbery. 'Oh, and I'm meant to be attending a rehabilitation programme in town as well, seeing as I can't be a soldier any more.' He looked Joseph squarely in the eye. 'I thought I might take up basketry.'

They both burst out laughing. They laughed until they had tears in their eyes, and then James was crying again, great noisy anguished sobs that almost broke Joseph's heart.

★　★　★

Christmas 1917 at Kenmore wasn't a happy one. Ian's absence was still keenly felt, and the mood was sombre, but Tamar insisted the family still

297

celebrate the holiday, even if only for the children's sake.

Duncan was almost three now, a bright inquisitive little boy who ruled the household. Everyone adored him, although he pushed even Tamar to the limits of her patience at times with his incessant questioning and fiddling — Mrs Heath's kitchen equipment, the offal pit, Tamar's cosmetics, Joseph's spare wooden leg which Duncan decorated with creosote.

The worst, most frightening incident was when Andrew left the car in the driveway while he went inside to get something, and Duncan got into the driver's seat, let the handbrake off and sat there crowing with delight as the car rolled steadily towards the solid stone gateposts at the end of the drive. Lachie had to run madly across the lawn after him, almost giving himself a heart attack, leap into the passenger seat and wrench the brake on. When asked what on earth he thought he was doing, Duncan said he was motoring into Napier to buy some lollies.

Joseph said there was a name for children like Duncan — *haututu*, which meant troublesome or a nuisance — but he was actually very fond of him, and the child spent hours alongside his uncle hammering together pieces of wood while Joseph laboured on the house he was building for Erin when she came home.

Liam, on the other hand, blond and slight against Duncan's ruddy chunkiness, was quiet and incredibly sweet. There was no doubt now in anyone's mind that he was truly Ian's son, although there had not been a single word from his mother since the day he was left at Kenmore.

James was fond of Liam, and seemed to reserve for him what little affection he could summon up. Perhaps, thought Tamar, it was because Liam so resembled Ian. James certainly wasn't very affectionate towards his own son, but then Duncan was still very stand-offish with James and there was an uneasy truce between them. Duncan seemed to resent James' demands on his mother's time, few though they were, and did his best to disrupt any moments they had together. Matters hadn't been helped by the fact that Lucy had allowed Duncan to sleep in her bed throughout the entire period that James had been away, and the little boy was very put out at being shifted to another bedroom, even if he did have Liam for company. His strategy to counter this rude and abrupt modification to his sleeping arrangements consisted of a steady yelling and a rather forced but nevertheless intensely irritating sobbing that began at 7.30 when both boys were put to bed, and went on for at least two hours.

The performance initially caused a spate of very terse and unpleasant exchanges between Duncan's parents — Lucy believed the boy should be allowed back into the marital bed to settle him down while James insisted that would happen over his dead body — until James informed Duncan that if he didn't shut up he'd get a good hard belt across the backside and would be sleeping outside with the dogs. This did nothing to improve relations between father and son, but when James finally decided to go into town for a period in hospital, it was noted by all that Duncan did not move back into his mother's bed.

James had resisted the idea of an enforced rest for some months, but by January it was clear his health was not improving. He was still unpredictable and short-tempered, could not sleep and sometimes seemed apathetic to the point of almost complete inertia. He would sit in the garden for hours with a packet of cigarettes and a bottle of spirits, not getting visibly drunk but certainly drinking enough to become uncommunicative and extremely withdrawn.

Tamar occasionally attempted to talk to him but when she did he would often be reduced to tears, and she couldn't stand seeing this. She, and Andrew, encouraged him to get out and about on the station with Joseph in the hope that physical work would help him, but he refused. He was still underweight and off his food, and Tamar worried that he would soon become seriously physically ill.

At the beginning of November she had suggested to him that he take advantage of the opportunity for a break at Napier Hospital, but he had walked away. However, when Lucy had broached the subject with him the following day, Tamar had been able to hear them yelling at each other upstairs from where she was in the kitchen. She wished fervently that James would not take his temper out on Lucy, because she of all people deserved it least. She feared her son was turning into a bully, willing only to lash out at women and children, perhaps even the sort of man he was insisting he had already become

— gutless and weak.

But, just after Christmas, after a particularly heated row that the whole family couldn't help hearing, Lucy came down to breakfast with a grazed and purple bruise on her cheek. Tamar was appalled and, struggling to control her own temper, deliberately refolded her napkin and laid it carefully on the table.

'Have you hurt yourself, Lucy?' she asked evenly. Out of the corner of her eye she could see Joseph watching intently.

Lucy's hand wandered up to her face in an unconscious effort to hide the bruise. 'I, yes, I walked into the door last night, on the way to the toilet.' As nervous liars often tend to do, she compounded the untruth by adding superfluous additional information. 'I didn't want to put the light on in case I woke James. And when I got out of bed I wasn't watching where . . . '

Joseph butted in. 'Is James still in bed?'

Lucy nodded. 'He had another bad night last night.'

'Clearly,' Joseph said and got up.

'No, leave him, he's . . . '

'No, Lucy, I'm sorry but this can't be allowed to go any longer and we're all just condoning it by doing nothing. I know he's had an absolutely bloody awful time, but he can't keep on taking it out on everyone else.'

As he left the room no one disagreed with him, and no one got up to follow him. They went back to their breakfast in silence, but all looked up when Joseph and James came in about twenty minutes later. Joseph's lip was slightly split, his

301

right knuckles were grazed and his shirt was damp down the front, as if he'd hurriedly sponged something off it. One of James's eyes was bleary and swelling visibly. They sat down at the table without a word and casually laid their napkins over their laps as if nothing at all untoward had happened.

Eventually, James said, 'I think I might go in to the hospital for a few weeks after all. As soon as I can arrange it. I'm, well, obviously things aren't going too well.' He looked up. 'I'm so sorry, Lucy. I really am.'

Lucy, her eyes filling with tears once again, immediately reached across the table and took her husband's hand. Tamar had to blot her own tears, and Andrew had a sudden fit of vigorous throat-clearing. Keely was on the verge of crying too, but somehow Tamar didn't think it was because of Lucy and James.

After breakfast she sat on the sofa in the parlour — her favourite room in the house — and contemplated her errant daughter while she worked on a piece of embroidery destined to become a bodice panel in a new dress. She was enormously relieved that James had decided to go into the hospital, but something would really have to be done about Keely as well.

The family knew more or less why she had come home — she'd made no secret of it, and in some ways almost seemed proud of what had happened — but they were all paying the price of her misery, which was showing few indications of abating. Tamar had been very cross with her daughter for getting herself into such an invidious position, but given her own history she certainly wasn't in any position to be critical. These things happened in wartime. But, of all things, to fall in love with a married man — Tamar really thought Keely should have had more brains than that and certainly a better sense of self-preservation.

When Tamar had heard from Erin that Keely had been utterly infatuated with the man, her heart had gone out to her daughter: her feelings may have been misguided, but she had obviously loved Ross McManus deeply, which would have only made the sense of betrayal even more bitter and hurtful.

She had tried to talk to Keely about it but had been fobbed off with some comment about all that being in the past now. But Tamar knew it wasn't. You only had to look at Keely to see that: her eyes lacked their usual sparkle, she had lost weight and she was very self-absorbed. When Keely had first come home, Tamar had invited some of the more attractive and eligible young men from the district to dinner now and again, but more often than not Keely wouldn't even come down from her room. She had decided to let her daughter sulk until she became sick of wallowing in her own misery, but that hadn't happened.

If Tamar needed any confirmation that Keely was still enamoured of McManus, it was provided every time the mail arrived — or didn't arrive. On mail day Keely would moon about in the morning, then go down to the box by the gates. If there was nothing from McManus, as there never was, she would be in a black mood for days. Andrew was of the opinion that she wasn't too old to be sent to her room without her dinner, but Tamar just laughed and said that would hardly make much difference since Keely spent half the day in her room anyway.

Tamar was worried. Keely had received a letter from the matron of Napier Hospital several weeks ago offering her work on the veterans' ward, which Tamar thought was very generous given Keely's escapades in England, but her daughter had mentioned the offer once, then never referred to it again. Whenever Tamar tried to discuss it, she changed the subject.

It annoyed Tamar, this lack of enthusiasm, but she didn't want to be too hard on the girl who, she believed, was enduring her own sort of shell shock. A woman, after all, couldn't nurse all those poor broken men month after month with no real rest and emerge from the experience emotionally unscathed. But Keely wasn't trained to be anything other than a nurse, except somebody's wife, and with her face and constitution as sour as they were at the moment, that was most unlikely.

Tamar still had hopes, though. She wanted her daughter to be happy, to know the delight of a man who loved and supported her, someone with whom she would have children and grow old.

In a fortnight's time there would be a welcome-home dance at the local school for the district's returned and mostly wounded service-men. James should be home from the hospital in time, if he could be persuaded to go, and there would be all manner of young men there. Perhaps one might even take Keely's fancy. Each man was to be presented with a wristwatch to acknowledge his service, and the proceeds of the entry fee charged to non-veterans would go towards the district's war memorial project fund, which Andrew declared somewhat cynically had become the country's latest pastime. Tamar had berated him for his sarcasm, but it was true that communities seemed to be competing to get the grandest, most ostentatious memorial up as quickly as possible, even before the war was over.

A few days later, though, everyone at Kenmore forgot about the welcome-home dance: Erin was finally coming home.

16

Well before Erin returned, however, Kenmore had a visitor. Fred Wilkes was a small, faded-looking returned soldier who knocked on the front door one afternoon and explained through a pronounced stutter that he had served with Ian in France. He had come to pay his respects, he said, and hoped to offer some comfort to Ian's family.

Tamar immediately ushered the man into the parlour, ignoring the state of his clothes and his rather rancid smell, and sat him down, calling out to Mrs Heath for tea and cake. She sat opposite him with her hands clasped in her lap, nervous in case Mr Wilkes might blurt out unpleasant details of her son's death. But he only looked at her with sorrowful eyes that blinked rapidly and teared frequently.

When the refreshments came he ate four slices of fruitcake one after the other and washed them down with great gulps of tea, which he spilled down the front of his mouldy-looking old jacket. Because it was a hot summer's day Tamar offered to hang up his coat, but he said, with a deep shiver, 'N-n-no thank you, Ma'am, it was sh-sh-shocking cold on the Somme and I haven't b-b-been able to get meself warm since.'

Then it seemed to occur to him that Tamar might not want his filthy clothes on her lovely brocade sofa and he jumped up. 'Oh, s-s-sorry.

Shall I go in the kitchen?' He looked down at himself ruefully. 'I'm a b-b-bit down on me luck, as you can s-s-see.'

'No, no, of course not, Mr Wilkes,' replied Tamar immediately, forcing herself not to finish his words to save him from embarrassment. 'In fact, if you like, I can probably find something else for you to wear and Mrs Heath can put your clothes through a wash.'

'Oh, no, I d-d-don't want you to go to any trouble,' he said. He coughed liquidly and thumped his chest. 'S-s-sorry, it's me lungs. But I'd b-b-be honoured if you'd call me F-F-Fred, Ma'am.'

Tamar stood. 'Of course, Fred. Wait here and I'll find you something else to put on.'

When she returned to find him staring miserably at his cracked and dirty boots, she was carrying an old pair of trousers, a shirt and some clean socks.

'I hope you won't be offended but I've asked Mrs Heath to run you a bath. You seem to have been on the road for some time. Nearly everyone's out at the moment, so you won't be disturbed.'

Fred looked up at her, his hands filled with Andrew's cast-offs, and a tear finally escaped and ran down his cheek.

'Th-th-thank you, Ma'am,' he said, his lips twisting in an effort to control his emotions. 'Ian s-s-said you were a kind and generous woman, and b-b-beautiful, and he was right.'

'Well, thank *you*, Fred,' Tamar replied. 'And please don't call me Ma'am. Mrs Murdoch is fine. I'll get Mrs Heath to show you to the guest bathroom, shall I? And perhaps she can prepare you something more substantial to eat after you've refreshed yourself. We can talk about Ian when you're feeling a bit better.' She turned to leave the room, but paused at the door and turned quickly back again. 'Which company did you say you served with in France?'

'I didn't, b-b-but it were the 3rd Brigade, 2nd Battalion, C Company,' Fred replied immediately, his voice full of pride. Then, 'I weren't in the same s-s-section as Ian but we served s-s-side by side.'

★   ★   ★

Once the grime had been washed off and he'd combed his hair, Fred Wilkes was revealed to be a moderately good-looking man of twenty-three or twenty-four. He'd had to roll up the cuffs and sleeves of Andrew's clothes several times, but they were a vast improvement on those in which he'd arrived. Mrs Heath refused to put his old clothes in her nice clean copper but instead set fire to them, standing back with her fingers holding her nose and a very disapproving look on her face as the rags went up in flames.

When Fred had waded his way through cold meat and salad with fresh, buttered bread and another pot of tea — according to Mrs Heath's muttered aside to Tamar, he had almost 'taken the pattern off the china' — he burped gently into his napkin and sat back with his hands spread across his stomach.

'B-b-best feed I've had in ages, thanks, Mrs,' he said, smiling up at the housekeeper and showing missing back teeth. She hmmphed and bustled about clearing the empty dishes from the table.

Tamar suggested, 'Perhaps you'd like to bring your tea into the parlour?' She hesitated slightly before adding, 'And then you can tell me about Ian.'

When they were settled, Fred ensconced in Andrew's favourite chair and Tamar on one of the sofas, he began.

'He were a lovely b-b-boy, Ian. Everyone's favourite, even when we were training t-t-together at Trentham. Always ready with a s-s-smile and a joke, nothing were ever t-t-too much t-t-t . . . God!' Unable to get the word out, he grimaced in embarrassment and frustration. 'S-s-sorry, Mrs Murdoch. It's me nerves!'

Tamar nodded in sympathy. 'Take your time, there's no hurry.'

Fred took a deep breath and continued. 'And strong! Carrying the other lads' gear if they was s-s-struggling, giving them a helping hand, b-b-bucking them up when they had long faces. He was good at it too, s-s-soldiering. Sergeant said he'd make officer if his luck held.' He stopped and bit his lip, blinked hard and cleared his throat. 'It were the s-s-same when we was on the t-t-troopship. T-t-tower of strength, he was. We were all reinforcements, you know, and s-s-some of us had heard the horror stories going round about life at the front, and I got to be honest here and s-s-say a lot of us were getting quite windy about it all, but Ian was always chipper. He reckoned give us a m-m-month out there and the bloody Hun'd be straight back to Germany with their t-t-tails between their bloody legs, pardon my language!'

Tamar asked hesitantly, 'Were you . . . were you there when he died?'

Fred nodded reluctantly. 'We were all there. I w-w-won't go into details . . . '

'No, please don't,' interrupted Tamar.

'But I will s-s-say he had his friends around him when his t-t-time came.' Fred looked at the floor for a moment. 'And it was quick. I know people always say that, but it really w-w-was for Ian.'

He looked up again, at Tamar sitting across from him, her face red from the effort of not crying and her throat working to keep the sobs at bay.

'But I won't d-d-dwell on that, Mrs Murdoch. Your b-b-boy died a hero, and that's all I'll say on the subject. I got plenty of other s-s-stories about him though, how p-p-popular he was and all that, if you got time to hear them before I set out again. And he t-t-told us so much about your place here, I feel like I'd know my way around s-s-straight off.'

Tamar plucked her handkerchief from her sleeve and blotted her eyes. 'Do you have to go today, Fred? Perhaps you could stay a day or two. I'm sure Mr Murdoch, Ian's father, would be very happy if you would. James and Thomas, our other sons, are both away at the moment — Thomas is still overseas — but my son Joseph is home, and Keely is here, of course, our daughter.'

Fred gave a watery smile. 'Yes, K-K-Keely. Still getting up to mischief, is she?'

Tamar stared at him. 'I beg your pardon?'

'Keely. Ian s-s-said she were a very outgoing young lady. Always matchmaking and that s-s-sort of thing.'

'Oh. Well, she's still recovering from her nursing experiences overseas at the moment. She was in Egypt and France, you know. And England.'

'Oh, right, of course. They was all real angels, our n-n-nurses, and they worked damn hard. Looked after me a t-t-treat, they did.'

'Were you wounded, may I ask?'

Fred coughed again. 'Just the gas. And me nerves. Had a rough t-t-time of it for a while. We all did. Went back to the front line after me first hospital stay but ended up flat on me b-b-back again. Then back to the front, managed for a couple of months, got another d-d-dose and that was it. Me CO said send this man home, he's done his bit. 'Course, getting work with a d-d-duff chest isn't easy. I can labour all right, it's just getting these b-b-blimmin' farmers round here to give me a go, that's all. What I wouldn't give for half a ch-ch-chance! But you don't want to hear about all that. I'm here to tell you about your son, not moan on about meself!'

Andrew, Lachie and Joseph came in at dinnertime. By then Jeannie and Keely, and Lucy and the children, who had all gone into town to visit James, had arrived home as well.

311

James had seemed more relaxed, Lucy said, after a spell in the company of other returned soldiers also attempting to come to terms with their war experiences. In fact, James seemed so improved that Duncan had consented to sit on his knee for ten minutes, a treat he didn't bestow on just anyone.

They were all surprised to find that Kenmore had a visitor but welcomed Fred, who had accepted Tamar's invitation to stay a few nights. Despite his stutter, he charmed the women — except for Keely, who couldn't be charmed by anyone. Andrew thought he was decent enough, although he said to Tamar later he wished the man wasn't quite so ingratiating, and even Joseph came to the conclusion that Fred was probably a reasonable enough bloke. He had interrogated the younger man — just to make sure, he said to Andrew the next day, he was who he said he was — but Fred had provided so much detail about army life and conditions in France it was clear he'd been there. Joseph did, however, raise his eyebrows when he claimed he'd been awarded the Military Cross but had given it away in a moment of drunken largesse in Wellington shortly after his honourable discharge from the army.

After several days, Andrew offered Fred a temporary job on the station, doing odd jobs and helping to move stock. Although he was accommodated in one of the shearers' huts, which were much more than just shacks and actually quite comfortable, he'd take his evening meal up at the big house and tell stories of Ian's popularity and his heroic exploits on the Somme. Everyone soon realised he was offering the same yarns over and over again, just changing the dates and locations now and then, but no one minded: he'd obviously had a tough time of it and the talking seemed to be having a cathartic effect. He still struggled to control his emotions when he spoke about the mates he'd lost in France, but his debilitating stutter had improved markedly.

Surprisingly, it was Andrew who didn't want Fred to move on, perhaps seeing in him a tenuous, final link to Ian; Tamar was usually the more sentimental of the pair. Andrew had in fact been more than charitable, giving Fred several more items of clothing and a pair of perfectly good if slightly unfashionable boots to tide him over, and discreetly slipping him money so he could go into town and buy himself a set of decent clothes that fitted him properly.

Once she had heard all of Fred's stories about Ian, and satisfied herself that her son had not suffered before he died, Tamar seemed to become less interested and even slightly suspicious. There was definitely something not right about the man and she was beginning to think he could in fact be suffering from the same sort of problems as James. She did not begrudge him sitting at the Kenmore dining table every night, but she felt uneasy and suggested privately to Andrew that it might be more prudent if he ate his dinner with the rest of the station hands. Otherwise there would be talk, she said, and perhaps even ill-feeling.

'I really can't explain it,' she said when Andrew pressed her about her increasingly negative attitude one evening.

'It's just that this is so unlike you,' Andrew replied. 'The chap's down on his luck, he's had a difficult time of it, and he seems to be doing so well here. Well, that awful stutter of his has disappeared, anyway. And he was close to Ian, after all.'

Tamar gazed at her husband with a look that somehow managed to combine tenderness with exasperation. 'He *knew* Ian, darling, but I'm not quite so sure now how *close* he was to him.'

'What do you mean? Are you saying he's making it all up?'

'No, of course not. It's just that he's been here a good few weeks now and he's told us all about Ian and we more or less know what happened. Well, as much as I want to know, anyway. And he seems to be feeling better so I just think it's time he moved on. He can't live here. And James will be back next week. I'm not sure it would be wise for him to still be here then. I hope you're not disappointed, but I am starting to feel quite strongly about this.'

Andrew was disappointed. He had come to like Fred. 'It's just a bit of a surprise, that's all. You're usually the first to open your arms to waifs and strays.'

'Yes, well, I've opened my arms to this one, and now I'm closing them,' Tamar replied sharply, and looked away to avoid seeing the hurt expression she knew would be on Andrew's face. She couldn't bring herself to tell him that

Joseph, too, was having doubts about Fred Wilkes.

There was nothing he could put his finger on, Joseph had confided to her several days ago, and there was no way of proving the truth of Fred's claims unless specific enquiries were made to the army. And Joseph didn't think that that would be fair. But he had a bad feeling about the whole business now, and was very worried that Andrew had taken such a shine to Fred — mainly, he suspected, because of his alleged association with Ian.

★ ★ ★

When James came home the following week he seemed much improved, although still somewhat on edge. He'd put on weight, didn't head straight for the brandy the minute he was in the door, smiled easily and even laughed once or twice. He seemed genuinely pleased to be reunited with Lucy and Duncan, and the little boy no longer hung back and hid in fear behind his mother's skirts.

But Tamar had been right — James didn't appreciate Fred Wilkes' presence at all. From the moment they met, James was ill at ease.

One evening, in the study with Andrew, James declared, 'He gives me the willies, Da. Don't know why, he just does.'

Andrew admonished him gently. 'He was one of the last people to see your brother alive, James, we can't forget that.'

James leant forward in his chair, two bright

315

spots of colour on his cheeks. 'We can actually, you know, if we try hard enough. You can't go on living Ian's life through someone else. He was killed in France, a year and a half ago. He's dead, we all know it, and nothing — no one's stories, no one's memories, and certainly not any pointless bloody *wishing* — will bring him back, all right?'

He sat back and watched as his father's face went grey. 'I'm sorry, Da. Keeping Wilkes on isn't going to change anything — Ian will still be gone, and you'll still have to come to terms with that. That's what's bothering you, isn't it? The fact that Ian really has gone?'

Andrew nodded jerkily, unable to speak.

'Oh, Da,' said James with weary compassion. He moved over to put his arms around his father, the young man comforting the old. 'I know it's hard,' he sighed. 'I know.'

It was decided by general consensus that Fred should be asked, as gently as possible, to move on within the next week or so.

He was very understanding about it, and at dinner that night expressed his gratitude to them all for the time he had spent at Kenmore and the generosity and support he had been shown during his stay. He declared that he'd already decided it was time for him to be going: he planned to leave on the afternoon of the welcome home social. When Andrew suggested he postpone his departure until after the event, because it might be good for him to meet some of the men he'd served with, he demurred politely. He wasn't sure if he was ready to see any of the lads yet.

'They're the heroes, not me,' he said. 'I don't really deserve to be there.'

'What about your Military Cross?' James asked, and immediately received an extremely withering glare from Andrew.

James gazed fixedly back at his father, but not before he'd glimpsed a hint of something close to fear in Fred's eyes.

★ ★ ★

The social was held on a fine March Saturday. Mrs Heath had loaded up the seat of the station truck with plates of food made especially for the event — cakes and sandwiches and cold meat, and coloured jelly for the children — while Tamar, Andrew, Jeannie and Keely arranged themselves in the car. Everyone else was to go in the truck, which Lachie would drive.

Tamar, Jeannie and Lucy had been at the school since lunchtime, helping the local ladies to decorate the big classroom with ponga fronds cut from the bush and an enormous hand-painted banner that read 'Welcome Home Sons, Brothers and Husbands of the Tutaekuri District'. It was suspended above the makeshift stage, where the band would set up and the dignitaries would sit during the speeches and the presentation.

The women had returned home at four to get themselves ready and were now in their finery. Keely insisted on wearing her burgundy suit and, according to Tamar, too much make-up for

317

someone who wasn't working in a brothel, but she refused to change into anything lighter or more festive. Tamar herself wore a dress in pale rose silk — nothing too grand as there would be all sorts of people at the event, including those who couldn't afford lovely clothes — with gloves and a small matching hat. Lucy wore a new mauve outfit Tamar had made for her the week before, and Jeannie was in a rust-coloured skirt and cream blouse. James and Joseph wore their service uniforms, and Lachie and Andrew had put on their second-best suits. Liam and Duncan were in their best clothes, although Tamar knew they would both be coated with jelly and a wide range of other foods before the evening was even halfway through. Blankets had been packed in the hope that they might be coerced into going to sleep in the car at their customary bedtime, but no one had high hopes of that.

Fred had packed his rucksack and was standing on the front steps at Kenmore waiting to wave them all good-bye before he left. He looked a forlorn little figure in clothes that were too big for him and with the dark smudges under his eyes that had never gone away, despite plenty of restful sleep and good food over the past weeks. Andrew looked very uncomfortable, but neither Keely nor Lucy even looked in Fred's direction. Lucy was too excited at the prospect of a night out with her handsome husband, and Keely, as usual, was too absorbed in herself to notice anyone else.

As the car turned down the driveway, Tamar glanced back at the house and saw that the truck hadn't started after them yet. Instead, James had jumped down from the back and was approaching Fred. He said something that caused Fred to step back, clutching his rucksack to his chest, and shake his head violently. Then James grabbed the other man's arm and marched him roughly over to the truck. There was another terse exchange of words and James pushed Fred, hard. He turned and, very reluctantly it seemed, put one foot on the tailgate and James gave him an almighty shove so that he shot into the back of the truck.

Tamar was mystified and uneasy. When they arrived at the school, everyone jumped out of the truck. James had a firm hold of Fred's sleeve, and was half leading, half pushing him up the steps when Tamar stopped him.

'What on earth do you think you're doing?' she hissed, appalled at her son's loutish behaviour.

James pulled Fred around to face her. The man looked extremely nervous. Tamar wasn't surprised; James was almost twice his size.

James said brightly, 'I thought Fred here really should see some of his old mates before he hits the road again. He might never get another chance, and we all know how strong the bonds are between fighting men, don't we, Fred old *mate?*' At this he administered another little shove.

'James, let him go,' Tamar snapped.

'When we're inside,' James replied just as tersely, and propelled Fred through the door.

Trestle tables had been arranged around the

walls, and many of them were already full. The social seemed to be well under way — there were bottles of beer aplenty and the air was hazy with cigarette smoke. The band had started but was easing into their repertoire with a medley of rather staid renditions of popular patriotic songs; the real dance music would came later after the speeches and the presentations, and also after the somewhat elderly band members had availed themselves of the free beer that was their fee.

The Kenmore party found themselves two empty tables and pushed them together. Fred was ushered into a seat by James and handed a bottle of beer, which he didn't open; he was too busy gazing desperately around the rapidly filling room.

Keely lit a cigarette — she had smoked almost constantly since she'd come home — and noted disdainfully, 'It's all a bit, well, *rural*, isn't it? Nothing like London.'

James, half an eye still on Fred, said, 'Well, we *are* rural people, Keely, and you used to be really proud of that. And thank God this isn't London, or we'd have been bombed to buggery by now.'

Keely raised one eyebrow, shrugged and looked away. This was all so very different from her experiences overseas, and even in Wellington. There was no excitement here, no sense of urgency and, worst of all, no men. Or, more to the point, not a *specific* man.

The band wound up 'It's a Long Way to Tipperary' and were moving their instruments back to make room for a row of chairs being carried onto the stage. These were followed by a line of representatives from various local war work and welfare committees who teetered up the narrow steps at one side of the platform and sat down self-importantly. A small folding table was also produced and on it were laid a stack of small black velvet boxes and a pile of official-looking certificates.

The mayor stood, cleared his throat loudly and clapped his hands briskly. No one took any notice, so he borrowed a drumstick and struck a cymbal a ringing blow. As the chatter gradually died down, the mayor began a lengthy speech, praising the hard work that been done by various committees in the area, the fundraising, the personal sacrifices made by all those involved. The expressions on the faces of many of the returned men ranged from sceptical to distinctly sour.

The veterans were called in alphabetical order. The first walked with a very stiff-legged gait and the aid of a stick, and seemed to take ages to get up the low steps. The second was helped by a friend, and it was soon horribly obvious that he was blind. The two who followed seemed physically unharmed, although one had hands which shook so much that he dropped his velvet box. No one in the hall made a sound. The man who came after him had one arm missing above the elbow and the other above the wrist; he smiled apologetically at the mayor when it became mortifyingly clear that he would have nowhere to wear his watch.

The names continued. Tamar felt her throat constrict and she swallowed painfully. This wasn't at all the joyous homecoming everyone had anticipated, but a sad and tragic line of shuffling, damaged young men who would bear the scars of their military service for the rest of their lives.

The next man to go up had a dreadfully burnt head and face.

To Tamar's horror, Duncan piped up in his clear, loud, little boy's voice. 'Nan, why's that man got no ears? Nan? He's got no ears. Why not?'

Tamar grabbed him and hugged him against her side to shut him up. 'Shush,' she whispered, praying his voice hadn't carried up to the stage. 'He's been in an accident, that's all.'

Duncan's muffled voice came from under her arm. 'But he looks funny, Nan. He's all *shiny*.'

Lucy scooped Duncan up and hurried him outside before he could say anything else.

The last man to be called was another amputee, whose artificial leg thumped hollowly as he awkwardly mounted the steps. A wide and ragged scar ran all the way down one side of his face and twisted what had obviously once been very handsome features. He was also very drunk. At the top of the steps he swivelled clumsily and lurched over to the mayor, who was extending a congratulatory hand and smiling welcomingly.

'Frank Wilson,' he began, 'in recognition of your service to King and country in France on the Western Front, we of the . . . '

He tailed off as Frank Wilson leant forward unsteadily and said something inaudible.

'I beg your pardon?' said the mayor, a deeply

322

shocked expression on his face.

Reaching for the table to steady himself, Frank Wilson repeated, significantly louder this time, 'I said, fuck the Western Front, and fuck the King.'

There was a gasp from the crowd, followed by a deep silence.

Frank Wilson then turned to face his audience and announced loudly, 'And fuck all of you sitting at home on your fat arses thinking you had a hard war, because you fucking well didn't. We had the hard war,' he added, pointing at the other returned men dotted about the hall, 'we had it, not you bastards moaning on about the price of fucking butter and how knackered you got doing all that fundraising. It's *my* leg and balls that are still in the mud in France, so don't tell me about how fucking hard *your* war was!' His voice cracked on the last word, and he raised his hand slowly to his face as if to make sure it was still there. He stood for a moment like that, then mumbled, 'And you can keep your wristwatch and your certificate, because it wasn't worth it.'

James was on his feet and had moved across the floor towards the stage. When Frank Wilson swayed dangerously, he bounded up the steps and put his arm around him. 'Come on mate, let's get you down, eh?'

Wilson looked at James blearily. 'Who the fuck are you?'

'Captain Murdoch, 1st Brigade, 2nd Battalion. You're all right now, come and sit down.'

Wilson nodded, then in a gesture that almost

323

broke Tamar's heart, he reached out and held James's hand and allowed himself to be helped down the steps and over to the Kenmore table. He was stared at briefly, then everyone started talking at once, and up on the stage the chairs were hurriedly removed so the band could start up again.

Frank Wilson sat down heavily and put his face in his hands. Close up his scar was quite grotesque, and Tamar unconsciously fingered the very fine white line at her temple.

What occurred next happened so quickly she couldn't initially comprehend what was going on.

Wilson looked up and suddenly spied Fred. 'What the fuck are *you* doing here, you thieving little shit!' he bellowed, and lunged across the table.

Fred scooted backwards and as Wilson lurched to his feet and grabbed at him his chair tipped over and he hit the floor. Wilson, his artificial leg conspiring with his inebriation to knock him off balance, followed, landing heavily on top of Fred and throwing wild punches as he went down. Everyone leapt back from the table and James reached to drag him off.

'No!' Wilson screamed, 'this is the little bastard who was stealing off the *lads*!'

'What?' demanded Andrew, moving closer again.

James pulled Wilson upright as Fred scrabbled away on his hands and knees. Wilson howled, 'He was thieving off everyone in camp, at Trentham. Got kicked out. Fucking good job

324

too,' he added, and took a wild swinging kick at Fred with his artificial leg.

Andrew asked quietly, 'He was in France though, wasn't he?'

Wilson spat in disgust. 'France? He's never been out of bloody New Zealand. Goes around conning people, says he knew their dead sons. He's wanted, he is.'

Andrew was rigid with shock until James shoved him out of the way in his hurry to get to Fred. He snatched the little man up by the collar and dragged him outside, knocking over chairs and a table as he went.

Tamar looked over to Joseph for help, but he just shook his head almost imperceptibly, righted his chair and calmly sat down again, indicating that everyone else should do the same. Tamar, her face white with shock and fury, sat down next to Andrew, and took his hand, stroking it gently and murmuring words to him that only he could hear.

Outside, while the band played a lively rendition of 'Pack Up Your Troubles in Your Old Kit Bag', James spun Fred around and punched him full in the mouth.

'That's for my mother and father,' he grunted, then lashed out again. 'And that's for the rest of my family.' Fred collapsed onto the ground but James pulled him up again and delivered one final blow. 'And that's for Ian. Now fuck off and never *ever* show your face around here again!'

17

Keely, wearing her gardening ensemble of an old pair of her father's trousers, a baggy knitted jersey with holes in the elbows and a scarf covering her unwashed hair, was loitering in the hall one morning just in case the postman decided to bring the mail up to the house, when she was startled by the sharp rap of the door knocker. Oblivious to the fact that she had a smear of dirt on her chin and that there was a snail inching its way up her sleeve, she leapt to the door and yanked it open.

Standing there was a man in his late twenties wearing a modest suit — although his shirt was open at the neck and he was without a tie — and holding a brown felt trilby hat in one hand. The other was jammed into his trouser pocket.

'Good morning,' he said in a deep and rather pleasant voice. 'Excuse me, I'm sorry to bother you, but I was hoping to speak to Mr and Mrs Andrew Murdoch. Do I have the correct address?'

Keely stared at him, her sense of disappointment written all over her face.

'If I haven't,' he continued, less confidently now, 'perhaps you could direct me to the right place? It's about the Murdoch's son, Ian. He and I served together in France.' The features of the stunning but rather sulky-looking young woman in the doorway immediately contorted into an expression of pure rage and he took a quick step back.

'Oh, bugger *off!*' she shouted at him. 'Go on, get out of it. We're sick of bloody shysters like you!' And she slammed the door in his face.

'Well,' he said to himself, standing alone on the steps and thinking it was a good job he hadn't taken the liberty of pointing out that there was a snail on her shoulder.

He took a measured breath and knocked again.

The girl opened the door a second time. The snail was on her collar now. 'What!' she snapped.

'Look,' the man said reasonably, 'if this is the Murdoch residence, could I please speak to either Mr or Mrs Murdoch? I don't mind waiting.'

Keely shut the door again and went to the bottom of the stairs.

'Da?' she yelled crossly. '*Da!* There's a man here saying he knew Ian. I've told him to go away but he won't.'

When her father appeared, she stomped away down the hall, muttering to herself.

Andrew hesitated at the top of the stairs, a sick feeling of anxiety stirring in his belly. He wasn't sure what to do: it would be rude to send a visitor away without even speaking to him, but he couldn't face another impostor pretending to have known Ian. He descended the stairs slowly, getting a good grip on his thoughts and his fears, and opened the door.

'Yes?' he asked the personable-looking young

327

man on the porch. 'How can I help you?' At least this one was clean, he noted.

'Good morning, sir. Would you be Mr Andrew Murdoch?'

Andrew nodded curtly.

'Oh, good.' When the man removed his right hand from his pocket and offered it, Andrew saw that the last two fingers and half of the middle finger were missing. 'My name is Owen Morgan. I served with Ian in France. I was passing through so I thought I might stop in and, well, if there was anything you might like to know about Ian, perhaps . . . '

He stopped. Mr Murdoch had a look on his face that suggested he was struggling with immense anger or profound hurt. Or perhaps it was both. This wasn't the reception he'd expected, but then grief did funny things to people.

'Look, I'm sorry if I've come at a bad time,' he said. 'If you'd rather, I could write to you in a few months. Or not at all, if you'd prefer.'

Andrew stared for a moment longer, then folded his arms defensively.

'Don't think me rude, please,' he said, 'but I wonder if you've got some sort of evidence. To, er, prove that you knew Ian, perhaps. We've had a spot of bother recently and, well, frankly we're just not prepared to go through all that again.'

Owen Morgan looked surprised, and somewhat mystified. 'Well, there's this,' he replied and reached into his jacket pocket, felt around for a second then handed Andrew a square of dog-eared card.

Glued to it was a rather curled-up and worn photograph of Owen and Ian standing together in uniform outside the *estaminet* in Etaples on the night of their leave there, with their arms around each other and silly, self-conscious grins on their faces.

Andrew gazed at it for almost a minute, then rubbed his thumb gently over the image of his dead son. He looked up.

'Come in Mr Morgan, please.'

★   ★   ★

He was asked to go into extraordinary detail, he felt, to prove he had indeed served with Ian, and that he'd been there when he'd died. But, after hearing the story of Fred Wilkes, he wasn't in the least surprised or resentful towards the Murdochs. They — in particular James and the dark chap called Joseph, the half-brother obviously, who was watching him like a hawk — asked him over and over again the dates of his service in France, exactly where his battalion had been and what they had done there, the names of other men in Ian's company and on and on. He suspected his story wasn't totally accepted, however, until Mrs Murdoch excused herself and came back with Liam.

Owen's long face softened. 'He's the image of his father, isn't he? I had no idea Ian was married, though,' he said in genuine surprise as he watched the boy playing happily on the floor. 'He certainly never mentioned a wife

329

and child.' He looked up at them all. 'Why on earth not, I wonder?'

A look passed around the room and there was an almost palpable easing of tension, leaving Owen with the distinct impression he had just passed some sort of test.

Mrs Murdoch, an extremely handsome woman and exactly as Ian had described her, said, 'He wasn't married, Mr Morgan. Liam is his illegitimate son. Ian was never even aware of his existence, and neither were we until he was deposited here the day after we held a memorial service for his father.'

'Do you know who the mother is?' Owen asked her, then immediately wondered if the question was perhaps a little indiscreet.

'No. She's never contacted us, and I sincerely hope she never does. Well, at least not while Liam is so young anyway. A child needs stability in his early years, and it wouldn't be in his best interests for his mother to appear out of the blue and want him back.'

Owen recalled the story about Tamar Murdoch's own illegitimate son, who was now sitting opposite her and smiling indulgently down at the boy on the floor, and understood immediately the hint of sadness beneath her words.

'Yes, I expect you're right,' he agreed.

'And you're a married man yourself, Mr Morgan?' she asked politely.

'Me? No, I'm afraid not,' he replied, and his gaze slid towards the girl who had initially answered the door. She looked back at him rather disdainfully.

She had been introduced to him as Keely Murdoch, Ian's sister. She had changed out of her tatty old pants, in which Owen thought she had looked very fetching, but surely this surly young woman couldn't be the vivacious, fun-loving creature Ian had so fondly described? She was certainly her mother's daughter in terms of looks, but there was a sense of such disillusionment about her. But then Owen remembered that she had served overseas as a nurse.

Tamar watched Owen watching Keely, and wondered. He clearly liked what he saw, although Keely just as blatantly didn't. She had always attracted the admiring attentions of men, but since her return home she hadn't shown the slightest interest in anyone. Tamar doubted that Owen Morgan would change all that. He was entirely unsuitable as a match for Keely, or at least he would be as far as her daughter was concerned. True, he was educated — he must be if he had been a school-teacher before the war — and he really was rather attractive, but he obviously wasn't a wealthy man. Above all he didn't seem to be at all *outgoing*. Confident and self-assured, yes, but in a quiet and steady way, not at all the flashy and smooth type of man who normally appealed to Keely.

She told herself not to be such a silly interfering old mother, but heard herself saying, 'Keely, offer Mr Morgan some more cake. Or perhaps you would prefer a pikelet, Mr Morgan?'

'Both, please,' he responded enthusiastically. 'And please called me Owen.' Keely stood up and, with her fingers, plonked a piece of cake on a plate together with the most thinly buttered pikelet she could find and ungraciously thrust the lot at Owen.

Tamar drew in a quick breath, shocked and embarrassed by her daughter's dreadful lack of manners. Lucy and Jeannie looked appalled, and so did Andrew.

'Keely!' he admonished. 'Whatever's got into you?'

'Nothing,' she replied, not looking at him. Knowing she had gone too far and to hide her own embarrassment, she lifted the lid off the big silver teapot and mumbled, 'We've run out of tea, I'll ask Mrs Heath to make some more.'

When she'd rushed out of the room, Tamar said, 'I'm terribly sorry, Owen, you must think us the most absolutely awful family. She's not usually so rude . . . '

Someone muttered, 'Yes she is' — James or Joseph, Tamar wasn't quite quick enough to detect the culprit. She was even more annoyed when Lachie snorted into his cup of tea, but she refused to be deterred.

'As I was *saying*, Keely isn't usually this, well, prickly, she's normally a very charming young lady, but she's not long been home herself and she hasn't quite been able to put it all behind her yet. Well, of course, you yourself will know how it is for returned servicemen and women. And then there was Ian. Losing him was an awful blow to all of us.'

Jeannie picked Liam up off the floor and carried him out.

Owen waited, then replied, 'Oh, I quite understand, please don't apologise. It can take a very long time to settle back into civilian life. And Ian, well, his death devastated us, so I can only imagine what it must have done to you as his family.'

There was a brief silence, then Andrew asked, 'Do you, ah, do you know the details of his actual death? The telegram we received didn't say much, they don't, you know, and the letter from your captain said he'd died a hero, but then I expect they all say that.' He turned to Tamar for confirmation, and because he needed to know she was near him if they were finally to be told how their son had died. 'We do want to know, dear, don't we? What really happened?'

Tamar's knuckles whitened around the handle of her teacup until Andrew was afraid it would shatter in her hand. Finally she said, 'Yes, we do.'

They all turned to look at Owen, and suddenly he wished he hadn't come. He put his plate down carefully and cleared his throat.

'He drowned. He was trying to rescue a pair of horses from a flooded shell crater, and he drowned. We got a rope in but it was too late. I'm so sorry, but there just wasn't anything we could do.'

And there's sod-all else I can say, too, he reflected sadly.

Tamar and Andrew were holding hands, as if they too were drowning. Andrew nodded slowly. 'And is he — is his body — still there?'

Owen nodded, his face despondent. 'Yes. So many men died on the Somme it was impossible to retrieve them. And the terrain, it was so completely and utterly changed by the time we withdrew. We had a full service for him though, and everyone who could be was there. And we all drank to him on our next leave.' He paused for a moment, then looked around at the faces gazing intently back at him and added, 'He was a good boy, your Ian, and he loved you all very much.'

Andrew sat in silence, then put his hand over his mouth so that when he did speak his voice was muffled. 'He ran away, you know, to join the army.'

'Yes, I know, he said. And he said he wished he hadn't done it like that.'

'Did he still think he'd made the right choice, though? Going off to the war like that?'

'Oh yes, he always believed he'd done the right thing. And he believed he was doing the right thing when he was trying to get those horses out, too. They were terrified, you see, and he couldn't bear it.'

James said, 'He was always good with the horses.' He looked Owen in the eye, veteran to veteran. 'Was he a good soldier?'

Owen held his gaze. 'One of the best,' he replied simply and truthfully.

'Good.' James' tone implied that the discussion about Ian was now closed. He nodded at Owen's maimed right hand. 'Did you get that on the Somme?'

'No, Messines, last June.'

'Shell?'

'Indirectly. One landed in the dugout next door and I copped a piece of flying metal. Had a month or so in the hospital while it healed and then the MO in his wisdom said I'd be useless with a rifle, so I was sent home.'

'Can you use one now?'

'A rifle? Of course, it was only a matter of practice. Been shooting rabbits quite successfully for the last couple of months.'

Lachie and Andrew looked at each other.

'Did you want to stay on? In France?' Joseph asked.

Owen shook his head with undisguised vehemence. 'No I didn't, frankly. I'd had just about enough by then.'

Joseph nodded and something passed between him, James and Owen, something that excluded everyone else in the room and that was all right.

* * *

'I think young Owen's taken a wee bit of a shine to Keely,' Andrew said to Tamar the following week as they were getting ready for bed.

He was sitting on the edge of the mattress trying not to let Tamar see how stiff his back was as he bent down to tug off his socks; he'd spent almost the whole day in the saddle and his old bones were protesting mightily. However, as he watched Tamar slipping a soft, lace-trimmed crêpe de Chine nightdress over her head — her arms up and a standard lamp behind her emphasising her shapely silhouette — he was very pleased to note that other parts of his anatomy were still working, and rather impressively, too, if he did say so himself. He pulled on his own nightshirt and eased himself into bed, turning down the blankets for Tamar when she had finished her evening toilette. He never knew why she bothered with all that greasy cream — she was beautiful enough without it.

'Yes, dear, I think you might be right,' she said as she examined her face minutely in her dressing-table mirror. She definitely had wrinkles now, she noted resignedly — there was absolutely no doubt.

Andrew chuckled as he fluffed his pillows. 'You spotted it almost straightaway, didn't you?'

Tamar turned to look at him and smiled fondly. 'Well, yes, of course I did. A woman notices that sort of thing, especially when it's her own daughter.'

'Well, you've certainly got to admire the man's courage. I hope he's prepared to be disappointed, though, you know how trying Keely's been since she came home. Can't say she'd be much of a prize either, given her current state of mind.'

'Andrew, that's a very unkind thing to say about your own daughter!'

'Aye, but it's true though, isn't it? She's been positively poisonous.'

Andrew knew that Keely had come home at least in part because of some business with a man, although he'd not been told the more intimate details. He thought she'd become exhausted by her work, had fallen prey to some predatory and unscrupulous man and had been returned home for her own safety, a course of action he thoroughly approved of.

'Yes, she has been a trial hasn't she? But she's so obviously unhappy, Andrew, we must try and see her point of view.'

'About what?' Andrew grumped. 'She did a sterling job over there and I have no doubt at all it was all very harrowing and demanding, but now she's home safe and sound so why is she still upset?'

Tamar returned to the mirror and began to brush out her long hair. 'I'm sure she's experienced things you and I can't even imagine, darling. I don't think we'll ever really know what she went through, and perhaps that's a blessing. It's the same for James and Joseph, and it will be for Thomas when he comes home too. We just have to be patient and offer them our support, and hope they can come to terms with it in their own time.' She turned to him again. 'Look at James, he's getting on very well now, and Joseph has settled down marvellously. You'd hardly even know he has an artificial leg.'

'Except for when he takes it off,' Andrew muttered. 'You can sort of tell then.'

'Oh, don't be so negative! He's adapted really well, don't you think?'

'Yes, I suppose so,' Andrew agreed grudgingly, because Joseph really did seem to be getting back into the swing of things.

'And yes, I have noticed the way Owen looks at Keely, but I've also noticed the way she looks back at him, as if she's stepped in something the cat has done on the lawn.'

Andrew laughed out loud at this. 'She does have a way of putting you in your place with just a glance, doesn't she?'

'Unfortunately yes. But I don't see much evidence of Owen being put off by it. I think he's taken the measure of Keely already. *I* think he has the gift of being able to look beneath the surface of a person at what they're really like inside, and I think he likes what he sees inside Keely very much.'

Owen had approached Andrew and Lachie privately about the possibility of some short-term work at Kenmore, and they had accepted his offer immediately. He rode well, knew farming, did indeed shoot adequately in spite of his missing fingers and didn't mind hard work. He was also very personable, had a good sense of humour and seemed to be level-headed and reliable. Even better, James and Joseph both liked him and the three of them had spent several evenings in the garden drinking beer and talking about their time overseas, and it did Tamar's heart good to see them. Owen took the occasional meal at the big house when invited, but was equally happy with his own company in one of the shearers' huts. He demanded nothing except a reasonable wage for a day's work, and gave of his best in return.

As for his interest in Keely, he'd made no overt overtures towards her but he wasn't reticent either. He seemed to enjoy watching her, even when she was in one of her moods, which only seemed to make him laugh. When he did this, however, and Keely happened to notice, she became enraged and more often than not flounced off with her face burning and a selection of very unladylike words on her pouting lips.

★ ★ ★

Keely was in the daffodil paddock behind the house. Even when there weren't any blooms she liked to come up here to get away from the rest of the family. She loved Duncan and Liam dearly, but sometimes they drove her almost mad with their incessant noise. Sometimes, she wished she had taken the offer of work at Napier Hospital, but then she wasn't at all sure if she could have coped with wounded soldiers again either. Life at Kenmore was stifling and dull, but at least it wasn't stressful.

It had been eight months now since her return to New Zealand, and she hadn't heard a single word from Ross McManus. She hadn't expected she would, but by God she had hoped. She still couldn't believe how effortlessly he had let her go, but was finally coming to terms with the fact that he really hadn't cared, that, for him, she had been simply a diversion. She had heard it said that there was sometimes a very fine line between love and hate, and now she understood exactly what that meant.

'Mind if I join you?'

She jumped at the sound of Owen Morgan's voice. 'What?' she responded rudely, annoyed that her reverie had been interrupted.

'Just say if you'd rather be alone.'

Keely shrugged. 'Please yourself.'

He sat down next to her and smiled pleasantly. 'Having a break from the children?'

'Yes, I am actually. They're being particularly noisy this afternoon.'

'Mmm, children do that. It's quite common I'm told.'

Tamar looked at him sideways. 'Know a lot about children, do you?'

'No, nothing actually. Well, not ones that small anyway. When I was teaching they were all six and above. That was young enough. Don't you like children?'

Keely picked a stalk of grass and began to tear the seeds off the end of it. Owen noticed that the scowl dissolved from her face as she replied, 'Yes I do, very much in fact.'

But she certainly wasn't going to tell him that other people's children reminded her of the family she thought she would have with Ross McManus.

Owen plucked his own piece of grass. 'You know, you're a very lovely young woman when you're not frowning,' he said conversationally.

'I beg your pardon?'

'You shouldn't frown all the time. It makes you look like a constipated sheep.'

Keely leapt to her feet. 'Excuse *me*!' she said, outraged.

'Certainly. You're quite striking when you're angry though.'

She was speechless — what rudeness! She turned and marched off down the hill, a satisfyingly dramatic departure spoiled only when she shut her skirt in the paddock gate.

'Need a hand?' Owen called, smiling widely.

Keely ignored him, tore a hole in her skirt in her efforts to unsnag herself and disappeared into the house. Owen watched thoughtfully as the back door slammed behind her, then he carefully tied a knot in his piece of grass and poked the end of it back into the ground.

Unfortunately, as far as Keely was concerned at least, Owen had been invited to dinner at the big house that evening. They sat across the table from each other, he with his customary smile and she even more frosty than usual. Andrew raised his eyebrows at Tamar, who shrugged in mutual incomprehension; God only knew what had upset their daughter this time.

Owen was asking Jeannie, 'When are you expecting your daughter back?'

'We're not entirely sure yet. We received a letter about six weeks ago saying her request to come home had been accepted — she's been away for over two years now so there was no problem with that — but we haven't heard exactly when she expects to be here. We hope it's as soon as possible, of course, but we assume she would have had to wait for a ship and all that sort of thing.' She smiled warmly, and in that smile Owen could see what had attracted Lachie to her. 'She and Joseph are to be married when she finally does get home. That's why he's building the house.'

Owen knew this of course; Joseph mentioned it often enough. He glanced at Keely and said, 'You must be looking forward to your cousin coming back — between you you'll have a lot of exciting tales to tell.' He thought, but didn't say, *and some bloody awful ones too, probably.*

Lachie said, 'Yes, Erin was on the *Marquette* when it went down. She was almost drowned.'

'My God,' Owen said to Keely, genuinely concerned. 'I hadn't realised you were on the *Marquette.*'

Keely looked at her plate and answered tersely, 'I wasn't. I had a very safe war.'

Did you? Owen reflected. *Then what was it that upset you so much while you were away? What transformed you from the lively and happy girl Ian described into the sad and bitter person you are today?*

It could certainly have been the strain of nursing all those poor wounded buggers like himself, many of them a damn sight worse off than he'd been, but somehow he felt there was a lot more to it than that. There had been Ian's death, of course, and then James coming home in a state the man himself had described as a 'bloody dog's breakfast' — those two things alone would be enough to sour and depress anyone. But he had a strong suspicion that something deeply personal had so shaken the poor girl's confidence in herself that she felt compelled now to hide her true feelings behind a mask of thoroughly obnoxious behaviour. He knew from James and Joseph that she hadn't been happy ever since returning from England, and that she had come home under some kind of cloud, but neither of them had explained, and he hadn't asked.

342

But by God she was a lovely girl. She had the sort of lush and welcoming figure he and the lads had yearned for night after night as they huddled in their dugouts, shivering and stinking and wondering why the bloody hell they'd ever signed up. Clean sheets — any sheets at all, in fact — and a warm, compassionate woman had been everyone's idea of paradise. But the closest they'd ever come to either was a mean little cot in a base camp somewhere and the services of whores — pleasant enough girls in themselves, Owen had always suspected, but sharing one with a dozen other men had never been his idea of an intimate interlude. And he hadn't been with a woman since arriving home six months ago, fearing that he'd be very poor company with his rough soldiers' ways and his preference for solitude, and that any intercourse with a woman, sexual or otherwise, would be a dismal failure.

But Keely Murdoch was different. She had set his pulse racing the moment she'd opened the door. He liked a woman who didn't mince words; he couldn't stand 'society' women, or men, if it came to that. Not that he'd known many. He'd had a horrible moment when he'd walked through Kenmore's gates — would he find a family of rich, affected and arrogant squatters dressed in their fancy clothes eating those little sandwiches with no crusts and sod-all in them, and with absolutely no idea of what went on in the world around them? But then he'd remembered Ian and felt easy again — no one as open and fun-loving and as *genuine* could ever have been raised by such a family.

343

It was true, though, that the Murdochs had money — Owen would have to have been blind not to notice that. Their homestead was, if not palatial, then at least very spacious, well appointed and comfortable. The house was plumbed and there was hot water (usually), there were two separate bathrooms and flushing toilets, there was power from a generator fed by a nearby stream and electric lights, the telephone was connected and the house was very elegantly decorated.

* * *

Erin's telegram arrived the following week: she would be docking at Wellington in about a fortnight's time and expected to be at Kenmore soon after that.

Joseph enlisted everyone's help to get the house finished in time. The roof and walls had been up for months, but the interior still wasn't quite completed as Joseph had been doing most of the building himself in between his work on the station. Lachie had offered to pay someone to come out and do the bulk of the construction but Joseph had refused: he would rather do it himself, even if it did take up almost all his spare time. Lachie understood and was secretly very pleased that Joseph was so keen on making a nest for Erin and himself with his own two hands.

And the house was certainly no shearers' hut, either. Nestled in a shallow valley about a quarter of a mile away from the big house, it had four bedrooms — because, Joseph had confided self-consciously, he and Erin wanted plenty of children — spacious living and dining rooms, a kitchen, a bathroom and an indoor toilet, and a small study for sewing and bookwork. The design was quite simple, but Joseph had spared nothing on the quality of the wood he'd used. Now there was only the kitchen and bathroom joinery to complete, the new stove to install and the interior of the house to furnish. But perhaps he should wait until Erin came home so she could choose the furniture, carpets and fabrics herself.

He had wondered whether Erin would want to live so near her parents, but her letters had made it quite clear she was looking forward very much to having her family around her. There had been the possibility of going to live at Maungakakari, but if Joseph was to continue working at Kenmore it made little sense to live so far away from the station. There was also the question of Erin adapting to life in a Maori community; Joseph was sure she would be happy to, but it was a hard and often very mean life, and he didn't want to subject her to that. Kepa agreed, having finally accepted that if his son was never going to be a famous politician, then he could do far worse than marrying Erin McRae and one day possibly managing Kenmore.

In fact, as a wedding present, Kepa had commissioned a very talented carver at Maungakakari to fashion an intricate, paua-inlaid wooden mantelpiece for the living room of his son's new home. The carver was Ihaka's older brother, a coincidence that made the gift even more poignant.

Joseph's building efforts had also reaped another, quite unexpected benefit. While chatting with the local miller one day he was introduced to a type of native wood called *whau*, as light as balsa and very easy to shape. For some time now he'd been thinking about what to do about his artificial leg. Both it and his spare limb were extremely heavy: more than once when he'd swung himself out of the saddle the momentum had thrown him flat on his back. And the complex arrangements of leather straps and buckles that attached the prosthesis to his body were not only irritating and restrictive, but failed to hold his leg on particularly well. He frequently fell over because his stump had slipped out of the socket in the artificial leg, which was extremely painful and moderately embarrassing. Now he managed to fashion himself a new leg out of *whau* that was much lighter, easier to wear and gave him more mobility, and didn't need so much strapping to keep it in place.

He was very pleased with it. In fact he was very pleased with life in general. He had come home from the war intact enough to live a fairly normal life, he had a good job doing what he loved, he was near his family, he had a new house and, best of all, his beautiful Erin was coming home.

18

June 1918

Oblivious to the wet grass, Erin sat down suddenly on the hillside and burst into copious, noisy tears. Holding out her hand to him, she said, 'Oh, it's beautiful, Joseph, it's just beautiful.'

They were looking down on their new home, and Erin thought she'd never seen anything more welcoming and wonderful in her life.

She'd arrived home too late the night before to make the short walk across the paddocks to see the new house. And no one would tell her anything about it: they'd all just sat around smiling hugely and conspiratorially, relishing the anticipation of her pleasure.

She was utterly exhausted — she had worked almost non-stop on the hospital ship all the way back to New Zealand — but nothing would keep her from visiting the house this morning. Instead of the little cottage she'd imagined, though, here was this rather splendid new home with big double-hung windows, a fancy front door, two chimneys, a verandah and a garden seat, although there was no garden yet.

'There's nothing in it, no furniture I mean,' Joseph said hesitantly. 'And no carpets. I didn't know what sort of thing you might like so I thought we'd go into Napier when you've settled in and have a look around. Oh, and Mam said we can have some of the old furniture from the big house, stuff that's been in the shed since she redecorated, if we don't mind used.'

Erin was blowing her nose on her handkerchief, and had to take her hand back to do it. 'Of course we don't mind,' she said in a muffled voice. 'Do we? I certainly don't. We can sit on boxes if you like, as long as we're sitting on them together.'

Joseph laughed delightedly. 'I was hoping you'd say that. I haven't exactly made my fortune since I've been home but I've a bit put away so we can buy ourselves a few nice new things. A new bed, perhaps.'

He felt slightly nervous saying this; it had, after all, been almost two and a half years since the first, the *only*, time they had made love. What if she'd changed her mind about marrying him? She'd never indicated that in her letters, but perhaps she was only trying to spare his feelings until she could talk to him face to face?

The idea had worried him so much that the night before Erin arrived he'd had a very nasty dream in which she had come back from overseas behaving like Keely and, even worse, not wanting to marry him at all. He'd woken in a cold sweat and had had to get up and make himself a cup of cocoa. It had been even worse than the dreams he still occasionally had about still having both legs: sometimes, in his sleep, he'd get out of bed, attempt to put both legs on the ground and fall heavily, more often than not banging his stump painfully on the way down.

And last night, Erin had been so tired after her

train trip from Wellington that after a quick supper she'd fallen asleep in her chair in the parlour. Joseph had been dying to get her away from everyone else and reassure himself that she did indeed still want to become his wife, but Jeannie had woken her and bustled her upstairs and into bed, saying, while looking pointedly at Joseph, that she wasn't to be disturbed until she awoke of her own accord the following day.

Now here they were, finally alone, and Joseph was suddenly feeling tongue-tied. She didn't *look* dismayed at the idea of sharing a house — and a life — with him, but he knew that, like most good nurses, she was very good at hiding her true feelings.

He took her hand again and gazed into her huge eyes until he thought he might fall into them. Eventually, he asked tentatively, 'Those things you wrote in your letters, about us spending the rest of our lives together, well, do you still feel that way? About us getting married?'

He must have unconsciously pulled a face of some sort because Erin laughed and reached out to touch his cheek.

'That depends,' she said, 'on how you feel about it.'

'I've never wanted anything more in my life,' he said passionately.

Erin's eyes closed and she sighed. 'Oh Joseph, you've no idea how much I was hoping you'd say that. I had such terrible doubts about staying overseas so long.' She dropped her damp handkerchief and lifted her other hand to

Joseph's face. 'Knowing you were here waiting for me was the only thing that kept me going a lot of the time. I know it sounds like something you'd read in a silly romance story, but it's true. So yes, I do want to marry you, very much.'

They didn't kiss, but rested their foreheads together in silence, feeling the gentle mingling of their breath and marvelling that their dreams of each other had managed to sustain them for so long.

Erin felt weak with relief; she had been so nervous that during her long absence he might have changed his mind about marrying her but hadn't been able to tell her. She'd been tempted several times to resign from the NZANS and come home but every time she seriously considered it, another huge influx of horribly wounded young men would arrive at the hospital and she knew she was needed more where she was.

It was a decision she'd had to make by herself, too, as most of the other nurses had told her she was a fool to stay on in England when she had a young man waiting for her at home. There were far too many girls looking for husbands in New Zealand, they'd insisted, and someone would be bound to snap him up if she wasn't careful.

Then she would remind herself sternly that if she was planning to marry Joseph — and she was — then she would have to trust him even though they were thousands of miles apart. And then one day she had the strange realisation that it wasn't Joseph she needed to trust, but herself. If she did indeed lose him, would she cope?

Eventually, she decided she would, and with that came a sense of security and the knowledge that everything would work out as it was supposed to if she just let it.

But sometimes — when her eyes burned with tiredness and her back ached as she hunched over the sluice sink scrubbing blood and pus off her hands at the end of a long gruelling night shift — a mean little voice still whispered to her that she might miss out, that if she wasn't careful she might lose the man she adored and who had brought colour into a life that had once seemed flat and grey. Now, though, at home at last, she knew that voice had been banished forever.

Joseph brushed his lips across hers and murmured, 'Well, *that's* all right then, isn't it?'

'Yes. I think I'm going to cry again.'

'You can't, you've dropped your hanky in something unpleasant.'

'Oh,' said Erin, seeing that her handkerchief had indeed landed on a small cairn of sheep droppings. 'Never mind,' she laughed.

'So, when then? Tomorrow?'

She stood up and brushed the wet off the back of her skirt. 'Tomorrow would be wonderful, but I wouldn't dare rob our mothers of the opportunity to make an enormous fuss and rush about organising everything. And Mrs Heath will need time to make one of her world-famous fruitcakes — she'd be scandalised at the idea of having just an ordinary old cream sponge, it wouldn't be 'proper'. What about the beginning of July? That's only three weeks away.' She had a sudden thought. 'Oh, I'm sorry, Joseph, would you rather be married at Maungakakari? How selfish of me.'

Joseph shrugged. 'To be honest I don't really care where we're married, as long as we are. Kenmore will do, won't it? There's more than enough room.'

They joined hands and went down to the new house together, Joseph managing the slippery slope on his new leg with impressive agility. He pushed the front door open and ushered her proudly into the wide central hall, then gave her a guided tour of the home he had built for her. For *them*.

He was a little worried because it didn't look anywhere near finished yet, not in his eyes at least. Many of the walls — those that were to be papered rather than painted — were so far only covered with a layer of scrim, and much of the woodwork was still to be oiled or varnished. But Erin seemed absolutely thrilled; she smiled delightedly as he showed her through the bedrooms, the largest of them with a set of glazed doors opening out onto a planned private garden area; she nodded appreciatively when he took her through the kitchen and pointed out the new 'wetback' stove with plenty of cooking surface and a spacious oven for roasts and loaves of bread; and she admired the bathroom with its deep bath and the adjacent indoor toilet.

But the carved mantelpiece in the living room took her breath away. 'Oh, I love it, it's absolutely *beautiful*.' She turned to him and said excitedly, 'It makes this house, well, *ours* — a union of who you are and who I am. It's perfect.'

'It's a wedding present from my father, so it's fortunate you've agreed to marry me, otherwise it would just be me sitting here looking at it.'

'No, that will never happen,' she said, taking his hands. 'I want this house to be a *home*, Joseph, for your people as well as mine. It's important, for our children as well as for us. I want everyone who comes here to feel welcome.'

Joseph kissed her again. 'I know, and they will. It's part of the reason I wanted us to have our own house. I know my Maungakakari family will always be welcome at Kenmore but, well, I think they'd probably be more at ease in a house that isn't quite so grand. *Papa* will be fine of course — he's used to flitting in and out of both worlds — but perhaps not some of the others.'

'Do you think it really would bother them?'

'No, probably not but, well, not everybody at Kenmore is as open-minded as my mother.'

There was a short silence as they contemplated the likely reaction of Mrs Heath and Jeannie and Lucy to great gatherings of Joseph's relatives camping out in the Kenmore parlour on special occasions.

'No,' Erin agreed eventually, 'you're probably right. Anyway, we should have a home of our own. I much prefer the idea of just you and I together.' She looked up at him with an expression of pure happiness. 'At least until the children come, anyway.'

* * *

Everyone was in the parlour talking at once about plans for the wedding. At least, the women were — the men seemed content to sit and watch. Duncan was cantering about the room on an imaginary horse with a lace doily draped over his head, chanting loudly, 'Here comes the bride, fair, fat and *wide*.'

Lucy said, 'Duncan, that's not very nice. Aunty Erin isn't fat, wide or fair.'

'No but she's a bride, and that's what you sing for a bride,' he replied knowledgably.

'Oh aye,' said Andrew, 'and how many brides have you met?'

Duncan ignored him and cantered out into the hall, followed immediately by Liam on his own invisible mount.

Tamar eyed the loose waistband on Erin's skirt and observed, 'Actually, you've lost a lot of weight. Was the food not very good at the hospitals?'

'Oh, no, it was fine,' Erin replied, blushing slightly as everyone looked at her. 'We all ate like pigs but with all the running around I suppose we never had a chance to get fat.'

She had lost weight, and she knew it. Her hip bones stuck out now, and had for some time; she suspected she appeared thin and tired. She looked better than Keely, though. She thought her cousin looked awful, agitated and somehow defeated at the same time. Erin thought they'd all changed, to a greater or lesser degree. Both of her parents looked older, especially her mother, whose hair was starting to go quite grey. Andrew was looking positively grizzled and the lines on

Tamar's face were more noticeable than they had been three years ago. Lucy looked tired too, and poor James seemed a shadow of himself; Tamar had hinted that he still wasn't quite right. Erin wasn't surprised that he looked older, and somehow harder: his expression of wary and slightly uneasy repose was very familiar.

The only one who really hadn't changed much was Joseph, although perhaps she couldn't see it because she'd carried such a bright and burning image of him in her mind while they'd been apart. His dark hair had grown long again and he'd clearly regained the physical condition he'd lost after he'd been wounded. In fact he looked rudely strong and healthy, and she'd been delighted to see him walking on his artificial leg with a limp that was only barely noticeable. He really was such a marvellous man and she was so proud to be the one he wanted. As if he'd heard her thoughts, he looked over at her and smiled.

Jeannie, watching her daughter, smiled too. 'Well, I'm sure Mrs Heath will do something about getting the meat back on your bones, dear. You know how she likes to force-feed people if she thinks they're under the weather.'

'Oh Mum, you make me sound like a sick ewe. I'm fine, really I am. I was too heavy when we went overseas anyway — on the ship some of the girls were calling me Onion instead of Erin because of the shape of my backside,' Erin said, and grinned.

James, Andrew and Lachie laughed immoderately.

'Really? How rude,' said Tamar, although she

couldn't completely suppress her own smile.

'I hope you took no notice,' Jeannie said, feeling insulted on her daughter's behalf. 'They were probably jealous.'

Joseph came over, perched on the arm of Erin's chair and gazed adoringly down at her. 'And were they jealous of your beautiful face too? And your lovely blackbird hair and your extraordinary compassion and your wonderful personality?'

Keely made a gagging noise. Joseph looked over at her. 'What?'

'You two,' she responded impatiently. 'Do you have to be all over each other all the time? It's sick-making.'

There was an embarrassed silence, then with a barely stifled sob Keely lurched to her feet and rushed out of the parlour.

'Oh dear,' said Tamar, and got up to follow her.

Erin reached out and touched Tamar's arm. 'No Aunty Tam, I'll go. I think Keely and I need to have a talk.'

She went upstairs and knocked discreetly on her cousin's door.

'Go away!'

'Keely, it's me. I want to come in.'

Silence, then the door opened to reveal Keely's tear-splotched face. She stood back to let Erin in, then flopped heavily onto her bed.

Erin settled at Keely's feet and asked gently, 'Do you want to tell me what's going on?'

Keely rolled over and buried her face in the pillow, her tears soaking the thin cotton pillowslip.

'I'm sorry,' she blurted, her voice muffled. 'You must think me the most ungracious cow. It's not sour grapes, really it isn't, I really am very happy for you both. I think it's lovely you're getting married so quickly and I would too, if it were me. It's just that, well, it's been months now and I haven't even had, well, I thought . . . ' She burst into a renewed fit of sobbing.

Erin patted Keely's leg. 'But you know what a rotter he was, surely?'

Keely rolled back over and sat up. 'Yes, I *know* that,' she snapped, wiping her running nose inelegantly on the back of her hand. 'I know that, but I thought he might at least have got in touch.'

Erin didn't think this was the time to tell Keely he'd probably been too busy with his new girlfriend to do anything of the sort.

Instead she said, 'I can't say I know how you feel because I don't, but I can see how much it's hurting you.' She took her cousin's hand. 'But Keely, was he really worth it? All this pain?'

'Yes, he was. And I hate him for it.'

'Have you talked to your mother about how you feel?'

Keely nodded. 'Sort of. She's been quite understanding, really.' She reached into the top drawer of her nightstand, withdrew a neatly folded and ironed handkerchief and blew her nose honkingly. 'According to her, though, I'm grieving for what I thought I had, not what I really had.'

'And is she right?'

Keely shrugged. 'I can't see how she can be.

How would she know about something like that? She and Da have always been so happy together.'

'Well, yes, they have, but what about her first husband? Obviously that wasn't an ideal partnership, otherwise Joseph wouldn't have come along, would he?'

'I suppose,' Keely agreed grudgingly. 'But she still can't know what it was like for me with Ross.'

'No, she can't, but she might be able to help you put the whole thing behind you. It's about time, Keely. After all, it's been nearly a year now.'

'Oh,' said Keely acidly, 'I hadn't realised there was a time after which a person's broken heart should suddenly be mended.'

Erin took a deep, measured breath. 'Being sarcastic won't help anyone.'

Keely's shoulders suddenly slumped dejectedly. 'I know, I'm sorry.'

She blew her nose again then took a few deep breaths herself before looking Erin directly in the eye.

'The thing is, I really don't know *what's* wrong with me. For a long time it *was* Ross, and the embarrassment of being sent home and all that, but I think I've come to terms with that now — well, with the fact that I'll never be with him. As you've said at least a hundred times, I'd have to be deaf and blind not to realise what a swine he was. No, it's more than that. I just can't seem to *settle*. I know I said when we were at Brockenhurst that I was finding it hard to look after sick soldiers day in and day out, and I was. It was really depressing me there for a while. And then Ross came along and it all seemed so much more bearable. I had something to look forward to every day then, and when one of the patients died, the fact that I had someone to talk to, someone who wanted to spend time just with me, made me feel not quite so useless. I always felt so insignificant whenever we lost one of the men. Oh, I know we all did the best we could, and looking back I'm amazed that we didn't lose more, but I just felt it was always ultimately hopeless.' She stared down at her hands, clenched together in her lap. 'They just kept on coming and coming, didn't they? Day in and day out, no legs, arms missing, paralysed, blind, hurt and crying and frightened. And I couldn't deal with it, in the end. And then when I came home, I found I really missed it all and I realised that I, we, *all* of us who were there, really had been making a difference.' She laughed, and it came out as a sob. 'That's funny, isn't it? I wasn't any good at it, but I really missed it when it was gone. And now my life feels empty and pointless and unbelievably boring and no matter how hard I try all I seem to be able to do is grump and snap and irritate people. Some days, *most* days, I dread getting out of bed because I just can't see the point.'

Erin sighed. 'Oh Keely, of course you were a good nurse. I think that was one of the reasons Matron was so angry with you, because she had no choice but to send you home after what happened, and she really didn't want to lose you. But she couldn't have let you stay, not after everybody found out about you and Ross.

Between the pair of you, you broke just about every rule in the book. You do see that, don't you?'

'Of course I see it, Erin, I'm not completely stupid. It's just that I seem to have lost all of my self-confidence and I just can't pull myself together. I know I should, but I can't,' she finished lamely.

It was beginning to occur to Erin that poor Keely might be suffering from some sort of nurses' version of delayed shell shock. Or was it delayed? Had she in fact been having problems at Brockenhurst but everybody had been too busy to notice?

'Have you talked to James about this?' she asked. 'Or Joseph? I'm sure they'd understand.'

'No, I didn't want to bother James. He had to go into hospital recently, did you know? For a rest. And, well, I felt too silly to talk to Joseph about it. Here he is, a leg missing and he's doing so well — riding and back at work and building your house and all that — and here's me not even able to get up in the mornings or speak to anyone with a civil tongue when everyone's been so kind to me. Of course, I've only told Mam the real reason I came home. I'm sure Da thinks I was sent back to protect my virtue or something old-fashioned like that.' She sighed heavily. 'God, what am I going to do? I can't go on like this. I felt so alive over there, but here I feel like I might as well be dead.'

'No,' Erin snapped back immediately. 'Don't ever say that, *ever*. What would that achieve? That really *would* be the cowardly way out. Look

360

at you, you're young, beautiful, intelligent, you've your whole life in front of you, which is more than can be said for Ian and all of those thousands and thousands of other men who have died.' She finally lost her temper and whacked her hand onto the bedspread angrily. 'How dare you say that, Keely, after everything we've seen and done? How *dare* you?'

Keely looked at her in alarm, shocked by the vehemence in her voice.

'Well?' Erin demanded. '*Have* you any right to say something like that, after so many people have lost their lives without even having the choice?'

'No,' Keely admitted grudgingly.

'No, you haven't. Look, I know nursing all those poor soldiers was horrible and hard and utterly depressing, but we all did it and so did you. And you were an excellent nurse, Keely. Don't discount all of that now that you're home again. Forget about Ross McManus, or if you can't forget about him, at least try to think of him as someone who was probably just as lonely and as frightened as you were. He probably needed you as much as you thought you needed him, but he was just more realistic about it. God, what am I doing defending him?' Erin shook her head in bemused wonder. 'But be *proud* of what you did over there, not ashamed and depressed. It's time to get on with life again, for me and for you. I'm going to start by marrying the man I love more than anything else in the world. What are you going to do?'

Keely opened her mouth, shut it again briefly,

then said, 'If it's all right with you, I'd like to start by being your bridesmaid.'

They looked at each other and smiled, and the smiles turned to tears and they hugged fiercely, clinging tightly as if they might never see each other again.

By the time they'd exhausted Keely's supply of clean handkerchiefs, they both felt enormously better. Together they went to Keely's mirror and set about tidying themselves up.

'Oh God,' Keely groaned as a matching pair of red faces, swollen eyes and shiny noses stared back at them in the glass. 'We look terrible. Do you think they'll notice, downstairs?'

'Probably,' Erin replied, 'but does it matter? We've been to a war, remember, we're allowed to cry. It's a pity the men aren't. There are three downstairs who might do well if they did, now and again.'

'Three?' asked Keely.

'Well, yes — James, Joseph and Owen Morgan.'

'Oh, yes, Owen. I keep forgetting about him.'

Erin shook a little of Keely's face powder onto a large brush, swept it across her nose and cheeks and frowned at the patchy result. 'Well, perhaps you shouldn't. This morning Aunty Tam suggested that there might be, well, a certain level of interest from that quarter.'

So had Joseph, adding that, in his opinion, Keely would be a fool not to make the effort to behave a little less unpleasantly towards Owen, as he seemed to be the only man within a hundred-mile radius of Kenmore who didn't seem to mind her behaviour.

'He's been very rude to me,' Keely said reproachfully as she applied a hint of pale rose gloss to her lips.

'Surely not? He seems to have lovely manners.'

Erin had only met him this morning, and briefly at that, but already she could see that he was a kind, thoughtful and very stable sort of person. And quite good-looking. Not as attractive as Joseph of course, but certainly appealing.

Keely said, with a moue of distaste, 'He said I had a face like a constipated sheep.'

Erin bit her lip. 'Well, had he any cause to say that?' she asked.

Keely put the lid back on her pot of gloss. 'I might have been a little sour with him once or twice, but really, what a vulgar thing to say!'

'Oh, don't be a prude. We heard worse than that every day in the hospitals. We've *both* said worse than that plenty of times.'

Keely ignored that, because it was true. 'Anyway, he's quite unsuitable. He has no money, he doesn't move in the right circles, and he's quite happy to do menial work.' She looked at Erin in the mirror, her own blotchy face betraying a momentary flicker of interest. 'He was a schoolteacher before the war, though,' she said, but then she frowned again. 'But he seems quite happy to trot around the station fixing broken fences and dagging smelly old sheep all day. I couldn't possibly develop a serious interest in a man who does that for a living.'

'Keely, our fathers do that for a living.'

'Oh, you know I don't mean it like that,' Keely

protested. 'It's just that he's not, well, I don't know what he isn't, really. I haven't really thought about it, to be honest. I've been too busy being rude to him.'

'Then perhaps you should stop. Perhaps you could start by apologising for your behaviour.'

Keely looked genuinely appalled. 'Apologise?'

'Yes, it wouldn't hurt. And perhaps you could have a talk with everyone else, too, about how you've been feeling and why. I'm sure they'd appreciate it.'

'Perhaps, perhaps, *perhaps*,' Keely mimicked. 'Why are you always so sensible and right all the time, Erin?'

But she glanced at her cousin and smiled, and her face, swollen though it was, looked relaxed for the first time in months.

★ ★ ★

The following week was a whirlwind of whizzing into town in the car to buy magazines and pattern books then back to Kenmore to decide on a style for Erin and Keely's dresses, then tearing into town again to purchase the fabrics, trims and accessories.

But before that there had been a very uncomfortable couple of days after Erin had announced that she intended to get married in her nurse's military uniform; she was due to start work at Napier Hospital when her leave ran out six weeks after the wedding, she had been a nurse for the past five years, she was still a nurse, so why not wear her uniform? Men got married in their uniforms all the time, so why couldn't she? Jeannie was appalled and refused to even speak to her daughter for an entire day, aghast at the idea of her only child marrying in a such a dreadfully dowdy grey dress. But Erin dug her toes in, and it took a period of intense negotiation, with Tamar acting as intermediary, before a compromise was reached. Erin finally agreed to wear a proper wedding gown, but it was to be of her choosing and her choosing alone — she flatly refused to wear anything frothy and extravagant, in which, she insisted, she would surely run the risk of being mistaken for a Christmas-tree fairy.

Then it was decided that the children needed new costumes as well, so back to town Lucy and Erin went, with Duncan and Liam bundled in the back of the car looking forward with tremendous excitement to a day out in Napier, unaware that most of it would be spent standing in various draughty shop dressing rooms trying on a succession of scratchy and uncomfortable little boys' suits. At Kenmore, the men, including Joseph, looked on in bemusement, and quickly found reasons to spend as much time outside in the paddocks as possible.

Erin chose a very simple design to be made up in lustrous ivory satin. There was a lace bodice trimmed at the neckline with seed pearls, and loose three-quarter sleeves generously hemmed with the same lace. The satin skirt fell from a high waist to just above the ankle, and a matching waistband fastened at the side with pearl buttons. Keely's dress was in the same style, but in a soft champagne-coloured crêpe with chiffon instead of lace. They would both carry bouquets of pale orchids and maidenhair fern.

The boys were not at all impressed with their little Norfolk suits, with short trousers and jackets, although Liam had initially been quite taken with his. Then Duncan announced he hated his with a vengeance and Liam soon decided that he did as well. Tamar thought the new outfits were really rather sweet, and was very cross when, four days before the wedding, she discovered both pairs of trousers in the daffodil paddock and the jackets under a pile of hay in the barn. She yelled at the boys very loudly and smacked them both across the backside. They both burst into tears, Duncan blurting between sobs that it wasn't fair because his suit made him feel like an itchy old hedgehog and why couldn't he just wear his farm clothes?

When Joseph tried on his own newly purchased wedding suit the following day, he muttered to James that he had to agree with Duncan, even if the boy was only three and a half.

He stood facing a full-length mirror looking this way and that, a little dismayed at what he saw. 'I look like a prize bloody ram,' he grumbled.

'Well, don't pull the trousers up so high,' James replied, amused.

'I have to, otherwise the waistband gets snagged on the buckle of my bloody leg harness.

And I have to wear it — I can't hop up the aisle, can I?'

'You're not going up an aisle, you'll be standing in the parlour in front of the fireplace.'

'Well, all right then, I can't hop up to the fireplace,' Joseph snapped back. Then, sheepishly, he apologised.

James was surprised, and a thought struck him. 'God, you're not nervous are you? How extraordinary.'

'Yes, I am actually,' Joseph reluctantly admitted.

'About the ceremony, or is it your leg? If it's the ceremony, there's nothing at all to worry about. It only takes a few minutes and it's all fairly painless.'

'I know, but I don't particularly enjoy being the centre of attention. Not even for a few minutes.'

'Oh, don't worry,' said James, waving his hand airily, the old married man of nearly four years. 'It's certainly no worse than hopping the bags at Gallipoli. Just take a deep breath, close your eyes and it'll all be over before you know it. If it's your leg, though, what Erin might think about it I mean, then I can't offer you much advice I'm afraid. Except to say that if a man has a good woman, then things like that usually turn out all right. And I should know. Lucy's stood by me splendidly, despite my abominable behaviour.'

Joseph removed his new jacket and hung it carefully over the back of a chair. 'No, I'm not bothered about that. She saw me in the hospital, remember. Bathed me and bandaged the bloody thing for weeks, in fact.'

There was a brief silence during which neither man looked at the other: Joseph because he didn't want his brother to see in his eyes that he and Erin had already been together, and James because he suddenly realised that they had, and he was too polite to let on that he knew.

Joseph continued, 'Anyway I suppose one stump's the same as the next, and God knows she's seen hundreds already.'

'Not when it's attached to the man she loves, I expect. And she does love you, you know, you can see it in her face every time she looks at you.'

'Yes, you can, can't you?' said Joseph, grinning widely. 'So, no, I suppose I'm not nervous, really. In fact I've never wanted anything more in my life than to be married to Erin.'

'Good. And we'll ask Mam to let the buttons out on your trousers, shall we? Then the waistband can sit under your straps and things won't be quite so, well, *on show*.'

19

July, 1918

Kepa was wandering around the garden, getting a breath of fresh air before the ceremony. Only immediate family would be attending the actual wedding, but this afternoon there was to be a reception for seventy guests out here on the lawn. He looked at the huge marquee erected yesterday, then at the ripe grey clouds gathering over the hills, and hoped that if it rained, everyone would fit under it.

Only Joseph's half-sister Huriana and her husband, and his foster-mother Mereana, would be attending from Maungakakari, but tomorrow Joseph and Erin would be guests of honour at a special wedding celebration in the village.

He checked his watch impatiently, and noted there was just over half an hour to go.

'It's a bore, all this standing around, isn't it?' said a voice.

Kepa turned to see James coming towards him, dressed, like Kepa, in his best suit and wearing a flower in his buttonhole. He lit a cigarette, shielding the flame of the match from the gentle breeze.

'Joseph's ready,' he added. 'He's inside having a quick brandy.'

Kepa raised his dark eyebrows. 'Not nervous, is he?'

'Yes, I think he is, a little — not looking

369

forward to all the fuss.' James looked skywards as a few desultory drops of rain darkened the fabric of his coat. 'Damn, I was hoping it would hold off.'

Kepa looked up as well. 'Oh, I think it will. Most of those clouds are not moving at all.'

'Well, I'm going inside anyway. Would you care for a snifter of something yourself while we're waiting?'

'Yes, thank you, James,' said Kepa, 'I would.'

They turned and walked back across the lawn. As they reached the back door of the house, James flicked his cigarette butt into the winter spinach in the kitchen garden; it lay smoking lazily until he stepped on it and ground it into the soil.

Kepa observed dryly, 'Do not let your mother catch you doing that. You know how she feels about her vegetable garden.'

James looked at Kepa sharply, at his immaculately tailored suit and his dark, handsome face framed by patrician silver wings in the black hair sweeping back from his strong temples, and felt an immediate pang of anger. Who was this man to imply ownership, or at the very least guardianship, of his mother's feelings? Yes, he was Joseph's father, and Tamar was Joseph's mother, but as far as James was concerned any further relationship between the pair of them was inappropriate and certainly unwelcome.

Even as a small child James had sensed, or imagined he sensed, something more between Kepa and Tamar than a mutual interest in

Joseph's wellbeing. He had never understood why his father tolerated it; if he had been in Andrew's position he would have gone to considerable lengths to prevent anything more than strictly necessary contact. But Andrew had welcomed Kepa at Kenmore and seemed quite happy with his presence at various family functions over the years. Tamar had never given any indication that her relationship with Kepa went any deeper than shared concern for Joseph's welfare, but James was still uneasy about the arrangement, particularly now that Kepa's wife had died. He was even more uneasy about the realisation that he saw Andrew's capitulation as a form of weakness, so he tried not to think about it too often. He genuinely liked and respected Kepa, and he found his own private discomfort confusing.

At least Kepa and his mother wouldn't be sitting together at the top table at the wedding breakfast. Everyone in the district knew the situation, but there was an unspoken under-standing in the family that there was little to be gained by actively advertising the fact, so it had been mutually agreed that although Kepa would of course attend the wedding, he would not take his place beside Tamar.

Today of all days, however, James had no wish to cause a scene of his own with Kepa, so he bent down and retrieved the cigarette butt. 'Probably right,' he replied lightly, and looked around for somewhere less noticeable to dispose of it as they went inside.

Spread across the vast kitchen table, two extra

tables brought in especially for the occasion, and every other available flat space, were arrayed the fruits of Mrs Heath's toil for the past week. There was a selection of cold meat, and, judging by the tantalising smell, hot meat dishes still on the stove and in the oven, plates of cakes, pikelets, scones, coloured jellies and junket for the children. Enough, in James' opinion, to more appropriately feed two hundred guests, not less than half that number.

In a corner of the kitchen, carefully out of the way so it couldn't be bumped, was the wedding cake. Mrs Heath had clearly ignored Erin's original request for something simple — or perhaps Erin had simply given in — and had outdone herself. The vision consisted of three individual cakes supported by pillars, each layer heavily decorated with marzipan and white sugar icing. A riot of incredibly intricate scrollwork was piped around each tier, and on the smooth tops had been arranged multiple sprays of tiny icing flowers interspersed with silver foil leaves, wedding bells, white satin ribbons and the odd horseshoe. On the top sat a slim, delicate vase made of icing and filled with trailing artificial flowers, and the whole lot sat on a gleaming, solid silver platter lined with paper lace doilies.

'That is, er, very clever,' said Kepa. 'Lovely work, Mrs Heath,' he added heartily as she bustled up behind them, her face red from cooking and her hair escaping from its pins.

'Yes, I think so,' she agreed proudly. 'It's probably the best I've ever done, I should think. No, don't touch it!'

James stepped smartly away from the cake, in mortal fear of accidentally damaging it, and muttered, 'Yes, very nice. I'm just getting Kepa a drink.'

'The liquid refreshments are in the study,' said Mrs Heath, employing her best vocabulary in honour of the occasion. Then her eyes skimmed over the food on the tables, checking again to make sure nothing had been omitted or was sloppily presented, and she dismissed the two men with a flick of her tea towel.

Also in the study were Andrew, Joseph and Owen, standing in front of the fire with drinks in their hands looking uncomfortable in their good clothes. Outside Duncan and Liam were racing noisily up and down the hall, almost apoplectic with excitement, their jackets unbuttoned and shirt-tails already hanging out.

James handed Kepa a drink and motioned him to a seat. He opened his mouth to speak but before he could there was a shriek of pain mixed with indignation from the hall.

'Oh God,' he said, 'that's Duncan. Where the hell's Lucy?'

He put his drink down and went out to see what his son had done to himself this time.

'Where are the girls?' Andrew asked bemusedly.

Joseph said, 'Upstairs helping Erin to get ready, I think.'

'All four of them?'

'Well, I think Mam might be in the sewing room but the others are with Erin.' He put his own glass down. 'In fact, I might just go and see how she's getting on.'

'Hang on, apparently you're not allowed to see the bride before the wedding,' cautioned Andrew quickly. 'There'll be hell to pay if you see her before she comes down those stairs.'

Joseph rolled his eyes as he went out.

'Perhaps he is a little nervous,' Kepa said in an amused tone.

'Yes, well, it's not every day a chap gets married,' noted Andrew.

'No, of course not,' Kepa agreed chattily. 'You know I initially cautioned him against it? Marrying Erin, I mean, not the institution of marriage itself. A man can never have too many *mokopuna*.'

There was a silence before Andrew said in an uncharacteristically cool tone, 'Did you?'

'Yes I did. Did Tamar not tell you?'

Owen suddenly decided he should go and ask Mrs Heath if she needed a hand with anything.

When he'd gone, Andrew asked evenly, 'And what were your reasons for cautioning him? Surely you don't consider Erin an unsuitable match?'

'Actually, yes I did. At first.'

'Do go on,' Andrew said, very frostily now.

'I wanted him to marry a woman from among his own people.'

As Kepa said this, he winced inwardly, hearing an unwelcome echo of his Uncle Te Kanene's voice. Years ago Te Kanene had cautioned him against — in fact actively campaigned to prevent — any possibility of a marriage between himself and Tamar after it had become clear that Kepa was the father of her child. It had sounded pompous and dictatorial then, and it sounded no less so now.

He added quickly, 'I consider Erin to be a fine young woman, and of course I am delighted that she has consented to marry my son and become a member of our family, but at the time I admit I did harbour some doubts as to whether the union would be wise. I know times have changed since . . . well, over the years, but the marriage of a Pakeha woman to a Maori man is still considered somewhat unusual, as you yourself are no doubt aware. People can still be very censorious.' He gestured at the brandy decanter. 'May I?'

'Of course,' replied Andrew. 'And I take it you also discussed this with Tamar?'

'Yes, or rather she discussed it with me,' Kepa said, pulling a wry face as he poured another measure of brandy. 'This was, oh, it must have been a month or so after Joseph arrived home. He had evidently told her of my concerns, and she approached me about it not long after that.'

Andrew felt rather disturbed by the realisation that Tamar had sought Kepa out and he had known nothing about it.

'She tore a strip off me actually, as they say,' Kepa went on conversationally, apparently oblivious to Andrew's discomfort. 'There is really no other way of putting it. She was most upset at the thought of my interference. She is like that with Joseph, as I am sure you have noticed. Will not let anyone say a word against him or do anything that might jeopardise what she sees as his happiness. She informed me that he is a grown man more than capable of making up his own mind about whom he wants to marry, and that Erin is a very lovely girl. And of course she was right on both counts.'

Andrew nodded, slightly mollified now at the thought of Tamar telling Kepa off. 'And what was Joseph's reaction? When you talked to him?'

'He told me to mind my own business. But then he always has.'

'Yes, children do that these days.'

'Indeed,' agreed Kepa. He drained his glass. 'And on that note, I think I will take a short walk and stretch my legs.'

★   ★   ★

At the top of the thickly carpeted stairs he stood quietly and listened. From behind a closed door to his left he could hear giggling and women's voices, and assumed correctly that the room belonged to Erin; the doors to the rest of the rooms on the first floor were all open, except for one at the far end of the hall which was only slightly ajar. He padded down and stood outside it for a moment, listening again. He heard a small sound from within and pushed the door open a few inches. Inside, at her sewing table, sat Tamar, dressed in all her mother-of-the-groom finery and with tears running down her face. He stepped in and closed the door quietly behind him.

Tamar turned with a small gasp. 'Kepa! I didn't hear you.' She ran her fingers under her eyes to collect the tears.

'Is something wrong?' he asked gently.

'No,' she replied, and tried to smile. She looked up at him, and shook her head despondently. 'Yes, there is.' She picked up a slim sheaf of crumpled and dirt-smeared note paper. 'This is from Thomas. It arrived this morning. I haven't shown it to Andrew yet, I'm not sure whether I should or not. Not today anyway. It's about Passchendaele and it's awful.'

She blew her nose and continued dully, 'Sometimes, in the mornings, especially when the weather's fine and warm, I wake up and hear Duncan and Liam galloping about the house, and for a few seconds I'm sure . . . ' Her voice cracked and she swallowed with a visible effort. ' . . . I'm sure it's James and Thomas belting about, and Ian, out of bed before anyone else like they always used to be, and then I remember they've all grown up and there's a war on and Ian won't ever be coming home and James is never going to be the same as he was before he went away and neither is Joseph. And Thomas, well, I don't even know whether Thomas will come back to us.' She glanced up at Kepa despairingly. 'Oh, I know he says he's doing all right and that he's a survivor, but how can I really know what will happen to him? How can *he* really know?' She stopped to blow her nose once more because she was crying again, and to take a deep breath as bitter anger pushed her sadness roughly aside. 'It all seems so arbitrary to me, who lives and who dies. There doesn't seem to be any *sense* in it. I'm so tired of it,

Kepa! Is it *never* going to end?'

Kepa stared back at her, surprised and dismayed at this sudden outburst. He wondered how many other outbursts there had been in the privacy of her room or while she was off across the paddocks on one of her frequent solitary walks. Too many, he imagined. Or perhaps not enough.

'I do not know the answer to that, Tamar,' he said eventually. 'God knows I wish I did.'

His heart ached for her and as she stood he reached out his hand to her. She took it and he gently laid her palm against the skin of his cheek.

'It will be over one day,' he said quietly as he briefly savoured the warmth of her skin on his, 'we can be sure of that. We just have to go on being strong until then.'

Tamar took another deep breath. 'I know. I know, and I will.'

'Come on then, dry your eyes and come downstairs. Our son is getting married today, remember. This is a day of celebration.'

★   ★   ★

The parlour was elegantly decorated for the occasion. The French doors had been closed against the chill in the July air and the curtains pulled back to frame the view of the manicured lawns and neat flowerbeds outside. In front of the doors a white-painted wrought-iron arch had been set up and entwined with fresh flowers and trailing greenery. Elsewhere about the room were arranged bowls and large vases filled with beautifully arranged flowers and foliage, all of which added a faint but delectable scent to the room. In fact, Tamar and Jeannie had gone so overboard regarding the floral arrangements, now placed strategically throughout the house and in the marquee outside on the lawn, that they'd almost denuded the garden and the hothouse and more flowers had been delivered from town.

By the time Andrew had herded everyone into the room, Joseph had reappeared and was standing a little apprehensively to one side of the arch, waiting for Erin to be escorted into the parlour by her father. When she appeared in the doorway on Lachie's arm, looking beautiful, serene and radiantly happy, Joseph's face relaxed in a slow and delighted smile.

Standing at the back of the room, Kepa saw this and allowed himself a small, sad little smile of his own as he realised what had been unsettling his son — the awful and obviously much-contemplated possibility that Erin might, even at the last minute, change her mind about marrying him. And, privately, Kepa understood Joseph's fear. As he knew from personal experience, there was no greater disappointment and sorrow than that which comes from having to accept that the woman you desperately wanted to marry would be forever beyond your reach.

* * *

Owen needed a leak. He pushed his chair back from the table, forgetting that the marquee was pitched on grass, and almost toppled over backwards. Clutching wildly at the tablecloth to right himself, he felt his face burn as both James and Keely, sitting across from him, roared with laughter. He straightened the cloth, wondered vaguely how his head was going to feel the following day, then got to his feet and carefully moved his chair back. He was drunk, but not horrendously so, and he made a mental note to keep it that way: matching James drink for drink was turning out to be somewhat unwise. He was a good sort, James, but God he could knock it back.

Suddenly aware of eyes on him, he glanced across the table again to see Keely staring straight back at him with a small, private smile on her face. She looked quite devastating today; the sherry she had been rather injudiciously quaffing had given her cheeks a rare rosy glow and her eyes far too much sparkle for her own good. Her champagne-coloured dress suited her colouring and the rich sheen of her auburn hair, and Owen imagined he could see a hint of shadowed cleavage through the chiffon of the bodice. As he looked, Keely winked, slowly and deliberately. It was extremely uncharacteristic, and oddly disturbing.

His bladder twinged suddenly and he was reminded of why he had stood up in the first place. Stepping back he only just avoided treading on Liam, who was squatting on the ground with Duncan and enthusiastically encouraging Strawberry the house cat to eat a bowl of pudding heaped with whipped cream. Strawberry already had cream on her whiskers and on her ears and her sleek belly was alarmingly distended. Owen hoped for the sake of Tamar's fine oriental carpets that the animal would be relegated outdoors for the night.

Outside it was almost dark; the clouds hadn't dissipated — they looked even more swollen if anything — but so far the rain had stayed away. Owen went around to the back of the house to use the toilet next to the washhouse, sighing with exquisite relief as his urine streamed noisily into the bowl.

He sat down on the steps of the back porch, retrieved his pouch of tobacco from his pocket and set about rolling a cigarette, a process that always seemed to fascinate Duncan and Liam every time they saw it. They thought it was very clever of him to do it one-handed, not realising that the maiming of his other hand had given him no choice. He closed his eyes as he drew the mellow smoke deeply into his lungs, then exhaled with exaggerated leisure.

'Enjoying yourself?' asked an amused voice.

Owen's eyes snapped open. Keely stood in front of him, her head to one side and her hands on her hips; he hadn't even heard her approach. He must be drunker than he thought.

'Yes, I am,' he replied.

'Good. I've come to use the toilet,' Keely said, brushing past him up the steps and pushing the toilet door open.

Embarrassed, Owen leaped up and moved

away from the porch to give her some privacy, but could still hear her as she yanked the chain with a clank and a rattle, then marched back out defiantly. God, he thought, why does she have to make so much out of everything? It was only a pee.

'That's better,' she stated, and burped gently. 'All that sherry, I expect. I don't like it myself, it's too sweet, even the dry stuff. I prefer brandy or whisky, but Da does go on about women drinking hard liquor in public. Says it's unbecoming.' She snorted inelegantly, wavering slightly in her high heels, then thought for a moment. 'Still gets you drunk, though. The sherry, I mean.'

'Clearly,' Owen said, although he was hardly in a position to talk.

'I suppose you think it's unbecoming as well, do you?'

'Women drinking hard liquor, or women being drunk?'

'Either.'

Owen shrugged and said truthfully, 'I try not to make judgements.'

'Yes, you would, wouldn't you? You're such a *decent* person, Owen.'

He ignored the sarcasm in her voice, although he was disappointed that her unpleasant behaviour seemed to have resurfaced.

As if sensing his disapproval, she said suddenly, 'Look, I'm sorry, it's the alcohol talking. Take no notice.'

They both knew this wasn't true — Keely was still rude and sarcastic to him most of the time

— but Owen let it pass.

'They make a lovely couple, don't they?' he said.

'Joseph and Erin? Yes, they do, and I'm happy for them, I really am.' She watched as he took a last draw on his cigarette then flicked the burning butt at a shrub. 'I am, you know,' she repeated. It was obviously important to her that he believed her.

'Yes, I know.'

'Good,' she said, then added, 'Can I have one of your smokes?'

Leaning against the potting table, Owen rolled two more cigarettes, lit them and handed her one.

'Da doesn't like me smoking, either,' she reflected. 'Although plenty of women smoke these days. Da's a bit old-fashioned sometimes.'

'He's your father. He's allowed to be.'

'D'you think so?'

'He loves you.'

Keely raised her eyebrows disdainfully at him. 'It's only smoking.'

Owen shrugged again, and they fell silent. There was laughter and a burst of applause from the direction of marquee and Owen turned towards it. 'We'd better get back, I suppose.'

Keely reached out and took hold of his sleeve. 'No. Come for a walk with me, up to the daffodil paddock. I don't feel like going back just yet.'

He considered her for a moment, her shining eyes and the gleam of the porch light in her hair, and then, against his better judgement, nodded and proffered his arm.

They followed the path that bisected the kitchen garden, picking their way carefully as the light from the house faded, but as they neared the gate leading into the daffodil paddock, Keely suddenly stopped.

'Hang on, I need to get something first.'

She reappeared several minutes later, with something clutched in her hand.

'What have you got there?' Owen asked.

She held it up and grinned wickedly. 'Da's brandy flask. Can't go on a picnic without brandy.'

20

From the summit of the hill Keely and Owen could see the warm and welcoming lights of the homestead below. Immediately to the left was the translucent glow of the marquee and the individual torches placed strategically about the lawn so guests could find their way to and from the house, and to the right the stables and the darkened sheds housing the vehicles and farm implements. Between the sheds and the lower slopes of the daffodil paddock sat the black shape of the hay barn that serviced the flatter reaches of the station.

It was cold, and Owen removed his jacket and draped it around Keely's shoulders. Reluctantly admitting to herself that you couldn't in fact climb a steep, grassy hill in high heels after more than five glasses of sherry, she had taken her shoes and stockings off halfway up and left them sitting incongruously on a tree stump. Owen couldn't see Keely's bare feet in the dark, but he had no doubt they were purple with cold. She didn't seem to mind though. Perhaps that was because since reaching the summit they'd imbibed at least half of the contents of Andrew's brandy flask. Owen wondered if anyone had missed them yet.

Something small and hard stung the back of his hand and he looked up. The moon was too obscured by clouds to see anything much at all but a nebulous darkness above them, but he could smell the tang of rain on the wind. Another drop hit him, and then another, and he clambered unsteadily to his feet, pulling Keely up with him.

'It's going to pelt down. Come on, we need to get back.'

She laughed and pulled away from him. 'Why? I like the rain!'

'You won't like this,' Owen warned. 'I think there's a storm coming.'

Keely shrugged out of his jacket and tossed it back at him, just as the skies let go, the sudden, violent rain accompanied by a brilliant flash of lightning and an ear-splitting crash of thunder. Within seconds they were both drenched. Keely spun around and around, her arms wide open and her face towards the sky, her eyes shut tight against the stinging rain.

Owen made a grab for her and she dodged out of his way, laughing wildly. He finally succeeded in hooking her by the neck of her dress, which was now plastered to her body, and began to half carry, half drag her back down the hill. She almost got away when he stopped to retrieve her shoes and stockings, but when another fork of lightning scattered sharp black shadows across the ground and thunder exploded almost directly above them, she seemed to suddenly appreciate the danger, and snatched at the front of his sopping shirt.

'Down there!' she yelled directly into his face, her breath heavy with brandy fumes.

'*What?*' Owen bellowed.

'*Down there!*' She gesticulated wildly towards the bottom of the hill as water cascaded from her flattened hair and down her face. '*The barn, it's closer!*'

Owen turned to where she was pointing, then grabbed her hand and started to run. They both slipped over repeatedly before they reached the huge barn doors, which they found firmly shut against them. Dodging around the side to a smaller door, Owen shoved it open and they fell into the deep, musty blackness inside. The sound of the rain on the corrugated-iron roof far above was deafening.

He swore as he ferreted through his pockets for matches. After several soggy strikes, one finally caught and he held it up, its weak flare illuminating a small sphere around them.

'Where's the light?' Keely asked.

Owen gestured back towards the door. 'It's over here somewhere.'

He groped around then tugged on a cord swinging gently down from the blackness. An insipid light came on. The barn was half empty, as some of the hay had already been fed out, but there were still stacks of it piled up in the back half of the building. In the gloom, halfway up the mountain of hay, Keely saw three pairs of unblinking yellow eyes — the barn cats, staring suspiciously back at her.

'Oh, *do* excuse us,' she said, and giggled.

Owen was smoothing water from his hair. 'What?'

She pointed. 'The cats. We've interrupted their

sleep. Or their mousing, or whatever it is they do out here.'

They both ducked instinctively as another peal of thunder crashed overhead, the rolling boom reverberating around the inside of the barn.

'Christ, that was close,' muttered Owen nervously.

He wasn't going to admit it but the thunder was disconcertingly reminiscent of the terrible and incessant racket of the big guns in France. He wondered how James and Joseph were faring.

He spread his drenched jacket over the closest heap of hay and sat down heavily, uncomfortable now in his wet clothes. Thank God it wasn't too cold in here; they'd go back to the house when the rain slowed a little.

Keely stood looking at him for a moment, then sat down with her muddy feet stretched out in front of her, a bedraggled sight with her rat's-tail hair sticking to her skull and her dress ruined. Owen thought she had never looked more beautiful.

He noticed the hairs standing up on her forearms. 'Cold? Do you want my jacket again?'

'No, I want this,' she replied, reaching for the coat and extracting the brandy flask from an inside pocket. She unscrewed the lid and took a long swig, then passed it to him.

'You'll be sorry tomorrow,' he warned.

'Then have another drink and be sorry with me.'

He'd already exceeded his limit and knew he was in for a headache in the morning anyway, so he accepted the flask. Brandy certainly had a warming effect on the body, if nothing else.

'Actually, I am quite cold after all,' Keely said and, scooting over to him, rested her head on his solid shoulder.

Owen looked down at the tracks the rain had sculpted through her hair. She smelled nice, of some sort of floral perfume with a heady, musky undertone, and he wondered whether the deeper scent was her own.

He also wondered what he should do next. He certainly knew what he wanted to do, but every facet of his conscience told him it would be wrong. Keely was the daughter of a family who had shown him nothing but generosity and kindness, she was the sister of a young man he had come to care about very much in France, she was a troubled spirit, and she was very drunk. And so was he. But, oh God, she was tempting, and a certain part of his body was acknowledging this fact in a very embarrassing manner. He hoped she hadn't noticed, and bent his right knee in an effort to conceal the rigid lump in his trousers.

She put her head up then, and said, 'My lips are cold too,' and reached up to kiss him.

Her lips *were* cold, but only on the surface. Underneath he could feel a soft, warm pulse that matched his own. He sat perfectly still for several seconds, struggling mightily with his principles, but when he felt her cool little hand begin to slide down the front of his shirt towards his groin, his principles found themselves suddenly and resoundingly defeated. In one swift move he had her on her back and was lying half on top of her, his right leg between hers and his pounding erection hard up against her thigh.

He was shocked at the depth of his lust. They were both fully clothed but he could feel every inch of her body, every contour and every curve, and every tiny movement she made. He gazed down at her for a moment and when he saw her lips begin to move in a slow, lazy, inviting smile, he was gone.

She arched her neck to give him unrestricted access to the smooth whiteness of her throat, and grunted in pleasure as he nuzzled and then bit. At the same time he moved his other leg between hers and began to rub himself against the firm mound at the junction of her thighs. She scrabbled with the buttons on his shirt, tearing the bottom two off in her haste. His chest was damp and his nipples erect, but not as erect as hers. Supporting his weight on his elbows now, he caressed the tops of her round breasts, swearing in frustration when he couldn't get his hands far enough down the front of her dress to touch the enticing flesh there.

He rolled off her and urged breathlessly, 'Sit up so I can undo it.'

But she beat him to it, reaching behind to unhook the row of fabric-covered buttons that fastened her gown at the back. Halfway down she gave up, tugged the sleeves off her shoulders and slid the top of the dress down to her waist. Underneath she wore a satin and lace bust bodice, and this too she pulled at frantically so she could bare her breasts to him. He sighed as he ran his hands over them, then lowered his lips and kissed the erect nipples until Keely moaned deep within her throat.

It was the last straw for Owen: he reached for the hem of her dress, hauled it up to her hips, yanked off her knickers and climbed on top of her. She was ready, warm and slippery and reaching for him as he guided himself into her. She uttered a single, unladylike grunt as he entered and began to thrust, hard and passionate and utterly out of control. He didn't feel her fingernails as they raked his back, and he didn't hear her as she gasped and cried out a name that wasn't his.

It had taken them hardly any time at all, but as they lay together in the prickly hay, sticky with sweat and giddy with alcohol and spent desire, it occurred to neither of them that their few minutes of wild, reckless passion would bind them to each other for the rest of their lives.

October, 1918

Keely had very reluctantly acknowledged her own pregnancy barely a week before Erin announced hers. The difference was that Keely hadn't told anyone yet. The entire household was absolutely delighted for Erin and Joseph, and the announcement gave rise to much good-natured teasing among the men about how busy Joseph must have been on his wedding night.

He had in fact been busy, and so had Erin, but not making babies. When the storm had broken, there had been a mad rush to get everyone and everything out of the rapidly disintegrating

391

marquee and into the house. It had turned into a sort of game, with most of the participants — already invigorated by the generous provision of liquid refreshments and then excited by the spectacular weather — dashing between the marquee and the house with armfuls of food and drink, chairs, children and assorted wedding decorations. How they all managed to jam themselves into the house Tamar never knew, but the resulting evening was thoroughly uproarious and memorable, and 'the night of the storm when Erin and Joseph got married' became a part of local history.

Those whose transport was not reliable or robust enough to navigate the weather stayed the night at Kenmore, sleeping in various makeshift beds and in assorted stages of semi-undress. Fortunately there was plenty of food left over and Mrs Heath was able to feed all of the impromptu guests the following morning.

Erin and Joseph, who had not been allowed to escape from Kenmore until around one in the morning, had been almost dead on their feet and collapsed as soon as they arrived home, wet and cold because the station truck — which Joseph had now mastered with the help of his new leg — first wouldn't start, then had leaked copiously during the short trip to their new house. They lay together naked and shivering in their recently purchased marital bed, between equally new and wonderfully crisp cotton sheets, and giggled hysterically about the whole affair. Then they settled, savouring their closeness after the long months spent apart, and fell asleep in each other's arms within minutes.

The following morning, though, they finally came together as husband and wife, and their lovemaking was as thrilling and as satisfying as it had been almost three years earlier, although this time their surroundings were infinitely more intimate. Erin calculated that it was then, the first morning of their married life together, that their child was conceived.

Telling the family was almost as rewarding as telling Joseph had been. She had suspected for some weeks, but she and Joseph kept the news to themselves until several months had passed, just in case something untoward happened. Nothing did — in spite of Erin's private fears because of what had happened after the *Marquette* — and at the beginning of October they made their announcement. Erin was worried that Keely would take the news badly, reminded yet again of her disastrous relationship with Ross McManus and the dreams and plans she'd been forced to abandon, but she seemed genuinely pleased, although Erin had been puzzled by the wry smile on her cousin's face.

'Are you all right, about the baby?' she asked the following day. 'I was a little worried that the news might upset you.'

Keely, who was stretched out on a chaise on the terrace making the most of the spring sunshine, smiled. 'I'm absolutely thrilled, for both of you.' She opened one eye and squinted at Erin. 'Of course, this means you won't be able to go back to nursing now.'

Erin nodded regretfully. 'I know, but perhaps later on.'

Keely laughed and sat up. 'You really are disappointed, aren't you? You can't have everything you want in life, you know!'

'No, I suppose you're right,' Erin replied. 'But, really, you're not upset about it?'

'No, not at all. In fact I'm delighted, because it means the two of them will be able to grow up together, like you and I did.'

Erin frowned. 'What do you mean, the two of them?'

'Well, there will be. Two, I mean.'

'But I'm not having twins.' Erin's hand crept to the barely noticeable swell of her stomach. 'At least, I don't think I am.'

Keely took a deep breath, let it out and said evenly, 'No, you're having one baby and *I'm* having one baby. And that makes two.'

Erin stared at her, unable to believe her ears. 'Are you saying you're *pregnant*!'

Keely nodded, quite cheerfully Erin thought, given the circumstances.

'But, you . . . I mean, you can't be! Who . . . '

'The ever-popular and thoroughly decent Owen Morgan.'

Erin's hand flew to her mouth. 'Oh my God! But, when?'

'The night of your wedding. We got caught in the hay barn when the storm came, remember?'

'And you . . . '

'Yes. We were both drunk. Just think, all those times with Ross and nothing happened, and now, after just the once with Owen and I've fallen.' She said this with a mildly puzzled note in her voice.

'Oh Keely. Are you sure?'

'I'm as sure as you are.'

Then Keely started to cry, great, silent sobs that were wrenched out of her. Her hands slid over the back of her head and she hunched over until she had curled almost into a ball.

Erin moved closer and placed her hand on Keely's back, patting and smoothing gently but firmly. She began to make the small, reassuring noises she had used to soothe the terribly broken young men in the hospitals overseas.

She let Keely weep for almost ten minutes, until her slowly subsiding sobs indicated she had done enough crying, for now anyway.

'Have you told him?'

A negative shake of the auburn head.

'Have you told Aunty Tam?'

Another short, sharp shake.

Erin said, 'Keely, listen to me.'

She gently pulled Keely's hands away from her face and lifted her head. Her cousin's eyes were red, her lips were swollen and dry and there was a long, thin thread of snot on her cheek. Erin used the hem of her dress to wipe Keely's face, and carefully pushed the damp hair back from her temples.

'Keely, listen,' she said again. 'You have to tell your mother.'

'She'll kill me.'

'No, she won't. She loves you. And, with all due respect, it's not as if this sort of thing is completely foreign to her, is it? She knows these things happen.'

'Well, then, Da will kill me.'

Erin nodded — there was no denying this. 'Yes, he probably will, so you have to tell Aunty Tam first. And then Owen.'

Keely's head jerked up in alarm. 'No! Not him. Why? He's barely even spoken to me since the night of the wedding!'

Erin realised that relations between the pair of them had in fact deteriorated even further over the last few months. 'Well, have *you* talked to *him* since then?'

'No. There didn't seem to be anything to say. I got drunk and I let him make love to me. In fact, I *encouraged* it. It was my fault. And I just assumed he wouldn't have much to say to me after that.'

'Would it have hurt you to at least *try* talking to him?'

Keely's eyes filled again as she confessed, 'Yes, Erin, it might have hurt me very much.'

And it suddenly occurred to Erin that Keely was right — she had had enough disappointment in her life already, and it was understandable that she should try to protect herself from even more.

She took Keely's hands in her own. 'Do you want me to come with you when you tell your mother? You have to, you know. You won't be able to hide it soon.'

'Yes, I know that.' Keely looked back at her cousin. 'Thanks, but I'll tell her. You're right, she does love me. I know that too.'

Andrew and Tamar sat in the parlour in brittle silence. They had barely spoken since Keely had broken the news to her mother that morning and she, in turn, had reluctantly informed Andrew. Keely herself was hunched in the corner of the couch opposite, her arms folded over her stomach and her face set in an unreadable expression.

They were waiting for Owen. Outside in the still garden the sun was warm and the hum of bees flitting busily from one flower to the next drifted in through the open doors. Joseph, who had been sent to fetch Owen and was looking as mystified as he no doubt felt, said from the doorway, 'He's just taking his boots off. Er, is there anything I can help with?'

Tamar waved her hand. 'No, thanks, darling. It's just something we need to talk about, the four of us.'

Joseph looked at her carefully for a moment, then said, 'Oh, right,' and disappeared as quickly as he could.

Owen appeared then, in his socks and shirtsleeves, arms and face tanned already. 'You wanted to talk to me?' he asked cheerfully.

Andrew said tersely. 'Yes, we do, Owen. Sit down.'

Owen perched on the opposite end of the couch to Keely, his hands on his knees, and waited expectantly.

There was an increasingly uncomfortable pause, then Andrew said without preamble,

'Keely has informed us that she is expecting a baby. And that you're the father.'

Tamar had heard the expression 'his face drained of blood', but had never actually witnessed it — until now. Owen had gone a deathly shade of white, and she wondered if he might be about to faint. He sat for a moment in stricken silence, then whipped around to face Keely.

'My God, why didn't you tell me!' he blurted.

Tamar closed her eyes in relief. At least he wasn't going to try and deny it.

'So it's true?' Andrew demanded.

Without taking his eyes off Keely, Owen replied, 'If Keely says so, it must be.'

'Don't speak to me like that, young man,' Andrew snapped, his own face white now, but with anger, not shock. 'We invited you to stay at Kenmore out of the kindness of our hearts. We wanted to do something for you because of the support you gave Ian in France. How *dare* you repay us like this!'

Keely spoke at least, but her voice was dull and without emotion. 'It was me, Da. You can't blame him.'

'What?'

'I said it was me. I pushed him into it.'

Owen opened his mouth to say something but Andrew got in first, appalled and profoundly embarrassed by this shameless admission from his daughter.

'I don't care *whose* fault it was, Keely, it's a bloody *shambles*!' he barked, his voice rising several notches in angry frustration. 'What the

398

hell did you think you were doing, the pair of you, eh? What the *hell* did you think you were doing?'

Sick with worry, and at the end of her own tether from listening to Andrew rant and rave in the privacy of their bedroom for the last two hours, Tamar snapped, 'Oh Andrew, what do you *think* they thought they were doing?'

She despaired; what on earth was wrong with her children? First James, then Ian, and now Keely! And because Keely was a woman, her indiscretion would be considered much more shameful than those committed by her brothers: people expected young men to venture far and wide and with occasional careless abandon. Only Joseph had managed to father his and Erin's child within the boundaries of wedlock. And that, Tamar strongly suspected, was only because they had been on opposite sides of the world for the duration of much of their relationship. She wondered briefly, but guiltily, whether it was her fault, whether somehow such irresponsible behaviour could be passed on through the blood, then dismissed the thought as absurd.

And perhaps, after years and years of being pushed away, repressed and ignored, a similar idea reared up in Andrew's mind, because, for the first time in the whole of their married life together, he turned on his beloved wife.

'Shut up, Tamar, for God's sake! You might think this is normal behaviour, but it bloody well isn't!'

Tamar recoiled as if he had slapped her across the face.

Andrew slumped, horrified at the cruelty of his own words and regretting them instantly. 'Oh God, Tamar, I am so sorry. Please, I don't know what I'm saying.'

He was distraught. Since being informed of Keely's condition earlier that morning, he had been relentlessly assailed by ghastly visions of his precious only daughter living the rest of her life a lonely, unwed mother, spurned by any men who once might even remotely have been considered suitors, all because of one stupid, thoughtless mistake.

He reached blindly for Tamar's hand. 'Please forgive me, my darling, I'm so sorry.'

And Tamar did understand his pain and his need to lash out, because she felt it too, possibly even more, although she had learnt years ago that the pain of one individual was not something that could be measured and compared with that of another. She felt for Keely and, as she took Andrew's cold hand in her own, she felt for her dear husband, sitting beside her with his grey-streaked head bowed, crumpled and defeated.

In the intimate tableau they presented, Owen saw something that touched him deeply, and it helped him to come to a decision. He stood up, uncomfortably aware of his rough, hand-knitted socks and informally bare forearms, and cleared his throat nervously.

'With your permission, Mr and Mrs Murdoch, I would like to ask Keely to become my wife.'

Andrew's head came up then, and Owen averted his gaze to avoid seeing what he suspected might be sudden tears of relief in the old man's eyes. He looked instead at Tamar, who was smiling at him gently. When she raised her eyebrows a fraction in Keely's direction, Owen took his cue and turned.

'Keely, I would be honoured if you would consent to marry me, as soon as possible, providing of course that your mother and father give their blessing. I won't allow a child of mine to grow up without a father.'

No one said anything for several moments, although all eyes were on Keely.

'Yes,' she said eventually. 'Yes, I'll marry you, Owen.' Then, as an afterthought, she added, 'Thank you.'

★ ★ ★

So the Reverend McKenzie journeyed out to Kenmore once again, although this latest wedding was a very quiet affair with only the most immediate family present. He had been briefed by Tamar regarding the circumstances, although quite rightly not in any great detail, and couldn't help feeling empathy for both the daughter and her parents, after everything else the family had been through. Naturally he didn't at all approve of intimate physical activity outside the bonds of marriage, but God knew people did it all the time these days, especially since the war, and who was he to judge? Unlike the clergymen of some faiths he could mention, he had never considered unsolicited criticism of his parishioners to be part of his vocation.

And this union seemed to be a sensible one, if nothing else. The groom was a personable young man, a war veteran whom McKenzie had met at the wedding last July and had rather warmed to. By all accounts a man of maturity and responsibility (apart from the presumably single rash act that had prompted this wedding, of course), he seemed a good catch for a girl who had allowed herself to fall so irreversibly from grace. And Keely Murdoch was a very attractive young woman, and quite bright, too, although he gathered she had been rather a trial to her parents since returning from overseas. Oh, well, perhaps motherhood and a husband would settle her down.

Tamar and Andrew fervently hoped so. They had both been somewhat surprised, not to mention extremely relieved, when Keely had agreed so calmly to Owen's proposal. The fact that he had made it without any prompting had gone a long way towards restoring Andrew's opinion of him, although Tamar had never wavered from her belief that he was an honourable man. She hoped, however, that he hadn't offered purely out of a sense of obligation. This possibility had preyed on her mind to the extent that two days after the confrontation in the parlour, and a week and a half before the wedding, she set out on horseback late one morning to talk to him about it.

She found him in one of the lower paddocks, using a pair of pliers to mend a fence through which a number of enterprising sheep had recently escaped. There were no fences up in the hill pastures, except for those defining Kenmore's boundaries, but down here on the flat the land was divided into large paddocks intended to confine stock when they were brought down for shearing and lambing.

As she rode up, Owen straightened, shoved his pliers into his back pocket and smiled up at her.

'Good morning Mrs Murdoch,' he said, politely touching the brim of his battered old work hat.

Tamar dismounted and pulled her smart kid riding gloves off finger by finger; they looked quite out of place next to the tatty old trousers and shirt she was wearing — her habitual riding outfit around the station — but she was a little vain about her hands, and the gloves protected them from the unyielding leather of the reins. She settled herself comfortably on a nearby rock, appreciating its warmth on her backside.

'Now, there's something I need to talk to you about, if you don't mind.'

Owen raised his eyebrows enquiringly.

Tamar patted the boulder in a wordless invitation to him to also sit, and looked up at him from under the brim of her hat, a rather smart stockman's affair imported from Australia by Andrew several summers ago after her nose had received a particularly bad sunburn. She smiled to put Owen at ease as he perched warily on the other end of the rock.

'It's about you and Keely getting married. Andrew and I are delighted of course that you will be joining our family, but there are one or two things that I would like to clarify before that happens, at least in my own mind.'

Owen remained politely silent.

'I'll be direct with you, Owen. I'm aware that, well, no, let me rephrase that. I *suspect* that had Keely not found herself in the situation, or condition rather, in which she *has* found herself, you would not have offered to marry her.'

She waited for Owen's response but as he seemed happy to remain annoyingly close-mouthed, she resorted to being even more direct.

'Would you have asked her? Eventually?'

Owen pushed his hat further back on his brow and reached down to pluck a leaf off his boot, which he proceeded to examine intensely. He didn't want to offend Tamar, but neither did he want to be dishonest. He suspected that of all the Murdochs, Tamar was the one least likely to accept half-truths of any kind.

'No,' he finally admitted in his deep, measured voice, 'I'm not sure I would have. In fact, I'd have to say it would have been highly unlikely.'

Tamar felt irrationally disappointed. Wouldn't this all be so much easier if it turned out that Owen had secretly been in love with Keely from afar from the moment he met her? But all she could say was, 'Oh. Well.'

Owen felt terrible. 'I'm sorry if you had hoped for something else.'

'Well, yes, perhaps I had,' Tamar admitted, adding briskly, 'I suppose then that there's no point in asking you whether you love her?'

Owen flicked his leaf away and considered his

future mother-in-law.

'Yes, there is a point in asking, and no, I wouldn't say love, not at this point, but I think I could love her, in time. If she'll let me.'

Tamar looked into his pleasant, open face: he was speaking the truth.

'Are you saying . . . '

'I'm saying that your daughter is the most contrary, bad-tempered, rude and infuriating woman I've ever met. And she fascinates the hell out of me. And no, I probably wouldn't have asked her to marry me had she not become pregnant, simply because, more than likely, she would have refused me. But the situation has changed — she needs a husband, I want to be a father to my child, and both you and Mr Murdoch, I believe, approve of the match.'

'Yes, we do. Andrew thanks God you did offer.'

'And you don't?'

'I don't thank God for anything any more.'

'That's not what I mean.'

'No, I realise that. Of course I'm pleased, and I think Keely could have done a lot worse for herself, pregnant or not. I believe you'll make her a fine husband.' Tamar paused briefly and rubbed at a speck of dirt on the knee of her trousers. 'If you can stay the course. Keely is rather, well, you know how she is.'

'Yes, I do. She's frightened, and she's got lost somewhere along the line. I hope she'll let me help her find her feet again. Well, me and the baby.'

* ★ ★

But Tamar was still worried about Keely, who didn't seem to be taking the idea of marriage seriously at all. When Tamar asked her why she had accepted Owen's proposal, she replied that it saved having to change the monogram on her luggage.

'What *are* you talking about?' Tamar was perplexed.

'The set of luggage you and Da gave me for Christmas a couple of years ago, before we went overseas, well, it has KM on it. When Owen and I get married, my surname will still start with M, so I won't have to have it altered.'

Tamar was hard-pressed not to whip out a hand and slap her daughter.

'Keely, this isn't about *luggage*! This is about your life, Owen's life, and a *child's* life. The one you and Owen made *together*, remember? You can't just ignore that.'

Keely looked at her mother with something approaching despair.

'No, I know that, Mam, but it all just seems so, I don't know, so *unreal*, somehow. It was bad enough before, when it was just me, but I'll be someone's mother soon! And by next week I'll be a wife. It scares me, Mam, it *scares* me!'

Tamar nodded. 'I understand that, love, but really, what's the alternative? Raising the child on your own? It's hard enough bringing up children when there are two parents. Although I've loved every minute of raising you and your brothers, I can't say it's been easy. And it would

406

wreck your chances of marrying in the future, you must see that.'

'You married after you had an illegitimate child.'

'Yes, but no one knew about Joseph.'

'Da did.'

Tamar sighed in exasperation. 'I doubt there are many men out there as big-hearted and as understanding as your father. And Joseph wasn't public knowledge.'

'He was eventually, though.'

'Yes, and we soon found out who our friends were then.'

'I don't remember that.'

'Keely, stop being so deliberately obtuse! You weren't even born at the time. Look, Owen is a good man, surely you appreciate that?'

'Yes, he is. And he's not bad-looking, and he's clever and all those other things 'good catches' are supposed to be.'

'Yes, so what's so bad about marrying him, especially given your predicament?'

'But Mam, I don't *love* him.'

'Perhaps not at the moment, but you might, given time.'

'And I might not, too. What then? Surely you don't want me stuck in a loveless, unhappy marriage for the rest of my life?'

'Of course I don't, but I really don't think you have a lot of choice in the matter. And if things go well for you, you might eventually find marriage to Owen Morgan far from loveless.'

Keely rested her hands on her stomach and closed her eyes for a moment. Then she opened them again and said wearily, 'Yes, I know you're right. It's just not the way I thought things would turn out, that's all. Owen's a good man, I know that, but he's not, well, he's not the man I wanted.'

Tamar felt a rush of sympathy for her daughter. She moved over and gathered her to her breast.

'My darling, Ross McManus belongs in another part of your life, a part that's over and done with. I understand how you feel, believe me, I really do, but you have to let him go.'

Keely nodded, her face cool against the silk of Tamar's blouse. 'But it's so hard, Mam.'

'I know, sweetheart, I know.'

21

November 1918

The final visitor to Kenmore in 1918 arrived silently and unannounced, and at first no one even noticed.

Keely and Owen had been married for almost four weeks, and had taken up residence in one of the larger bedrooms upstairs. Both Erin and Keely were faring well with their pregnancies, although Erin was having a tougher time with morning sickness. Not that she complained to anyone, but she was often pale and needed a rest by lunch time. Jeannie and Tamar both assured her that the nausea would pass very soon, and Erin had to admit that she wouldn't be at all displeased when it had. It was rather irritating, having to lie down in the middle of the day, as there were plenty of other things she would much rather be doing, such as sewing for the new babies and decorating the room she and Joseph had designated as the nursery.

She also cooked for Joseph, of course, although there were occasions when he had to feed himself if she wasn't feeling up to handling raw meat or anything similarly stomach-turning. It made her feel guilty, although he insisted he was more than happy to prepare food for both of them, despite the joking accusations of unmanliness from the visiting shearing gang.

Keely, on the other hand, didn't appear to be

lifting a finger in terms of housework, although Mrs Heath did a lot of it anyway. Owen was not comfortable living in the big house, but the idea of Keely relocating to one of the shearers' cottages was absurd.

Keely did, however, seem to have found a certain, rather unexpected contentment in being pregnant. It certainly suited her; her face had filled out and she had colour in her cheeks at last, she was sleeping extremely well and seemed much calmer within herself than she had for a long time, for which everyone was very grateful. And, at only four months, her belly was already a very full, round bump. Erin had a belly too, of course, but it wasn't nearly as obvious as her cousin's. Tamar had a sneaking suspicion and a subsequent desire to ask Owen whether there were twins in his family, but decided to put that possibility aside; the idea of one baby was probably enough for Keely at the moment.

On the 8th of November, Tamar was in the garden cutting flowers after lunch when the tranquillity of the early summer day was shattered by the sound of a truck back-firing noisily up the dusty driveway, and a cacophony of horn-blowing and cheering from what appeared to be a group of larrikins hanging precariously off the back. The dry crunch as the truck skidded to a halt in the gravel was followed almost immediately by a fevered knocking on the front door, and Tamar hurried inside to see what on earth the fuss was about. Andrew was already in the hall, trying simultaneously to calm Mrs Heath, whose feathers were severely ruffled by such improper behaviour, while also attempting to get some sense out of the revellers, who were all shouting at once on the front porch.

Suddenly, his face lit up as he realised what they were saying.

He turned to Tamar and exclaimed with utter delight, 'The war! It's over! They've signed an armistice in France!' He snatched a copy of the *New Zealand Herald* out of the hands of a man with a Union Jack tucked jauntily into his hatband, and waved it at her. 'It's in this morning's paper! Just think, we might not have known until our mail arrived!'

Tamar immediately felt a knee-wobbling sense of relief that Thomas would finally be home soon, and a fresh and painful reminder that Ian never would.

But she pushed that thought away and exclaimed, 'Really! How absolutely *wonderful*!' and took the paper from Andrew, who was grinning like an idiot.

'I must go down and tell the boys,' he said, and hurried off.

He must have run across to the shearing shed as barely five minutes later Tamar heard the faint but unmistakably jubilant shouts of the shearing gang, the motley but efficient crew of men, boys and a handful of not too badly disabled returned veterans. Andrew declared the rest of the afternoon a holiday, and a small convoy of trucks was soon heading through the gate to join the celebrations in town. Andrew didn't accompany them, grateful instead just to sit quietly with Tamar. Owen and Joseph stayed home too, but

James joined the crowds in Napier.

When he arrived back that night, very late and rather the worse for wear, he entertained everyone with stories of constantly shrieking sirens and pealing school bells, Union Jacks run up every flagpole, vehicles decked out with bunting, children marching about banging tin cans and making the most of the opportunity to create as much noise as possible, ecstatic crowds dancing and singing in the streets, and strangers tossing formality aside and shaking hands and embracing.

The Kenmore household stayed up late that night, and no one started work until the extraordinarily late hour of ten o'clock the following morning. But then came the disappointing news that yesterday's celebrations had been premature: although the war was almost certainly coming to an end, an armistice had not in fact been signed yet. Apparently England and France, except for the town of Brest where the rumour of armistice had originated, had not begun to celebrate and were waiting instead for the official hour of ceasefire, which was to be at 11 a.m. on the 11th of November.

But only days later, jubilation at the end of the war ended abruptly as news began to spread of an influenza epidemic that was sweeping New Zealand at a horrifying rate. Everyone at Kenmore was shocked by the increasing newspaper reports of flu deaths in the cities, and as close as Napier, and terrified that the illness would reach them. They hoped, though, that they would be safe because of their distance from town. No more visitors were allowed at the station. They had enough basic food and other supplies to last them for months if necessary, even for the shearers who had been stranded at Kenmore when Andrew closed the gates, a well-stocked vegetable garden, their own water supply, and plenty to do without having to go off the station. They thought they were safe.

That was, at least, until Andrew began to cough on the evening of the second Thursday in November, and couldn't stop.

15 November, 1918

He wasn't the only one. By the following morning, four of the shearers had reported sick, and neither Lucy nor James could get out of bed: their limbs and heads ached and they had high fevers and racking coughs. Duncan was fine, but annoyed that his parents would not get up and play with him. Eventually Tamar removed him from the bedroom and sent him off with Liam to 'help' Mrs Heath with some baking.

Tamar was very worried, particularly about Andrew, who looked really very ill. His face had gone completely grey, except for two flaming red spots high on his cheeks, his skin was burning and he was sweating profusely. He said his head hurt, and whenever he tried to speak it took him some time to get his breath. Erin and Keely had conferred and then administered an infusion of supplejack for the fever, a dose of Bonnington's and a liniment of camphor to his chest to assist breathing. None of this helped, however, and by

413

late that afternoon Andrew's condition was clearly worsening.

During the day Erin and Keely had gone down to the shearers' cottages to help there, much to the consternation of everyone else, particularly Joseph and Owen, who were both terrified that their pregnant wives would get sick themselves. Erin and Joseph had the first real argument of their marriage, which ended in Erin walking resolutely out of the back door of the big house with a bag of medical supplies under her arm and a very determined look on her face. Owen, who had learnt some time ago that Keely did whatever she pleased regardless of what anyone else thought, simply let her go. Anyway, he privately suspected that the virus was already rife at Kenmore.

By late Friday afternoon one of the shearers had died, and Lachie, as acting manager of Kenmore Station, made no objection when the rest of the gang decided to leave. There were subdued goodbyes when the small convoy departed just as the sun was setting, some of them heading for town where they felt they would receive more specialised medical care, and others towards the Ruahine Ranges in the hope of outrunning the epidemic.

Andrew lay very still except for the laboured rise and fall of his chest as he struggled to breathe. In the last hour or so the skin of his lower legs, arms, neck and face had begun to turn a dark mottled colour. He was barely recognisable as the man she loved so dearly, and spread over his chest was something that terrified her even more — a large square of linen, once white but now spattered with the bloodied sputum that erupted from his mouth every time he coughed.

'Tam? Is that you?'

Tamar sat on the side of the bed and took hold of Andrew's hot, clammy hands, shocked at how much they suddenly resembled veined and yellowed claws.

'I'm here, darling. It's all right.'

There was a sticky, clicking noise as Andrew ran his tongue over his mottled lips and then swallowed. His eyes were sunken and red-rimmed, and Tamar wondered when he turned his head whether he was seeing her or not.

'I was asleep,' he said. 'I don't feel well.'

'I know, my dear,' she said as she gently stroked his grey-bristled cheek. 'You have a touch of the flu.'

'We have to bring the lambs down, it's too cold,' he muttered, then closed his eyes. 'Get Ian. He can help.'

Tamar felt tears fill her eyes. 'Oh darling, Lachie can organise that, you need to rest.'

Andrew relaxed for a moment, then his face contorted as he fought to suppress a cough. Tamar lifted his head and shoulders to help him, and grimaced as flecks of blood flew from his mouth onto the linen bib and the front of her dress. When he had finished, his breath rattling and bubbling in his throat, she used a cloth to wipe the strings of mucus from his chin and the tears that had been forced from his eyes.

'There, there,' she crooned, 'try to rest now, you need to sleep.'

He sank back on the pillows, and Tamar held his hand as he slid into sleep, or perhaps unconsciousness, almost immediately.

'Mam?'

Tamar turned towards the door, where Keely was balancing a cup of tea on a tray.

'I've brought him a hot drink.'

'That's very thoughtful, dear, but he's asleep again. Why don't you put it on the nightstand in case he wakes up soon?'

Keely moved towards the bed, her swollen belly already changing the way she walked. 'How is he?' she asked.

'I think he's holding his own.' Tamar replied, looking back down at Andrew. 'What do you think?'

Keely bent over her father, took his pulse, put her ear against his chest and listened for almost a minute. 'His lungs sound very fluidy. When were you expecting the doctor?'

Tamar, noticing the blood spots on her dress, dabbed at them ineffectually with her handkerchief. 'Damn, I'll have to put this in cold water. Around three or four, he said.'

Glancing at the clock on the mantle, Keely observed, 'But it's after seven now.'

Tamar didn't reply but instead folded the handkerchief neatly and with exaggerated care and tucked it into her sleeve.

At ten that evening she had to admit that the doctor wasn't coming. They found out later that he'd been forced to take to his own bed and had died the following day.

Andrew's breathing deteriorated through the night, and the family, seriously concerned now, took turns to sit with him. Tamar refused to leave his side until Erin insisted that she go downstairs for a ten-minute break and a cup of tea.

She had barely taken her first sip when Erin appeared at the parlour door.

'I think you'd better come, Aunty Tam. He's awake and he wants to speak to you.'

Tamar put her cup down, slopping tea into the saucer, and hurried back up to the bedroom.

Andrew was on his side now, and she could hear his ragged breathing from the door. She went over and settled herself on the bed.

'Darling? Did you want me?'

Andrew's eyes opened slowly, the shallow breath wheezing through his parted lips smelling like the water in a vase of week-old flowers. Tamar didn't flinch.

He murmured, so quietly that Tamar almost didn't hear him, 'Aye, I'll always want you, my love.'

Then she felt his hand creep into hers and give a single weak squeeze before it fell limply away again.

She sat up and looked at him. His eyes were open and still, his chest had stopped moving, the dreadful rattling sound coming from his lungs had ceased. She watched him intently for perhaps five minutes more, and when it became horribly clear that he had gone from her, she stood up, jammed her hands on her hips and set her mouth in a straight, angry line.

Then she turned and marched downstairs to the parlour where she said to her daughter, 'I'm sorry, Keely, but your father has passed away. I'll tell James. Oh, and we must let Thomas know as soon as possible.'

Oblivious to the stunned and dismayed expressions on everyone's faces, she spun on her heel and walked back upstairs.

In the bedroom she had shared with Andrew for so many years, she kissed his cool lips one final time, fell to the floor in a whisper of skirts and let out a howl of such anguish and despair that Kenmore was haunted by it for years.

★　★　★

Lachie telephoned Riria, Tamar's most cherished friend, to ask if she would consider coming down from Auckland to be with Tamar for a few weeks, to help her over the shock and grief of Andrew's death. She arrived two days later, carrying two large travelling bags and a case crammed with a range of traditional Maori medicines; much more effective, she declared, than all this Pakeha rubbish in which people were putting all their faith and which clearly was not doing anyone any good at all.

Almost everyone at Kenmore was in bed. Mrs Heath was running about doing her best to tend to everyone, including Tamar, who had refused to leave her room since Andrew had died, even when they had buried him in the small family cemetery in the daffodil paddock. Keely was also working tirelessly, with the added burden of trying to keep Liam and Duncan entertained and, more importantly, quiet. Lachie was looking out for the station by himself, and it would be a godsend, Mrs Heath said, to have another pair of hands to help. That was, if Mrs Adams was not averse to helping.

'Of course not,' said Riria briskly, as she heaved her bags into the front hall. 'That is what I am here for.'

She removed her hat — a large black straw trimmed with a purple satin ribbon and matching berries — and hung it over the newel post at the bottom of the stairs, then undid the buttons on the sleeves of her black blouse and pushed them up to her elbows.

'Now, where would you like me to start?'

Mrs Heath hesitated, not at all sure about giving her orders. She had always been rather uncomfortable with the undeniably handsome Maori woman who dressed perpetually in black widow's weeds, even though she had been coming to Kenmore for years. And it wasn't just her costume (a woman *should* wear permanent black after the loss of her husband — Mrs Heath herself did, and so of course had Queen Victoria), it was also her striking physical appearance. The long copper hair worn unbound, the smooth, barely lined face (even though Mrs Adams was in her fifties) marred only by that really quite barbaric tattoo on her chin, and the still voluptuous figure that Mrs Heath disapprovingly suspected was not being supported by undergarments.

But it was more than that — something about

her imperious manner and the authority she effortlessly commanded, which Mrs Heath didn't think was quite fitting. But she was Mrs Murdoch's very dear friend, and was obviously loved by the rest of the family. She still didn't feel comfortable, though, about telling the woman what to do.

Embarrassingly, Riria read her mind. 'Mrs Heath, I realise that this is an unusual situation. I also realise that you run this household, and very well, according to Tamar. I have no wish to intrude upon your domain, but clearly you and Keely need help. I am here to provide that, and to tend to Tamar. Please let me know what needs to be done, and I will be more than happy to oblige.'

Mrs Heath raised a hand and fiddled with the collar of her blouse, hoping to disguise the blush she could feel creeping up her neck and face.

'Oh. Oh, well, yes, thank you very much, Mrs Adams. I'm very pleased you're here. We all are. Mrs Murdoch will be delighted.' She paused, then added quickly, 'Well, not delighted perhaps, but certainly . . . '

'Yes, I know what you mean, Mrs Heath,' Riria interrupted. 'Where is Keely at the moment?'

'She went over to Joseph and Erin's house, to see if they need anything, although it worries me, Keely traipsing up hill and down dale in her condition. They're both confined to bed, Erin and Joseph I mean, and with Erin expecting as well it's quite a worry — she's very under the weather. I wanted them to stay over here but Erin said I had enough sick people to look after with James and Lucy and Mrs McRae and Owen. Of course, Keely's looking after Owen, really, which is a wonderful sign, as I'm sure you'll appreciate.' Aware suddenly that she was prattling, and referring to what was possibly supposed to be a family secret, Mrs Heath shut up.

Riria, who had received several letters from Tamar on the subject of Keely and her hasty marriage to Owen Morgan, smiled slightly.

'Yes, I am aware of the situation. And Keely shows no signs of becoming *mauiui* herself?' When Mrs Heath frowned, she translated, 'Sick. With this influenza.'

'No, she doesn't seem to be. She's very fit, although devastated by the death of Mr Murdoch. They all are, not to mention myself.'

Mrs Heath led Riria upstairs and knocked softly on Tamar's door. When there was no answer, she opened the door a crack and asked in a loud, reverential whisper, 'Mrs Murdoch? Mrs Adams has arrived. Would you like to see her?'

There was no audible reply but the housekeeper stood back and ushered Riria into the darkened room, closing the door behind her.

Riria wrinkled her nose at the stale air, and it was stiflingly hot. The heavy drapes had been fastened across the windows and the light was very dim. Tamar lay sprawled across the big unmade bed, her face pressed into the rumpled sheets, wearing nothing more than her shift and clutching one of Andrew's work shirts to her stomach.

Riria crossed the room. 'Tamar?'

Tamar moved her head slightly and looked blearily up at Riria through swollen eyes and a curtain of long, unbrushed hair. 'Oh Ri, he's gone. I've lost him.'

Riria gathered her friend in her arms, as she had once before many years ago, and began to rock her gently.

★ ★ ★

Joseph woke to someone calling his name, in a persistent, irascible voice that sounded as old as the hills themselves.

He sat up, then slumped dizzily back onto his pillow; he was so weak and disoriented he barely knew where he was. His head pounded, his chest and throat burned and his limbs felt utterly drained and useless. For a moment he thought he might have gone blind, then realised he must have been asleep for hours and the sun was setting. The little light that remained had a strange yellow cast and there was a metallic taste to the air.

He turned his creaking neck and saw Erin's dark head on the pillows beside him — she appeared to be asleep, but his heart leapt in fear as he realised she didn't seem to be breathing.

'Erin!' he rasped, and shook her shoulder roughly.

And then she did breathe, a long ragged inhalation that seemed to tear into her lungs before it wheezed out again.

Joseph was terrified. She had not been this ill

this morning, but while he had been sleeping she seemed to have deteriorated drastically. He laid his ear against Erin's chest and listened. Yes, she was definitely breathing, but there was an ominous and very frightening bubbling noise coming from deep down inside her.

He would have to go over to the big house for help, if he could get that far without passing out himself. Keely said Riria Adams was arriving today — perhaps she would be able to do something. He would bring Keely back, anyway. He ran his hand across Erin's hot cheek and then down her body until it came to rest on the bump in her belly that was their child. Yes, he would have to get help.

And then it came again, that dry, sibilant voice calling his name. He almost recognised it, but then the memory sidled away from him. There was certainly no one else in the bedroom, and surely he would have heard footsteps if there was someone walking around outside under the verandah?

'I'm going to get help,' he whispered to his wife, although there was no sign at all that she heard him. 'I'll be back very soon, all right?'

He sat up again, but much more slowly this time, and waited for his head to stop spinning before he reached for his false leg. And where were his trousers? Oh God, they were draped over a chair on the far side of the room. He knew any attempt to hop in his current condition would surely result in falling over, so he buckled his leg on first, then staggered woozily across to his clothes and dressed as quickly as he could.

Outside, as he glanced briefly at the swollen and bruised sky that heralded an unseasonable summer storm, there was a silent flash of white lightning followed seconds later by a deafening thunderclap. Christ, he thought fuzzily, not another one, remembering the tempest that had interrupted his wedding. No rain yet though, which was a blessing.

The station truck was parked in the driveway, and from where he stood on the verandah, clutching at the rail to hold himself up, it seemed miles away. What if he fell over or fainted even before he got to it, or passed out while he was driving? 'Bugger it,' he muttered, because there really wasn't any choice. He had to get help.

But no matter what he tried, he could not get the truck to start. So he gave up and headed for the horse paddock with a bridle thrown over his shoulder, feeling sicker and dizzier with every step and almost weeping with fear and frustration. He didn't bother to saddle up, but threw himself over the horse's back, swearing viciously as the skies opened and rain began to pelt down.

He was soaked within seconds but he didn't care. It was almost completely dark now, and he gave the horse his head; together they had made the short ride to Kenmore hundreds of times and the horse knew the way well enough.

At the top of the hill separating his house from Kenmore homestead, Joseph thought he might finally pass out so he bent forward onto his horse's neck. But still he felt himself sliding, and as the horse and the hill seemed to tilt up and over his head, he crashed down onto the wet grass with a breath-snatching thump.

He lay there coughing and gasping while his horse stood placidly over him. The wet grass felt pleasant against his cheek and he was very tempted to just let himself drift away, but a sharp, rasping voice, speaking in Maori, yanked him back to consciousness. 'Get up, boy. I want to talk to you.'

Joseph dragged himself to his knees and peered into the darkness. Was he dreaming now, or had he lost his wits completely? He could see, but just barely, a scruffy shape perched like a huge black bird on a rock about ten feet in front of him.

'Who is it?' he muttered.

'Never mind that,' replied the voice grumpily. 'Where have you been, boy? I have been calling and calling you.'

Too exhausted and confused to get to his feet, Joseph crawled closer and peered up at a sunken, toothless, milky-eyed face.

And now he knew to whom the voice belonged. He also knew he must be either dreaming or delirious. It was Te Whaea, the old crone who had told his fortune when he was a boy at Maungakakari over twenty-five years ago. She had been ancient then, so surely this must be her *kehua*, her ghost?

He shut his eyes and shook his head to dislodge the apparition, and winced at the pain the movement brought.

But she was still there, staring down at him, her rags flapping in the wind and the intermittent lightning outlining the spindliness of arms hardly thicker than the carved *tokotoko* she gripped in her gnarled right hand.

She pointed the stick at him and said, 'Get up. It does not become you to grovel. Te Kanene would turn in his grave.'

Joseph struggled to his feet, and stood swaying unsteadily in the gusting wind.

The ancient woman examined him with her one good eye. 'Ae, you have grown into a decent man. I said you would. But you are *mauiui* and so is your woman. She will die.'

'No!'

'Hold your horses, boy. Let me finish. She will die if you do not give her the right medicine.' She rummaged in her tattered skirts and withdrew a small, brown glass bottle. 'Five drops of this, every hour, until she recovers fully. There will be plenty for the others, too.'

'What is it?'

'Magic,' came the blunt reply. 'Or not. It depends on what you believe.'

Overcome by another wave of faintness, Joseph sank to his knees again. Then he bent over and vomited onto the grass.

The woman waited patiently until he had finished.

'Charming. Have some yourself,' she added, and handed him the bottle.

He took it and stuffed it down the front of his shirt, then tried to get to his feet again and couldn't.

'Oh Christ,' he said wearily, 'I'm not sure I can get back down the hill.'

Sighing audibly, the old crone climbed nimbly down from her rock, reminding Joseph of a scuttling, over-sized spider. She stepped towards him, stretched out a bony brown finger and touched his throat briefly.

'You always were touched by the gods,' she muttered, 'but this will give you a little extra help.'

And Joseph did start to feel a little better. His breathing was suddenly easier, and he could swear that the fever had eased slightly. Of course, if this was all a fevered and delirious dream, as no doubt it was, he might sprout wings next, and head off on a great soaring flight over the thousands of acres that made up Kenmore.

But instead he bowed his head in silent thanks to the old woman, and turned and started back down the hill, his legs stable and strong beneath him, for the moment anyway. When he turned and looked back, she was staring after him, the flapping rags wreathing her body like the remnants of a winding sheet, but when he looked again a moment later, she had disappeared.

22

'And that's all I can remember, really. I gave the stuff to Erin, and it worked,' said Joseph, joggling baby William on his knee.

Erin didn't really like him bouncing the baby up and down, but at three months he could already hold his head up by himself, and Joseph had a firm grip around his fat little stomach, so he was perfectly safe. And thoroughly enjoying the game, if the wide toothless smile on his round face was anything to go by.

Thomas scratched the side of his nose thoughtfully. 'Do you really think it was the old woman, Te Whaea? I mean, you were pretty *non compos mentis* yourself, weren't you? And if she was ancient when you were a boy, wouldn't she be about a hundred and thirty by now?'

Joseph shrugged. 'Who knows? I don't. And I don't think I care, to be honest, given that everything worked out all right in the end.'

'What about Aunty Ri? What did she say?'

'Nothing, really. She just smiled and said you shouldn't look a gift horse in the mouth.'

'And it wasn't her?'

'I doubt it. I might have been delirious, but even so I expect I still would have been able to tell Aunty Ri from an ancient old hag.'

At this point a low rumbling sound issued from the region of William's rompers, followed almost immediately by a smell that made both men flinch.

'Christ,' said Joseph, screwing up his face. 'He's my pride and joy, but my God he can stink sometimes. Where's Erin?'

Tamar was in the office going over some of the station accounts, a job she had taken over since Andrew's death. She was still tired and pale but, thanks to Riria's constant support and ministrations, she was beginning to look and feel more like her normal self again. She still mourned Andrew dreadfully, but after several months had forced herself to take a good look at the wonderful things she still had in her life.

The death toll in New Zealand from the influenza epidemic had been disastrous, and for Maori in particular, although there had been no deaths at Maungakakari, thanks to Kepa's foresight when he quarantined the village. His father Te Roroa died during the epidemic, but of old age, not as a result of the flu.

Kepa had not attended Andrew's funeral, but had sent Tamar a long and sincere letter of condolence. More letters had arrived from him since, but these Tamar had read in private then locked away in the small drawer of her dressing table. He did not come to visit: he understood Tamar's need to grieve in private.

Now she looked up as Thomas and Joseph went past.

'Ah, Thomas, just the person I want to see. My God, what's that smell? Oh, I see. Erin's in the garden, Joseph, so go and find Keely. She's actually condescended to change Bonnie herself.

She's up in the nursery.'

Tamar swivelled in her chair and took yet another good, long look at Thomas. She couldn't gaze at him enough, it seemed, and was only just getting used to the fact that he was finally home. He wasn't quite the same man who had gone away to war, but he was close enough for her. And his face would certainly never be the same, but he was home, he was well, and that was enough.

Seeing him still reminded her vividly of the terror she had felt when, just before Christmas and less than five weeks after Andrew's death, she received an official telegram which she hadn't had the strength to open. Riria had had to do it for her.

It seemed that God had finally taken his hand off Thomas: he had been wounded in Belgium on his way to Germany as part of the British occupation force. They found out later, in a letter from his commanding officer, that he had been standing next to an undetected mine when it had exploded, and that although his wounds were not fatal, they were serious. He had been in hospital in England for several months after that, before being sent back to New Zealand.

The right side of his body had taken much of the blast, but he was steadily regaining full use of his limbs, for which he was incredibly grateful. He would be physically scarred for ever, and the moderate disfigurement caused by shrapnel across his right cheek and jaw would be permanent. But, he said he wasn't particularly bothered by it, and if he wasn't, no one else should be either.

He had been home less than a week and Tamar didn't want to push him because he was still very tired, but she was keen to know what his plans were.

'I'm not sure, Mam. Catherine will be up from Dunedin in a couple of days, and I expect we'll sort things out then. We'll be getting married as soon as we can. God knows she's waited long enough.'

Tamar nodded. She had only met Catherine once, but she seemed a very sensible, intelligent and gracious young woman.

'I imagine she will want to get married in Dunedin, near her family,' she said, then added hopefully, 'Or perhaps she'd like to think about getting married here? The grounds here are perfect for weddings.'

'I don't know. Dunedin, probably. Sorry. But we'll talk about that when she gets here.'

Tamar said, 'Well Thomas, where do *you* want to get married?'

'To be honest, Mam, I don't care, as long as we do.'

Smiling at him fondly, Tamar replied, 'I know, I understand. And whatever the pair of you decide, we'll all be there, I'm sure of it.'

Thomas cleared his throat, then sat staring at his knees.

'Mam,' he said after several moments, 'I'll probably be going back down south to carry on with my law career, you do understand that, don't you? I was offered an associate partnership

431

at my firm just before I went away, and they still want me, apparently. I telephoned yesterday and the offer is still open. I really feel I should take the opportunity. They're a good firm and well disposed towards returned servicemen, which is the area of law I'd like to work in.'

'I didn't know there was a field of law specifically for veterans.'

'No, there isn't, really. I mean I'd like to represent the ones who haven't had the benefit of the sort of education I've been lucky enough to have. There'll be all sorts of things a sympathetic lawyer could help with, like employment discrimination and badly assessed war pensions and disability allowances. Oh, I know the men are all being feted madly now that they're starting to come home, but that's going to wear off pretty soon, and when it does it will be back to normal and to hell with returned servicemen.'

'Do you really think so?' Tamar was surprised.

'Yes, I do. There are signs of it already. Don't look at me like that, Mam, it's just the way the world works. We were all heroes when we went off to war, but now it's over nobody really wants to know. And not just about those men who are maimed and mentally disturbed, either — there are also the ones who won't be able to settle very well — there'll be a lot of those.'

'Like James, you mean.'

'Yes, like James. Not every returned soldier is going to be as well balanced as Joseph, you know.'

Tamar leant back in her chair and sighed.

'Well, I'm sure you know what you're talking about. And you have to do what your heart tells you to do. I'd be the last person to try and stop you.'

'Thank you, Mam. I knew you'd understand.' Thomas stood, then stooped and kissed his mother on the cheek. 'We'll only be a telephone call or a letter away. And we'll come back every chance we get.'

'I know,' said Tamar as she gave her son a quick hug. 'Go on now, off you go and see if that nephew of yours has been changed. It will be good practice for you.'

Tamar sighed again. She wanted Catherine and Thomas to at least settle in Napier, if not at Kenmore, especially now that Andrew had gone, but she knew her son had earned the right to a life of his own. He had never really shown any interest in the station, much to his father's disappointment, but James and Joseph were here, and Owen, although Tamar wondered just how long James would stay. He was slowly recovering from his shell shock, and was immensely better than he had been when he had first come home, but he was still short-tempered at times, still drank too much, and continued to be plagued by nightmares that snatched him from the deepest of sleeps, yelling and thrashing and frightening the life out of the rest of the household. He had talked about moving into town and considering banking as a career, or even taking his family to Auckland, but was happy in the meantime, it seemed, to stay on at Kenmore. Lucy was pregnant again, and perhaps they would stay until after the new baby was born. Tamar certainly hoped this would be the case.

So, when Lachie retired, Joseph and Owen would probably run the station between them — providing Owen and Keely were still married by then, and Tamar was having serious doubts that they would be. She was happy with that prospect, although she was thoroughly enjoying doing the bookwork for the station and had decided she would very much like to continue. It was quite a lot like running the brothel, at which she had excelled. And it gave her a break from the children and stopped her dwelling on the loss of Ian and Andrew. Thank God Riria had been here. She had ended up staying at Kenmore until April, when, in her opinion, Tamar was able to get on with her life again and the babies had arrived, an event, Riria had declared, she wouldn't miss for anything.

William Te Roroa Deane had arrived exactly on time in the second week of April. Erin's labour was straightforward and, she insisted, relatively easy, although Joseph hadn't thought so as he paced backwards and forwards across their living room listening to her grunts and cries of pain. The baby had yelled his head off the moment he was born, which everyone thought was a good sign, especially Riria, who approved of such lustiness in infants. He was a long baby, and would probably be tall like his parents, but still lovely and chubby with a shock of black hair and the most attractive pale coffee-coloured skin.

He suckled enthusiastically and was in every way a delightful child.

Keely, on the other hand, had delivered early, two weeks before Erin. And she had produced twins. Neither Tamar nor Riria had been surprised, Owen had been delighted, and Keely had been, and still was, horrified.

They were both girls, small but healthy and with lots of hair that looked as though it might be auburn like their mother's. After much family debate, they were named Bonnie and Leila. Tamar had thought Angharad and Aelwyd might be nice, to mark their Cornish and Welsh heritages, and James suggested Morag and Megan, but the former were declared a tad unpronounceable and the latter, added to Morgan, would be too many 'm's. In the end Owen put his foot down and selected their names himself.

Although Keely had blossomed during her pregnancy, she certainly didn't enjoy giving birth, and became irascible and withdrawn again soon after. She seemed unable to cope with the twins, could not feed them herself and left much of their care to the other women. Erin didn't mind, although she did find three babies at once a bit much at times. Duncan and Liam were delighted, pushing the twins enthusiastically around in their pram until, on one unfortunate occasion, they tipped them out on the lawn. But the girls seemed happy, they were loved dearly by their father, and they were certainly healthy and bright. Their mother, however, spent a lot of time on her own, going for long solitary walks across the paddocks and only occasionally spending time with her daughters.

Tamar couldn't understand why Owen continued to be so patient with her, but he was. He left her alone whenever she requested it, took the girls away at every opportunity and was largely responsible for their care in the evenings. Tamar wondered how long it would last, how long it would take for him to finally lose his tolerance for his fickle and indifferent wife and walk away.

⋆　⋆　⋆

Keely had received several letters over the past two months. They were from Ross McManus and she hid them as carefully as Tamar concealed those she received from Kepa.

Ross had returned home just after Christmas, made another attempt at reconciling with his wife, failed and left the family home for good in the New Year. He was still in Auckland, and planned to stay there to continue his medical practice. But he realised now what a terrible mistake he had made allowing their romance in England to end and he missed Keely dreadfully. He was so sorry for the way in which he had treated her. Could she ever possibly find it in her heart to forgive him and perhaps even consider renewing their relationship?

It didn't take long for Keely to decide how to reply. She looked at her boring but dependable husband, her sweet but extraordinarily demanding twin daughters, the empty days and nights that made up her life at Kenmore, and most of all in the mirror at her own weary and joyless face. Yes, she had enjoyed being pregnant, mainly because she felt it gave her a purpose in life, but once the twins had been born she had begun to feel redundant and had become depressed again, especially when she discovered she couldn't feed them. And she was sick and tired of Owen telling her to take more interest in them: that he could tolerate being shut out, but they couldn't.

So she wrote back to Ross. She *would* consider resuming their romance; she too was in a loveless marriage from which she desperately needed to escape. But how could they, when she was living in Hawke's Bay and he was in Auckland?

Easily, he replied. He would come down and collect her — he would let her know when the time was right — and take her back to Auckland to live with him. They would build a life together there, and to hell with what anyone else thought.

So she began to prepare. She walked for miles every day and ate as little as possible to make sure that when Ross did come for her she would have her figure back. She very publicly renewed an acquaintance with a girlfriend who lived in Napier so she would have an excuse to go into town when the time came and no one would wonder where she had gone or why. Everyone at Kenmore thought this a very positive sign, which made her feel guilty. And she deliberately detached herself even further from her children so that when she did go, they would not miss her.

Finally the letter came from Ross saying that

he would be down to pick her up on the evening of the 30th of July. She was to wait for him in the foyer of the Masonic Hotel on Marine Parade where he would collect her at five, and she was to bring nothing but a single change of clothes as it was imperative no one knew what they were planning. She hid the letter with the rest of his correspondence, and began to count down the hours and minutes until their rendezvous.

On the day, there was hardly anyone at the big house when she left. So she said goodbye to Mrs Heath, who remarked on how sensible Keely was, going out on such a cold day in that lovely suit from England, and told her to have a good time and to drive carefully, although she didn't approve of women driving and never would.

As she walked around to the shed where the car was kept, pulling on her duster coat and her leather driving gloves, Keely was startled to feel tears beginning to prick the backs of her eyes. Then, just as she was climbing into the car, she heard rowdy squeals of delight from the daffodil paddock behind the big house where Erin, Lucy, Tamar and Jeannie had taken the children to play, and she was suddenly unable to stop her tears from spilling over.

But by the time she had driven through Kenmore's gates, she had her emotions under control. It would be best this way, easiest for everyone. Her mother would understand, eventually, and perhaps one day she would even be able to bring Ross home. They might even have their own children by then. Bonnie and Leila would be fine, there were plenty of people to love them. After all, look how well Liam was doing, and he didn't have any real parents.

She did not know that Owen was standing on the terrace at the side of the big house, with Ross' most recent letter crumpled in his back pocket, watching her as she drove away.

★ ★ ★

The weather was closing in by the time Owen reached Napier. Nothing too violent, he thought, just a touch of winter rain. At ten to five he drove down Marine Parade and parked a short distance from the ornate and verandahed façade of the Masonic Hotel. Then he climbed out, buttoned his coat, pulled his hat well down on his forehead, and wandered casually up the hotel steps and looked inside.

There she was, sitting in the foyer in her best suit and hat with a small case at her feet, fortunately not looking in his direction. He stepped back out of sight, thought for a moment, then went outside again. Up the street at a tobacconist's he bought a newspaper and a packet of tobacco, then went back to his truck, rolled a cigarette, opened his paper and settled down to wait.

Keely looked at the clock above the hotel desk. Five thirty-five. Well, Ross had always been an unpunctual sort of person, except when it came to performing surgery. There was no need to worry yet.

An hour later, she did start to worry. It was raining quite heavily outside now and the

439

concierge behind the desk was starting to give her strange glances. She had already explained that she was waiting for a gentleman friend, but now he was looking at her very suspiciously.

She blushed and called across the foyer to him, 'He must have been held up by the rain, don't you think?'

'Yes, madam, I'm sure,' came the dour reply.

By seven forty-five, Keely felt awful. She was hungry, and desperate to go to the toilet. But what if she did and Ross arrived, couldn't find her and left without her? Twenty minutes later she decided that if she didn't go to the toilet she would wet her pants, so she dashed into the ladies' room, then rushed back to the foyer and straight over to the desk.

'Did a man come in, tall, dark hair, moustache, grey eyes?' she asked in a rush. 'He would have been looking for me.'

'No, madam, I'm sorry. No one at all has come in during the past minute and a half.'

Keely sat down again, and looked around. There were several other people in the foyer now, but none of them was Ross McManus.

What should she do? She opened her bag to retrieve the letter in which he had outlined the time and place for their meeting, then realised she had left it behind at Kenmore. But she was sure she knew the details off by heart.

He was now three hours late.

At ten p.m., Keely started to cry.

'Look, miss, is there anything I can do for you?' asked the concierge, a different, younger man now because the other one had finished his shift. 'You can't stay here all night, you know.'

Keely bit her lip and nodded. 'Yes, I do know that, but I really am meeting someone. He promised he'd be here. Just give me another hour. He's sure to have arrived by then.'

The concierge looked at his wristwatch. 'Well, until eleven. But we close the doors then.'

But at eleven Keely was still sitting by herself. Her face was swollen from crying, much to the ongoing embarrassment of the concierge, and she felt sick with dread that Ross wouldn't turn up at all.

And then she was asked politely to leave. Would a taxi perhaps be helpful? Or would she like to book a room at the Masonic for the evening?

Keely, who didn't have the money for a room, and nowhere to go in a taxi, picked up her case and walked out onto the steps of the hotel, not even turning her head when the doors were closed behind her.

She stood outside in the cold rain until her head ached, her hands were almost numb and she could barely feel her lips. And she was still crying, quietly but with dreadful persistence.

Then a man came walking up the street, the shoulders of his coat wet and his boots splashing in puddles of rainwater.

'So he didn't turn up then?' Owen asked mildly.

Keely looked back at him through bloodshot eyes and shook her head.

He held out his hand. 'Come on home, girl. Let's call it a night.'

She didn't take his hand but when he turned to go back to the truck she followed him. He took her case, opened the door and helped her up.

When he'd settled himself in the driver's seat, he said quietly, 'I have to ask, Keely. Why?'

'Because I don't love you, Owen.'

'But I love you.'

'It's not enough.'

'And Ross McManus would have been?'

Keely closed her eyes and rested her head against the back of the cab. 'I don't want to talk about Ross McManus.'

'No, neither do I. I want to talk about us.'

Keely looked at him then. 'Oh, Owen, you just don't *understand*.'

'Because you won't *let* me!'

'Because it just wouldn't do any good.'

Owen lost his temper then. 'It fucking well would, you know. You're not the only one who's come home from the war feeling lost and utterly hopeless. There are thousands of men — and yes, quite a few women too, I suspect — out there right now who don't know whether they're Arthur or bloody Martha because of what's happened to them. You're not unique.' He shifted in his seat so she would have to look at him. '*Talk* to me, Keely, for God's sake. I don't give a toss what you tell me — we all did things we'll have to bear for the rest of our lives. I killed people, ordinary decent blokes like your brothers. I don't want to live with that but I have to. And you had to watch them die, and to protect yourself you made up a dream and fell

442

for someone who turned out to be a right bastard. So what? I couldn't care less if you went to bed with *twenty* blokes, all right?' He was looking directly into Keely's eyes now. 'It was the *war*, Keely, and it's *over*. You have to leave it behind, do you hear me?'

Keely put her hands over her face and sobbed, 'But it's so bloody hard to *do*!'

'Yes, but you can do it. I know what you're made of. I've known since that first day you told me to bugger off at the front door.'

Hesitantly, Keely turned to him and asked, 'Will you make everything better for me?'

Shaking his head, Owen replied softly, 'No, Keely, I won't.'

She regarded him for a moment in silence, then turned her face away and watched the raindrops as they chased each other down the windscreen. When she moved to open the cab door, Owen grabbed her hand.

'No, don't run away from this. I can't make everything better for you, but you can do it for yourself. And I can, I *will*, stand right beside you while you're doing it. You don't have to do it alone, you can always have me. You never have to be by yourself again, Keely. There's me, and our babies, and your family. We'll all be there. Only you have to stop running, do you understand that? Going off with that bastard McManus is just another form of running, and you can never outrun the things that live in your head. You have to make *them* run. Believe me, I know, I ran for a *long* time. But I've made my peace now, with those men I killed and, more to the point, with Ian.'

'Ian?' Keely was confused.

'Yes, Ian. I thought for such a long time it was my fault he died. He was so young and I'd promised to look out for him, and I failed. But then I realised that if I was serious about coming to talk to you, to his family, I couldn't make my own guilt a part of that. So I did some serious thinking, and talked to quite a lot of other veterans, and that helped me to finally put it all to rest. You have to do that as well.'

'And you'll stay by me while I'm doing it?'

'Every second of the day and night, if you want me to.'

Keely thought for a moment, then inclined her head towards the steering wheel.

'Then drive,' she said.

Epilogue

It was very late when they arrived back at Kenmore — past two o'clock in the morning. But Tamar was still awake, watching from her bedroom window as the truck came slowly up the driveway.

When, by the light of the moon now that the rain clouds had moved on, she saw Owen and Keely alight from the truck then embrace tightly, she closed her eyes and murmured a very uncharacteristic prayer of thanks.

She sat for a while longer, then moved over to her small writing desk, took a fresh sheet of paper from the drawer, and began to write a letter to Kepa.

She thought it was about time she answered his question.

*   *   *

Further along the hall, in the darkness of the bedroom they shared, James and Lucy lay in each other's arms. James' hand rested protectively over the small bulge of his wife's stomach that would be their second child, and in his sleep he smiled.

*   *   *

In the nursery Bonnie and Leila slept side by side in their cot, unconsciously touching hands and completely oblivious to the fact that although their mother had been away, now she had come back to them.

Duncan and Liam snored peacefully on the other side of the room. They neither knew nor cared about the tribulations of the wider Murdoch family. And why should they? For them there were trees to climb, creeks to dam and endless hills to conquer.

* * *

Thomas was dreaming. He dreamt that James had killed an entire company of his own men, and he, Thomas had been assigned to defend him even though it was horribly clear to everyone that James was guilty. But then the vision changed and he was with Catherine, and he settled almost immediately into a deeper, more peaceful sleep.

* * *

Jeannie and Lachie were also asleep, although neither dreamed. They knew they were moving into the twilight years of their lives, but found to their surprise that they did not mind. Although times had often been difficult, and occasionally very painful, their lives together had been good and they had no regrets. When the time came, they would be ready.

* * *

In the next small valley, in the home he'd built with his own hands, Joseph lay propped up on one elbow, watching the sleeping faces of his beautiful wife and son. There would be no more wars for him, not even if the New Zealand Army did one day have to resort to recruiting men with only one leg.

He had finally come home. All those years of fighting and roaming the world and he'd found what he'd been looking for right here. He had the land, he had both his Maori and Pakeha families, and he had his beloved Erin and now William. But most of all he had peace of mind because he had done his best, and would continue to do so for as long as he lived. And that, he understood now, was true *mana*.

We do hope that you have enjoyed reading this large print book.

Did you know that all of our titles are available for purchase?

We publish a wide range of high quality large print books including:
Romances, Mysteries, Classics
General Fiction
Non Fiction and Westerns

Special interest titles available in large print are:
The Little Oxford Dictionary
Music Book
Song Book
Hymn Book
Service Book

Also available from us courtesy of Oxford University Press:
Young Readers' Dictionary
(large print edition)
Young Readers' Thesaurus
(large print edition)

For further information or a free brochure, please contact us at:
Ulverscroft Large Print Books Ltd.,
The Green, Bradgate Road, Anstey,
Leicester, LE7 7FU, England.
Tel: (00 44) **0116 236 4325**
Fax: (00 44) **0116 234 0205**

Other titles published by
The House of Ulverscroft:

TAMAR

Deborah Challinor

The first volume in a three-volume family saga. When Tamar Deane is orphaned at seventeen in a small Cornish village, she seizes the chance for a new life and emigrates to New Zealand. In March 1879, alone and frightened on the Plymouth quay, she is befriended by an extraordinary woman. Myrna McTaggert is travelling to Auckland with plans to establish the finest brothel in the southern hemisphere and her unconventional friendship proves invaluable when Tamar makes disastrous choices in the new colony. Tragedy and scandal befall, her, but unexpected good fortune brings vast changes to Tamar's life. As the century draws to a close, uncertainty looms when a distant war lures her loved ones to South Africa.

I'LL BE SEEING YOU

Margaret Mayhew

When Juliet Porter's mother dies, she leaves her a letter and an old Second World War photograph, which reveal a shattering secret. The father she had loved dearly until the end of his life had not been her father after all. Instead, it seems that she is the daughter of an American bomber pilot who is completely unaware of her existence. Without knowing his name and with only the photograph to help her, Juliet sets out to find her real father. The task proves both daunting and difficult, but she feels compelled to go on. Her search takes her back to the old wartime Suffolk airfield where her mother fell in love with the American pilot in 1942, and, eventually, to California, where in the end she meets not only her past but also her future.

THE TURN OF THE TIDE

Alexandra Connor

Rose Bradshaw is brought up a stone's throw from Blackpool's bustling promenade. She's quick-witted and ferociously loyal, but the boys aren't interested. Her father is one of the town's best-known bookies and, the trouble is, few take kindly to his daughter working on the track. The rapacious Widow Miller, a former neighbour, will take Rose in hand, but she has her own devious reasons for wanting to manipulate the Bradshaws' lives. Guided by the Widow Miller, a new, glamorous Rose moves up the social scale. Unfortunately, Rose can't forget the ambitious lad across the street. Then comes World War II, and she is called upon to risk everything for the man she has always loved.

JOSEPHINE AND HARRIET

Betty Burton

Josephine turns her back on the conventional role for respectable young women in Victorian England. She has an indomitable spirit, but her chosen path is far from easy, as female journalists are practically unheard of — let alone ones who specialise in crime reports. Harriet is content to drift from one opportunity to another, from man to man, living by her singing, resorting to occasional prostitution when times get tough. It's an uncertain life, cut short by tragedy. Josephine is fascinated by the case. If circumstances had been different, could this have been her? The two women are close in age, their families not so very different. What made one life turn out this way?

RACHEL

Irene Carr

Orphaned at a young age, Rachel is left penniless and alone in turn-of-the-century Newcastle. Determined to follow her mother's advice, she must embrace her opportunity of an education so she can rise to the position of governess. When she lands a post with a good family she believes her struggle is over — until she is blamed for a crime she hasn't committed. Moving to another job, Rachel finds herself at the mercy of an unscrupulous employer. Then she learns that her eccentric uncle has left her his house in Sunderland. But it comes with a heavy price: she must marry her childhood friend, Martin, a man who has caused her embarrassment in adult years and who she has vowed never to befriend again . . .

SECOND CHANCE OF SUNSHINE

Pamela Evans

1950s: No one would blame Molly Hawkins if she envied her best friend, Angie. Blessed with financial security and a loving husband, Angie has everything that Molly lacks. Brian Hawkins is too idle to seek regular employment, and there's never enough money to provide for Molly's six-year-old daughter, Rosa. What's more, Molly is forbidden to go out to work. But when Angie's father, George Beckett, dies suddenly and leaves Molly a share in the Beckett pottery, it's on the condition that she takes a job there. Seizing the chance to bring in much-needed income, Molly gains strength from her new-found independence — a strength she will need to take her through the tragedy that lies ahead . . .